]

Divulgent

BOOK TWO
OF
THE TIRANIMEITH
CHRONICLES

R. Allen Jones

Copyright © 2022 R. Allen Jones

ISBN: 978-1-9163693-2-0

IREDAN PRESS
3 The Quay, Looe, Cornwall PL13 1AQ

LIGHT DIVULGENT
ISBN: 978-1-9163693-2-0

First published in Great Britain
In 2022 by Iredan Press

Cover design by: Haley Rust & R Allen Jones
Printed in the United Kingdom

FOLLOW THE AUTHOR

On his Facebook page www.facebook.com/RAllenJones2/

CONTENTS

Acknowledgments v

About The Book v

PART 5 – DOWN THE RIVER

1 Katina's Trip To Kersladen 1

2 We'd Better Join The Party 19

3 The Escape 33

4 Katina Leaves 47

5 The Castle 61

PART 6 – ACROSS THE PLAINS

6 Odd Footprints 71

7 Heading West 81

8 What The Hell Is That 90

9 The Lost 103

PART 7 – SOME PLACE ELSE

10 Down The Tunnel 121

11 The Mist 137

12 The Great Plains 147

13 The Great Tree 164

PART 8 – THE LONG TRIP HOME

14   The Polished Wall   182

15   The Gateway   194

16   We Don't Want to Get Lost   203

17   Heading South   216

18   The Thin Line   234

19   Mr. A. Farmer   249

20   The Final Stretch   262

PART 9 – THE LOST TEMPLE

21   The Meeting   276

22   Leaving Again   290

23   The Temple   301

TAIL PIECE

Back At The Valley   314

ACKNOWLEDGMENTS

To Amanda Miles and Roxie Ray for in-depth, invaluable, detailed, long-term help and encouragement.

To Louise Bobbitt for her invaluable aid in the description of some of the medical matters.

To Hayley Rust for such excellent artwork. If you are interested in Hayley's work, she can be contacted through the author.

ABOUT THE BOOK

This book of the Tiranimeith Chronicles follows on from Katina leaving Warameth in Chapter 16 of Book One - Light Emergent. Chronologically it runs parallel to the events covered in Book One from Chapter 16 onwards and continues, happening side by side with those events contained in Book Three - Light Ascendant. Virtually the whole book covers the adventures of Katina and those that travel with her.

Please note that in this book some speech is in *"Quotes and Italic words."* This is to denote that the conversation is spiritual communication. This is a form of telepathic speech used by spirits and gods. The existence and content of those discussions will be known only to those few who can hear spirit speech. Everybody else will be oblivious.

PART 5 – DOWN THE RIVER

1 - KATINA'S TRIP TO KERSLADEN

Katina saw Helghyer circling high above. The huge falcon then plummeted towards the ground heading for a patch of tall grass a few hundred yards away. Then there was the sound of galloping horses and combat.

'Ablamon, we should go and help.' She shouted.

'I am afraid not. We must keep going.' He replied.

'But Ablamon, they're fighting Plains Devils. We must help.' Shouted an anxious Katina.

'No, we must not.'

'I'm going to help.' Said Katina as she stood up and prepared to jump off the cart.

'Sit down NOW. You have your orders to get home and tell our tribe what is happening here. Our job is to see you safely down the valley. You will follow your orders no matter what. Do you understand?' Ablamon replied in a loud stern voice.

Hawkyn gently put his hand on her arm. When she looked at him, an understanding face looked back.

'Yes, sir.' Was her reply muffled by a downcast face.

Worriedly Katina watched the tall grass as they continued past the noise of weapon on weapon and the screams of pain. After a few more minutes, she could stand it no longer and prayed out loud, trying to remember the words used by Oswald and Lord Mord at Luka's ceremony.

'Huntress, I beseech thee, hear my prayer. I know I am not one of your true worshippers, but can you please see fit to tell me what happened to my friends.'

'I don't think that works for us.' Hawkyn commented, then a disembodied female voice replied aloud.

'Katina of Iredan. You and your friends have served us Gods of Light beyond all expectations in recent weeks, so just this once. There is a proper divine miracle for this kind of thing which requires a lot more precision and detail of what you wish to see.'

Katina's mind slowly slid away from looking at the grassland beside the road. All went a mid-grey colour for a second. Then she was looking at the Plains Devil fight from above. When she came around, the two carts had stopped, and everyone had gathered around her.

'Are you alright, were you shown anything?' Asked Ablamon.

'The Huntress saw fit to grant me a vision. It looks like the Plains Devils are all dead. The two scouts are beheading them while Oswald heals Agnes and Tara. Freki has a bandaged paw and Helghyer is missing some feathers. Everyone is up and about.' Katina responded.

'To be given a vision like that is incredible, though it sounds like a tough fight. We must keep moving. There may be more of them.' Ablamon concluded. Without further command, they resumed their places and moved out.

The wagons rolled slowly along the road to Izellameth. Ablamon and the guards were ready for immediate action, looking like the warriors they were rather than the merchants they were supposed to be.

Katina noted the return of the animals and wildlife in general so relaxed, watching the long grass sway in the gentle wind. Despite what the warriors believed the presence of small animals meant there were no more Plains Devils about. Given the defeat the Goblins received earlier, more attacks from them were unlikely for some time.

Katina thought reflectively on recent events and realised she considered Oswald, Arturous and Agnes the strongest of friends and battle companions despite only knowing them for a few days. Katina didn't want to go home but knew she must do it. She had also learnt the importance of following orders. They taught hunter/scouts that independence and self-reliance were paramount. While that was undoubtedly important, not appreciating the need to follow orders meant that when working with warriors, hunter/scouts lacked perspective in battle, namely the requirement of being where you were supposed to be and aiding with communication to those in charge.

Further, not only had she seen spiritual magic but had a prayer made to a god answered and received a vision in return. That was a definite culture shock for someone who did not readily believe in any god. Although The Huntress made it clear answering a prayer was a once-off, she would need to take great care when asking for something.

As they approached Izellameth, someone spotted them and ran towards the village. Soon others were following. By the time they got to the half wooden half stone houses, a large crowd had gathered.

Several persons who appeared to be village elders, led by a tall older man of superior bearing, approached them. Katina also noticed a vagrant leaning on a log at the side of the street.

'Master Ablamon, several of our outlying farmers, have seen large numbers of Goblins and other horrible monsters between our two villages. They appear to have gone now. Can you give us more details? People are concerned.' Said the tall older man.

'You are correct. Warameth defeated some Goblins. Those that survived have left the area.' Responded Ablamon.

'You are travellers by nature of your business. Without your guards, there is no one to defend the villages.' The man said.

'That is not correct. The villagers of Warameth are

doing their bit too. Regular armed patrols to help outlying farmers. Your two villages have a lot more capability than you give yourselves credit for.' Replied Ablamon.

'But not the leaders or those to train us.' Said the man.

'Incorrect.' Ablamon replied. 'Our tribe has been fighting these things for hundreds of years. The Sheriff of Warameth is one of our best warriors and tacticians. Also, your own Major Partten and family live in the village. The tales I have heard of him are incredible. Your up-river friends can do well in this.'

'Did you mean Major Partten from the Goblin raids?' The ragged Vagrant asked.

'Yes. A few former soldiers identified him.' Ablamon replied.

'Former soldiers. That is an interesting way to describe the captured bandits those youngsters dragged through here a few weeks ago.' The tall older man commented.

'They defended the village from a sneak attack, fought Goblins, killed several and got wounded in battle. Placing a positive view on their situation seemed fair in the circumstances.' Replied Ablamon.

'Are the villagers forgiving banditry then?' An older man asked in a worried voice.

'The accused made an offer which in light of service in battle the village elders are seriously considering. Full or partial forgiveness will be up to the elders and Magistrate.' Ablamon replied.

'I must get through to Warameth and see for myself. Thank you.' The Vagrant said.

'So, you knew Major Partten then, did you, Vagrant.' The tall older man asked with a sneer in his voice.

'I fought under him, yes.'

'Your family name is Trehillion, isn't it?' A dawn of realisation overcoming the man's face as he said the words.

'Yes, it is.'

'Then that would make you Major Trehillion.

Commander of the infantry unit raised in Porarpen. You ended up second in overall command to Sergeant Major Michael after the command staff decided to abandon the fight.'

'That is true I was, but my actions before Sergeant Major Michael's brutal intervention would not bring me great acclaim.'

'But I take it you stayed, commanded troops and fought in a battle you won?' Asked Ablamon.

'Not just me, but yes, I did.' Was the Vagrant's reply.

'Then you are still worthy of honour.' Ablamon concluded. The village elders nodded in agreement.

'I must try and get through to Warameth and see if this is Major Partten for myself.' The Vagrant concluded finally.

'If you don't see or hear wild animals, turn around and come back. Trust me.' Katina told the Vagrant who was packing up his meagre possessions. He looked at her and nodded.

'Major Trehillion, when you have satisfied yourself of the authenticity of Major Partten, I would ask you to return to us. Help with our training and defences.' The senior village elder asked with, Katina noted, the look of someone eating a healthy portion of humble pie. The Vagrant looked at him for a second, considered the offer, then smiled and nodded before walking up the road.

Ablamon approached several families and concluded various negotiations quickly. They exchanged goods and tools for many bags of grain.

They headed off downriver to Treenys. A trip that on this occasion was uneventful. The last remnants of the fight at the copse were now gone, the only reminder being the grave markers. At places, the Great Forest came close to the road and on one occasion spread across it to the river, elsewhere the terrain was flat unoccupied grassland, this gave ample opportunity for ambushes, so Katina often went scouting. Several poorly concealed Humans watched the group head down river but showed no hostile intent. The group ignored them and continued to Treenys.

The passage across to the island village was uneventful. News of the attacks upriver had not filtered through this far. Ablamon secured accommodation at the village inn, leaving most of the guards with the carts. After eating an evening meal of mutton and vegetables, they retired to bed. Katina took her turn watching the carts, which passed without incident. They left at first light with a bleary-eyed ferryman transporting the heavily laden carts across the river one at a time to the road to Kersladen.

Ablamon insisted that Katina cross with the first cart and go scouting while the ferry brought the second one across. Again, Katina found a few unkempt, poorly dressed and armed Humans, watching. They posed no threat, so Ablamon ignored them and continued downriver.

As they approached Kersladen, Katina noted the clear signs of mounted patrols on the roads and countryside. Initially abandoned farms, their fields left unattended and overgrown, boundary hedges dilapidated, as were the farms walls and buildings. The farms then became inhabited, but poorly kept, with insufficient labour to run them.

As they approached Kersladen, the farms improved. When within about five miles of their destination, the farm complexes had taller than man height stone walls, well-kept buildings and a proper labour force. A mounted patrol of soldiers approached from the city.

'Good morning, Corporal. We haven't seen you outside the city walls before.' Ablamon enquired.

'Good morning Ablamon. The usual crew I see with two carts of grain and wool.' The Corporal responded formally, looking at the carts and escort.

'That is correct, although I have both sheep and goat wool this time. I am heading for the central market, then the warehouses and back as usual.' Replied Ablamon politely.

'Good. That's the boring stuff done. These patrols are a new thing. The sheer scale of the attacks on you a few weeks ago has scared many farmers hereabouts. They need reassurance as they provide the bulk of our food.'

'I wouldn't worry too much about the bandits. They attacked us twice and got hammered. We have either killed or captured over sixty in the last few weeks.' Ablamon said.

'It didn't work out for them then.' The Corporal said with a smile.

'Not really, no.' Hawkyn added.

'The bandits, in committing themselves to us in such a manner, are pretty well played out. The public executions in Warameth will deter recruitment. It's not the end of it though, there is more I am afraid.' Ablamon added.

'Go on.'

'Goblins have attacked Warameth.' Ablamon informed a stunned Corporal and his soldiers. He paused a moment before he continued.

'The village, though, have some excellent scouts, so they knew they were coming and prepared defences. The Goblin's lost over half their number in the first attack. When they withdrew to regroup, they were hit on the flank by a mounted charge led by a former commander of yours, Major Partten.'

'Yes, brilliant.' A soldier interrupted.

'They were pretty much wiped out. That won't be all, however. It never is.'

'Is Warameth lost then? I have relatives there.' Asked the earlier soldier.

'Warameth has a lot going for it. They will be able to defend themselves.' Ablamon stated to surprised looks from the soldiers. 'I would suggest larger patrols though. Ten is enough for bandits, but Goblins operate in groups of twelve. If you are surprised, your numbers may be insufficient.'

'You have had a busy few weeks haven't you?'

'Eventful, but successful.'

'You fought the Goblins?' The Corporal asked.

'Yes, some in the line, some in the mounted charge.' Ablamon replied.

'Thank you for all the information, Ablamon. We must be on our way now.' The Corporal turned and, looking at his men, said

'We are supposed to be soldiers, time to look like it.' The patrol formed into two columns and, with a nod of acknowledgement, rode off upriver.

The carts continued their slow journey towards the city. Katina watched the patrol as they rode up the river behind them, then turned inland, returning to the city cross country significantly before the heavily laden carts got there.

The merchant train drove on slowly to the city's upriver gatehouse. It was one story higher than the tall stone city walls. The dozen stood to attention as they approached the gatehouse. A hard-bitten Sergeant walked up to them in a professional yet respectful manner.

'Greetings Master Ablamon. My Corporal has updated me on your discussions with him, so no need for further inspections. As a mark of respect for those who have recently served in the battle against followers of the Evil Lord, six of my guards will escort you through the city to your usual accommodation. They will guard your wagons while you rest and do business.'

'Thank you, Sergeant. I also need to see the High Priest too. I have a letter for him.'

'We can certainly escort you to the gates of the temple complex. Can't say beyond that.' The Sergeant motioned to some of his men, who quickly formed up in front of the wagons and banged their swords against their shields in unison. A path soon cleared in front of them.

'Thank you, Sergeant, we appreciate this.' Ablamon replied.

They passed through the gatehouse, which had two

thick solid wooden doors. The passageway through the walls had a room on each side. As they emerged into a wide rectangular unpaved open area, streets were either directly in front or to left and right immediately behind the city walls. Katina noted the walls were about twenty feet tall, fifteen feet thick, made of large stone blocks about a yard in each direction and very old. The buildings of the city were much newer and mostly made of dark stained wooden timber frame with poorly maintained whitewashed plaster.

After a short while, the muddy streets became paved with cobblestones as they approached the central market itself. It was a large area with many tents and stalls of traders. A large walled warehouse complex was on one side. Ablamon directed them to an inn on the opposite side. It was not flashy or fancy, but large and certainly well-kept with armed guards on the main gate. Katina noticed one of the escorting soldiers had a brief word with what appeared to be a senior guard and they all passed through without incident or question. Inside was a fair-sized yard with either buildings or stout walls on each side.

'I must go and conduct business with my usual merchants.' Ablamon informed them. He motioned two of his guards to follow him, took a set of shears from a compartment in the side of one of the wagons and told Katina and the others to guard the carts. The soldiers stayed to help protect the wagons also. With her companions, the six soldiers and the inn's guards, there were about twenty fully armed guards looking after two carts. Like Ablamon's men, both the soldiers and the inn's guards wore chain mail armour, carried a large shield and a sword. After about three hours, Ablamon had concluded negotiations, took the carts to the warehouses, exchanged goods and they were back at the inn.

'I must now go and see this High Priest that Oswald was on about and give him the letter. You two come with me.' Ablamon ordered, looking at Katina and Hawkyn as he turned to leave. As Katina picked up her bow and quiver of arrows, she noted the six escorting soldiers looked at each other. Three nodded and led the way.

After passing through the market, they followed the main street a little way down the river, where on one side stood the temple complex. A ten feet high stone perimeter wall encompassed many acres, within which stood several large buildings including the Temple itself. When they approached the solid wood double gate, several members of the clergy and some temple guards stood on duty.

As Ablamon approached the gate, a clergyman spoke.

'What is your business here? You may not proceed unless I say you can.' The clergyman said in a superior voice and looking at them with a sneer on his face.

Katina did not think Ablamon liked the clergyman's attitude and neither did she. This discussion probably would not end well, was her next thought.

'My business is with your High Priest and not you, so underling take me to him.'

'My name is Curate Shanks. I am the High Priest's Personal Assistant and arranger of his appointments. You will not be seeing him today or tomorrow or, in fact, next week. So, go away and come back in a few weeks and I will reconsider your request then.'

Katina noted Ablamon reach down to his sword. There was a quiet groan from Hawkyn. They both reacted appropriately.

'I have a letter from one of your Initiates whom he sent to Warameth. I am entrusted with its hand delivery to His Grace and I will see it done. Now, if you value your teeth, either take me to your superior or get out of my way.' Ablamon stated, looking down on the Curate. He also partially drew his sword with a metal on metal scraping sound. The six temple guards drew swords. Katina, Hawkyn and the three soldiers also drew swords.

At this point, a petrified novice tugged heavily on the

annoying Curate's robe. Bowing about as humbly as Katina thought it was possible to do.

'Please Curate, allow me to escort them. I know you have many tasks, allow me this simple one for you. It's only the delivery of a letter.' The novice said in a very shaky tone. The Curate looked at the prostrate novice in a very hostile manner. Then he noticed all the drawn swords and seemed to reconsider his attitude.

'You are not entitled to enter that part of the temple, novice.'

'I can take him to Priest Shamus. He will be at the High Altar now. He will know how to proceed with this and show both His Grace and our guests the proper respect. I am sure they do not intend violence in the house of The Light Bringer.' The novice continued.

'We only commit violence when necessary.' Ablamon interrupted. There was an eerie calm for a few seconds as everyone considered the next move. Then a booming voice broke the silence.

'Novice Mark, why did you not come to me as soon as word of my cousin arrived.' Said a tall, lean clergyman in a long white robe who stood in the doorway to the temple at the top of a set of wide stone steps. Katina noticed he appeared very similar in physical and facial appearance to Oswald Shamus but a bit older, more confident, and wiser.

'He was trying to prevent our Curate from losing his teeth.' Said an only slightly shorter man who had appeared out of a side alley. He was a much broader, muscular, dark-haired man of middling years dressed in a brown cowl and holding a quarterstaff.

'He would have lost more than his teeth.' Was Katina's inadvertent comment. That produced a slight grin on the face of the new entrant.

'Curate Shanks, these are Southern Plains People. They are not interested in or tolerate church politics and petty displays of self-importance. They kill without a second thought those who offer impertinence. They are pleasant enough to deal with, only if you show respect and are useful to them. Pretty much everyone else they kill on the first excuse.' Said the new entrant.

'Lord Guardian, I presume to guess by your demeanour.' He continued looking at Ablamon.

'Technically, I am his qualified second.' Ablamon said.

'Lord Guardian rank, though.'

'Yes.'

'These others of your tribe also?'

'Our senior hunter and one of the High Priests personal guard.' Ablamon replied.

Looking around the courtyard, the new dark-haired man continued. 'I doubt there are enough temple guards in the entire complex to stop these three if they decide to come through.'

'Apart from you, Brother Michael.' Said the white-robed priest.

'In my day, Priest Shamus maybe, but it would have been a tough call even then.' He replied.

'Enough of this talk.' Priest Shamus replied sternly. Then looking at Ablamon, he continued, 'I request you not harm our Curate.'

'So long as I can personally deliver the letter and the Curate ceases to be rude to my companions and me, I will not harm him, ... today.' Ablamon replied.

'That will do. Now everyone, put up your weapons. Brother Michael, Novice Mark, assist me in escorting the visitors to His Grace.' Priest Shamus ordered sternly. Everyone sheathed their swords with visible relief from the very worried temple guards.

'Please follow me.' The white-robed priest said politely to Ablamon and led them all into the church itself. When clear of those in the courtyard, he stopped briefly and genuflected to the altar, muttering some words quietly. He rose and turning to Ablamon said. 'My cousin, is he alright?'

'He is fine, though tired and bruised and has seen much combat in the last few weeks.' Ablamon replied. The priest looked shocked.

'I must say he is a credit to your family. He has survived assassination attempts, fought in combat against bandits, fought in the line against Goblins, cast divine magic spells to counter dark magic and conducted religious ceremonies at which both your God and ours were present. Lastly, he has saved several lives, including mine.' Ablamon replied to a stunned silence from the attending clergy.

'It was a pleasure to serve with him, though his sermons are terrible.' Katina added.

'You must be the famed Brother Michael. Your expert training of our priest was most fortunate. It has enabled him to make such a huge difference simply by tipping the scales slightly.' Ablamon said.

'Glad to hear it.' Commented Brother Michael.

'We must proceed now, or our annoying Curate will notice the delay.' Priest Shamus said as he led them into a transept.

'Not for long he won't.' Katina replied.

From there the priest took them through the plain stone corridors of the cloisters and into a double fronted house at the end with a large dark oak door. Then up some stairs to more opulent accommodation. They walked along a wide corridor with dark wood panelling, side doors and hanging tapestries. A decorated door waited for them at the end of a passage.

Then the voice that had responded to her prayer, spoke in her head.

"Don't any of you eat or drink anything. Trust me on this."

Katina sighed. Being an atheist, she had difficulty with all this direct divine communication. In the circumstances, though, there appeared to be little option for either of them.

"Thank you for your understanding." The voice in her head

13

responded.

Priest Shamus knocked on the door in front of them.

'Your Grace, we have visitors who wish to see you.'

'Please come in.' His Grace responded from behind the door.

'You three had better remain outside.' Priest Shamus said to the soldiers who had accompanied them since entering the city.

'Novice Mark, you will remain with them also.' The novice responded by bowing respectfully, having appeared to have recovered some of the wits he lost in the courtyard.

Brother Michael opened the door. The Priest entered the room first, followed by the rest of them with Brother Michael closing the door behind him. It was a large room with polished wooden floors and fleece rugs. The centre piece of the room was a large oak desk with a matching ornately carved chair facing the door. The room also had several simple chairs.

'Your Grace, the leader of this group wishes to see you. They have a message from my cousin.' The priest stated, pointing to Ablamon.

The High Priest stood at one side of the room next to a small table with a carafe of wine and some goblets on it. He looked at Ablamon and smiled as he returned to his ornately carved chair.

'I have to mention that Curate Shanks overstretched his authority and failed to be polite. As you can see, these are Southern Plains People, they are intolerant of such behaviour.' Priest Shamus said. The High Priest solemnly nodded.

'Luckily, Novice Mark was able to delay a potential incident from occurring until I could intervene.' Priest Shamus continued.

'I see. Please accept my full apologies, master merchant. That was regrettable. Sit down, all of you. How may I be of assistance?'

'I am Ablamon, and these two are my guards. While we are indeed Southern Plains People, we are also merchants. Having accompanied us to Warameth and made himself useful, your Initiate asked me to deliver a letter to you personally when I next came through.' Ablamon reached inside his cloak to a leather bag and retrieved a sealed scroll which he handed to the High Priest.

'Thank you, Master Ablamon. I will make sure my overzealous Curate understands the literal nature of your people so that impolite behaviour does not happen again. Please, all of you, take some wine while I read my Initiate's letter.' He responded as he broke the seal on the scroll.

'Thank you for your kind offer, but we are all on a religious fast right now and must respectfully decline.' Katina instantly interrupted before anyone had a chance even to sip the goblets they now held. She also made a put-down gesture behind her back. Katina saw Brother Michael turn away from the High Priest while he read the scroll. There was a sniff of the wine and a brief scowl on his face.

'I won't be leaving until tomorrow. I could take a letter back if you wish. I will be heading that way again eventually.' Ablamon responded by putting the goblet down untouched.

'Thank you for your offer. I will send Priest Shamus to you after first prayers in the morning.' The High Priest responded. Then, looking at the priest, continued, 'Sorry to send you on such a small task, but in the circumstances, my Curate would not be appropriate.' Priest Shamus nodded.

'It is always a pleasure to serve the Gods of Light. Good day to you, and thank you for your time, your grace.' Ablamon responded formerly. They rose and left with Brother Michael shutting the door behind him.

The three soldiers and Novice Mark, who had been waiting quietly, followed Ablamon and the others along the corridor away from the High Priest's quarters. When they reached the bottom of the stairs to the senior clergy accommodation

Brother Michael asked Katina.

'How did you know?'

'The Huntress told me.' Was the indifferent reply. There were some shocked faces.

'There are several people I have come across lately that various gods talk to directly. Katina here appears to be one of them. They give advice, warnings and similar. Your Initiate was the first.' Ablamon stated.

'It's rather disturbing. Even my own thoughts aren't private.' Katina added.

'But it has been quite useful.' Ablamon suggested.

'True, but still disturbing. I don't even believe in any god.' Katina concluded.

'You might want to reconsider your personal beliefs.' Priest Shamus suggested with a smile.

'Just as well she did, the wine contained poison. It would have killed us all. I think it was a concentrated version of Arsenic due to a slight smell of almonds.' Stated Brother Michael.

'I will arrange for you to be met at first light by the temple gates.' Ablamon said, looking at the priest.

'It will be Katina here and a few others.' He said, pointing to her.

'The first service will be at dawn. We will be a little later than that.' The priest replied.

'I would consider missing it. If we can get you out of here alive, then your cousin will protect you.' Katina replied sternly.

'My cousin, protect me. That is a new one.' The priest said in a surprised voice.

'Trust me, priest, he will. If you stay here, we may all be dead by tomorrow evening.' Was Katina's curt reply. The priest nodded glumly in agreement.

Ablamon then looked at Novice Mark and the soldiers.

'One word of this, and we are all dead.' The novice and

three soldiers also nodded.

'Excuse me, sirs, did you say the High Priest tried to poison a Priest, a Brother of the Infirmary and three guests?' One of the soldiers asked a short while later.

'Bill, aren't you forgetting the bit about Gods speaking to people directly.' Another soldier added.

'I was trying not to think about that.' Bill replied.

'I am afraid so.' Brother Michael responded.

'If the killing has started, then we need to leave too. We are known to have accompanied you.' The last soldier said.

'Excuse me all. There is something I must do. I will be at the front gate at dawn. If I am not there, do not wait for me.' Novice Mark said. He turned on his heels and left them, opening the large front door before anyone had a chance to say anything, heading back along the cloisters to the Novices quarters.

They followed the novice out of the building and walked through the cloisters to the temple, entering via the transept. There were several more groups of Temple Guards, one in each aisle and one in the choir area. She noticed the three city guards starting to get nervous.

'There are only supposed to be a half company of them. There are more than that just in this church.' Bill commented quietly.

Without a further word, Brother Michael and Priest Shamus led the visitors through the middle of the Nave, keeping maximum distance between the various groups of temple guards. They left by the main door descending the broad marble steps into the long courtyard. Those in the Temple followed a discrete twenty paces behind them.

When they approached the main gate, Priest Shamus looked at Ablamon and said.

'I will bid you good day here. Brother Michael and I will deliver His Grace's reply to my cousin's letter to you at first light tomorrow.'

'First light it is then.' Ablamon replied, bowing politely.

Both the Priest and Brother Michael responded in kind.

Katina took her place to one side and behind Ablamon, Hawkyn doing so on the other side. The three city guards formed up in front and led the way back to the inn. Soon Katina and the others were back with their comrades.

2 – WE'D BETTER JOIN THE PARTY, OR WE'LL MISS IT

With Brother Michael stood next to him, Priest Osgood Shamus watched Ablamon and the others leave. The pair went back to the infirmary in silence. Brother Michael was furtively looking around from time to time, checking if anyone was watching, he then beckoned Osgood inside and closed the door behind him.

'My friend, we must both leave. I would prefer now, but waiting and travelling with the merchants tomorrow may well be safer. The more professionally trained warriors we travel with, the better.'

'You are right, but if I start packing, the High Priest will find out.' Osgood Shamus replied sadly at the thought of leaving the only home he had ever known.

'Then don't. Do your tasks for today as planned and come back here an hour before first light. I will arrange essential clothing and equipment for us both. Just get yourself here.' Brother Michael replied firmly.

'Thank you, Michael. I am ill-prepared for this journey, much to my shame.'

'With hindsight, we should have both seen this coming as soon as your cousin banged his head.' Replied Michael. Osgood nodded.

'Those merchants know more than they are letting on.' Osgood suggested.

'Much more.' Michael replied.

'What has my cousin got himself into now.' Osgood wondered.

'Whatever it is, it's serious enough to warrant your god talking to him directly. For the first time in my life, I am worried.' Michael replied.

'And we must help him now more than ever.'

'We wouldn't be much of a family if we didn't, would

we.' Michael said

'We probably won't survive long enough to see my cousin again.' Osgood replied sadly.

'Wrong. From what we have seen this afternoon, at least one of the Gods of Light rides with the merchants. That will change things a lot. We must part now, or the High Priest will know. Remember, here an hour before first light.' Michael replied finally. Osgood nodded solemnly and left.

Osgood checked if anyone had seen him leaving the infirmary. It didn't look like it, but there were lots of Temple Guards about, many more than usual. He went straight to the High Altar in the temple. The preparations for the evening service took longer than usual as there were no novices to help him, he said nothing but wondered what Novice Mark was up to.

After Osgood had finished conducting the evening service, he walked distractedly towards his quarters, lost in thought. He considered that if they were to go at first light, his Grace would already have to have given him the scroll. It would look suspicious if he did not have the scroll when leaving the temple complex with Brother Michael. As he could not disturb his Grace before dawn, there was only one choice. Risking it all, off he went.

'Your Grace, it is Osgood. May I have a word, please?' He said after knocking on the door of the High Priest's chambers.

'Please come in, Osgood.' Replied the High Priest. He entered. The High Priest bid him be seated with a smile.

'Thank you for handling the earlier matter with the Southern Plains People so diplomatically. We managed a cordial meeting despite the genuine possibility of serious violence. I am most grateful to you and Brother Michael.'

'Thank you, Your Grace. That is why I have come to see you. While undoubtedly Brother Michael and I must deal with the delivery of the reply to my cousin, there's a lot to be done tomorrow and wondered, if it is ready now, could I take it and deal with it first thing. The merchants will want to be leaving early anyway.'

'That is an excellent idea. I have the reply scroll already prepared and more money for your cousin. There is a separate smaller bag of coins for the merchant's trouble. Your cousin appears to be doing well. He has approached matters differently than I would, but the villagers appear to be considering allowing him to set up his church. He is far more practical and pragmatic than I gave him credit for.'

'Thank you, Your Grace. Thinking quickly and working out key issues was always his strongest points.' Osgood replied politely. He picked up the scroll and two bags of coins the High Priest handed him, they said their pleasantries and he left.

After returning to his quarters, he changed robes for one with internal pockets. Osgood realised that most of his possessions would have to be left behind but placed a few items, such as his religious symbol and a small revision scroll containing some of the more complex rituals, in his internal pockets. That was the best he could do. Then he lay on his cot pretending to be asleep.

At what he believed to be an appropriate time, somewhat before first light, Osgood got up quietly, left his quarters for the last time and headed to the infirmary. Unusually for this time of night, the priest passed several groups of temple guards. Nodding politely, he continued his journey. None of the guards questioned him or commented on his movements probably, he thought, because they did not wish to justify their own to a priest. When he reached the infirmary, he knocked on the door and just asked.

'May I come in.' The door opened. Osgood entered, Brother Michael, closing the door behind him.

'Please take your cassock off.' Michael asked. Osgood complied with a puzzled expression. Michael opened a large chest and took out a long leather jacket.

'We will put the leather jacket on you first, followed by chain mail armour. Those will cover your chest, abdomen, and upper arms. We will then put the cassock back on over the top, and hopefully, that will cover it all.' Michael said.

Osgood complied and although a tight fit for the cassock afterwards, the idea worked. They each took a large bag and placed them on their backs. Brother Michael gave Osgood a sizeable stout oak stick while he picked up his war mace and motioned to the door. As they left, Osgood noticed Michael looking sadly at his home. Then shut the door and the pair headed for the main gate.

They walked through the herb and vegetable gardens along the well-trodden paths to the alleyway between the church and guardhouse that led to the main gate courtyard. By the time they arrived at the temple's one hundred feet long paved courtyard, the merest sliver of light projected across the sky.

Katina, Hawkyn and Ternan sat quietly on the single-story guardhouse roof, having climbed over the perimeter wall unnoticed about half an hour earlier. She saw the priest and the Brother from yesterday enter the courtyard from a side alley. Signalling the other two, Katina silently got to her knees.

The pair approached the gate when a guard stood in their path and blocked the way.

'Revered Priest, may I ask your business.' The guard requested.

'While you are not entitled to question the movements of the higher clergy, on this occasion, you might as well know. His Grace desires a letter delivered to the merchants who visited yesterday. After the difficulties with Curate Shanks, the High Priest deemed appropriate for Brother Michael and me to deliver it.' The priest replied in a quiet and polite tone.

'I am not satisfied that you are entitled to leave and must refuse permission.' The guard replied. The priest immediately stood tall and with a face of thunder.

'You, refuse me. How dare you. Get that gate open now.' He ordered angrily.

'No, my priest, I am forbidden from obeying your orders and must place you under arrest.' The guard replied. A dozen or so temple guard came out from the guardhouse and took position behind the pair, oblivious to Katina, Hawkyn and Ternan sat on the roof a few feet above them.

'I, as a senior member of the clergy whom you are supposed to protect, am giving you a direct order. Get that gate open now, or I will cast you out and ban you from the temple for all eternity.'

'Sir, my orders are to refuse you.'

'So be it then.' Said Osgood Shamus with a face that emanated blazing fire and a voice so hard it would knock down a stone wall. He then started the ritual of casting out.

'Lord God, The Light Bringer, I beseech thee to hear your humble priest's prayer . . . .'

'Take them.' Came an order from behind the pair.

Katina, watching the exchange, realised that the priest was not in the slightest bit concerned at their predicament.

'I would seriously recommend you get out of the way.' Said Brother Michael in a casual voice to the guard at the gate.

Before she had a chance to process what was developing below, the now familiar voice in her head said.

"This priest doesn't mess about, does he. I like him. Shame my Light bearing Brother isn't around."

With that, from nowhere, a beam of sunlight reflected off something on a nearby roof, illuminating the chanting priest who continued his ritual.

"Eww, he is about. Today will be fun." The voice in Katina's head said in an amused tone.

The guards stopped dead in their tracks at the sight of

the illuminated chanting priest. That is until their Sergeant bellowed.

'Kill him before he completes the ritual, or the priest will condemn all our souls to hell. Now move.' The guards, now more frightened of their Sergeant, advanced.

Light glinted off the Brother's previously hidden chain mail armour as his cloak opened slightly. Before Katina had time even to think, the Brother whipped out a mace and, with his left hand, swung it at the open helmeted head of the guard in front of them. The blow removed the guard's jaw, who collapsed immediately.

Then in one move, spun around to face the other guards, while drawing a short sword from beneath his cloak Brother Michael stepped forward in front of the still chanting priest and said with a vindictive sneer.

'Now, let's see how good you are.'

He advanced alone on the temple guards. He was simultaneously swinging both his war mace and short sword at opponents on either side while dodging an incoming slash from the one to his front. The mace caught the inside of the left opponent's shield and pulled it around, blocking the soldier's attempt to strike. He flicked it back hard, hitting the left arm below the shoulder with an audible crack as the arm broke. With his short sword, he caught the sword of the guard advancing from his right. He pushed the guard's sword sideways into his shield, then flicked his sword up to the guard's neck and lunged, forcing his sword through the throat. The short sword swung back, slicing the neck of the guard who had missed him half a second earlier. At the same time, he swung his mace at the side of the guard's head. He was advancing through them before they finished falling.

'Blimey, this brother is good. We'd better join the party, or we'll miss it!' Katina shouted to her comrades while shouldering her bow and jumping from the low guardhouse roof.

One guard tried to strike her before she recovered from landing. It didn't work. While still on her knees, Katina simply pre-empted him by swinging her sword upwards at his legs. There was a cry of pain as her sword created a large gash in her opponent's left leg. Standing up, she sliced the distracted opponent in the neck.

The courtyard was fast running out of temple guards. In the time it had taken Katina and her companions to jump off the roof land and put down one each, Brother Michael had put down another five. Of the fifteen or so guards that had been in the courtyard at the start of unpleasantness, Brother Michael had put down nine trained and equipped guards in less than half a minute. The remainder started to run.

'Leave them to go. We must depart the temple now.' The priest ordered as he turned and opened the gate. Katina nodded to Brother Michael.

'What about that novice?' Katina asked.

'He said not to wait for him and we dare not stay here with what has just happened.' Osgood Shamus replied, sombrely looking around the courtyard at the dead and dying. They all stepped through the front gate.

As soon as she left the temple compound, Katina could hear fighting in what sounded like the whole city. It was clear from their faces, the others heard it too. She led them across the twenty feet wide cobbled stone street to a recessed doorway of a large timber-framed house opposite the entrance to the temple complex. When they were all gathered.

'We must get back to Ablamon and the others at the inn as quickly and discretely as possible. To the edge, quietly now and stay in the shadows.' Katina ordered without thinking to whom she was speaking. As the sudden dawn of realisation came to her face.

'Do not be concerned about your orders, scout. We will follow your guidance on matters of sneaking.' Brother

Michael replied in a quiet tone.

They all crept in the dawn shadows, moving slowly from the doorway to doorway of the large wooden houses along the half-mile of the main street towards the city centre. There were many dead city guards and clear signs that others had changed sides.

As they approached the central square, they hid in a shop doorway and looked on. She saw a giant bonfire in the middle. The city mayor and his family dressed only in their nightclothes were being dragged onto a raised platform at the front of which stood a tall, lean middle-aged man.

'You have been charged with heresy and service to the Lord of All Evil. Admit it and I will only execute you and your wife. Deny it and watch your children burn on the fire before I also torture you to death.' It was the High Priest.

'We must save them.' Katina said with a voice of fire.

"No, you must not. Let's just say it's the pot calling the kettle black." Said the voice in her head.

'Your face went blank. Have you been spoken to again?' Asked the priest.

'Yes, I was. The Huntress just told me that it's the pot calling the kettle black.' Katina replied. Everyone froze for a second as the enormity of the statement sunk in.

'Then we must go on immediately.' Concluded the stunned priest.

'To the inn on the market square, it is.' Said Hawkyn, drawing his sword.

'Please, good sirs, there is a series of servant alleyways that lead to a building on the central market.' Said a hidden voice from under some blankets at the back of the doorway.

'Show this lady the way to check what you say. Know that if you betray us, she will kill you without hesitation. It is simply the nature of her people.' Brother Michael stated calmly. A dirty, shabby man got up from under the pile of blankets, looking pale-faced and shocked.

'After you.' Katina said to the Vagrant politely while drawing her sword from its scabbard with a rasping sound.

Hiding in the shadows, he took Katina a few yards back the way they had come to a nearby doorway. Then looking across the street at the meeting of two large houses, she saw a side alley no more than two feet wide. Protuberances obscured its entrance from the neighbouring stone and wooden shop fronts. They crossed the street to the other passage and entered. The wood-frame buildings were three or four stories tall, making the journey airless and bereft of direct sunlight. It contained everything from domestic refuse to decaying body parts, but it was free of soldiers. The vagrant led her some significant way up the alley, then a sharp left turn that led to the main road at the back of the Mayor's Manor after some further distance. Katina noticed a similar small opening nearly opposite her.

'That goes where?' Katina asked quietly, looking at the other opening.

'To the warehouse complex.' He replied. Katina nodded an acknowledgement.

'That will do. We had better get back.' Concluded Katina. They retraced their path to the others. When they arrived, they found them pulling six bodies and bits back into the shadows.

'The mayor and family are all dead. Beheaded and thrown onto the fire. Even the baby.' Hawkyn informed her with a voice that dripped pure hatred.

'One day, I am coming back to settle this, but unfortunately, I have a more important job to do first.' Said Katina with a flat, unemotional voice while staring at the distant burning corpse of a baby on the fire. Brother Michael looked at Katina's two companions, and they both nodded, their faces full of anger.

'It appears, good lady, that you will not be alone in this.' The vagrant said while looking at Brother Michael and the two warriors.

'No, she will not.' The priest said with an icy tone. 'The High Priest must answer for this, but as our good scout said, not now.' They all looked at Katina.

'It is narrow, dark, smelly and dirty, but it takes us to the road at the back of the Mayor's Mansion. Nearly opposite is another one that I am told leads to the warehouses on the central market. We did not venture that far.' Katina replied to the implied question.

'We cannot remain here, Michael.' The priest said, looking at the bodies. Brother Michael nodded.

'What do you want in return for your help.' He asked the vagrant.

'After what I have seen today, quite simple. Passage out of here.' He replied.

'Then we are agreed. Lead on.'

The vagrant led the way, with Katina following closely. Brother Michael and Priest Osgood Shamus next, with Katina's two companions in the rear. The group traversed various narrow, smelly alleyways to the main road at the back of the Mayor's Manor. Temple guards were at the entrance to the manor but appeared to be having trouble with an angry mob of civilians and not watching.

The small group quickly scuttled across to the opposite alleyway and were soon away from the distracted temple guard. The vagrant led them through a similar series of narrow, dark, oppressive alleys, but this time there were a few small courtyards no more than six feet wide surrounded by small slum houses. The occupants were looking out hopelessly at the passers-by. Katina doubted they cared who was running the city.

As promised, the group were quickly looking at the warehouse courtyard from between several large stacks of boxes and sacks. About a dozen temple guard held various workers tied up. Katina looked at her two companions, who nodded. The three of them quietly prepared their bows and snuck into the warehouse yard. Staying near the alleyway entrance and hidden behind some abandoned barrels.

One soldier moved his sword to strike at a prostrate worker. Katina took careful aim and released her arrow. Straight through the neck. Both her companions shot too. Three temple guards went down. The remaining guards turned to see who fired but otherwise did not act and appeared shocked. This was a severe mistake. Quickly another three went down to chest and leg hits.

Brother Michael, sword drawn and mace in hand, ran at the six remaining guards who turned to engage but not collectively. As a result, he quickly dispatched two more. Even as Katina and the others ran in to fight, the four remaining guards fled to the market. Katina and the others retrieved arrows speedily and carefully looked across the market from the yard entrance.

Ablamon, during the night, had sent Katina and two of his guards to retrieve the priest before somebody killed him, while he and the others prepared the carts to leave as soon as they got back. Then at first light, all hell broke loose as the temple guard took over the city. He and his guards were at first-floor windows. They had for some time kept the temple guard at bay with archery fire, while the inn's guards, together with the city guard that had made it to the inn, protected downstairs. They kept it secure predominantly by keeping the inn's heavy gates and window shutters closed. So far, it had worked quite well.

The others though, were worried about Katina and the companions. So was he. This morning's trouble was on an entirely different scale than was anticipated. He watched the warehouse courtyard expecting to witness another batch of senseless slaughter. Instead, he saw many temple guards go down to archery fire that originated from out of vision. He then saw a charging monk kill two more with ease. The remaining temple guard ran.

'I have found the others.' Ablamon shouted.

'About bloody time, where are they?' was a reply from one of his guards.

'In the warehouse complex across the market square.' Ablamon explained. He continued looking to see someone he didn't recognise free tide up workers who left his vision. Katina, two of his guards and the monk now secured the entrance to the warehouse complex. Ablamon noted that Katina and the others wouldn't have seen the two hundred or so temple guard between them and the inn. Katina disappeared behind a wall, reappearing a little while later, head chest and bow above the stone gate pillar next to the entrance. True to form, she was looking around the square.

Things paused for a few minutes, then a concerted attack on the inn occurred by about a hundred temple guards. However, the inn had stout stone walls several feet thick and fully boarded windows on the ground floor. In addition to Ablamon and his guards, and a dozen inn guards, there were double that of the escaped city guard. The main doors held, but some enemy gained entrance through a window. Concentrated archery fire prevented further reinforcement of those who had got inside. The city guard butchered the attackers, seeking vengeance for earlier temple guard atrocities committed on their families and comrades. After several minutes of withering archery fire from various first-floor windows, the temple guard withdrew.

The attackers then did what, with hindsight, turned out to be a serious tactical blunder. They dispatched two full squads to deal with Katina and her associates at the warehouse single cart width gate and started a full-frontal assault. That in itself was not the error. It was the unforeseen actions of one of the guards that caused the issue.

Ablamon saw his two guards taking a position somewhat reverentially on either side of the monk. Katina, as expected, fired arrows from the top of the warehouse courtyard's wall. Hawkyn, Ternan and the monk systematically butchered the charging soldiers. Many fell quickly, with it would appear, no one getting anywhere near the monk. After about a minute, the three advanced beyond the gateway as the casualties started to cause the attacking guards to step back. It was at this point the error occurred.

Katina had been happily standing on some convenient wooden boxes to get a good vantage point when she realised the others were advancing beyond her immediate vicinity. She jumped down and followed them through the gate.

'Brother Michael behind.' She didn't get the chance to finish the sentence as he immediately leapt forward, dicing the soldier in front of him and creating space. Then spinning around and dropping to one knee, easily parried a clumsy attack from a soldier on the ground. Sheathing his short sword, he picked up the struggling, wounded guard by his neck and, with one hand, lifted him off the ground, the guard's feet kicking aimlessly in the air. He turned around to face the attacking temple guards. With eyes of fire and a face angrier than Katina had seen in a very long time, Brother Michael bellowed.

'You dare attack your Blade Master from behind after I spared your life. It and those of all of your comrades are now forfeit.'

Then letting his mace dangle on its strap with his left hand ripped off the struggling man's helmet. He recovered the dangling war mace, threw the struggling man a few feet away, then with a backhanded swing, he hit the guards unarmoured head just below his left ear. Katina failed to move quickly enough as parts of the head hit her legs.

'I will now kill all of your wounded before I kill all of you.' Brother Michael shouted loud enough for the whole square to hear. He casually walked over to the next wounded guard.

Katina had stepped into the space left in the line by the fuming Brother Michael, although it transpired she didn't need to. When Brother Michael picked up the next screaming, struggling guard by the hair, he drew his short sword and beheaded him in one blow. He casually walked over to the third and beheaded him too. Katina noted the temple guards' enthusiasm for the fight dissipated rapidly. Several more beheadings, including some with the mace and all fighting ceased.

'Brother Michael, stop this now.' Said the Priest Osgood Shamus, which Brother Michael wholly ignored as another head sailed through the air.

'Brother Michael, Blade Master of Light I, Senior Priest of Light, order you to stop this now. Such violence is not permitted against other humans unless they are in the service of the Evil Lord.' Priest Shamus shouted in tones similar to those Katina had heard in the temple compound at daybreak. Brother Michael appeared to come to his senses, dropped the head he was holding and walked back into line with a face of death to all those who got in his way. Katina wondered if it might have been better just to leave Brother Michael to get on with it.

'Temple Guard, now hear me. You are trying to kill Warriors of Light, including several Lord Guardians and your Blade Master. So far, you have not even harmed us and have lost over a quarter of your number. Withdraw now or die. I will not protect you again.' Osgood Shamus shouted in a harsh voice, having turned to face the Temple Guard. They broke and ran. The battle left behind a destroyed market and at least fifty dead and dying temple guard on top of butchered civilians and city guard.

3 – THE ESCAPE

Katina started to walk across the devastated market. Brother Michael and Priest Shamus quickly flanked her. Hawkyn and Ternan were on the outside. All walked with weapons drawn. As they approached the Inn, she could hear removal of the barricades from behind the gate and noticed people looking out of first-floor windows.

Ablamon came out smiling. 'I am glad to see you all safe.' He said as they all approached. Then looking about with a sorrowful face, he asked. 'No novice?'

'He didn't make it.' The priest replied sombrely.

Pausing for a second of thought, Ablamon said, 'We must leave the city right now. From what we can see, the temple guard has taken the whole city bar this market.'

'Brother Michael here, who you met yesterday, is the one who trained our priest in combat. He is extremely competent. Certainly, he is better than Major Partten, though I hate to say it is probably better than Lord Daxx.' Katina continued.

'I am pleased to have you on our side this time. Are you able to accompany us up the valley?' Ablamon asked.

'I will. If I remain here, The High Priest will kill me.' Brother Michael responded.

'Please excuse me for asking, but when you were angry, you referred to yourself as "Blade Master". You are an excellent swordsman, even by our standards. However, it is not a title I am familiar with.' Katina requested humbly, not wishing to insult new comrades who possess such skill at arms.

'Neither would you have heard of it, Katina. We have not had a warrior of that standard in a long time. It is a title given to a Lord Guardian of extreme competence and a cut above the other Lord Guardians. In our culture, a Blade Master is of Lord Guardian skill in three different types of weapons in either hand plus some other stuff.' Ablamon responded.

'Forgive the extreme impertinence. Even from what I have seen, you are very competent, as Katina said, but are you by right the current Blade Master?' Ablamon continued.

'There is no impertinence in an honest question in these circumstances. I probably shouldn't have said that. I was a Blade Master while serving as a soldier and Regimental Sergeant Major many years ago. Technically I ceased being eligible when I became a Brother of the Infirmary, but once I did hold that title.' Brother Michael replied.

'Was it passed on to someone else?' Katina asked.

'No, I was the last Blade Master.' He replied.

'That's good enough for me. It's a privilege to have you accompany us, Lord Blade Master.' Ablamon said, bowing respectfully. This shocked Katina as she had not seen Ablamon bow to anyone other than the Chief.

'Kind sirs, they are coming back.' The vagrant stated.

'Who's this?' Ablamon demanded curtly.

'A homeless person who guided us through various alleyways in return for being escorted out of the city. Because of him, we were able to bypass many hostile areas. He has earned his passage.' Katina informed Ablamon, who merely looked at the vagrant and nodded an acknowledgement.

'Ablamon, we are being approached.' Hawkyn stated.

A party of about a dozen or so from the now rallied temple guard walked towards them.

'They appear to want to talk.' Said Brother Michael. 'Vagrant, go to the inn and wait. Your request for an escort out of the city will be honoured.' The vagrant bowed respectfully to Brother Michael and ran for it.

'We had better see what they want.' Added Ablamon. They all visibly sheathed swords and slung bows on shoulders as they slowly walked partway towards the advancing temple guard contingent.

'Greetings and well met. I am here to ask for your

honourable surrender and invite your terms for our consideration.' Opened what Katina noticed was a more ornately dressed Temple Guardsman.

'You have already lost nearly a third of your men for no casualties on our side. Many City Guards, Southern Plains Warriors, several Lord Guardians, and a Blade Master oppose you. You are badly overmatched. You have also committed heresy by attempting to kill a priest. I have already cast out and cursed to hell many temple guards this morning. I am happy to do it again unless you withdraw immediately.' Priest Osgood Shamus replied. Brother Michael raised his hand to stop the priest from talking further.

'You are not in a good position, Captain. What are your orders?' Brother Michael asked.

'Lord Blade Master, my orders are to capture and occupy the inn using any means necessary.' The captain replied.

'Then let us, our people, and families, leave unmolested. That would allow you to carry out your orders without further bloodshed. Either way, we are leaving. You can agree, or we go through you. The choice is yours but be quick to decide, or we will depart anyway.' Brother Michael responded curtly.

'I am not in overall command. I can only agree to your terms until a superior officer overrules me. Subject to those limitations, I will agree, but you must leave soon as my superiors will arrive shortly.' The Captain replied.

'If you cross us, you will die, painfully.' Brother Michael responded with an unemotional tone. The captain acknowledged nodding with a sad face.

'After I have cast you all out and cursed your souls to eternal damnation in hell.' Added Priest Osgood Shamus. A very pale-faced captain and escort bowed respectfully and returned to his remaining men.

'Any chance they will honour the agreement?' The priest

asked.

'The captain will until he is relieved of command. He will have already requested reinforcements. We must move quickly.' Ablamon said.

The big doors to the inn opened. Katina noted that Ablamon's carts, two others and some spare horses were ready to go. All crammed with women and children. The non-warrior men stood at the sides of the carts.

'The captain of the temple guard has allowed us safe passage out of the market square. We will head for the upriver city gate, but we must leave now.' Ablamon shouted.

There was no argument. Ablamon, his guards and Brother Michael mounted various horses. Katina mounted her horse and the priest climbed onto a cart. Two women drove each of the four carts. She noted in addition to Ablamon, his guards and the innkeeper's guards, there was roughly twenty-five city guard. Overall, approximately fifty fully equipped and trained warriors defended four carts and civilians.

The gate opened with the best and mounted warriors at the front. The soldiers and inn's guards were at the sides. As they passed through the remains of the market, unarmed men ran out and collected swords and shields from the fallen. A fair number of wounded city guards were recovered and placed on the back of the carts. True to their word, the temple guards stood aside and let them pass without question.

'Katina, take some city guard and watch our rear.' Ablamon commanded.

She dismounted, tied her horse to the back of a cart and beckoned several city guards. About a dozen dropped back with her. They formed a line and followed the others up the twenty feet wide cobblestone paved street. Looking backwards constantly, sure enough, half the temple guards from the market square followed. More squads joined the temple guards from side streets.

Several families also joined the convoy as it progressed passed their houses. In a short space of time, the civilians outnumbered the combatants by two to one. They proceeded slowly about a quarter mile when Ablamon shouted,

'Prepare for battle.'

Katina looked to the front to see the street blocked by about a hundred temple guards. When she looked to the back, those followed had now closed ranks and quickly advanced with swords drawn.

'Get ready, chaps.' Katina shouted as she climbed onto the back of the last cart, retrieved her bow from over her shoulder and prepared to fire.

'Remember, concentrate on staying alive and holding the line. Strike only when it is safe to do so. Archery will see them off.' She continued.

The attack on the rear came quickly and was brutal. The city guard would not usually have held the line against those odds, but the screams and cries of fear from the women and children emboldened them in the desire to protect the weak. Katina's archery fire with a fatal shot every few seconds had devastating results. The street was not wide enough to allow her new comrades to be outflanked or succumb to numbers.

After several minutes of this, when Katina was worried about her stock of arrows, she spotted the Temple Guard Captain from earlier. He was not covering himself with his shield. She aimed and released her arrow. A hit in the stomach, the power of her longbow and the narrow head of the arrow easily penetrating the captain's chain mail armour. He went down screaming. That was enough for the attackers. They retreated, being chased by the city guard. The temple guard lost several more soldiers during the withdrawal. Her squad retrieved many of her arrows, with some swords and scabbards being taken from the dead and dying.

Katina quickly checked over her new command. There appeared to be some injuries and a fair amount of blood, but they still functioned as individuals and a unit. None had got past them to the civilians. Her soldiers quickly put the spare swords on the rear cart. Katina then remembered something she had heard senior warriors do during battle.

'Those under my command, very well done. You followed my orders, and we saw them off. I am most pleased with you all.' She said and noticed several smiling faces.

Katina then stood up on the rear cart and looked forward. It was clear that a significant engagement had occurred at the front. There had been a mounted charge by Ablamon and his guards. Brother Michael and the city guards holding the line at the front of the carts. There were many casualties. The injured city guards were placed on the front cart and the line reformed.

'Advance.' Came the booming voice of Brother Michael, and the three-deep line at the front slowly walked forwards shortly followed by the carts. Katina looked back to the temple guards following them and decided on some intimidation.

'You have two choices. Let us go and live, or like your friends at the front, die trying to stop us. Oh, I forgot, how is that cursed captain of yours.' Katina shouted backwards to laughs from those under her command. She motioned to those with her to follow the carts, the enemy behind them decided on discretion rather than valour. After a short while, Katina saw evidence of the violence of earlier encounters.

'Can we take the bodies of our fallen comrades, please? We know most of them.' One of the soldiers asked Katina. No one was following them, so Katina nodded. Four were quickly placed onto the rear cart. One moaned as he was laid down.

'I've got this.' Said an elderly lady who started giving orders to the women around her. Katina had other things on her mind, so she just let the woman get on with it.

When they reached the point of the fighting at the front, Katina saw several dozen dead or dying temple guards. Looking forward, a mounted Brother Michael was fighting side by side with Ablamon. His guards were flanking them, with city's and inn's guards backing them up. The less well trained and equipped temple guards it appeared were having a bad morning. After some time, they withdrew to a courtyard in front of the upriver gatehouse, which still flew the city flag proudly at the top.

The retreating temple guard spread out several ranks deep across the entire square in front of the gatehouse a fair way away. A second company were behind them, facing the blockaded gatehouse. Ablamon halted the advance at the edge of the courtyard but did not enter it.

'Katina, get up here. You take command of the rear squad.' Ablamon ordered. The surprised city guard nodded and ran to the back. Katina noticed that he looked down the road and saw the group that had attacked Katina's squad earlier had not moved. As they had time, Katina noticed him speak to each soldier of his new command in turn and ordered several to get wounds cleaned and bound. With the assistance of the women in the rear cart, the elderly lady accomplished this quickly. Katina also noticed the elderly lady still working on the wounded soldier. Seeing everything was in hand, she ran to the front.

'Our situation appears dire, but neither of you seems the least bit concerned.' Priest Osgood Shamus said to Ablamon and Brother Michael.

'We aren't bothered, and our situation is secure revered priest. We are in no danger. We will stay here a while, then leave.' Ablamon responded.

'I am missing something.' The priest commented.

'Lord Blade Master, may I.' A soldier asked Brother

Michael, who nodded. The soldier then spoke loudly enough for the four carts to hear and probably the temple guards too.

'It goes something like this revered priest. The Southern Plains People make the best longbows there are, and we have about ten of them. Any one of them could probably fire over the city wall from here. If the temple guards do nothing, then the longbows will kill them. Like us, the Temple Guard are men at arms and have no bows. They can't fire back. If they attack, we simply stay on this street so they can't outflank us, removing the advantage of numbers. Then our Blade Master here, the Lord Merchant and his guards, will simply cut them to bits. Either way, they are dead.' The soldier stated.

'Especially as the gatehouse is still in city hands and they also appear to have bows as well.' Brother Michael added. The scared faces of the civilians on the four carts eased substantially at the reassurance.

Brother Michael stepped forwards. 'Hear me all, you cowardly incompetent heretics and servants of evil. I am Brother Michael, Blade Master and Servant of Light. Leave us to go or die and be condemned to hell for all eternity. Archers, on my mark, shoot. Five, Four.' Various people readied bows. 'Three, two, one. Release.' Brother Michael ordered. Ten shots fired with ten hits. Katina noticed frantic movement in the gatehouse.

'Archers prepare to shoot. Five, four, three, two, one. Release.' Brother Michael ordered again. Another ten hits, the arrows from the longbows going straight through hastily raised shields. 'Ceasefire.' He ordered. 'I take it that I have made my point.' He said finally, and as if to emphasise it, the gatehouse fired a volley into the second company of temple guards. Both companies withdrew to the centre of the square.

'Where did the extra two bowmen come from?' Ablamon asked. Two civilians raised hands.

'Please excuse the impertinence. We used to be poachers, spotted the spare longbows and thought we might help. It seemed appropriate at the time.' One thin, ragged civilian replied.

'Apology accepted. Stay on duty and accompany the tall blond lady with the bow. Her name is Katina.' Replied Ablamon.

'Yes, sir.' They both replied in unison.

The temple guard commanders discussed matters for a few minutes, after which the two companies withdrew to the wide streets that circumvented the city just inside the city walls, reformed ranks and waited.

'Brave but foolish. The temple guards plan to attack our flanks as the wagons go past and our forces are split.' Stated Brother Michael.

'Sounds appropriate.' Commented the priest.

'But they have forgotten the gatehouse. Anyone not fully engaged will get slaughtered by archery fire from the gatehouse walls.' Ablamon added.

'Katina, take those two poachers, go to the rear wagon and kill any temple guards who get within one hundred paces.' Ablamon ordered. She looked at the two poachers, who nodded an acknowledgement and the three ran to the back of the last cart.

'Soldiers hear me. Brother Michael take the town guard and form a line along one side of the four carts. I will take my guards and the inn's guards and do the same on the other side. The lines must hold. Given time Katina, the Poachers and the gatehouse bowmen will see them off. If they breakthrough, we are all dead.' He ordered. Then looking at the two women driving the first cart. 'When everyone is ready, move as quickly as you can.' Ablamon concluded. They both nodded through teeth gritted against fear. After a brief period of reorganisation, all combatants were ready. Ablamon gave the order and they all moved out.

As predicted, they were attacked from both sides simultaneously. The temple guards from the marketplace rushed the rear cart. Suddenly the carts stopped. Katina briefly looked between bow shots to see the lead cart had reached the barricade, which was being hurriedly cleared to let them through. Katina and her two poachers concentrated on the rear attack while the gatehouse archers took shots at the two side companies as and when the opportunity arose. The city and inn guards focused on defending and holding the line leaving the killing to the more experienced warriors. Katina was too busy to see how the rest were doing, but the rear cart she was on lurched forward after a few minutes.

'Step back slowly.' Katina shouted to her rearguards. She jumped down off the cart and stayed with them as step by step they withdrew, holding their line until they were past the barricade at the gatehouse. Katina noted that several city guards were down, others were wounded. One of Ablamon's guards was down and several others also injured.

The temple guards tried to press forwards, but archery fire from behind the barricade and the gatehouse walls soon took a terrible toll, and they hurriedly withdrew. It was clear to Katina that the temple guards were much worse off, though. Everything paused as their enemy considered the next move.

'Permission to recover our fallen sirs?' Asked the soldier who had spoken earlier and was now covered in blood.

'Granted. Archers cover them.' Brother Michael ordered.

Several soldiers and women moved a small part of the barricade then rushed out to check the fallen. There was a cry from a middle-aged woman and her teenage daughter as they lifted a man by the arms and dragged him back, both weeping profusely.

'My husband. I watched him die and did nothing.' The middle-aged woman wailed. The elderly lady jumped down off her cart, gave the woman a hard slap around the face.

'Pull yourself together, woman. He is still bleeding, so he is not dead. Put him on the cart and prepare yourself to help me. You are of no use in your current condition.' The elderly lady said in a very stern voice.

Several others helped the middle-aged woman with her husband and the various other wounded and dead. The elderly lady ordered women and older teenage girls around like a general for the next several minutes, giving precise commands to be obeyed immediately, or you got slapped hard.

'Get that wrong again and the soldier dies.' She said to a posh looking woman, who she slapped around the face leaving a significant red mark. Very quickly, though, the women removed bloodied armour and dirty clothes, wounds cleaned, potions and ointments administered. Katina noted that the elderly lady examined each wound before bandaging it herself. On a couple of occasions, having checked an injury, she used a small device and pulled something out before putting an ointment and very tightly binding the wound. Katina also noted that her bandages were clean, and any equipment used was wiped down and stuffed in a large bottle of liquid. After some time, when the elderly lady had treated all the severely wounded, she came over.

'My lords, a private word, please.' The elderly lady asked. Ablamon motioned her to a corner near the gate where Brother Michael and Priest Shamus were already talking. Katina followed out of curiosity.

'Thank you, madam, for all your efforts.' Ablamon said. She waved that off.

'I am what you would call a wise woman. It is my duty. By some miracle, the only dead we have are the six we picked up along the way. An additional six that we also collected still live. Somehow none of the soldiers that fought with you at the inn is dead, though we now have a dozen of them seriously wounded. Many others, including the merchant's guards, are wounded but still functional. Unfortunately, most of that dozen will die after a few days when I run out of ointments and herbs. Many will die anyway, your man too, I am afraid.' She said, looking at Ablamon.

'Did you not bring enough then, madam?' Brother Michael asked in a respectful tone.

'I came prepared to treat an ill niece, not deal with a full-scale battle. For once in my life, I didn't see this coming.' She replied wryly.

'Luckily, I did. Here have this.' Brother Michael said, handing her a large pack from his back. 'Until this morning, I was a brother of the infirmary. You should find all you need inside the bag.' He continued.

'Can you keep them alive for two weeks?' Ablamon asked.

'If kept warm, no rain, careful movement, some probably yes. Especially now I have the brother's medicines too. They will all be dead by three, though. I can't stop the bleeding long term.' She replied.

'We know someone who can, but he is two weeks away.' Ablamon retorted.

'That is a big ask of Oswald. There is no way he can do all. Last time he passed out after four serious cures and didn't wake up until morning.' Said Katina.

'Many will have already died. Of the remainder, some will be worse than others. Four per day may just work for those who are left. I know of no healing that will deal with these wounds, though.' She replied sternly.

'Some ancient knowledge has returned, and there is now one priest who can wield it. The problem is he is two weeks away. Is there no way to keep them alive for the two weeks?' Said Ablamon.

'Unfortunately, that is beyond me. One week and we will start losing people. Mainly due to blood loss. That is the best I can do. I must return to my duties.' The healer replied. The others all nodded respectfully.

One of the soldiers came through a side door and approached the group.

'Sergeant, am I glad to see you and your men.' Ablamon said to the approaching soldier.

'The feeling is mutual, Ablamon. Is there anywhere else left, the main barracks perhaps?' The sergeant asked hopefully.

'I don't think so. The mayor and family beheaded and burnt. They have either changed sides or are dead.' Ablamon replied.

'Then we must leave. My corporal and twenty-five mounted guards are a few hundred yards up the road outside the city.' The sergeant informed Ablamon.

'Then we must get the gates open, get the carts, civilians and wounded to them and then organise a retreat for the rest of us.' Ablamon informed him.

'After that?' The sergeant enquired.

'We head straight to Warameth. We have wounded that need treating there if they are to live.'

'Will they take all of us?' The sergeant asked.

'For sure. How many men do you have?' Ablamon asked.

'Nineteen here, plus twenty-five and my corporal outside. We are down the six that escorted you yesterday. That is how we knew something was wrong.' The sergeant explained.

'They weren't supposed to say anything.' Ablamon stated sternly.

'They didn't, but when they got back, their faces were white as sheets. They took all their equipment home with them, even took spare swords, bows and arrows. When they didn't show up today, we knew something big was up.' The sergeant stated. Ablamon nodded.

'We have equipment from neighbouring towers. There

are horses packed full of spare swords, bows, arrows and food.' The sergeant continued.

'Great, get them out now and have them leave with the carts. Tell your men to be ready to run for it. As soon as the carts are safe with your Corporal and out of bow range, we shall leave.' Ablamon told the sergeant, who nodded and left.

'Priest, you go with the carts. No arguments. You have not had the training your cousin has. Sorry to be blunt, but you are of no use here.' Ablamon ordered. Priest Osgood Shamus nodded sombrely.

The city guard brought out four horses. Within moments, the Sergeant opened the gates and the carts left, leaving just the combat-capable behind. The horseman beyond the gate rode forwards towards the gate immediately. The sergeant ran towards them.

'Corporal, escort these wagons and civilians clear of the city walls and out of bow shot. Then wait for us. When they are safe, we will run for it. I will explain later. Now go.' The sergeant ordered. After a few short orders, the mounted patrol formed a rear guard and two protective flanks as the wagons proceeded up the road.

Within minutes of the gates opening, the temple guards attacked once more. Yet again, withering archery fire stalled the attack as they tried to cover the one hundred paces between the two sides. As the temple guard ran back to the safety of distance, Brother Michael shouted.

'NOW'

They all abandoned their posts and ran as fast as possible to where the carts and mounted patrol were waiting. The temple guard did not try and chase but just stood and watched. When they were all finally together, and clear of the city, Priest Osgood Shamus breathed a loud sigh of relief.

'I've made it.' He didn't mean to say out loud.

4 – KATINA LEAVES

Katina kept watch on the City of Kersladen as they progressed down the road, but there were no attempts to follow them. Looking around, the first thing she noticed was the lack of activity on the farms. Several were utterly devoid of people or animals. The rest eyed them warily or with open hostility from behind shut gates and high stone walls. Peasants with pitchforks was not a concern to mounted soldiers in armour so the refugees kept going.

Looking at the procession of carts and people, the civilians appeared visibly relieved now that Kersladen and the horrors within were slowly disappearing into the distance. The warriors' demeanour indicated they considered the matter far from over. The wise woman treated those with minor injuries who then returned to service. Ablamon asked the civilians about former military experience. For the first mile or so out of Kersladen, the four-cart wagon train was a hive of activity. A few miles later and the military element was looking much better.

The best of the city guard increased Ablamon's five remaining guards to ten men and all on horseback. The mounted company that had waited outside the city gates were fully functional and yet to see action. Despite nineteen-foot soldiers being severely wounded, replacements from the rescued civilians improved the situation dramatically. Although many soldiers were now a bit long in the tooth, they had one mounted company and two companies of infantry, each twenty-five soldiers. The captain of the inn's guard commanded one of the infantry companies, the sergeant from the gatehouse the other. All soldiers were engaged in practising weapons and company shield wall tactics while on the march. By the time night was falling, they were looking quite good. Eighty-Five fully equipped soldiers plus commanders all had chain mail armour, large shield, and a good sword.

Ablamon and his guards rode at the front. The mounted town guard that had waited outside the city gates were several hundred yards behind the procession to discourage pursuit. One company of foot soldiers walked on each side of the wagons and their civilians.

Then at dusk, some ten miles out of Kersladen.

'Katina, front, please.' Ablamon shouted.

Katina, who had been dawdling, quickly rode forward.

'You have orders for me?' She asked.

'Yes, I do. You will need to be dealing with your mission soon, won't you?'

'Sorry, but it must be done.'

'I agree, so please take those two poachers and see if they are any good at scouting.'

'Yes Ablamon. We shall go upriver a few miles, circle around the farms and return from the back.'

'Poachers, come here please.' Katina shouted. One thin, ragged looking civilian of middling years and another of medium build and similar age, both poorly dressed, quickly ran to her, carrying longbows horizontally in their left hands.

'Are you two any good at scouting for enemy soldiers and Goblins?' Katina asked.

'We were passable at sneaking up on sizeable wildlife and even escaped from sheriffs occasionally.' Replied the thin, ragged poacher.

'We weren't that good, though. We got caught.' The medium build one added.

'Is that vagrant who guided us about Kersladen still here.' Katina shouted.

'I am, mam.' So responded a voice from behind a wheel of the lead wagon.

'Are you any good?'

'I heard mam. Town work I was passable but never done open country. I doubt now is the time for learning.'

The vagrant replied.

'No, it is not. Are you willing to stay with us and learn?' Katina replied.

'I am staying for now. I cannot promise long term though. Maybe I can learn later.' The vagrant responded.

Katina simply nodded at the vagrant, looked at the two poachers, dismounted and tied her horse to the rear of the front cart. The three scouts ran off up the road at a fast jog ignoring the derelict stone-walled farm complex they were passing. Finally, after about half a mile, Katina stopped.

'We will have to start looking now. Careful, though, there is still a lot of farm traffic. We will have to tell the difference between those and ambushers.'

The two poachers just nodded. One went towards the river, the other towards another abandoned farm away from it. Katina followed them for a while, double-checking their observation skills, though in truth, it was impossible to determine anything given all the travel on the road and it was almost dark. After about fifteen minutes of fruitless searching near the river.

'Hey, we had better join your friend. It's impossible to see anything here.'

'His name is Nate. For what it's worth, mam, I doubt the temple guards could have gotten past us.'

'The temple guard is not the concern.'

They jogged away from the river about a mile, where they saw Nate crouched in the long grass on the other side of the last of the abandoned fields. Signalling to her companion to keep low, she crawled along the hedges and through the tall grass to the hollow Nate was hiding in.

'No need to be cautious, mam. They have seen me. Sorry, I hadn't considered the level of care needed. I will do better. Those watching us are withdrawing. When I got here, they were about a quarter-mile away.'

'Who was it?'

'They weren't Human, mam, so that makes Goblins.

Several dozen, but not loads.'

'Not necessarily. Just because our enemy isn't Human, that doesn't make them Goblins. How tall were they, my height?'

'About average height, not as tall as you, green and brown.'

'That would make them Goblins, as you say. However, if they are my height or taller, green, reptile skin with no wildlife about, then they are Plains Devils and serious trouble.'

'No wildlife? You mean no birds and animals.'

'Correct.'

'It wasn't them then.'

'Let's check where these Goblins were hiding.'

'They were behind that group of small trees over there.' Nate said, pointing further inland and upriver.

'After you then.' Katina ordered and the three crawled in the dark onwards through the long grass towards a small group of crab apple trees about five hundred yards away.

'You were right, Nate, Goblins. Look at the misshaped feet and the wide stance they take when walking or running. It looks like one team here. You said several dozen Nate.'

'Yes, mam, there was a second group a few hundred yards downriver.'

'Are they still about?'

'No, mam, I can see them in the distance over there. Very messy and careless, these Goblins.' The medium build poacher responded.

'They are. That's the reason The Lord of All Evil hasn't already won. You two go back and tell Ablamon and the Blade Master what is going on here. I will circle round for another mile or so to make sure there aren't any more.'

'Yes, mam.' The two poachers responded in unison and ran back to the group of refugees. Katina continued cautiously across the grassy plains in a downriver direction, but all she found were the occasional tracks of Human and animal movement. After about a further mile, she returned to her friends.

When approaching the wagons, Ablamon and Brother Michael rode towards her.

'We've been told. They are a long way down the valley. Do you think the others are alright?' Ablamon asked.

'If something serious had happened upriver, I am pretty sure I would know.'

"Yes, Katina, I would have told you. They have had a fun time lately, but everyone is unharmed." The Huntress interrupted.

'And?' Ablamon said in an exasperated tone.

'Your face went blank again.' Brother Michael added.

'Apparently, it has been entertaining for them, but they are unharmed.' Katina responded.

'There are no further patrols about, just the two that have left.' She continued.

'So, we are currently in the clear and everyone can rest.' Brother Michael said.

'Yes, but not for long. Those two groups will not be all this far down the valley without being part of a much larger one. If they return, they will be on us quickly.'

'We know senior Huntress. So how did the two poachers do?' Asked Ablamon.

'They appear to have reasonable skill but are not used to applying our level of care, patience and attention to detail. The need for it has sunk in, though. In time and with further training, they will be adequate.'

'The three of you will need to keep watch while we rest. Now get some food, then take your two trainees and watch our flanks for a few hours.' Ablamon ordered.

Katina nodded and headed for the lead cart. Her two poachers were sat on the grass nearby, eating a small amount of bread and cheese.

'I am afraid we are to go out again to make sure we are not visited while the soldiers and horses rest.'

'Presumably, mam, if we are seen and avoided, then the

people here die.'

'They will be asleep, so yes, Nate, they will all die.' Katina replied.

'I guess we had better be doing a proper job then.' The other poacher concluded.

'I am not doing this anymore.' Came a loud female cry from a middle cart.

'Neither am I. We are high born noblewomen. This is servants work and they are only soldiers. I don't care if a few die. I am covered in filth and blood, and no one has given me my wine all day.' Added another voice.

Then there was silence. The elderly healer stood up, looked them both up and down. Then with a calm but loud voice said.

'Both of you get up and leave now.'

'What. You can't do that.' The first noblewoman replied.

'You women of noble birth are good for only one thing, being broodmares. You are both too old for that. You have no skills or strength, have brought no food to share. Your money is useless here or where we are going. You inhibit our chances of success, so you must leave.' The elderly healer responded.

'I shall not go. You do not have the authority for that.' The second noblewoman stated firmly.

'Oh yes, she does.' The vagrant replied. 'As the only wise woman here, anything non-military falls under her or the priest's decision. Judging by the look on his face, he won't be supporting you.'

Priest Osgood Shamus got down off the lead cart and slowly walked over to the arguing women, face full of sorrow.

'My ladies, please let me help you down. I would suggest you head back to Kersladen. I doubt you will make it to Treenys. There are Goblins in the way, according to our scouts.'

'We're not going.' Was the loud reply from the second

noblewoman.

To Katina's surprise, the priest grabbed both her arms just below the shoulders and pulled her off the cart, dumping her on the road. The two shocked women started to cry.

'Which way?' The priest asked gently.

'I have family in Treenys.' One of the noblewomen said.

'Treenys is that way.' The priest said, pointing onward up the road.

'We'll die.' One of the noblewomen said.

'Probably, now leave.' Replied the priest.

The sobbing pair slowly walked into the darkness while the other civilians watched in silence, eating a small piece of bread each. A few minutes later, there was a shout from up the road.

'If we promise to look after our two soldiers, can we come back please?' Shouted the first noblewoman.

'You must do as you are told and learn how to treat the wounded. Agree to that and you may come back.' The elderly healer lady replied.

The two noblewomen came running out of the darkness amidst guttural shouts and curses from the night. Both were panting with exhaustion and crying.

'The place is crawling with monsters off to the side of the road.' The first noblewoman exclaimed through tears of fear.

Priest Osgood Shamus turned to the train of carts and said.

'That is why we need living soldiers.' Everyone sat in silence.

The vagrant walked up to Katina. 'I think it is time I started my tuition.' He said sombrely.

'Changed your mind?'

'Yes, mam. I didn't think those in charge had the guts. I was wrong. This is a fight that can be won.'

'Oh yes, this fight most definitely can be won. You stay

with me, behind, eyes open and silent.' Katina responded.
She then looked at the other two.

'Nate, head up the river where the women went.
Quarter mile no more. Don't get caught now.' Then
looking at the other poacher, 'You go inland from the carts,
again no more than a quarter-mile. I will be between the
two of you with the vagrant here.' Katina said. The two
poachers got up, nodded and disappeared into the darkness.
Then looking at the vagrant, she said. 'Our turn now.'

'Yes, mam.' Was the reply as he stood up. They both
jogged low to the ground, away from the road and ahead.

After a few minutes, Katina whispered. 'We keep watch
from here.' They both knelt, observing the darkness ahead.

Many minutes passed in silence, then she heard the
familiar twang of a longbow to their left, followed by a
guttural scream. Katina went to get up.

'No, mam, you are needed here. I have no chance of
doing your job, but I can help Nate.' He got up and silently
disappeared into the darkness.

Katina heard movement in the distance. Similar sounds
to her left and right joined the twangs of longbows. She
wanted to help her new pupils but could now see shadows
closing on her too. Katina knew she must hold her position
and hope her new pupils were up to the job independently.
Screams augmented the sounds of the longbow to her left.
There was a shadow that was a head taller than the others.
Carefully she aimed and released the arrow. It flew true and
the shadow fell with a cry.

The vagrant then returned, a pair of blood-covered
long-bladed daggers in his hands. Katina looked at him and
said.

'A homeless vagrant, my arse.' The vagrant just smiled,
putting his index finger to his lips as he cleaned both his
daggers on the grass. The noise of moving wagons
penetrated the sounds of the night.

'They are not remaining here. Go tell the other poacher

to move upriver in time with the wagons. Then come back to me.'

'Yes, mam.' Was the response as the vagrant ran off in a downriver direction. Katina got up, slowly walked through the tall grass, keeping as low as possible while watching the darkness beyond. This continued for a few more hours, the carts progressing even more slowly than usual, the vagrant regularly moving between Nate, Katina and the second poacher, who it turned out was called Inan.

While the Goblins watched the refugees, they did not make any more incursion attempts. The wagon train stopped several times for rest and a little sleep, but never for more than a few hours. As first light approached, patrols from the company of mounted city guard started and the Goblins rapidly withdrew. Finally, the wagons rested, allowing the three scouts and vagrant to get some well-earned sleep.

By noon they were on the move again. The sight of a dockside lined with Kersladen river barges and Temple Guards, dashed any hopes of relief at Treenys. After a quick discussion, they kept going into the night, stopping slightly upriver of Treenys with many of the guards awake at any one time, the three scouts and vagrant a quarter-mile further out on watch. Katina thought something was out there, but whatever it was, it did not approach. They broke camp at first light and continued the journey.

After a while, Nate and Inan approached Katina.

'Excuse me, mam, but something is wrong. There is still lots of evidence of farm carts and animals on the road. There shouldn't be any given we are past Treenys.' Nate suggested.

'I agree, something is not right. We had better tell the others.' So, she went over to Ablamon.

'Lord Blade Master, Ablamon, may we have a word with you and the other commanders, please.' Various calls went out and within a few minutes, all company commanders,

Brother Michael and Ablamon, were gathered around.

'My scouts here have pointed out to me that there is still evidence of significant farm movement to include carts, animals and people on the road upriver. We are beyond Treenys now. That sort of traffic doesn't happen this far up the valley.'

'The others?' Suggested the Corporal from the company of mounted city guard.

'It could be.' The Sergeant replied. Looking at Brother Michael, he went on. 'The six guardsmen that escorted you through the city when you first arrived were previously farmers. Their families work on four of the farms near the city. Having got wind of events, they may have made a run for it.'

'Huntress, please look. You should be able to recognise them.' Brother Michael ordered. Katina looked at Ablamon, who nodded. 'Poachers, cover the plains to our right.' He continued.

'Yes, my lord.' And off they ran.

Katina nodded at the commanders and proceeded up the road. Progressing at a fast run, she covered several miles quickly. The great forest to her right closed on the road, crossing it to the banks of the river Emor. Just before that, she saw a group of carts and animals blocking the road. As she drew nearer, there were shouts from the people in the carts. Several soldiers dropped back, blocking the road between her and the stationary carts.

As she got nearer, one of the soldiers said. 'Oh, it's you. Thank the Light Bringer. Are the others with you? We could do with some help.'

'We are trying to get through to the upper villages but have broken a wheel on the lead cart. We're stuck.' Continued another.

'I will ask. There are a lot of us. We had to fight our way out. Your company made it out along with other soldiers, my people, Brother Michael, the Priest, and many civilians.

There is bound to be somebody who can fix a cartwheel. How many of you are there?'

'A dozen equipped soldiers, four farms worth of family and hired hands, several dozen cattle and oxen, and four carts with tools and grain.' The soldier replied.

'I will go back and ask what help is available. You will see us soon anyway.' Katina then ran back.

'Ablamon, the Corporal and Sergeant were correct. The families and hired hands of the soldiers that escorted us through the city, plus animals, grain and tools. They have a problem, though, broken cartwheel.'

A wheelwright and his son fixed the broken wheel, but it took several hours. By then, unfortunately, it was too late in the day to be travelling through a forest, so they made camp for the night. The intention was to leave at first light.

When settling down for some long needed rest, there was a wail of despair from one cart, followed by gentle, soothing words from neighbouring women. Then, finally, the elderly wise woman, tired, drawn face, came over to Ablamon.

'This trip is tough beyond words. None have yet died, but several are very close now. I have to watch them all die by the inch. In a day, maybe two, and we will start losing them. Three are hanging by a thread. So, I told the women, hence the wailing.' The wise woman said.

Katina, who had got up, then noticed something, claw marks on a cart tailgate.

'These are new. When did this happen?' Katina asked those on the cart.

'While you were out scouting this morning, mam. The biggest falcon I have ever seen. Huge grey and white thing. Stared at our priest for ages, then flew off like the devil was chasing it.'

'Ablamon.' Katina shouted.

'I heard. They know, don't they?' Katina nodded, smiling. Then looking back at the elderly healer, Ablamon said. 'Continue to do your marvellous work, madam. Do not give up. I don't care how you do it. Just keep them alive.'

The elderly lady shrewdly looked at Ablamon. 'Something is at work here, isn't it? Something is fiddling with things.'

'Several somethings. Two are active currently that I know of.' Ablamon responded.

'That will attract attention.'

'Everything comes with a price.' Replied Ablamon. She nodded with a resigned look on her face and returned to her patients.

After some rest, the four scouts were put to work for the night. At first light they ranged through the forest checking for surprises and found evidence of hasty departures. Inan and Nate continued near the forest and the grassy plain on the other side of the wood. The vagrant went through the grassland and Katina up the road. They waited patiently for the eight lumbering wagons with several hundred tired, hungry, and frightened civilians to clear the woods.

The vagrant came running over. 'I have just spotted Nate running hell for leather across the grassland. No Inan, though.'

'Trouble then.' Then Katina listened. 'Oh shit. No birds, no animals. Run now, move.' Katina ordered.

The startled vagrant turned on his heels and ran for the wagons. Several arrows that came too close for comfort followed them, but they both got clear. Those at the carts had seen the mad dash runs. The companies were already taking defensive positions and forming a perimeter around the wagons. Nate arrived at Ablamon a few seconds before Katina and the vagrant.

'Lord Blade Master. Goblins out of the forest, hundreds of them. We killed several scouts, but Inan was too slow leaving. He's climbed a tree and hidden.' Nate reported.

'Senior Huntress, I have not seen you run from anything.' Brother Michael asked.

'Plains Devils, hidden. I couldn't see them. I think they block the road.'

Brother Michael Looked at Ablamon. 'You know these things?' he asked.

'Regretfully, I do.'

'Then you must take them. I will deal with the Goblins.' Said Brother Michael.

'You won't get many of us back, if any.' Replied Ablamon.

Brother Michael nodded then shouted, 'First Company, Second Company shield wall now. Mounted, take the flank.' The soldiers of each company quickly formed a line two ranks deep and began interlocking shields.

Ablamon looked at the dozen soldiers from the farmers they had just joined. 'Farming company, back my guards up. None must get through. Some of our enemies will be invisible.' The oldest soldier simply nodded, his squad formed a single line behind the horseman and interlocked shields.

'Advance.' Came the shout from Brother Michael who had taken position in the front row between the two infantry companies.

'Step.' Came the shouts from the two company commanders, and the whole line took a step forward.

'Step.' and the whole line took another step forward.

Katina mounted her horse and walked it towards the line of Ablamon's guards.

'Katina, what the hell are you doing. Get your arse across that river and complete your mission now.'

'You are not serious, Ablamon.'

'Do your duty girl. Follow your orders. The tribes must know, now get going. Survive this and get home.'

'Ablamon, they're coming.' Came the shout from the road. He then turned his back and rode into line.

Ablamon looked around quickly and shouted, 'Hawkyn, go with her.'

'What?' Was his surprised response.

'Follow your orders man. Get gone. Now.' Was Ablamon's shout as he joined the line.

'Yes, sir.' Hawkyn said as he pulled away from the others and rode towards Katina.

Knowing that her orders must overrule the hatred of the Goblins, with tears of anger, Katina wheeled her horse and spurred it on, jumping it into the deep, wide river. She did not look back but could hear Hawkyn following her. As the pair struggled across the half-mile-wide freezing water, Katina thought.

"Huntress, you Gods of Light, ask too much of mere mortals."

"We know, but you must do it." Was the response.

5 – THE CASTLE

Katina clung to the saddle of her horse as it swam through the freezing water of the half-mile-wide river. Well, it was better than swimming it herself, she thought. That was about the only positive thing in her current situation. Not only were her body and mind reeling from the thermal shock of cold deep water, but she had also just run from a battle for the first time in her life. Not only leaving her tribe and battle companions behind but civilians too. That went against every second of her training and experience. The women and children of the valley folk had no hope against either Goblins or Plains Devils who would butcher them. She appreciated that her tribe must know about the valley, but the cost attached to the taking of that message weighed heavily on her soul.

To distract herself from turning around and going back, she considered, as her horse dragged her across the river, whether all the tribes could come here? Would that be wise? Well, it would increase the combat power of the Humans in the valley. There was enough space for all the tribes, in the short term at least. Humans controlled only half the valley's length, and even that was largely vacant. From what Arturous had told her and what she had seen herself, the valley must be about three hundred miles long. Warameth, the furthest the Humans now were, was only halfway. There were just a few routes into the valley, all guarded by castles. She wasn't a tactician or strategist, but if they could get control of the whole valley, defending it would be a lot easier.

She stopped her musings as they both struggled up the steep bank out of the river. While the horse briefly shook itself, Katina looked back. Hawkyn was nearly at the bank too. The entire focus of the enemy was on the caravan, none had followed them across the river. She could see and hear the battle from here, but not who was winning.

Hawkyn and his horse approached. Eventually they scrambled up the bank and shook themselves off.

'Good to have you along. Unfortunately, we are far too close to hostilities to dry off here. We must keep moving.' Said Katina. Hawkyn nodded.

'Our horses will be far too cold to ride for a while. We are going to have to walk in wet clothes.' She continued.

'I figured as much.' He replied.

They walked roughly southwest across the grasslands to where she thought the castle in the Southern Mountains was. Katina checked the area leaving the horses with Hawkyn. There was no evidence that the Goblins were on this side of the river, so she returned to Hawkyn. When the sounds of battle receded into the distance, she briefly stopped, rid herself of water in boots, clothes, and bags, then slowly walked her horse through the waist-high grass. The sun started to dry out her sodden clothes.

After several more hours of walking, Katina decided it was time to get on their horses and move more rapidly. The pair travelled across the grassland, the cold biting wind whistling up the valley from the sea a hundred miles east. They struggled on until nightfall when they stopped and made camp.

'I will go and have a look around. Check we are alone and see if I can find any firewood. We both need to get warm.' She said.

'I will set up camp.' Hawkyn replied.

An hour later, Katina returned. He had dug a small deep firepit, placed the bedrolls near it, and tethered the horses.

'Not much of anything out there, but I did find a small dead tree, so we have some firewood.'

'I will take cold salted beef over a raid by Plains Devils anytime. You look very sorrowful. Anything I can help with?'

'Recent events are weighing heavily on me. Twice now, I have had to walk away from trouble, leaving others to face the horrors of our enemy. It goes against every fibre of my being and training.'

'The news of what is going on here must be taken home. The valley folk have potential, and with Major Partten and Brother Michael, two great warrior leaders. Alone they will lose, but with the return of the Gods of Light, spells from Oswald and Luka, and our tribes too, we may just be able to hold somewhere.'

'It's too big an ask of me.'

'You are wrong Katina. I have watched you since you were a little girl. I have seen your dogged determination grow, your ability to learn new skills improve, your amazing abilities in the wild. You are easily equal to Luka and the Elf and are the only one who can make it home and warn the tribes.'

The night past uneventfully, both huddled around the meagre fire. They moved on in the morning, riding at a modest pace and by the evening could see the low hills that marked the beginning of the Southern Mountain Range a few miles away. The following morning, they broke camp again and rode slowly through the low hills to the mountains and up the ten feet wide path that led to the castle.

'The gates are shut.' Observed Katina.

'I wonder if that is a good or bad sign.' Said Hawkyn.

'Hello. Can we come in, please?' Katina shouted.

A head looked out of a narrow arrow slit in the gatehouse, then a minute or so later peered over the crenulated battlements of the castle wall.

'It's two of the Southern Plains people. Can we let them in?' The guards shouted from behind the wall. A few minutes later, there were sounds of moving wooden bars and the rattling of large chains. Eventually, a door opened.

'Hawkyn, you and your friend may come in, but keep your swords sheathed.'

'Thank you, Walgund. You are being far more cautious

than previously.' He replied.

'We have had many refugees arrive from the outlying farms of Kersladen. They have told us about the takeover by the High Priest.' He replied as the pair passed through the gateway.

The inside was a hive of activity. There were carts, horses, cows, sheep and crowds of people. Many were walking through the other gate carrying farming tools or bags of grain. Others were taking food to a storage building. There were also men working on dilapidated buildings, clearing them out and repairing roofs.

'You have a lot more people here and a lot going on.' Said Katina.

'Yes. We have about five hundred people now, most of whom are farmers or labourers. The new refugees are cultivating the valley on the other side of the castle. Unfortunately, we will run out of food long before the wheat is ready to harvest. Do you know if Ablamon can bring us more food soon?' Walgund enquired.

'You could ask her to pass a message on. She may help. They've asked enough of you lately.' Hawkyn suggested.

'I am not a priest. Not only that, but I also don't believe in any gods, at least not for worshipping. I doubt she will be listening.' Katina said.

'Can't hurt to ask.' Hawkyn replied.

'Ask who?' Enquired Walgund.

'It's a bit of a long story, but the Gods of Light have returned. I have seen miracles carried out on behalf of The Light Bringer and The Huntress. I have seen Katina here be spoken to by The Huntress. If she asks nicely and the Goddess is listening, then just maybe The Huntress could arrange some help.' Said Hawkyn.

'Everyone here would be most grateful if you could ask for help on our behalf.' Walgund said.

'Alright, I will try. Is there somewhere peaceful I can pray in?' Said Katina.

'How about that building the newcomers finished re-roofing this morning. No one is in it yet.' Suggested a gate guard.

'I will try that. Please lead on.'

Walgund and two men who had stood near the gate took them to a small building attached to the other wall of the castle. While it had a roof, four stone block walls and was clean, it did not have a door or windows, just rectangular spaces where they should have been.

Katina went inside. It was clean and dry but devoid of contents. She went to the middle of the room and knelt on the floor. It took a few seconds to compose herself. Then in her mind, she called out.

"The Huntress, are you there?" Then waited a few minutes. Nothing.

"The Huntress, are you there? Some people need your help." Again nothing. Katina waited and repeated the call. Again, no response. She stopped, got up, brushed herself off and left the building.

'I am sorry, it didn't work.'

'It was worth a try.' Responded Walgund. 'Please join us for dinner. It's about time for the first group.'

He led them to a big fire surrounded by some large logs on which various people sat eating. Katina, Hawkyn, Walgund and the two gate guards sat on an empty log. The meal consisted of a modest piece of bread and a small lump of cheese each.

While sat there eating, listening to Hawkyn explain to everyone the incredible events of the last few months, she saw him look upwards and frown despite the sky being clear. That was when Katina realised that the air felt heavy, like it is just before a big thunderstorm. There was, however, no sign of any storm.

As she returned to her meal, she noticed a pair of ladies walk through the other gatehouse. These ladies were both as tall as she was. One was blond-haired, wore supple leather armour with a longbow and quiver of arrows over a shoulder. She carried several rabbits in each hand. The other woman had long dark hair, wore a homespun brown woollen dress and held a wickerwork basket on her head. As they walked nearer, the air felt ever heavier and more charged. They walked with a purpose way beyond refugee farmers and headed directly at Katina.

When they got near the fire, the blond one turned and said. 'Master Walgund, my sister and I have come to visit my friend Katina of Iredan. We understand that it is custom with your people for visitors to bring a small amount of food with them. To this end, we have brought you a few rabbits and potatoes.'

'Thank you, ladies. Please take my seat.' He responded while getting up off his log.

'Thank you, sir.' The blond-haired one said as they both sat down. Then she looked at Katina and said, 'You called. What's the problem?'

After a second of pure shock as realisation dawned, Katina responded, 'I thought you couldn't appear this way. Anyway, aren't you busy with the others?'

'You are correct. It is dangerous. My light bearing brother has given me a few hours off. Besides, my sister wanted to meet some of you.' Hawkyn went very pale and started to shake while looking at the two ladies. Walgund and several others around the fire had puzzled expressions on their faces as it dawned on them that something unusual was happening.

Looking at the dark-haired lady, Katina said, 'Pleased to meet you. Am I correct in assuming the potatoes are your thing?'

'Pleased to meet you too and yes, you are correct, potatoes are my thing.' Was the lady's deep, resonant response.

'Why did you call me?' The blond lady asked.

Katina raised her hand, indicating the man who had

offered the two ladies his seat and said.

'Walgund, because of the recent issues in Kersladen, has more mouths to feed than he has food. We were wondering if you could pass a message to either Luka or Oswald to have some brought down.'

'I could do that for you, but they are all busy and have a lot more people to feed anyway. I don't think they could supply enough food in the time frame required.' The blond one responded.

'I could help, but I would need people to like me. Even unofficially would give me enough power to fiddle with the timings.'

'You can't do that. Unless Katina is willing to become an Oracle, only one of us can talk and advise her. Mortals can only handle one of us. More than that kills them. They don't have the energy for it.' The blond lady replied in a very shocked tone.

'With Hawkyn here, she's got a good chance of completing the trials. We haven't had one in a long time.' The dark-haired lady responded.

'How many lives will be saved if I succeed?' Katina asked.

'Several thousand at least. So long as I get the worshippers too.' Said the dark haired one.

'You must know that these tests will most likely kill you, and even if they don't, you will be very different.' The blond lady added.

'Walgund, if you and your people agree to worship the goddess The Farmer and I can pass these tests, then that may solve your problem with food.'

A stunned Walgund looked at the two ladies. His face drained all colour. Then with a very shaky stammering voice. 'May I have the pleasure of knowing which Goddesses I am in the presence of?'

The dark-haired lady offered him her hand in greeting and said, 'I am The Farmer, and this is my sister, The

Huntress. If you and your people agree to worship me and pray to me often, I can speed up the growing cycle for you. It will be tough, but I think a harvest could be achievable just before you run out of food.'

He thought for a second. Then took the Farmer Goddess's hand and said, 'I must do it, or we will starve. If it could solve the food problem, I will willingly pray to you and ask others to do so too. I am so very grateful for your attempts to help us. We now have hope.'

'Divine ones, please forgive my impertinence of daring to speak to you, but may I ask something to check if I have understood things correctly.'

'Go ahead, Hawkyn.' Replied the blond one.

'Katina is to go on a divine quest, and you desire me to go with her, assist her and protect her until death if necessary.'

'We do.' The dark-haired lady responded.

'I would be honoured beyond measure. Of course.'

'If she succeeds, then you will have to be her intermediary. Protect her, determine who gets to see her for advice and provide for her physical needs in all capacities.'

'Of course, I will do that for my Katina.'

'Then it was worth the risk of coming.' The dark-haired lady said.

'We are all grateful to you for your willingness to participate. You must understand that the physical and spiritual cost Katina and the others, who are our representatives here, are huge and will last for all eternity.' The blond lady said to those around.

'It has to be done though.' Katina responded.

'That doesn't lessen the level of bravery and commitment you have all given. We must go now. Until next time.' The blond lady replied.

The pair nodded to those around the fire, got up, turned and walked back towards the gate they came through, disappearing as they crossed the threshold.

'Were those two who I think they were?' A grubby, muddy man in his mid-thirties asked.

'The Huntress was the blond one, and the dark-haired one was The Farmer.' Katina confirmed.

'Can you be sure?' Another asked.

'Yes, I recognised the voice of The Huntress.' Katina said.

'That's good enough for me.' The first muddy worker replied.

'Her word, is that all it takes?' The second questioned.

'I am not in the business of accusing two Iredan warriors of lying. I don't have much of a life right now, but it's the only one I've got and I want it to last beyond the next half minute.' The first concluded.

'We have a large basket of chitted potatoes given by a Goddess. Anyone going to help plant them?' A third worker asked. Several other people nodded and got up.

"They're just normal spuds, nothing special." A deep, resonant female voice said in Katina's mind.

"They are to these people." She responded.

'Walgund, mind if we stay the night.' Katina asked.

'In the circumstances, we would be honoured.' He replied. They managed to find an unused corner and set up camp. They checked the horses and equipment, then went and helped others with various chores. Katina found herself very tired and fell asleep quickly.

She was still tired in the morning, but got up at dawn, ate breakfast and broke camp. Then while Hawkyn packed away their equipment, Katina went in search of Walgund. She found him about to enter the mine.

'We are going now. Thank you for your hospitality.'

'I think we've got by far the larger benefit here.' He replied.

'You will need to raise a militia and have one company on duty at any given time. I would suggest you find out if you have any former soldiers to train and lead them. Things are rough out there just now. You will need them, or you will be overrun.'

'I will see what I can do.' They said their pleasantries and parted.

Hawkyn had finished packing the equipment and saddled the horses. The pair led their mounts through the other gate. Many people of all ages were busy preparing the soil or planting seeds. They just casually looked at the two strangers as they passed but nothing more. They worked feverishly to plant as much food as possible in the large flat valley protected by the castle. Katina took her horse through the new fields to the narrow gap in the cliff at the end, then led Hawkyn down the barely six-foot-wide crack in the mountains that took them to the Southern Plains.

PART 6 – ACROSS THE PLAINS

6 – ODD FOOTPRINTS

They led the horses down the narrow path between the two cliffs. Katina and Hawkyn were both covered in mud and soaking wet from mountain runoff water in no time at all. It was just as difficult going down the pass as it had been coming up those months before. She was not looking forward to the blocked part at the bottom, and judging by the increasing resistance of her horse, neither was he.

'Katina, any ideas where we have to go to start this quest.'

'I don't think it will work like that. The gods know we are heading home and why, so, we keep doing that and let them decide when and how we get tested.'

'You said "We", surely you mean you.'

'No, I don't. Becoming the Oracle is as much about you as me. Only with you can I succeed, so we both have to be up to scratch.'

'I hadn't looked at it like that. Any idea how many tests?'

'I don't even know how many Gods of Light there are. I know of five.' Said Katina.

'There are twelve, or so I was taught.'

'That's a lot of tests.'

'Perhaps they don't all test you.'

'Maybe.' Katina said unconvinced.

After several more hours and many slips, bumps, and

scrapes, they reached the large pile of rocks at the bottom of the pass, with a deep puddle of water in the way.

'Oh, this is going to be fun.' Hawkyn observed dryly.

'Not nearly as much fun as the other side, that's covered in brambles.'

'Great. No one's going to find this path in a hurry or be that keen on using it if they do. We went by the coast.'

Katina tried to lead her horse through the pooled water towards the boulders, but he became increasingly resistant. Finally, when they reached the boulder they had to climb over, the horse stopped and refused to go on. When Katina tried some persuasion, the horse attempted to bite her. Eventually Katina got her horse to the top of the boulders when, looking on, he gave her a long hard flat eared stare.

'No, I'm not keen on fifty yards of ten feet high thorn bushes and brambles either, but unless you can fly, we don't have a choice. Sorry, but we must go through this.' She said to her horse.

Hawkyn's trained war horse lost patience and forced Katina's horse onwards. With reluctance he let Katina lead him into the brambles. The next few hours were extremely unpleasant, but eventually, the two of them and the horses got through. Katina did her best to remove evidence of their passing, but the damage was just too extensive. She led Hawkyn northwest along the edge of the cliff of the mountain range. Then it started to rain heavily.

'This will be horrible.' Observed Hawkyn.

'The gods are covering our tracks. It happened with The Huntress' temple we found on the way over. It will be uncomfortable for several days but will make tracking us virtually impossible.'

They trudged on. Despite the weather, Katina slowly became less tired. Eventually, the rain stopped, they made camp and dried out most of their equipment. In the morning, after they ate a meagre breakfast, Katina checked her horse. While brushing him down, she noticed some unusual tracks.

'What are you looking at, Katina. Why the puzzled expression?'

'There are some tracks down here, and I don't recognise them.'

Hawkyn came over. 'Eagle, though its size would put Helghyer to shame.'

'It's not an eagle. Aside from having four forward-facing talons instead of three, it's got four feet. Those other marks would be a tail.'

'Four feet and a ground dragged tail would be a reptile, but with eagle style feet. Any ideas, Katina?'

'None at all. I'd like to see what it is and whether it has sided with our enemy. How do you feel like following them?'

'We will have to be careful. Judging by the spacing of the legs, this is one big lizard, but it shouldn't be difficult to follow the tracks.'

They packed up camp and started chasing strange footprints, which after several hundred yards, reached the top of a gorse covered hill and disappeared.

'I suppose it was going too easily.' Observed Hawkyn.

'Whatever it is must have gone somewhere. It's large, so we should be able to see it.' Katina dismounted and looked at the tracks again. 'Do those back imprints look deeper to you, Hawkyn?'

'Looks like it, now you mention it.'

'So, it either jumped or flew.'

'We'd better search the area, see if we can find where it landed.' They split up, starting their search several hundred yards ahead of them and circling round to the rear. They found nothing.

'We are going to have to try further out and do another circle.' Observed Hawkyn.

'How about a quarter-mile?'

'Right then, quarter-mile it is.'

The pair separated and started another search. An hour or so later, they met up again.

'Anything?' Asked Katina.

'Nothing. We need another plan. We can't track something that flies by looking on the ground.' Responded Hawkyn. Katina considered the situation for a few minutes.

'I think we need to try and figure out where it is flying too. So, let's go back up that hill and look around.' She said.

The pair trudged through the bushes back to the top of the hill. Looking around them, they stared at the wilderness.

'There's no sign of tracks nearby, so we must guess where our lizard has gone.' Said Katina.

'How about the next hill in the direction of the tracks.' Suggested Hawkyn.

'Can't hurt to look. It's only a few miles away.'

So off they trudged. The top of the next hill was a mess, with lots of torn up bushes covered in blood.

'Something had a bad day.' Hawkyn observed looking at the chaos.

'Not surprised. Whatever it was, got hit by a flying lizard about the size of a horse with four clawed feet.'

'So, it was our lizard then.'

'Definitely, I can see a few footprints but can't work out what it was that got eaten. There's not enough left.'

'Human?' Asked Hawkyn.

'Dunno.'

'You think that huge tree a few miles away in the valley should be our next stop.'

'Probably, it's the nearest vantage point.'

'Let's go then, but I'm not climbing it to see if a horse-sized lizard with wings and claws is sat at the top.' Hawkyn responded.

Off they went down the hill heading north-west towards a giant oak tree several hundred feet tall.

'That is one big tree.' Observed Katina.

'How are we going to check what's up it.'

'I am going to have to climb some of it at least and have a look.'

'Please be careful, it's a long way down.'

Katina took off her leather armour and equipment, keeping only a dagger attached to her belt. Hawkyn held her horse still while she stood on the saddle, just reaching the lower branches. She managed to haul herself up into the tree with effort, then scrambled up the trunk using its many branches. After about fifty feet, her hand touched something wet and sticky when reaching for the next branch.

'Hawkyn, our lizard has been here but appears to have gone now without finishing its meal. Wonder why it left?' Katina said as she looked up.

'You had better come back down. No point in going further up.'

Katina climbed back down and jumped the ten feet drop from the lowest branch. She cleaned her hands and put her leather armour back on.

'What do you think about checking out that next hill in the same rough direction.' Asked Hawkyn.

'I agree, but we will have to give some consideration to backing away when we find it. A horse-sized lizard with this level of violence will be beyond just two of us. If there is no clear allegiance to our enemy, leaving it alone may be the best choice. But, on the other hand if it could be a friend, the benefit would be significant. Either way Gods of Light or no, we must get back to our village.' Said Katina.

'Reluctantly, I agree.' Replied Hawkyn.

They continued through the long grass and bushes towards the next hill. As they approached the summit.

'There's something up there. It looks asleep. We'd better dismount and approach cautiously.' Katina advised.

The pair crept silently from bush to bush towards whatever it was lying at the top of the hill. Katina slowly peered into the clearing. She had never seen anything like the creature lying on the grass. Hawkyn gasped. Katina motioned him to be silent.

Overall, from the mouth to the tip of the tail was at least three horses long, nose to tail. Its cylindrical body and tail were about one horse each. The head was nearly half a horse long. She couldn't tell the size of the neck due to the position the creature was lying in.

Its long head consisted mainly of a protruding nose and mouth covered in a thick bony plate with two horns at the top above the eyes and forehead. From its back, just below its shoulders, were two enormous leathery wings, each at least as long as it was. Its skin consisted of a lot of thick grey scales that sparkled with gold flecks.

'Look at the size of that thing. You any idea what it is?' whispered Hawkyn.

'None, but judging by the mess, it doesn't like Plains Devils.'

'Do we approach?'

'It doesn't like our enemy and is wounded, so we should try and help. But we will have to be careful of that mouth.'

'And that tail, have you seen the size of the barbs on the end.'

Using extreme caution, they approached the creature. There were many sword marks on the scales and two spears stuck into the wing on the other side that they couldn't see from afar.

'Do we pull them out?' Asked Hawkyn.

'They will have to come out, but the creature must know we are doing it. If it wakes up to pain and a person holding a spear, then we're lunch.'

As they walked round to the spears on the other side of the creature, a gruff sound came out of the mouth, the head lifted slightly and its neck extended as it turned to look at them, mouth open. The pair stopped. Katina raised her hands above her head, leaving her sword and dagger in their scabbards. Hawkyn followed her lead.

This situation was unlike anything Katina had encountered before. The creature did not immediately attack them, so it was not overtly hostile and probably did not follow The Lord of All Evil. Act correctly and they may have a helpful friend. Get it wrong and she would be dead, first bite. She looked at Hawkyn. His face was pale, so he was frightened too. A new experience for them. The large green and orange reptilian eyes stared at her, and her fear grew. Stop being stupid, she told herself. Then something occurred to her.

'Magical fear doesn't work very well on our people. We've been fighting Goblins and training for over a thousand years. We're too used to dodgy situations.'

The creature's eyebrows raised as it tilted its head to one side slightly.

'Magical ability from a creature not a follower of our enemy, I've never heard of such a thing. What a gift from the Gods.' Said Hawkyn.

'It may not be. Gods of Light are all about symbols and strange words. There's none of that here. It may not be aligned to anyone.'

'Then this must be the first test, to make a friend.'

Katina motioned to the spear stuck into the underside of the wing near its body. 'May we remove that? It must come out.' The creature nodded. 'Hawkyn, please bring a cloth and some water from the horses.' He nodded and left, walking backwards away from the beast for several dozen yards.

After a few minutes, he returned with several waterskins and some bandages.

'Ready?' Katina asked, looking at the creature. There was a nod.

Katina had learnt a lot simply by watching the healers at work after the fight at Kersladen. Firstly, she checked the spearhead. It had a narrow long diamond-shaped head but no barbs so she could pull it out. Then looking into the creature's eyes and asked

'Ready?'

It nodded, so she continued 'Three, two, one.' Then yanked the spear out.

The creature gave a loud, low-pitched grunt. Katina checked the wound. There was some gungy stuff in it. Katina wiped it away and cleaned the injury. She then looked at the creature's face. It was crying.

'That one is clean, but I must attend to the other.' The creature nods. 'Ready. Three, two, one.' Yank. It gave another loud, low-pitched cry and the tears flowed.

'It's alright now the spear is out. I will clean the wound as I did with the other one. They will heal now.' Katina said to the creature while soothingly stroking its wing. She then walked to the head.

'Keep the wounds clean and they will heal. We have a long and dangerous journey home. We must be on our way.' The creature got up, stretched its wings, winced, and looked at her.

'We can't take it with us. The horses will go nuts. Freki was bad enough.' Observed Hawkyn. The creature looked at Hawkyn, sighed and then shimmered, leaving a long brown-haired hunting dog puppy in its place that sat down, looking up at Katina with a pair of puppy dog eyes.

Katina and Hawkyn just stared at it utterly amazed for a while. Then the puppy frowned momentarily, angled its head to one side slightly and whimpered a bit and continued to look up at Katina. Those puppy eyes seeming to bore into her soul as puppies tend to.

'It can change shape.' Said Hawkyn.

He got a flat stare from the puppy, followed by Bark. Then those eyes returned to Katina.

Although Katina was just as surprised as Hawkyn was, it was time to get herself together.

'I suppose that if we try and go on without you, you will just follow us anyway.' Said Katina.

Bark.

'Oh, alright then, come along if you wish, but our path is long and dangerous. We'll probably both die. You too if you come.' Katina replied.

There was a shrug of the shoulders, a look round at the mess of the combat and the discarded spears, followed by Bark.

'I guess that means it could die here anyway.' Hawkyn suggested.

'Probably and it has a point.' Replied Katina.

'Well done, Katina and Hawkyn, you have passed the first test.' Said the disembodied voice of The Huntress.

'Please, Goddess, if you don't mind me asking, what is it.' Hawkyn asked.

'It's a lost baby dragon.'

'Baby.' Hawkyn replied in surprised tones. 'How big do those things get?'

'Very big.'

'What's a dragon?' Asked Katina.

'A special creature that is predominantly magical but can also do some spiritual things too. When fully grown, they are a good deal more intelligent than humans or elves. They have kept themselves isolated and have not been involved in the world's difficulties with my uncle.'

'How old is it, in human growth?' Asked Katina.

'About a year in your development terms.'

'So, it can't talk much yet, has only just started to walk and is on special food.'

'That's about the size of it. We would be most appreciative if you could care for it until mum and dad come to take it home.'

'Mum and dad. If that's a baby, meeting mum and dad should be interesting.' Added Hawkyn.

'Of course, Huntress, but are we the best choice? Our road is dangerous.' Said Katina.

'True, but presently you are the only choice.'

'Come along then.' Katina said to the puppy, and they walked towards the horses. Katina mounted her horse, and Hawkyn handed the puppy up, who sat on the front of the saddle. Hawkyn mounted his horse, and they rode off away from the hills towards the rolling grassy plains.

7 – HEADING WEST

The puppy sat on the front of Katina's saddle, happily dozing as they plodded gently through the rolling hills towards the endless flat plains that eventually were her home.

'Are we going the right way? We appear to be heading West. Our home must be South.' Said Hawkyn.

'I am following my nose. I think the gods want us to head this way for a while.'

'So much for you being an atheist.' Said an amused Hawkyn.

'It's a bit difficult to hold on to an atheist belief when two of The Gods of Light are stood right in front of you. I must acknowledge that beings like that exist, but our relationship seems more of a trading situation than a worshipping one. They do something for me, so I do something for them.'

'You can't treat gods like that. They are to be honoured, respected and regarded with awe.'

'They don't seem to mind, or at least The Huntress and The Farmer don't.'

'That's a thought. You are going to have to be careful.'

'How so?'

'Well, just because The Huntress and The Farmer seem down to earth and pragmatic, others might not be. It makes sense for a farmer or hunter to be practical. That kind of goes with the job description. I would imagine a farmer that is not practical starves. So, you could expect a casual practical attitude from The Huntress and The Farmer. Being a warrior is all about backing up the soldier next to you, even if the situation is ridiculous. If you do not, then you both die. So, the casual attitude would not work with the Light Bringer or The Warrior, they will expect you to follow orders.' Said Hawkyn.

'Then, that is why we have these tests. Seeing if we can

act in a manner that each of the Gods of Light is comfortable with.'

'And to convince them that you are someone each god should talk or listen to.'

'I am confused why the gods want me to do this. They have priests now. Surely they will talk to them.'

'But the relationship between a God and their Priest is a worshipping one. The Priest looks at his god with awe and will not consider or question the orders given. You, however, will question and discuss.'

'So, you think an Oracle needs to be more independent and not a simple "Yes man"?'

'I think they will be looking for someone who can understand the attitude they each wish but also has some strength of will and independence. That's my view anyway.'

'It's worth bearing in mind.'

They continued out of the mountains, generally heading west for several days, camping each night beside a small fire. One day, the puppy jumped down off Katina's saddle and wandered off. The first time he was gone for ages. So long they stopped and waited for him to return. The next time, being concerned, Katina tracked him to check he was alright. It didn't take long to find him and when she did, he was trying to catch some rabbits. He was not doing very well due to inexperience. She cautiously backed away and left him to it, returning to Hawkyn and the horses.

'He's teaching himself to hunt.' Katina told Hawkyn.

'We'd better stay put and wait then.'

It was quite a while before the puppy came back, but he returned with a rabbit. These hunting trips occurred daily, but the time spent away reduced each trip and always resulted in a wildfowl or rabbit of some sort, which he gave to whoever was handy.

Slowly they came out of the hills that separated the cliff at the edge of the mountains from the vast grassy plains. Katina was of the distinct opinion that they were heading in the desired direction. Sure enough, about lunchtime, they came across a small single-storey stone building about forty-five feet long and fifteen feet wide running roughly east-west. It looked in an extremely poor state. The roof had collapsed, as had the doorway on the west wall. So had parts of the other walls. There was a large window on the east wall pointing towards the sunrise, and it was completely overgrown with vegetation and brambles.

'This is it. I know it.' Said Katina.

'Any idea what the test is?'

'Unfortunately not.'

They walked around the outside, then went in. The long since collapsed wooden roof structure had rotted away. Remains of the stone tiles lay scattered amid the brambles growing inside. The pair carefully walked to the largest clump of bushes near the eastern end of the building. The puppy sat in the doorway watching. Katina, with leather gloved hands, pulled the brambles apart to reveal a large rectangular stone block.

'This is starting to look like a small place of worship.' Katina said. 'My first thought is to tidy the place up, clean the altar and try and see if we can work out who the chapel is too.'

'We will not be able to fully restore the building. We lack the skills, time and equipment, but I have no problem with a general clean up.'

Using axes, a spade and a large knife, the pair set to work. For several days they removed the brambles and vegetation from inside the chapel, stacked the remains of the stone roof tiles in one corner out of the way and put the rest of the waste into a large pile on the north side somewhat away from the building.

The work revealed a previously well laid solid floor of large stone slabs which now needed the attention of a skilled craftsman. First, Katina and Hawkyn removed the plant growth from the walls outside the building and put it in the large waste pile. Next, the pair carefully stacked the stone blocks from the collapsed walls at the edge of the building. Attention then focused on the altar by removing brambles and washing it with water from a nearby stream. All in all, the place looked a lot better. Those with the proper skill could finish the job. People could even use it if they did not mind getting wet when it rained.

'As there's no disembodied voice, I take it that we haven't completed the task yet.' Suggested Hawkyn.

'That is my view too.'

'Any idea who this place is for?'

'As there's an equal-armed cross with a sun symbol on it carved into the front of the altar, I would think this is a Chapel to the Light Bringer.' Observed Katina.

'So, the test will be either something to do with Undead or something to do with this place of worship.'

'I can't see us being able to fight undead. We don't have the spells of the priests, so that only leaves bringing the place back into operation. Any ideas?' Asked Hawkyn.

'The big temple of The Huntress we found on the way to Warameth had a door on the back of the altar. If there is one here, perhaps there will be a clue in it.'

'It's worth a look, though I didn't see anything when cleaning the place.'

Katina, then on hands and knees, started to examine the altar. While it was not anywhere near the standard of the large Huntress altar, it had a polished marble top several inches bigger than its sides. All she could see at the back was one irregularly shaped crack from top to bottom a few inches in from the righthand edge.

'There is no secret back panel.' Stated Katina.

'Could it be somewhere else?'

'Can't hurt to look.'

Katina sat on the ground a few yards back from the altar and stared at it for some time. Then, finally, the puppy walked in, dumped a rabbit at Hawkyn's feet, ran over to

Katina and jumped up on her lap. It took some time, but she eventually realised the puppy had been staring at the same place for several minutes. Looking again, Katina noticed on the righthand edge a second crack a few inches away from the front of the altar. Considering the position of the two cracks, if they both went right through the stone, it might be possible to remove the side.

She went back and looked closer at the edging strip around the base. It came up a few inches above the altar's plinth. The front and sides were rock solid, but the back appeared to have some marginal give in it. She continued to try and push the right-hand end up, but the fit against the two side pieces was too tight.

'Hawkyn, help me. Try and push the other end up when I do mine.'

'Alright.' He responded while kneeling at the left-hand end of the back of the altar.

'Ready, three two one push.' It moved up a fraction of an inch.

'Again. Ready, three two one push.' It moved up a further fraction.

They continued for some time. Eventually, the base of the edging strip came sufficiently above the stone plinth for fingers to get underneath. Then finally, the edging strip came free.

'Now what?' Asked Hawkyn.

'Now we slide the side piece off.' This revealed the sides of the altar were stone slabs some four inches thick. The inside was hollow with something wrapped in a piece of soft leather. Katina took it out, placing the parcel on the altar top. Unwrapping it revealed a large cut clear crystal that seemed to sparkle in the middle.

'I've never seen a sparkling crystal.' Observed Hawkyn.

'It's extremely hard, sharp and tingles to the touch.'

'Presumably, we do something with the crystal.'

'Arturous mentioned mining some special crystals that

tingled. The Goblins very much demanded them. Given where we found this one, it must have some religious significance.' Replied Katina.

'We'll have to put it somewhere or do something with it then.'

'We'd better have a good look round. Perhaps there is an item or alcove to put it in, though nothing has jumped out at me over the last few days.'

'There must be something, Katina.'

After a long look around, trying to move loose stones in walls or floor to find somewhere to put the jewel, they stopped.

'Katina, we're missing something obvious.'

'Agreed.'

'Any ideas.' Hawkyn said to the puppy that lay curled up on the top of the altar. The puppy just raised its head and looked back with an expressionless face.

'I think that means "our problem".' Hawkyn observed.

'He did help me find the hidden compartment.'

'True.'

'This chapel is to do with the Light Bringer, so the crystal will be a Light Bringer artefact.' Katina said.

'Can the sunshine through it?' Suggested Hawkyn.

'It's nearly transparent, is cut and polished rather than rough, so it should do.'

'Then we need to put the crystal where the sun can shine through it.'

'That would have to be somewhere in the east window. So, we'd better go and have a look.'

They went over and examined the stonework. The middle of the window had a column of stone from windowsill to lintel.

'Is that a hole halfway up that stone column?' Katina said.

'Looks like it's full of dirt. It might be large enough to put that crystal in when cleaned up.'

'I will have to climb on your shoulders to get up there.' Which Katina did, holding on to the stone column with one hand while cleaning the hole out with her dagger.

After several minutes. 'Can you hurry up? It's not easy being a ladder.' Asked Hawkyn.

'Everything is so dirty, pitted and gummed up. It will take a fair bit longer. I'll give you a break?' Katina asked while she put the dagger back in its scabbard and jumped down, allowing Hawkyn to rest his shoulders. Katina repeated climbing up and cleaning several more times before she achieved a clean empty hole. Finally, Katina put away her dagger, got out the crystal and held it up against the now clean hole in the stonework window column.

'There's a slot in the middle of the hole. I think the crystal would fit if I could work out how I could get it in there.'

Hawkyn appeared to think for a few seconds then said. 'Does any of the stonework move? So far, we have had virtually invisible doors, amazingly well-carved statues, huge stone buildings. Our ancestors were a lot better at stonework than we are.'

'Pull out, you mean?'

'More likely slide or twist.' Replied Hawkyn.

Katina shoved and pulled things in various directions, then noticed the slimmest of circular cracks centred around the just cleaned out slot in the stone column. Pulling and pushing did not work, so she tried twisting. It was tough, but it did start to move slightly.

'It's moving. It twists.' Katina eventually said. Slowly a central stone ring about four inches across started to come out of the stone column.

'It's threaded and a very tight fit. I think I can take it out, put the crystal in the slot, then screw the stone back in.'

The struggle continued for some time, but it did come out revealing a socket. Handing the removed stone plug to Hawkyn, she tried to work out how to fit the crystal into the socket. One side was flat and the other convex but made up of several smaller flat faces. It seemed to position better with the convex side facing outside the building. She then slowly replaced the stone plug until everything was a snug fit and jumped down off Hawkyn's shoulders.

'Any other ideas?' Asked Katina.

'Afraid not.'

'The crystal is in the right spot for the sun to shine through it. So why is nothing happening?'

'Because it's too late in the day, the sun is no longer in the east.'

'Then we camp in here until sunrise.' Suggested Katina.

'Agreed.'

So that is what they did, although they did not build a fire inside the chapel. The puppy, who had been taking it in turns on who to sleep with, chose Katina this time. A gentle furry headbutt to the face woke her. Katina opened her eyes. The puppy padded over to Hawkyn and gave another gentle headbutt to the face.

They both got up to the first sign of light in the eastern sky and watched as the sun slowly peeped up over the hills. Then, as its rays hit the crystal, a focused beam of sunlight illuminated the altar, which then radiated light.

The building filled with the overwhelming sense of something more than human. Hawkyn fell to his knees and Katina looked at the altar. Then, a disembodied voice said in stern tones.

'I am the Light Bringer. Congratulations, you have passed my test. You are the first to re-establish one of my temples. A correctly positioned carved crystal to illuminate the altar is essential. Well done.'

'Thank you, divine one. Your satisfaction with our efforts is most appreciated.' Katina said while looking at the glowing altar, then briefly thinking continued. 'May I be so bold as to suggest something.'

'Humble suggestions for consideration are the

difference between an Oracle and the subservient nature of a Divine Priest. Please continue.' Replied the disembodied voice.

'The Gods of Light are in for a shock with Oswald and Luka then. I don't see either of them neatly fitting into the subservient category.' Hawkyn observed smiling.

Giving Hawkyn an exasperated look, Katina replied, 'The existence of the crystals and their use is unknown to the Followers of Light. If it is necessary, then they will have to be told.'

'We will consider this. The others, as you put it, have already worked out the need for a cutting from the Tree of Life and Arturous knows where the raw crystals are. The crystals of power have other uses too. You are right though, they must know the rest. And yes, Hawkyn, the strength of personality and disregard of authority has come as a shock to us.'

'To be fair divine one, Oswald hasn't had the best of role models in his former High Priest. Also, we teach our scouts independence and self-sufficiency. As a result, they don't have the same respect for authority we warriors have.' Hawkyn replied.

'That is true, Hawkyn. You three must now continue to your next test. Good luck.'

8 – WHAT THE HELL IS THAT

'Well, that's two down. I wonder who's next?' Enquired Hawkyn as they packed up the camp.

'I'm more worried about where's next. If we keep going west as we are, we'll end up further away from home than when we started.'

'We must assume the gods know what they are doing.'

'Big assumption.'

Hawkyn laughed. The puppy dumped two rabbits at Katina's feet when he returned from his morning's hunt, then padded over to the now mounted Hawkyn, barked and looked up expectantly.

'I think he wants to go with you this time. I'll lift him.' Katina walked over to Hawkyn, picked up the puppy and placed him across the pommel of Hawkyn's saddle. After some squirming, the puppy settled to a relaxed dozing position. Katina mounted her horse, and the three headed west at a slow walk.

'Why is it always west?' Asked Hawkyn.

'It feels right.'

'I can't argue with you on that one, though I never thought I would hear you saying it.'

Several days later, they ran into many tracks of horses. A few miles further on, it was rusty scimitars and bits of armour, shortly followed by decayed parts of Goblins.

'What's this about do you suppose Hawkyn?'

'My thinking is our peoples have started using more aggressive tactics and are attacking Goblins on mass. About time, I think. Unless we start killing whole tribes, they will just keep coming in ever-increasing numbers.'

Soon Hawkyn was proved correct when they came across the aftermath of a battle. The decayed remains of several thousand Goblins lay strewn over an area of about a square mile.

'It looks like they got completely run over. No signs of

any Human casualties.' Said Hawkyn.

'Looks that way, doesn't it?' Replied Katina. The puppy still sat on the pommel of Hawkyn's saddle, looked terribly upset.

'Unfortunately, dear puppy, war is an unpleasant affair and losing doubly so. To be defeated in battle has dreadful consequences.' Hawkyn said.

'We're also better trained and equipped. The numbers of Goblins are the only reason we didn't win decades ago. Let's move on. This place is a dreadful sight for a youngster.' Added Katina. The group continued and, after a further half-day, found the exterminated Goblin baggage train.

All three of them were in a sombre mood that night in a small forest and spoke little. The sights of the day affected the puppy greatly, but also, to Katina's surprise, affected both her and Hawkyn despite being hardnosed Iredan. While they predominately won fights with the Goblins, these rarely resulted in total annihilation on such a scale.

'After we win, we will have to become a better people.' Katina said.

'We have survived by being brutal beyond words for over a thousand years. For our people, there is no way back from that. We have simply spilt too much innocent blood for too many years. We will have the satisfaction of knowing that Humans survived because of us.' The puppy looked at the pair of them with a sad face.

It was a fitful sleep for them all, with the puppy going hunting before daybreak. Katina watched him quietly pad off and returned to dozing. After about an hour, the puppy came back without the usual food offering, barked while gently putting his teeth around one of Katina's hands and pulling.

'I think he wants us to follow him.' Suggested Hawkyn.

'You stay with the horses. I will go and see. If it is too far away, I will come back and we both go.' Suggested

Katina.

'Sure. I will start to pack up here, then follow you with the horses anyway.'

Puppy took Katina through the undergrowth, around bushes and dodging low branches. She trusted Hawkyn to follow the trail as they seemed to go on for a long time. Then at a large bush, the puppy stopped and barked. Katina peered over it, seeing a clearing, perhaps some fifty feet across, that was devoid of any vegetation at all. In fact, there was no life of any kind, just a heap of mainly black boned skeletons. The one in the middle wore rusty armour and was holding something. Then she noticed the absence of either birdsong or any animals in the area. Immediately Katina crouched down, remembering the telltale signs of Plains Devils. She carefully looked at each bush and tree in case it was the blend into the background type.

Before completing the task, she heard Hawkyn leading the horses through the forest. Thinking quickly, she decided to do something rarely used by her tribe these days and hoped Hawkyn would remember what it meant. She gave a bird call like a particular brown owl found near her village but not the same. The sounds of Hawkyn and the horses stopped. Good, he remembered, she thought and continued looking. After about a further ten minutes, Katina satisfied herself there was nothing in the area.

'Approach.' She shouted while keeping watch. Hawkyn dismounted, tied the two horses to a large branch, then, sword in hand, quietly approached the crouching scout.

'What's up.' He whispered.

'No birds or animals of any kind. I suspected Plains Devils, but I can't see any sign. Look at the area beyond the bush.' She replied quietly.

Hawkyn looked where shown. 'I have not seen skeletons like that before. Although the guy in the middle may be normal, it's hard to tell. I am not familiar with the armour, though. We'd better take a closer look.'

They both got up, Katina drawing her long sword and Hawkyn with his larger bastard sword. They walked around the bush and approached the first black boned skeleton. It had several broken limb bones and a shattered spine just below the neck.

'The bones look burnt, but I can't imagine they would be uniformly charred.' Said Katina.

'They wouldn't be and besides, the bones are black all the way through. Any fire that can do that would have consumed at least some of the bones.'

'That means some creature of The Lord of All Evil then.'

'That's what I think. Perhaps some form of undead or top-end cursed creature. We've not fought those in living memory. It appears destroying one affects where it falls.'

'There must be at least half a dozen of these things. If the guy in the middle killed them, then he's someone who should be honoured.' Suggested Katina. 'Let's see if we can get rid of the undead corpses.'

Loud growl.

'No touching black boned corpses then.' Added Katina.

Bark.

'Can you deal with them?' Asked Hawkyn. The puppy just stared at the nearest one.

'I take that as a maybe.' Continued Hawkyn.

'I believe he's thinking about it. Let's leave the puppy do his thing and go check out the armoured guy.' Suggested Katina.

The pair walked carefully over to the centre of the clearing, making sure to avoid any black boned skeletons on the way. They then looked down on the central corpse.

'Can't see much inside the armour, but the bones I can see look pale like ours would.' Said Katina.

'Judging by the blade under the armpit, he received a mortal blow then chopped the last ones head off before dying. I didn't think our swords could do that to the undead.'

'I don't think they can either. How do you feel about giving the guy a proper send-off?'

'It will take us some time, but anyone who kills six creatures of The Lord of All Evil deserves it, so I agree.' Said Hawkyn.

The pair separated, hunting down many roughly eight feet and four feet long logs, with which they created a rectangular pile several feet high. Then Katina and Hawkyn reverentially placed the skeleton of the lone warrior on top. Armour still on him, arms across his chest with hands-on the sword hilt, which lay vertically down his body.

'I would like to keep that sword and armour, but it would just not be right. Our warrior's possessions should go with him.' Said Katina.

'I agree. It would just not be right to keep them.'

At this point, Katina noticed the puppy had returned to his large, winged lizard form. He took a step back, pursed his mouth and breathed a narrow jet of blue-white fire over one of the black skeletons. The bones vaporised. A small cloud of black dust gathered in the super-heated air above where the skeleton had been. There was then a small explosion, an unearthly scream and the body was gone.

'It appears lizard fire beats Undead. Useful.' Said Hawkyn.

'Can you do it with the others?' Asked Katina.

Puppy nodded.

'Katina, look at the stone where the body was. It's melted.' Katina just stared, stunned.

'Blimey, not even our metal furnaces get that hot.' Katina replied.

The puppy repeated the process with the other black skeletons, then the three of them went over to the funeral pyre of the fallen hero. They stood looking respectfully for several minutes, then Katina said.

'We honour you fallen warrior, who dared to fight

unspeakable evil and paid the ultimate price in your victory. We commend your spirit to the everlasting care of your God. Go in peace.'

And with that, the puppy took a deep breath and breathed a gentle red-orange flame onto the wooden logs on which the body lay. They all stood and watched as the fire took hold, quickly engulfing the body. Katina looked up and noticed several birds of prey perched on nearby branches looking down. At the base of the tree stood a stag and doe looking on respectfully. Across the other side stood a large brown bear and several Great Wolves. Hawkyn simply added.

'Nature seriously liked this fallen warrior.'

'The animals are back, so our puppy's fire must have destroyed our enemy's curses.'

'I think we should stay until the fire has completely consumed the body, then bury the remains.'

'I agree.' Concluded Katina.

After about half an hour, the animals and birds left the vigil. Katina, Hawkyn, and the puppy stayed all day until the fire went out, digging a hole nearby while they waited. Once the fire was out, they approached.

'The sword and armour are not affected. Black, covered in soot, ash and bits of wood, but they look solid. Perhaps we should take them.' Said Hawkyn.

'I will ask.' Katina knelt on the ground and cleared her thoughts.

"The Huntress, The Light Bringer, can you hear me."

"Yes, we are here. You may take the sword and armour. Although hundreds of years ago, your hero was a direct male ancestor of Hawkyn. It is right for him to take the armour and sword. They are still sound, though they will need some work to clean up." Came the voice of The Light Bringer.

"Well done." Added The Huntress.

"Thank you." Replied Katina, stopped her concentration and got up. Both Hawkyn and the puppy were looking at

her.

'Apparently, our hero is one of your ancestors Hawkyn. He is of your direct male line, but hundreds of years ago. Yes, we can use the items.' Responded Katina to the implied questions.

Hawkyn turned back to the burnt remains, knelt on the ground, and said a few private words. Then, with thick leather gloves, removed the sword and each piece of armour from the funeral pyre. Katina tried to help, but he refused her. Hawkyn put the skull and larger bones in a saddlebag that he carefully placed into the hole with reverence. Next, he covered the bag with the other burnt remains and finally covered both with earth. Katina and Puppy waited patiently as a small burial mound took shape.

When finished, Hawkyn distributed the various bits of armour between the two horses.

'Katina, do you mind wearing this one over your back? I don't have space.'

'Certainly Hawkyn, I would be honoured.'

Katina went to pick up puppy and place him on Hawkyn's saddle.

'Puppy, you now seem several inches bigger?'

Bark.

'I think you are now too large for sitting on a saddle.'

There was a sorrowful looking puppy.

'Katina is right. You will have to run alongside.' Said Hawkyn.

The now bigger puppy ran alongside them as they continued the ever-westward journey. Each night Hawkyn took time to clean the sword, scabbard, and armour. Despite the fire and the hundreds of years lying exposed to the weather, all three items seemed structurally sound and functional. Completely covered in surface rust, soot, and ingrained dirt, but that was it. It took about a week to restore all items to a reasonable state. Then Hawkyn commenced the laborious task of sharpening a three feet long sword blade with a pocket-sized whetstone.

'The whetstone does not so much sharpen the blade as remove what little remaining dirt there is from the edge. The metal is the hardest I've ever seen.' Hawkyn said.

'Is it sharp enough to use?'

'What I have cleaned so far is very sharp, so sharp I think you could cut parchment with ease. Like the bits of armour, it has strange symbols carved into it near the hilt.'

The following morning while Hawkyn packed up the camp, Katina went scouting. Puppy stayed with Hawkyn curled up by the remains of the fire. About half a mile from the camp, she realised something was watching her and quietly cursed herself for not noticing sooner. Casually looking around while proceeding onwards, Katina tried not to give anything away. Despite all her best efforts, she could not find her follower so looped around and headed back to camp, by which time Hawkyn had packed up and erased all sign of it.

As soon as Katina got into the small clearing, the puppy jumped up onto all fours and instantly changed from happy waggy tailed puppy to serious all business ears back tail down bared teeth dog. A split second later, Hawkyn was on his feet and drawing his bastard sword out of its scabbard on his back.

'I think something is following me, but I can't work out what or where.' Katina said.

'Puppy agrees with you and that's enough for me.' Replied Hawkyn.

Katina mounted her horse and drew her sword. The three waited. After ten minutes, nothing came.

'Perhaps I was wrong.' Suggested Katina.

'Not a chance. That is doubtful, and there's no way both you and the puppy would be. Whatever it is, it's there.'

'We had better get moving. Our guest doesn't want to play right now.'

'Let's head out of this forest and get to the plains.

Perhaps we can get an advantage.' Suggested Hawkyn.

They rode at a steady trot directly away from where Katina had come. Puppy loped alongside. The forest was small, so they quickly found the endless grassy plains again. After about a quarter of a mile, Katina looked back.

'The grass is moving, so something large is following us, but I can't see what it is.'

'There's a small hill over there. Let's go to that and see if our visitor will join us.' Suggested Hawkyn. They galloped over, Puppy running at full speed close behind. On reaching the low flat-topped hill, they turned to face their pursuer.

'I can't see anything.' Said a surprised Hawkyn. Puppy clearly could, though, as he was staring at a specific spot in the wilderness growling with full bared teeth. Katina thought that the pursuer was now at the bottom of the hill, about one hundred yards away.

'I should have remembered dragons can see hidden things.' Came this deep gravelly, booming voice. The air at the bottom of the hill shimmered, and Hawkyn said.

'What the hell is that?'

What stood at the base of the hill was a twenty feet tall humanoid creature with greeny-brown leathery skin. Its arms and legs were like tree trunks, and its torso had the best six-pack Katina had seen in a long time. Two tusks jutted out of a protruding lower jaw, a mass of dark brown and black head hair and beard covered the face. Two sharp horns were sticking out of its skull above the ears.

'I want a human sacrifice. The male human and the dragon must watch me slowly eat the human female alive. They can leave when I have finished eating. I will not molest them again. Refuse, and I will kill and eat all three of you.'

'You are a Giant Ogre, aren't you?'

'Yes.' The puppy walked to the outside of Katina and changed into its dragon form. Turning its head to the Ogre breathed fire. The flames stopped short.

'I take that as a no then.' Replied the Ogre. Roaring, it ran up the burning slope of the hill, taking a large club in each hand from around its belt. Katina and Hawkyn charged the creature swords to the fore.

The three met with a resounding crash as the two horses collided with the creature's legs. Hawkyn's sword connected with the Ogre's right side, slicing into his ribs, while Katina's took a chunk out of the left arm. They were then both sent flying as the enormous club in the Ogre's right hand hit the rump of Hawkyn's horse, sending it flying sideways into Katina's.

The impact knocked her out of her saddle, so she rolled to her feet, as did Hawkyn. Both the horses slid sideways down the hill, screaming with pain and fear.

Hawkyn swung his sword again, hitting the left leg, followed by Katina's sword a split second later.

The creature's right club swung at Hawkyn, who parried with his large shield. The force was just too great for him. Katina heard the bones break as the giant club hit Hawkyn's left hip. He landed in a screaming heap several yards away.

Katina rolled forward at the last second, putting her sword in the way. The roll and the sword took most of the force, but the club still connected with her right ribs, which she felt break and blood came out of her mouth. The creature stood over her, so she thrust her sword up into its abdomen. A foot then caught her in the chest and knocked her onto her back. Desperately she swung her sword at the left arm, hit heavily, and it dropped a club.

The Ogre put a foot on her chest, looked down at her and said. 'Now you die.' Down the right-hand club came. Despite the agonising pain, she swung her sword at the pinning foot but lacked the force to cause any harm. She watched the giant club come down towards her head.

Then the puppy was there. His front left claw swiped the giant club to one side, and a three-foot-long mouth with six-inch teeth clamped around the Giant Ogre's forearm.

The dragon form puppy stood up on his hind legs and tail, wrenching the Ogre upwards and pulling its foot off Katina. With enormous force, he hit the Giant Ogre's jaw with a right-handed clawed uppercut. Katina could hear the flesh-tearing from the Ogre's right arm as it flew back down the hill pulling the arm out of the clenched teeth of the dragon. Before the creature could do anything, puppy followed it up with a swipe from his tail, several foot long barbs sinking into the Ogre's abdomen.

'Ouch, that's gotta hurt.' Said a prostrate Hawkyn. Katina got to her feet, still spitting blood from her mouth. This time, she sheathed her sword and picked up Hawkyn's sword. Puppy looked at her and nodded.

The Ogre picked himself up, muttered some words and the torn and missing flesh on its right arm repaired itself.

'Damn.' Hawkyn said out loud.

'I think I would prefer Plains Devils.' Commented Katina.

'Good fight, you bring honour to your tribe, well done. Now I eat you.' Replied the Giant Ogre.

With a roar, the monster charged up the hill for a second time. Katina went to charge down, but the puppy put a claw up to stop her. She heard the intake of Puppy's breath, followed by an explosive exhalation of blue-white fire from his mouth. The Ogre's remaining club and the lower part of its right arm simply vaporised. Katina swung the sword hitting the lower left leg biting to the bone.

The creature's left fist solidly struck puppy on the side of the head. Puppy's eyes rolled up and he collapsed. Katina struck again, sinking the sword deep into the creature's stomach, but a backhanded counter strike caught her in the head and dropping the sword, she went flying.

Groggily she got to her feet as the Ogre approached the helpless Hawkyn.

'Stop.' Katina shouted.

'Don't worry. I will eat you next.'

Picking up a sword, she advanced on the Ogre. 'Kill Hawkyn, and his family's sword will cut you to bits. Take me only and let the others live and leave unharmed.'

'They must watch you die. Then they can go free unharmed.'

'The Gods of Light will keep you to this. If you attempt to betray this pact, all of your family will die by nightfall.' Katina wasn't sure if the Gods of Light would help her here, but it was worth a try. She certainly knew they were watching.

'I accept. Now kneel so I can cut your head off.' Katina knelt, put the two swords in front of her and bent her head forwards. She heard the monster draw a long blade knife from its belt and felt the edge of the blade against the back of her neck.

'No.' Shouted Hawkyn.

Katina felt the blade slowly cut into her skin.

'Katina, you are willing to die for this Hawkyn and your puppy?'

'Yes, I am.'

'Then you have passed The Warrior God's test. You may rise. Congratulations. To be willing to fight against impossible odds, to be prepared to die for your friends and the helpless, are the key points of The Warrior.'

'Do we have the honour of being in the physical presence of The Warrior?' Asked a shocked Hawkyn, 'No wonder we lost.'

'No, I am Odran, his chief Vaettir. Head spirit and advisor.'

'I have heard before that the Warrior is missing. May I ask if those who wish to follow The Warrior God can become initiated through you? I can think of several that may want that.'

'I can't bestow full Divine Priests or Divine Lord Guardians. I can do everything else though.'

'You must let those we left behind know. Can I call you

like I can The Huntress or The Light Bringer?'

'Yes, you may. By morning, you will be fully healed if you stay on this hill tonight. There are special enchantments placed on Hawkyn's sword. It can harm spiritual beings and the undead when most normal weapons cannot. I must leave you now.' And with that, Odran vanished.

9 – THE LOST

Katina staggered over towards Hawkyn. 'I have a broken pelvis and hip joint. I can't move. Without some serious Oswald type healing, I am toast. So sorry dearest, it looks like you will be continuing without me.' Hawkyn said.

'I've got internal bleeding and far too many broken ribs that feel like they are sticking into things they shouldn't. So, I won't be far behind. Perhaps the Gods will allow us to travel the spirit plains together.' Then Katina stopped talking suddenly. 'Dearest?' she asked.

'Yes.' Hawkyn replied. Katina thought for a few seconds or so. He was a good man in many respects. Then said, 'I would be honoured.' Hawkyn smiled.

Wracked with pain and coughing up blood, she dragged herself over to the puppy. He lay on the grass, still in his winged lizard form, eyes were open but unfocused. There was a large fist mark on the side of his head. The scales were depressed into his skull. Katina shuddered at the force of blow necessary to do that to Puppy.

'Thank you most deeply, Puppy. It was extremely dangerous to take part in that fight. If you had not, both Hawkyn and I would already be dead. I am sorry, but your injuries look permanent.'

The large scaly head lifted and looked at her smiling. He shimmered into a boy form then said. 'I am most honoured to be allowed to accompany you. It is a privilege to be considered a companion on such a journey. Even our elders can only dream of being part of the tests for a new Oracle. Didn't that Odran fellow say something about being healed? Perhaps you could ask for details. If it doesn't happen soon, none of us will be doing any more tasks.'

Katina thought of loads of questions to ask Puppy, but he was right, she needed guidance on healing immediately, or they would die. She cleared her mind of thought and tried to ignore the pain.

"Is anyone there?"

"Yes, I am." Replied The Huntress. *"The three of you and your two horses get yourselves up to the top of the hill right now. It's consecrated ground. As a special favour, we will help you. Sleep, and you will all be fine by morning, but do it quickly. Your injuries are serious, and you are all weakening rapidly."*

"Thank you, divine one." Katina replied.

"You're welcome. If you both make it, your next task is to your north."

'We need to get to the top of the hill and spend the night there.' Katina said to the others. The puppy slowly got to his feet, headed over towards Hawkyn, and offered him an arm to help him get up.

'I don't know I can move enough to get up. That Ogre shattered my left hip. Thanks for the thought, though.' Replied Hawkyn with a pale white face and gritted teeth.

'Perhaps a litter from tent poles and canvas. We did that with our equipment for a time on our way to Warameth. Should work for you, Hawkyn, for the fifty or so yards to the top of the hill.' Katina said. He just nodded, the pain showing on his face.

She went to the two horses. Both were standing but injured. Katina's horse was battered, bruised, and frightened but still functional. Hawkyn's however, was in a bad way. His left hind hip joint looked broken, and the leg was hanging loose. Still, she had to get it to the top of the hill for the night. If the Gods did not heal Hawkyn's horse by morning, it would have to be put to sleep.

Carefully she grabbed the reins, slowly and gently leading the horse up the slope to the top of the hill. Luckily, her horse followed. She unpacked the tent canvas and poles laying them on the ground next to Hawkyn, then created a litter. Puppy changed back to his dragon form and put a front claw under his legs while Katina put her arms under his shoulders.

'Three two one, lift.' Said Katina. Quickly they placed

Hawkyn on the canvas of the litter. He screamed and passed out. Katina collapsing to her knees coughed up more blood.

'You two need to get up that hill right now.' Urged Puppy.

Katina nodded and picked up the two poles at the head end, slowly dragging the litter up the hill. When she reached the top plateau, she continued several more yards then collapsed herself. Laying on the ground, feeling herself fall into unconsciousness.

Katina slowly came round feeling very cold. Opening her eyes, saw from the sun position that it was early morning. Idly she wondered which morning. Looking around, the first thing she saw was puppy in his young dog form leading a horse by holding the reins in his mouth. Then she realised there were now three horses. Hawkyn was still at her feet, lying on the impromptu litter, but he was on his side and, judging by the noise, still asleep.

Stiff and sore, with caution, she got up and checked her ribs. They felt like they were in the correct place. Hawkyn's left hip and pelvis looked normal. He was pale but sleeping naturally. Remembering the words of endearment they had exchanged, Katina decided to honour them. He was a good man and had chosen the task of being her protector. She went over to the puppy.

'Can we talk?'

Shake of the head.

'Have we been out long?'

Puppy looked at the sun and barked twice.

'Two days.'

Bark.

'You found another horse.'

The puppy barked while looking roughly north.

'That's the way we have to go next. Any sign of the owner?'

Shake of the head.

'Alright. Although it is thin now, it looks well cared for. Probably a human owner, Goblins are not known for looking after anything. You look a fair bit bigger. You've suddenly grown.'

Bark.

'So, you don't develop as we do then.'

Bark.

'Perhaps we can talk about that sometime, but I guess we need to get things sorted out and be on our way.'

Bark.

Katina went over to Hawkyn and gently shook him awake. Finally, he opened his tired eyes.

'Good morning, apparently we've been out for two days. Your hip and pelvis look alright, but you are very grey. My ribs are all in the right place now and I no longer cough up blood, but everything is still quite sore. I think we should be moving but will need to take it gently for a while.'

Hawkyn started to get up, so she grabbed him. 'Gently dearest. You are recovering from injuries that should have killed you. Be careful and patient.'

'You remembered my words. I....'

She put a finger on his lips and stopped him from talking further. 'I am fine with it. Unexpected, yes, but that is all. Now, let's get you on your feet. Slowly does it.' Katina helped Hawkyn up.

'I am very stiff. I think I will walk for a while today. Do you know where we are going next?'

'North apparently.'

'North. That's about as wrong as it gets for going home.'

'I know, but north it is.' Hawkyn shrugged. The pair packed up their belongings and redistributed them amongst the three horses, using the new horse as a pack animal. They then headed north, walking through the tall grassy plains.

By late afternoon, they saw a settlement in the distance. A wooden palisade wall with a solid gate surrounded the buildings within. A river ran to the right-hand side of the settlement and a large low flat-topped hill lay to the left. Tall blond people were working sun-parched fields of wheat and tending cattle, sheep or horses.

'Looks very much like home.' Said Hawkyn.

'It does, doesn't it. Apart from our hill.' Katina replied.

As they neared the settlement, a group of six armed warriors walked towards them. When some fifty yards away, one shouted.

'Who approaches?'

'I am Katina, and this is Hawkyn. We are of the Southern Plains People and travelling north for personal reasons. We would like to stay the night if possible.'

'We are also Southern Plains People. We and a few other settlements nearby are all that remains of the once-mighty Iredan tribe.'

Hawkyn and Katina looked at each other. 'You must tell them.' Said Hawkyn.

'You are of the Iredan Tribe, you say. May we please speak to your elders? There are things you must know.' She replied.

'First, you must be inspected by our Shaman. It is the Iredan custom.' One of the Warriors replied.

'We are aware of this.' Said Katina.

'Then please follow us.' Was the response.

The warriors led them past several dozen roundhouses made of logs and mud, with thatched roofs. The central meeting hall was a sizeable rectangular wooden log building with a stone floor and lower part of the walls, also with a thatched roof. A tall elderly wiry looking man with a quarterstaff stood at the entrance.

Katina decided to take an idea from Oswald Shamus and cut through the laborious greeting rituals designed to sniff out those with dark auras.

'Good evening, revered Shaman, pleased to meet you.' Katina said, holding her hand out in greeting. He looked surprised.

'Over the last few months, I have learned about those rituals. Letting you shake my hand saves us some time. Hawkyn will comply too.' Said Katina.

The Shaman took Katina's hand, looked amazed, then Hawkyn's. He led them both into the building. About two dozen people were waiting inside already, with a group of six family elders at the far end of a large hall.

'Good evening. You are not the only Iredan tribe, and it is an honour to meet you all. I am Katina. My companion is Hawkyn, and we are both Iredan Tribe also. Our homeland is several hundred miles south, south-east of here. We moved there in the great migration about fifteen years ago.'

The crowd looked at the Shaman. 'She speaks the truth. I can see an aura around her. What I don't understand is why I can see three different shades of white. Same with her companion.' The Shaman responded.

'Ah, well, our journey, which currently takes us north, has been challenging and full of unexpected events.' Katina replied. She continued. 'Where to start. Well, just as you are not the only Iredan, we Plains Tribes are not the only free peoples. The other side of the mountains to our north-east is a wide valley with shorter dark-haired humans who live at the eastern end. There are several cities, plus towns and villages. You are not, by any means, alone. The bulk of the free humans are several hundred miles south or east of here.' Katina explained the problems with Goblins for both the Southern Plains Peoples and the other valley folk Humans. She also explained about the return of the Gods of Light and spellcasting priests.

'Revered Shaman, the reason that you can see three shades of white on Hawkyn and I is that the Gods of Light have given us a series of tests to see if I am worthy of speaking to them. So far, I have passed three of the tests. We are on our way to the fourth.'

'So, you're being tested as the next Oracle then?'

Suggested the Shaman.

'Yes, that is correct.' Replied Katina.

'I take it your tests, and recent experiences have been difficult and dangerous.' Said one of the elders.

'They have all been challenging with a substantial risk of failure. However, not all have been physically dangerous.' Katina replied.

'Could you help us with the failure of the crops and harm to our livestock?' The elder asked.

'I presume you have tried irrigation and praying to The Farmer for help?' Said Katina.

'Irrigation, yes, but it gets destroyed at night, as do our crops and animals. The Gods of Light do not interact with us anymore.' The elder replied.

'They do interact with you, or your Shaman wouldn't be able to sense our auras. So there must be a connection with at least one of them. All you will need to do is try and contact them.' Suggested Katina.

'We pray to them often.' Said the Shaman.

'A set of prayers defined by the leaders of the Iredan hundreds of years ago.' Added an elder.

'We know the ones. They don't work. The Lightbringer told his new initiate that.' Interrupted Hawkyn. There were various shakes of the head.

'We've both met the Farmer. She is a practical and approachable goddess. If you can get her attention and offer regular worship, she will most likely help and advise you. You need to clear your mind of thought and interruption and call out within the privacy of your soul.' Said Katina.

'Do you have the time to help us?' The Shaman asked.

'We could manage a few days, but not weeks.' Katina replied while looking at Hawkyn, who nodded.

'Thank you. Your journey has been long and arduous, with plenty more difficulties ahead. We will find a room for you for the time you are with us so you can rest. We will care for your horses. Once settled, if you would share an evening meal with us, we would be honoured.' Said the Shaman.

'That is most kind, thank you.' Said Katina.

'Please follow me.' One of the farmers in front of them asked. Katina, Hawkyn and the puppy followed him to a large hut quite near the meeting hall.

'My name is Barr. This is my wife, Fiona.' Then looking at his wife said, 'They will be staying with us a few days. They are from the Iredan tribe a few hundred miles south of here and are travelling north. I will explain later. How about letting them have Thena's area.'

'Of course, it's tidy.' Then looking at Katina, she added, 'Our daughter has married into a family in a neighbouring village. Her space is over there, pointing to a partitioned off area of the hut. The bed is a bit small for the two of you. The space to the right is our two sons, the space to your left is where my husband and I sleep.'

'That will be fine, thank you.' Katina said before Hawkyn had a chance to say anything. Fiona showed them to an area of the hut where they could store their equipment. Once they had unloaded everything and the horses were in the village paddock, they went for a walk.

The river was about a quarter-mile away but a fair bit lower than the village and fields. However, they did discover a three-sided hollow built into the side of the hill above the village. The fourth side consisted of a broken dam.

'Looks like the village created an acre of pond several yards deep with a straight downhill run to the fields.' Said Katina.

'And a water source, but it's smashed.' Said Hawkyn.

'Let's have a look around.'

'What have you got in mind.'

'I'm not sure; the area doesn't feel right.' Said Katina. 'We'd better head back for dinner. It looks as if they have finished on the fields for the day.'

The Shaman and several families were waiting for them in the meeting hall. Dinner consisted of bread, cheese, a little beef and a few vegetables. The hosts explained that a large chunk of the Iredan and some other tribes became separated in a storm during the great migration. Several thousand had stayed here in six settlements. The rest continued searching. With the remnants of the other tribes, there were roughly ten thousand Southern Plains People within fifty miles. About one thousand were warriors or hunters. Katina showed them the map, told them roughly where they were now and where everyone else is. They spent the rest of the evening talking and telling stories until well beyond sunset.

Once the evening had finished, they retired to Barr and Fiona's hut. Before Katina had a chance to do anything, she got a strange feeling. That was when she realised that Puppy was not curled up near the fire but stood up and looking around.

'Hawkyn, I wouldn't.' Katina said as he was about to get undressed.

At first, he looked a little hurt. Then his expression changed when he looked at Katina and Puppy. Without a single word, he slipped on his chainmail armour and picked up his family sword. They went outside and walked towards the paddock.

'I can sense something. A strange feeling.' Said Katina.

Puppy barked.

Hawkyn's horse came straight over to him. Stroking his horse's neck, he said, 'We know, something's wrong. We're going to look.' The horse glared at him.

They walked to the fields. Half the crops looked as if they had suffered from a severe case of frost. Not dead, but severely damaged. The rest looked fine.

'There looks like enough left for a bare minimum harvest, but that's it.' Said Hawkyn.

'Seems as though they won't starve, but little above subsistence. Shall we check the sheep out on the hill?' Said Katina.

There were a few dead sheep at the top, but most were just frightened.

'I don't think this is the doing of our enemy. That would have destroyed the lot and tried to kill the tribe.' Observed Katina.

It wasn't until Katina started looking at the whole area that she noticed the shape of the original hill before part had been removed to make the pond.

'Hawkyn, if the pond cut out from the hill was still there, what do you make of the shape of the hill?'

'I don't know, rectangular, flat-topped, not too high, perhaps twenty feet.'

'Yes. And what does it look like a bigger version of?'

Then Katina heard what sounded like a dog groan. Well, that's one who's spotted it, she thought.

Hawkyn looked about, looked at Puppy, then admitted, 'I'm sorry, I just don't see it.'

'It looks like a much bigger version of what you ended up with after you buried your ancestor.' Said Katina.

'So, our hosts have taken a large chunk out of someone's grave.'

'Possibly, yes. I don't think we should investigate at night, though.' Said Katina.

'No, neither do I.'

The three headed back to Barr and Fiona's hut.

'Some form of Undead then?' Asked Hawkyn.

'I'm not sure. I don't know what Undead feels like, not had this sensing thing before. I'd have thought it would be malevolent and pure evil. However, this doesn't feel like that. Somehow it seems very angry rather than evil.' Replied Katina.

'Well, if someone took a chunk out of my house, I'd be angry too,'

'It may be that simple.' Replied Katina.

'The solution won't be. That kind of thing is never easy to rectify.'

'That's true, isn't it. Whatever it is, we'll have to try to talk it down.' Said Katina.

'We're going to have to find it first.'

'That's for tomorrow. Now for some sleep.'

After returning to the hut, they spent some time talking with Barr, Fiona and their two sons. Then everyone retired to bed. Katina openly watched Hawkyn while he undressed. He looked as if he would make a good husband. Then she undressed and cuddled in. They kissed for a while. Then she let him drift off to sleep.

She closed her eyes cleared her mind and started her meditation.

"Hello." Asked Katina.

"Good evening." Responded the Huntress. *"I've been listening. You two have been busy, haven't you."*

"I am not sure if she can help, but the Farmer may be able to get some worshippers and help some lost Iredan in the process."

"That was our thought too. My sister will listen to the village Shaman and see what she can do."

"As for the local trouble, is this a test or just a problem?" Katina asked.

"While it is a long-running local problem, if you solve it, then we will consider it a test passed."

"Can you give me any information? I've not had these feelings before."

"Not for a test, no. Now get some sleep."

"Thank you, Huntress."

Katina quickly fell asleep, feeling refreshed in the morning. She got up, they both dressed and breakfasted with their hosts. When they left the hut, both the Shaman and one of the elders were talking nearby. Katina led the others over.

'Good morning, Katina. I saw you all take a walk last

night. Do you have any thoughts that could help us?' Asked the Shaman.

'We do. We may know what that hill is and if we are correct, it would explain your problems.' Replied Katina.

'Where did all that cut stone come from?' Asked Hawkyn.

'The side of the hill when we created the irrigation pond. It was part of a buried building and wall.' Said the elder.

'And you've had difficulties ever since?' Said Katina.

'Now that you mention it, yes.' Responded the elder.

'Thank you. We will go and look around now.' Said Katina.

'I think that settles it. This place is a barrow and the burial site of someone important.' Said Hawkyn.

'Now, all we need to do is work out how to get in.' Added Katina.

'There probably won't be one. The builders will have put stones around each burial room. It might be a planned building, but as they intended to cover it with earth, they will not have left a doorway.' Said Hawkyn.

'So, we dig further in from where the pond is and hope we can find something.' Said Katina.

'Sounds the best course.' Replied Hawkyn.

They got their spades and set to work. After a while, as they achieved progress into the side of the hill, Katina could feel a growing sense of anger bordering on rage.

'We are not welcome. You don't need to be a divine type of person to feel it.' Said Hawkyn.

'Agreed, the feeling is quite unpleasant.' Said Katina. She looked at Puppy who was walking around looking unhappy. They kept digging.

'I've found the edge of a wall.' Said Hawkyn after a few more feet.

'Great, let's see if we can get further in.' Said Katina, so they continued digging.

'What's your thinking?' Asked Hawkyn.

'That, once we can get into an indoor room or space, we may be able to get whatever it is to appear so we can talk to it.'

'And if it is hostile?'

'Then we get your family's sword out and chop it up.' Said Katina.

A few feet further and they dug themselves into a modest-sized room with three stone walls and a ceiling. It was dark, partially covered in earth, with a roughly eight feet by four feet stone sarcophagus in the middle. In the other wall was a closed door. There were assorted items around the room, a large ornately carved wooden chair, a rack of spears, a rack of bows with quivers of arrows and a rack of large shields.

'Can you see if whatever it is will talk to us here? I don't like the idea of wandering about an underground building in a situation like this.' Said Hawkyn.

'Sure, let's give this a try.' Said Katina.

She closed her eyes and cleared her mind as she would do when contacting one of the Gods of Light, but rather than saying only in her mind, she said out loud. 'Please, may we talk with you?'

She heard a growl from the puppy, then felt a growing fear within her that dissipated quickly.

'Fear spells won't work on our puppy. He's not what he seems. They won't work on us either. We're Iredan Tribe. We mean you no harm and only wish to talk. Perhaps to negotiate a settlement between you and the villagers.'

While the overwhelming sense of anger remained, the fear attempts stopped. Then a tiny sphere of light appeared above the stone sarcophagus, about half the size of a thumbnail.

'Here we go.' Said Hawkyn.

Then the tiny light started to grow. The air became heavy, cold and full of energy. There was a rasping sound as Hawkyn drew his ancestor's sword. Puppy positioned himself where they had come in. He was outside looking in. Just in case Katina thought, not enough space in here.

The light grew. An energy discharge came from the ball directed at Hawkyn, who put his sword in the way, deflecting the blast to a wall with, what Katina thought, was an angry hiss coming from the blade.

'It's a spirit sword. Pull that stunt again, and we'll cut you to bits.' Katina said.

The light continued to grow, with, after a bit, arms and legs becoming visible. Slowly the shape changed into a white glowing light shaped human about seven feet tall, head to knees in white shining chain mail with longsword and large shield.

'Wow.' Was Hawkyn's comment.

'Going to cut me to bits are you?' Came a sarcastic hollow deep voice.

'If we must, yes. You are not aligned with our enemy, so we would prefer not to.' Replied Katina.

'I, however, am quite happy to kill you.' The creature replied, swinging his glowing white longsword at Hawkyn. He blocked it and swung a counter stroke into the opponent's side. There was then a movement of the creature's fingers. Hawkyn doubled up in pain and fell backwards.

The enemy then leapt forwards with his longsword to the fore. Hawkyn, the experienced warrior, simply knocked the weapon to one side and, using his long blade dagger, stabbed the glowing creature in the neck. This achieved nothing, the blade passing straight through, but Hawkyn's headbutt to the nose did make contact. He then rolled to his feet.

'Former Light Bringer Priest, stop this now, or we will destroy you. How many shades of white do our auras have? Look and think. It is not allowed for us to fight each other. You will be destroyed if you do not see sense. Which do you want?' Katina shouted angrily.

Strangely, she could feel the Gods losing patience. Finally, the creature stopped, and Hawkyn stepped back to Katina.

'Three shades of white. The Light Bringer, Huntress and Warrior. Explain yourselves.' Was the response.

'I'm questing to become an Oracle and have passed three tests. Hawkyn is my Protector. You, I believe, are a spiritual being of the Light Bringer. Therefore, we should not be harming each other.'

'Then why are you here if it is not to desecrate the tomb of myself and others.'

'We are here to see if we can negotiate peace between you and the village outside. You are killing the village's crops and animals. They are at risk of starvation when at war with the Goblins.'

'They desecrated and damaged our resting place.'

'Not deliberately. We do not know of your kind. The villagers did not know what this hill was. They still don't, but we will tell them. They needed to build irrigation for their crops and found cut stone, so used it.'

'Surely their priests taught them not to do such things and the consequences.'

'There has not been your kind of priests in hundreds of years. There's little or no knowledge of true divine things. Currently, there are only two true Initiates. One for the Light Bringer and one for the Huntress. There are no proper priests yet. I didn't even know you existed and don't know what you are.' Said Katina. There was a stunned silence for a while.

'I am still angry at the desecration as the others will be, but you have explained the reasons. In answer to your question, we are Spectral Guardians. Spiritual beings who are protectors of the consecrated areas of the Gods of Light.'

'The Light's version of the wraiths, ghosts and vampires of the Lord of All Evil then.' Hawkyn asked hopefully.

'Pah, they are nothing to us. We are far stronger than they are.' The spirit replied.

'Oh wow. Can we bring your kind back to help us? We are really up against it.' So asked Katina, who was deliberately trying to avoid the phrase "Summoned".

'It is possible to Summon us by ritual, but it must be by the highest rank of Divine Priest and needs certain other things too. It is difficult to do. No disrespect meant, but that ritual is well above the capability of an Initiate.' Replied the Guardian.

'You'd better have a word with your God about that one. There seems to be a large amount of rule-bending going on. In the meantime, we will find out what the villagers are going to do about the desecration. May we return later and discuss things with you further?' Asked Katina.

'That would be sensible.' Said the Guardian.

'Then, for now, good day to you.' And they quietly left.

After walking some distance from the hill, Hawkyn said. 'Well, that was different. I'm going to have a few bruises, I think.'

'To get away with nothing but a few bruises in a situation like that is incredibly lucky.' Said Katina. 'Oh well, here goes.' She continued, seeing the Shaman talking with a few village elders. They walked over.

'Was all the digging worth it?' An elder asked.

'Yes. What we thought had happened was correct. Spirits are haunting your settlement. The reason is that the hill is a burial mound. You took the large stone blocks from the grave room of one of the occupants. Their spirits are angry with the village because of the desecration of the grave. I am hoping I can negotiate something between everyone to settle this.' Said Katina.

'What do you think?' An elder asked the Shaman.

'I know of no lore or teachings covering this. An apology and putting the removed stones back are certainly worth a try. It may go deeper than that.' The Shaman replied.

'They're part of buildings, though.' An elder commented.

'The stones belong to someone else. We need to give them back. That's all there is to it.' Concluded the Shaman.

The elders organised a small cart and had several unused large blocks of stone placed in it by various workers nearby. Katina and Hawkyn took these to the entrance made earlier and properly put them back in the remains of the wall. Katina, followed by Hawkyn, entered the sarcophagus room.

'May we speak with you again?' Katina asked after clearing her thoughts. Hawkyn stood next to her and Puppy just in the doorway.

The small white ball of light appeared and, like before, grew into the Spectral Guardian they met earlier. There were loud gasps from the elders and Shaman stood just outside.

'Hello again. I have explained the situation to the elders of the village and the Shaman, who are just outside. They will try and replace the removed stone and make good the damage caused.' Katina said.

The Shaman walked forward, bent down on one knee. 'We are most sorry for what we have done and will endeavour to make good all damage suffered. We hope that is satisfactory to you.'

'So long as you carry the repairs out quickly, and no further issues occur, then that will satisfy us on this occasion.' The Guardian replied.

'We thank you, gracious spirit.' The Shaman replied and they all left.

That evening they went to see the Shaman and village elders again. 'We think that we must be moving on tomorrow. We've got a long way to go and more tasks to do. Good luck with the restoration. If you choose to find the rest of the tribe, my home should not be hard to find. We range a fair way. You should pick up signs of our people.

In the morning, they gave their thanks and said their goodbyes to Barr and Fiona. Then with gear packed, they headed north again. When they were a mile or so clear of the village.

"Thank you, Katina. The Shaman has made contact. That and the help with the Spirit Guardian, I consider my task for you completed. You can now add me to your list. Four down, well done." Said the Farmer.

"Thank you. Where next?"

"Keep going north, then turn west ish when you near the mountain range. The next location is visible for a long way."

PART 7 – SOME PLACE ELSE

10 – DOWN THE TUNNEL

'We're doing well, four down. I don't suppose you know what's next?' Asked Hawkyn.

'Afraid not. All I know is that we go north until we hit the mountains, then head west. We will see it clearly from miles away.'

'The further north and west we go, the more likely we are to bump into Goblins or the like. So, we will need to start taking precautions.'

'More appropriately, do we fight our way through or hide and sneak.' Wondered Katina.

'While I don't like it, but if we start clobbering Goblin scouting parties, we'll leave a trail a mile wide. So, they'll know what direction we're going in.' Said Hawkyn.

'And will probably know where we're going better than we do.' Added Katina.

'Hide and sneak it is then.' Said Hawkyn. Puppy looked up at the pair.

'Are you listening and learning?' Katina asked Puppy.

Bark.

They continued heading north for several days, the tops of the mountains now showing themselves out of the mists of distance. They found signs of well organised mounted patrols and concluded they were Southern Plains People rather than Goblins. Katina decided to take a wild leap of faith and started to train Puppy to track. It was an unusual task requiring some different teaching strategies than when she had conducted the early training sessions of the tribe's fourteen year olds. Puppy, however, was quick to learn. The quality and quantity of his daily foraging improved dramatically.

When they reached the foothills, evidence of Goblin scouting parties became common. Katina showed Puppy the tracks, teaching him to recognise numbers and direction. They then headed west, returning them to the plains. Katina took Puppy on the regular daily scouting, showing him how to track and follow things. Within a week or so, Puppy had become reasonably competent. They were splitting scouting between them, leaving Hawkyn and the horses to follow up behind. With care, the various parties of Goblins continued their travels, blissfully ignorant of what was within a few hundred yards of them. After one particularly close walk straight past Puppy, he developed a "Surely they aren't that stupid" expression.

'Puppy, they are not stupid. Not by any stretch. Goblins are just careless, they don't get taught skills and they don't practice.' Katina then considered that perhaps Puppy was right after all.

It was a little later that a huge, peaked mountain came into view.

'I didn't think mountains smoked.' Said Hawkyn.

'I didn't think so either.' Replied Katina.

Puppy Barked.

'I think that mean's "They do".' Added Hawkyn.

'A mountain that burns, great. That must be where we are going. We'd better head towards that.' Said Katina.

'I suppose if it smokes, it must have a fire. Does that make it a fire mountain?'

'A good a name as any.'

They continued roughly northwest towards the fire mountain that continued to smoke in varying amounts.

After about a day, 'Hawkyn, stop, watch out.' Hawkyn halted at once. In front of him was a crack in the grass where the ground raised slightly. As he backed his horse away, the ground gave way. The three of them stared into the ten feet diameter hole. Katina looked further on and could see a gap in the grass heading off towards the fire mountain.

'It looks like some sort of fissure has opened up in the grasslands.' Katina said.

"You need to go down that." Said The Huntress.

'You're kidding.' Katina replied out loud.

"Afraid not, sorry. Be careful. The terrain is dangerous."

'I am missing half of that, I think.' Said Hawkyn.

'I am sorry to say The Huntress has advised that we have to go down that fissure and follow it. However, we need to be careful. The terrain is dangerous.'

The roof had collapsed into an oval tube with a flat base that gently went deeper into the ground. At this point, the base was only about four feet deep, but the height of the tube quickly increased to about ten feet. Fallen roof material made the floor impassable as it was, but looked smooth after the collapse.

'We'll have to clear that lot and collapse some roof to make enough headroom to get the horses through. Once past this entrance, by the looks of it, we should be alright.' Suggested Hawkyn.

'It's worth a try.'

They secured the horses and climbed down the few feet to the rock covered floor of the hole. Initially, they hacked away at the low ceiling on either side of the gap in the grass. Slowly they headed into the tunnel pulling more rock, stone and earth down until the opening was tall enough to get the horses through. Then Katina and Hawkyn moved debris to create the base of a ramp onto which they packed earth dirt and grass. The horses were in the tunnel by nightfall. They made camp under cover of the entrance, evading the cold never-ending easterly wind.

In the morning, they proceeded into the depths following the smooth-sided tube ever onwards and gradually downwards. The light of day from the entrance shone, illuminating the way forward. But, as they led the horses onward, slowly, the sound of above ground diminished and the light turned ever greyer. Without reference to sun or daylight, both time and distance became impossible to judge. Slowly the beacon of light at the end of the tunnel became fainter until finally, after what seemed to Katina like days, the illumination from the entrance disappeared altogether.

'Now what do we do? I don't have candles or torches. Luka or Oswald's light spell would be useful now.' Stated Katina.

'I have a few slow-burn tallow candles, about six, but that's all. They'll provide a little light, but not much.' Hawkyn replied.

'That may be enough. You'd better check how many you have. We must make sure we have enough to get out. That will limit how far we can go.' Hawkyn then rummaged through one of the packs on the spare horse.

'I was right. I have six.'

'Then we use three. When the candles are used up, we'll have to turn back. We won't achieve anything if we can't see.'

'We'll have to think of something else and come back again. We can't abandon one of the tests because of a practical difficulty. Maybe we can make more candles.'

'I don't know how.'

'I've seen it done a few times, so maybe.' Hawkyn said as he lit the first candle.

A dim orange light radiated out, slightly illuminating the way a few yards ahead. The three and their horses continued the descent through the silent near darkness for endless hours. The only sound being the horses' hooves on the rock surface. The tunnel remained roughly oval, and the sides had little in the way of protuberances. The floor was rippled but otherwise was flat stone covered with dust and dirt. Two candles later and Hawkyn observed.

'Am I imagining it or is it getting slightly warmer.'

'Now you mention it. I think it is.'

They continued onward through the near darkness, the gradual warming becoming more noticeable until.

'We have an orange glow at the end of the tunnel.' Observed Hawkyn.

'We'd better keep going. At least we may not need that candle for a bit.' Hawkyn blew his candle out and put it away.

Now they could see the end of the tunnel. It appeared to open out. However, Katina could not see anything but the glow. Moving forward, the air temperature around her increased significantly and the orange glow became brighter. As she approached the end of the tunnel, even the rocks started to warm up.

'What is this place?' Said Hawkyn.

'I don't know. If these rocks get any hotter, we'll have problems with the horses. Puppy, are your paws alright?'

Bark.

As they approached the entrance to the cave.

'I think we should secure the horses and leave them here, at least until we know what's in there.' Katina said. They found various boulders that occasionally lay in the tunnel and secured the reins with rope to a pile of rocks.

'Hawkyn, Puppy, forgive me for saying the blindingly obvious, but something giving this much heat is extremely hot. So please, both of you, be careful.'

They all walked forwards the last hundred yards or so to the end of the tunnel. The heat was staggering. What Katina saw shocked her. A large cave, perhaps three or four acres in size. The ceiling was some thirty feet above them. The floor, some thirty feet below, was molten rock, slowly swirling and moving. To the left and right was a ledge some six feet wide that went round the cave. It did not go far to the right. However, to the left, the cave and path went round a corner out of sight.

'To the left, it is then.' Said Hawkyn after a quick look around.

'Me first, I think.' Said Katina as she went to the corner and cautiously peered round and came back.

'The cave continues for a few acres then goes around another corner out of sight. There is a stone bridge across the cave to a tunnel. Someone in a hooded long black cloak is chained to a stone column at the start of the bridge.'

'We've arrived at the test then.'

'Seems like it.'

'Wonder who is chained up.'

'Don't know.' Said Katina, although she had an idea.

They walked around the corner, continuing a hundred yards or so to the bridge. At the entrance were two square stone columns about one yard across each going from floor to ceiling. The bridge itself was a two yards wide and seventy yards long stone arch with no railing. Katina approached the seven feet tall man chained to the left-hand column. She gasped in shock when pulling back his hood revealed a living skeleton covered in taught hairless grey skin and no eyes.

'The Bridge-Keeper. We're at the entrance to the Underworld.' She said. The grey-skinned skull nodded slightly.

After a few shocked seconds. 'How the hell do you chain and gag The Bridge-Keeper. We'd better try and free him.' Responded a pale-faced and Hawkyn.

Chains bound his wrists and ankles and those two were themselves fixed together by a larger one anchored into the stone pillar. They tried as hard as they could but could not free wrist, ankle, or pillar chains. Then, finally, they were able to remove the tight metal gag.

'These chains are demonic steel. You cannot break them with what you have. Over the bridge is the passageway to the gates to the underworld. The Lord of All Evil's demon Cruach has captured The Lord of the Gates and his wolf.

He has also chained the Gates to the Underworld shut. Cruach must be defeated, and the gates opened to allow the souls of the unclaimed dead to pass to the other side.' Said the Bridge Keeper with a deep, gravely hollow voice.

'How can we possibly defeat a demon if we can't even break the chains he uses?' Asked Katina in an exasperated tone. 'Although we have completed the tasks so far, we lost the last fight.'

The Bridge-Keeper looked at the pair of them for several seconds, then Puppy. 'You have the skill, strength and bravery, but simply lack the tools. Your spirit sword will harm Cruach. He has in his possession the Hammer of the Dwarf God. He used that to imprison both The Lord of the Gates and his wolf. Steal the Hammer, use it to free the wolf. Then help the wolf defeat Cruach. He cannot do it on his own, but if the Hammer allows one of you to use it and the other uses the spirit sword, then maybe. This is no place for a six-month-old puppy, though.'

'Puppy is not what he looks like, just takes that form while travelling. He has proved quite useful recently and is a good friend. But, still Puppy, an immortal demon is probably too dangerous for a youngster such as you.' Replied Katina. Puppy gave a flat unfriendly stare.

The three crossed over the bridge. Katina could see the looks on the faces of both Hawkyn and Puppy. They were going to fight an immortal demon powerful enough to beat a God of Light and two supernatural beings. Her legs shook, her blood raced and her skin was pale. So, this was fear then. She walked on. Then some thoughts occurred to her. The Gods of Light believed she was up to this or would have gotten someone else to do it. Winning was possible and despite the flat stare, she still felt this was no place for a baby, dragon or not. As they got halfway across the bridge, Puppy changed into his boy form and they all became a little transparent.

'You are a good deal bigger now.' Said Katina.

'Us dragons advance our stages of growth by both age and personal development. I am quite old but haven't had the opportunity for the personal development necessary to grow while being stuck in a cave up a mountain on a small island. It's why I ran away.'

'You should have stayed with your family. They will be worried about you.'

'That's what my brothers and sisters said when I left.'

'Do your parents know where you are.' Asked Katina

'No.'

'They will be angry with you, but that will be because you will have frightened them.' Suggested Katina. 'You will have to go home when we can arrange it.' Said Katina.

'No.'

'I take it that mum and dad are a good deal bigger than you.' Added Hawkyn.

'Yes, lots.'

'We can't defy a child's parents wishes. We will care for you and teach you as best we can, but you need to return to your family as soon as possible and take the punishment for running away. Subject to that, you will always be welcome.'

'I would prefer to stay here. Life is much more interesting than my cave. All I get to see back home is the odd rat.' Said Puppy.

'Can't be done long term, unless your mum and dad say you can stay.' Added Hawkyn.

The other side of the bridge opened to a large ornately paved area, about one acre in size, carved into the side of the cave. A thirty feet tall stone arch stood in the middle of the back wall directly opposite the bridge. There were fourteen stone statues, each about eight feet tall, stood on a plinth three feet high. Seven each side of the archway.

'You know what's weird?' Added Hawkyn.

'The whole thing is weird.' Replied Puppy.

'What Hawkyn?' Asked Katina.

'Look at the stone archway.'

It took Katina a few seconds to realise what Hawkyn was talking about. You could see another tunnel descending into the rock through the stone arch, but the arch was forward of the back wall and it appeared you could walk behind it.

'Oh.' She responded.

Puppy walked up to one of the statues and said, 'Isn't this the one that got you into this mess in the first place.' It was a statue of a lithe young woman, carrying a longbow and with a falcon perched on her arm.

'Yes, I think that is The Huntress.' Replied Katina.

'I can see both the Warrior and the Light Bringer. I think I know what these are. The younger statues could be the twelve Gods of Light. Don't know who the other two are.' Said Hawkyn.

'I wonder if the Gods of Light have a father and mother?'

'I was told they did.' Added Puppy.

'A statue for each of our proper gods. Suppose it makes sense to have those at the entrance to the underworld. I suspect there's a choice of where you go. Perhaps you choose a statue.' Wondered Katina.

'And if it goes wrong, you end up going through the arch.' Observed Hawkyn.

'We'd better get on with this. Quietly now, no more talking. I need to try and steal a hammer.' Said Katina.

They peered through the arch. The tunnel disappeared into the distance with no immediate signs of occupants. She signalled them to move forward.

The arch-shaped tunnel was thirty feet high with perfectly smooth walls and floor. Once they entered the tunnel, Katina could see a lit chamber several hundred yards away. All three kept tight to the walls, difficult for Puppy, who had changed his shape again and was an over thirty feet long dragon. They all trod carefully, making no noise as they progressed. Finally, about fifty yards from the end of the tunnel, Katina signalled the others to stop and continued alone along the left-hand wall.

At the corner, she slowly peered in. What was beyond struck her with awe. It was an impossibly large cavern with perfectly smooth sides. Taking up the middle and back part of the cavern was a whirlpool of translucent white mist that slowly descended into impossible depths. It was this mist that created the light. Immediately in front of her was a ledge that extended for hundreds of yards into the cavern. At the edge was an iron grating that ran to the roof. A path starting at the tunnel entrance slowly rose from the ledge until it reached the gate in the iron grating about a hundred yards above the ledge.

To her left on the ledge, several hundred yards away, was a large white stone mansion. To her right, a man chained to the wall and a wolf in a cage. She couldn't see any demons or hammers, so she went back and whispered to the others.

'I think we need to speak with the two chained up, see if we can help them and find out where this hammer is.' Said Katina. The others nodded and off the three crept. This time there was light coming from some of the windows of the mansion.

'Somebody's home.' Katina said quietly.

The three crept to the right, sticking close to the cavern walls. The only sound was the quiet hum of the whirling mist in the distance. They approached the human-looking figure so tightly chained he couldn't even move his head. Next to him was a twenty-five-foot iron bar cage containing a twenty-foot black and grey-furred muzzled wolf lying on the ground, all four paws chained together.

'Blimey, that thing makes even Freki look small.' Said Hawkyn quietly. The wolf's ears pricked up and the man's eyes opened. Katina signalled Hawkyn to keep watch, then went over to the chained man.

'Are you The Lord of the Gates?' Katina asked quietly

while removing the metal gag.

'Yes, I am. Do you know Freki? Are him and his brother Geri still in existence?'

'Yes, they are. Geri runs with his pack, and Freki runs with a warrior friend from my tribe. Currently, they are trying to stop The Lord of All Evil from wiping out valley folk Humans. Here please have some water.'

The Lord drank eagerly. 'Thank you.' Katina then tried to remove the chains, but like the Bridge Keeper, they wouldn't budge.

'You cannot break them. Only the Hammer of the Dwarf God can do that. It's hanging on the wall in the hall in my house. The only problem is Cruach is there.'

'Does he ever leave the house?'

'Yes. Each day he comes over here to gloat for a while. That will be your opportunity. The Hammer is intelligent and will not let anyone use it. Your only chance is to tell it first who you are and why you want to use it and hope. Now, gag me, or Cruach will know someone has been.' Katina complied.

The three again crept along the cavern's edge towards the stone mansion house around the other side. As they approached, Katina said

'There's a fair-sized gap between the back of the mansion and the cave wall. We can stay there until he goes visiting the others. After that, I will sneak in and get the Hammer. Then we hide until he goes back into the house. Once the coast is clear, we free those trapped before the demon notices.'

Hawkyn and Puppy nodded. They hid around the back of the house and waited. Puppy then shimmered and changed into a four-year-old dark-haired Human boy. Hawkyn and Katina looked at him.

'My normal form won't fit through the door.' Puppy whispered. They waited all crouched on the floor.

After about half an hour, the front door opened,

followed by steps going away from the house. Katina leading, the three snuck low around the side of the house furthest away from the cavern's entrance and the departing footsteps. They climbed onto a raised platform two feet off the cavern floor and, using the surrounding stone balustrade as cover, crept to the front door.

'Phew! it's open.' Said Katina, and they all walked through the eight foot tall double doors leaving them in a partially opened position. They entered a large double-height hallway with a wide staircase in front of them. The floor was of white oak boards and the walls were half-height dark wood panels. On the left-hand wall were stuffed heads of various creatures, none of whom Katina recognised. The right-hand wall had but one item above the dark wood panelling. An unassuming four-foot-long war hammer, eighteen-inch wide by nine-inch deep plain dark grey metal head with a white crystal in its centre.

'That thing's huge. Oh well, here goes.' Said Katina.

'Remember, introduce yourself.' Said Puppy.

'I will watch for the demon returning.' Added Hawkyn.

'Hello Hammer of the Dwarf God. I am Katina of the Iredan tribe. Please may I use you to free the Lord of the Gates, his wolf and reopen the gates to the underworld?'

The crystal glowed brightly then flickered between red and blue. Finally, after a few seconds, it settled on blue.

'Hopefully, that means yes.' Katina went forward and clasped the silver coloured metal handle. The Hammer came free in her hand. It was heavy, but she could just about carry it. As soon as she walked away, Puppy muttered some strange words and moved his hands in an intricate pattern. A duplicate hammer appeared on the wall.

'Elemental magic. It's not real and will not last long, but if he doesn't look closely, it may fool him for a bit.' Puppy explained. Katina nodded. 'Let's go.' and walked towards Hawkyn and the door.

'All clear, let's bail.' Hawkyn responded to the implied

question.

Katina led the way out the door, turned left and, hiding behind the stone balustrade, crept to the end of the mansion furthest away from the cavern entrance. Then jumped over the stonework and ran around the back of the building. The others followed close behind.

'If the demon is outside the house, we'll never make it across unseen. There's nothing to hide behind.' Katina said.

'We'll have to wait here until he returns, then try and get back before he notices the hammer is missing.' Suggested Hawkyn.

A few minutes later, 'Here he comes. He looks Human.' Said Katina.

'Don't be fooled. Cruach actually looks quite different. About the only thing that is correct is the number of legs.' Replied Puppy. They both hid back round the corner.

'He's a shape-changer and you can see through it?'

'Yes, he is. It is just a magical manipulation of matter. As for me, I am what is called an Emperor Dragon. We can see all things for what they are regardless of magic or anything else.'

Katina could hear footsteps climbing the stairs to the house. Then with the sound of unearthly laughter, the double doors slammed shut.

'We'd better move and try and get this done.' Hawkyn ordered. The three sticking close to the edge ran as fast as they could to the cavern entrance. Just as they got there, a loud ear-splitting shriek brought them to their knees.

'He's just destroyed the illusion.' Shouted Puppy. Hawkyn removed the gag as Katina lifted the heavy Hammer and tried to hit one of the chain anchors.

'Forget me. Destroy the cage.' Shouted the Lord of the Gates.

Hawkyn looked over Katina's shoulder towards the cavern entrance. 'Shit, shit, shit.' He drew his family sword from over his shoulder and, with his shield in his left hand, ran past Katina, shortly followed by a dragon form Puppy.

'Leave Cruach to your friends. Don't look. Just destroy that cage. NOW.'

Deliberately not looking at the cavern entrance, she ran the few yards to the cage amidst sounds of something heavy on a metal shield, the unmistakable sound of sword against armour and the sound of a dragon breathing fire.

'Do not look. Destroy the cage. You can do it, just believe.'

Katina raised the Hammer and swung it as hard as she could at a door hinge. The power flowed through her as her hand burned. The massive hinge screeched as it strained and twisted. The unmistakable sounds of Puppy and his six-inch teeth wrenching and tearing flesh drowned out the sound of the straining hinge. She also heard Hawkyn hacking at something.

The twenty-foot long wolf strained at his chains, desperately trying to pull free.

'Do not look at the fight. Just channel the power. Believe. You can do this.'

Again, she lifted the massive Hammer and felt the power burn her hands and arms. Finally, she cleared all thought and, remembering what she heard about spell casting, pictured the destroyed hinge, then swung the Hammer with a grunt.

The power flowed through her and the Hammer. The entire cage shone with red light, there was the screeching squeal of metal twisting and the top hinge snapped. Again, she swung. Her hands and arms felt like they were on fire as she hit the second hinge, which too cracked. Then using the Hammer as leverage forced the cage door open and entered. One swing of the Hammer and the lock on the muzzle broke. Two more and an anchor holding the chains attached to the wolf's legs shattered. A split second later and the wolf was out the door. Only then did she turn round and stand stunned at the sight. Hawkyn and Puppy were fighting a twenty foot tall grey scaled bipedal creature with four large tentacles for arms, a horned head and a protruding muzzle for the mouth. Each tentacle used a heavy mace. It also had a full plate armoured body.

Katina decided to free The Lord of the Gates and ran over. She swung a single blow to one of the chain anchors.

'That'll do, now help the others.'

She ran up to the fight at the cavern entrance. It was still evenly balanced, but Cruach, with both Puppy and Wolf, was now facing too many teeth. Slowly the demon was losing ground, and tentacles too judging by what was at Puppy's feet.

When Katina arrived, Puppy grabbed one tentacle just below the shoulder, and the wolf grabbed one on the other side. Katina swung her Hammer at the demon's legs, knocking them out from under him and down Cruach went. Before she had time to think, Hawkyn was at the neck, sticking his family's sword into the demon's throat. There was a cough of green goo from the mouth and Cruach collapsed.

Katina looked round. Hawkyn was a mess, covered in blood, holding a shattered shield in a dangling left arm. Puppy was limping badly and had one eye closed. Even the wolf had a bleeding face from a contusion on the snout.

The Lord of the Gates walked over. 'Finish this. Smash his head with the Hammer, or he will come back.'

Katina walked over to the head, swung the Hammer squashing the skull flat.

'I will give you the honour of opening the gates. Just remember, don't go over the threshold. I will go and free the Bridge Keeper.'

'Yes, lord. Thank you for the privilege.'

Katina, Hawkyn, Puppy and Wolf walked up the ramp to the pair of shut ornate gates that lead to the underworld, each some thirty feet high and fifteen feet wide, with the same demonic iron chain locking them together. Again, she concentrated and cleared her mind. Then, feeling the power flow, she swung the Hammer at the chains, which broke, then screamed with the burning pain of her arms and hands, dropping the Hammer. After a few seconds, she looked at the others who were standing there watching.

'Dearest, the honour of opening the gates is yours. When you are ready.'

Katina tried to ignore the pain and got up. Loosened the now broken heavy chain and let it fall into the whirlpool beyond the ramp. She grabbed the two gates and pulled. They swung open.

'You had better come down quickly. It will soon get cramped up there with thousands of years' worth of souls to pass through.' Said The Lord of the Gates.

'Yes, My Lord.' Responded Katina, and they all promptly descended.

'Katina and Hawkyn, two of my sisters, have spoken with me. I am aware you are questing to become the next Oracle and The Protector. Consider your test for me passed.'

'Thank you, Lord of the Gates.'

'I would suggest you stay a while to recover from your injuries a little. Unfortunately, you cannot stay long. This place has a strange effect on mortals.'

'Thank you, Lord, that would be most welcome.'

11 – THE MIST

Hawkyn sheathed his sword and put his shield down. His left arm hung limply at his side. Katina put down the Hammer and dropped to her knees, crying with pain.

'Let me have a look at you, dearest.' Hawkyn said gently, walking over to her. He went to touch her then stopped. 'Your hands, they are burnt.'

'I think it's arms and shoulders too. Feels like it.'

'I am going to have to undress you, top half anyway. Sorry, but we've got to get the raw skin cleaned and washed at the very minimum.'

'Hawkyn, we're to be together as partners in all senses for life. So it's not a problem.' He just smiled and softly kissed her. Then he went to remove a piece of armour from her lower left arm.

'Do you want help? Two people are likely to cause Katina less pain.' Asked the Lord of the Gates.

'It would be much appreciated, especially as I am having difficulties with my left arm.'

They started by removing her leather armour. Loosening the holding straps caused her to scream, but once undone, the armour came off easily.

'Mind if I undo a few top ties and look at your shoulders.' Hawkyn asked Katina.

'Please do. Both the shoulders and arms hurt a lot.' She replied.

Hawkyn carefully undid some narrow cloth ties at the top of her shirt. Then, while the Lord of the Gates held one side away from her skin, Hawkyn opened it to reveal a shoulder.

'It is like the hands, all deep red and blistered. I am sorry, but you are going to have to go topless for a while. There is no way your skin will handle having anything covering it.'

'That is to be expected.' Katina replied.

Carefully Hawkyn undid all the cloth ties holding Katina's white linen shirt closed, then gently opened it. The Lord held the sleeves clear of her shoulders while Hawkyn freed the fabric from the skin of her arms. They then carefully removed the shirt.

Both shoulders and arms were deep red and blistered to the tips of her fingers.

'What happened?' Asked a concerned Hawkyn.

'The Hammer of the Dwarf God is a divine weapon that channels enormous power, far more power than any mortal can handle, hence the burns. I have never known anyone who isn't a God survive using it for even one swing. However, no Oracle has tried to use a divine weapon before. As more than one God is connected to them, they can channel more divine power than other mortals. However, it was still more than Katina could handle and should have killed her.' The God replied.

'Oh.' Said Katina.

'I've seen our healers deal with serious burns. A long cool bath to reduce heat, a long time with a cold wet towel to cover the burns, honey to act as an antiseptic and lots of clean bandages. You will need washing carefully.' Said Hawkyn, then looking at the Lord of the Gates, he asked. 'Is there a possibility of a cool bath? Not ice-cold, just cool.'

'Yes. We'll have to clear the house first.' The Lord replied.

'I will go and collect your horses before I become busy. Those burns are going to take a few days, even here with my help.' The Lord of the Gates walked up the tunnel towards the bridge.

When he returned, 'Let's go to the house. We can secure the horses and check my place over. It's been a while and my squatter may have left things behind. I must get that done before the crowd arrive.'

They all walked over to the large mansion, tying the horses to the stone railings of the front balcony. The Lord waved his left hand again. Troughs of water and hay appeared in front of the horses, who at once started to consume the contents. The group walked up the steps and stopped at the front door.

He lifted his hands slightly above his shoulders and briefly closed his eyes. 'Nothing divine or spiritual. I am surprised. I would have thought there would be something.' Then looking at Puppy, 'Forgive me for asking you, but are you able to check for magic?'

'Despite my age, I am only a stage two dragon, and even that is very recent. Detection at short range, maybe, but I haven't tried it yet. However, we are not at my home anymore, but yours. I don't think our elemental magic works at your place. Essentially, we are on the Spirit Plane. There's nothing from back home on which my magic can work. The only thing that will work here is an illusion. That affects what is seen rather than what is actually here.'

'I hadn't thought of it like that.' The Lord admitted.

'Katina, you any idea what they are talking about.'

'No Hawkyn, I haven't.'

'When you become the Oracle, you will need to understand how the various planes of existence work, but it isn't needed now. Let's go inside.'

The Lord of the Gates opened the double doors. Puppy changed into a dog, and they all entered. Cruach had lost his temper when he had discovered the Hammer was a fake. He had smashed all the wall panels, torn the tapestries, broken the floorboards, and thrown furniture everywhere.

'He certainly had an anger problem did your demon.' Said Katina, looking at the mess.

'My uncle's demons are not known for their self-control. It's easily fixed, though.' The Lord again raised his hands and concentrated. Everything repaired itself.

'My patch, so it does what I say. Through the door over there, baths are waiting. I will check the rest of the house and prepare dinner. Katina, I have left a sleeveless shirt with less shoulder covering for you to wear if you wish to. The choice is yours.'

'Thank you.' Katina and Hawkyn went to the door shown while Puppy found a comfortable rug and lay down.

The room for their baths was a sizeable one with a log fire, half-height wood panelling on the walls like in the hall and tapestries hanging above. Two large oval metal tubs were in the middle of the room, each long enough to stretch ones' legs out.

Katina walked over and put her fingers in each of the two thirds full baths. One was nice and warm, the other significantly cooler. The colder one was probably for her. Because of the burns, the warmer one would be painful. Each bath had a stool next to it with a bar of soap and multiple cloths for washing and drying. The one next to the colder bath had a shirt folded upon it. There was also a large pot of honey and lots of soft, clean bandages.

Katina casually removed the rest of her clothes, Hawkyn allowed her privacy. He then came over and helped her into the bath before undressing himself and getting into the warmer one. They lay soaking and talking for some time, then washed.

Hawkyn got out of his bath, dried, and dressed, before helping Katina out of hers. First, he dried the unburnt areas of Katina and helped her partially dress. Then he gently dried the burnt shoulders, arms and hands. Next, he placed a large towel soaked in cold water over her shoulders and arms.

They sat talking for a while as the burns cooled further. Finally, he applied honey as an antiseptic and wrapped her shoulders and arms in the soft bandages. The new shirt, which had no sleeves and little shoulder material, was a lot more comfortable than the old one had been.

After at least an hour, they left the room. Puppy had moved from his rug and was lying in a doorway on the other side of the hall. He looked at them and barked, got up and went into the room. They followed. Like the other rooms they had seen, it was large with part panelled and tapestry covered walls. This time there was a lit fireplace on one wall that puppy headed straight for and a large rectangular wooden table with six chairs. The Lord of the Gates stood at the head of the table carving a joint of roast beef. The table also had bowls of vegetables and a small cask of ale sat in the middle.

'Please, come in and sit down.' Asked The Lord of the Gates. They both sat on opposite sides of the table.

'Take some ale while I serve dinner.' Hawkyn filled the three pewter tankards. The Lord handed them both plates with carved roast beef on them. Katina held the various bowls of vegetables for them to choose the amount desired. Then she realised the hands had healed enough for use, which was itself miraculous.

'I have been imprisoned for several thousand of your years. I wonder if you can bring me up to date with history and how things are in the world at this time. Maybe I can explain a few things to you too.'

'Certainly, Divine Lord.' Said Katina.

'Firstly, although I am the Lord of the Gates to the underworld, I am also the God of your race. If you wish to get married now, you can exchange vows before me if you both desire it. The other Gods of Light would honour the marriage, although obviously, your relatives and friends would not be present. Your choice.'

'Thank you for the offer Divine Lord. Hawkyn, what do you think about getting married now?' Katina asked.

'For a God to officiate over our ceremony is incredible. The honour of your offer my Divine Lord is well, I have no words. However, the ways of our people insist that families must give permission, both sides. While I can't imagine them saying no, given our possible status of Oracle and Protector, we must be seen to be adhering to the rules, I think.' Hawkyn said.

'Unfortunately, while I am happy to go ahead now, I suspect, Hawkyn, you are correct. We will most definitely get married and would love you or one of the others to officiate. However, if I make it as Oracle, then both Hawkyn and I will be of significant political power. We must be seen to obey the rules. Your offer is very kind, but I don't see there is much choice.' Responded Katina.

'You are correct, I think. You must obey your tribe's laws if your people are to accept your influence. Are you able to fill in on the history of Tiranimeith?' The Lord replied.

'Some, I think. Our elders told us that the pure races and the Gods of Light banished The Lord of All Evil. For some time, everyone was in harmony.'

'Yes, I was a part of that. But, of course, I had real power then.'

'Then us humans found elemental magic, developed professional soldiers and started conquering everyone else, forming a massive empire over the whole continent. Once the empire achieved that, the priests of the Gods of Light were persecuted and killed. They stopped being worshipped. At some point, The Lord of All Evil returned with his host and defeated the empire. However, he could not destroy the last pockets of humans in a valley in the north-east of Tiranimeith or in the plains in the east. Now Goblin tribes' control everything, bar a few thousand square miles. There can't be more than a couple of hundred thousand Humans left, if that.' Said Katina.

'And the largest human population centre in the valley has just been taken over by a priest who secretly worships The Lord of All Evil, even if the general population don't know it yet.' Added Hawkyn.

'Who do they think they are worshipping?' Asked The Lord of the Gates.

'Humans are mostly agnostic, but a chunk thinks the High Priest's church worship The Light Bringer. There is also the Monastic Order of the Infirmary who care for the sick and injured.'

'So, if my deranged uncle has all but won. Why then is my sister, The Huntress, so ecstatic?'

'Best guess, because of what is happening around a village called Warameth in the valley to our east. Not only are there now several divine spell casters and proper worshippers of the Gods of Light, but just about every Human warrior hero worth anything is either there or on the way. With improving divine and combat capability, the place will become a serious obstacle in fairly short order.' Said Katina.

'And given the place now includes Light Bringer spell casting capability, very soon our opponent will not be able to throw Undead at the village to solve the problem.' Added Hawkyn.

'The beginnings of the force necessary to defeat The Lord of All Evil now exists. If I can convince my people to help the valley folk and Oswald Shamus can train more divine spellcasters, perhaps humans could secure the whole valley.' Said Katina.

'Does The Lord of All Evil know this?' Asked The Lord of the Gates.

'Probably. We knocked a fair-sized hole in the High Priest's soldiers when we left the City of Kersladen during his coup. He certainly will know about the spell casters.' Replied Hawkyn.

'I see, then some or all of his Host of Evil will be on the way. Your saving grace is the continent is huge. They will have a long way to go.' Replied the Lord. 'Let's eat.'

While discussing the current situation and history, the three ate plentiful amounts of roast beef and drank a significant quantity of excellent clear brown ale. By the end of the meal, they were both full and tired.

'I suggest you sleep now. You must leave in the morning and continue your quest. I will show you to your room.'

The Lord took them up the solid wooden carved staircase and showed them through a door to their left. They entered another fair-sized room, part panelled like the others, with a large double bed, two large chests and some stands onto which you could hang clothes. They both undressed for bed and fell asleep quickly.

Katina awoke in the morning to a quiet indistinct murmuring of thousands of voices, but just a little too loud to be ignored. Hawkyn was already awake and dressed.

'Disturbing, isn't it.' He said.

'Indeed. Time to be on our way, I think.'

'Yes, I believe so. Do you need help?'

'The shirt over the shoulders if you please.'

As asked, Hawkyn helped Katina get dressed. Then opening the door, she found Puppy asleep on the other side. Katina bent down, gently shaking him awake.

'I am afraid it is time to go.' He looked at her bleary-eyed, then got up and followed them down the stairs to the hall.

A tall strange skeletal man with blue fire eyes, shoulder-length tied back blond hair and a calf-length long leather cloak stood downstairs waiting for them.

'Good morning. I am the Lord's assistant. Please let me take you to him.' He put his hand on the door handle and added, 'This will be very strange for you. Be prepared.'

The double doors opened, and they all stepped through. The sight that befell Katina was unlike any other. The previously huge empty smooth cavern was now half full of a light grey mist that came out of the tunnel they had entered from. Slowly the mist coagulated into people as it went up the ramp to the gates themselves.

The Lord stood at the gates. He occasionally pulled a soul out of the mist and stuffed it headfirst into a glowing cage of white bars that rose from the ground to the level of the top of the ramp.

'My Lord, shall I take over now?'

'If you please Cainnech. I won't be long.'

'Yes, my Lord.' Cainnech jumps the hundred or so feet vertically to the top of the ramp. The Lord of the Gates then jumped down.

'The mist is the souls of the dead. The ones who go through the gate go to the underworld. A few, however, are not allowed, for various reasons, hence the cage. They are disposed of periodically.' The Lord informed them.

'Is there no heaven then?' Asked a worried Hawkyn.

'Heaven as you mean it is the place inhabited by your chosen God. That bit happens at the statues by the stone bridge.'

'If you don't mind my asking, what happens to those in the cage and why are they there?' Asked Hawkyn.

'Those are truly twisted, perverted cursed souls of darkness. They must be separated from others and destroyed.'

'Evil, you mean?'

'No, not the Human concept of evil. These are souls that have become something else and are a drain to life itself.'

'The Undead and high ranks of the Lord of All Evil then?' Asked Katina.

'Yes. The souls of beings attached to my uncle have to be destroyed.'

'That's one drawback of playing for the other side we didn't know. Our enemy would be a lot less popular if having your soul killed soon after death were common knowledge.' Added Hawkyn.

'While the gates were closed, it couldn't happen. I will be quite busy for some time on catchup. Cainnech has already tendered to your horses and belongings. He has attached a jar of honey and a few skins of water to your packhorse. I have kept you asleep for several days to start off healing your injuries. Neither of you is fully cured but you are well on the way. I will take you as far as the bridge.

You simply go back up the tunnel you came down and you will get back to your world.' Said The Lord of the Gates.

'Thank you.' Replied Katina.

'You're welcome. I would be obliged if you could return The Hammer of the Dwarf God to my brother. If you can't find him quickly, then keep it with you and carry out your primary responsibility.'

'Certainly, Divine Lord.' Said Katina.

The Lord of the Gates led the packhorse, Katina and Hawkyn took the reins of their horses and walked towards the cavern entrance, which was now devoid of grey mist. They walked up the tunnel and as they approached the bridge, a beam of white light came out of The Huntress statue and pulled in what looked like a young lady in a long woollen dress.

'This is where I must leave you. Follow the path back around and go up the lava tube. Thank you for everything. I will be watching.'

'It was an honour, my Lord.' They both bowed and walked back over the stone bridge.

12 – THE GREAT PLAINS

On the bridge's far side stood its keeper, blocking the righthand path around the lava lake. A mist of humanoid shapes waited behind his outstretched hands. The group walked across, Hawkyn and Katina between them leading three wild-eyed and skittish horses.

As they approached the other side, the figure turned and looked at them. The grey hairless skin-covered skull was just visible beneath the hood of a long dark cloak of tightly woven heavy linen. Katina wondered how she had become so blasé about meeting such beings. His response was a nod. It radiated thanks rather than saying or showing it.

'It has been a privilege and an honour to help.' Replied Katina.

'So much knowledge of the spiritual world has been forgotten. Presumably, that's why we lost.' Added Hawkyn. There was a further nod and the Bridge Keeper turned back to the souls waiting to cross.

'We'd better keep moving and get out of their way.' Suggested Katina.

They continued along the left-hand path around the large lava lake back the way they had come. The group walked in a single file with Katina and Hawkyn, each leading their horse. Puppy had taken his dog form and was following behind, the reins of the packhorse in his mouth. The scorching heat of the lava caused Katina significant pain in her burnt arms and shoulders. At last, they reached the mouth of the tunnel and continued up it before stopping once the heat had subsided.

'I'd better get the candles out as we will lose the last of the light soon.' Suggested Hawkyn.

'Good idea.' Katina said as he rummaged in his saddlebags for a few minutes before getting out a couple of tallow candles with his flint and steel.

'Do we have enough?'

'I think so, provided we don't dawdle. Somehow, we will have to make some more though, if we have to explore any more caves.' Replied Hawkyn. Katina nodded.

He led the way holding the lit candle out in front of him as they progressed gently uphill in the near darkness. The hours dragged on as they continued. Regularly someone tripped over a rock. Katina became tired and irritable after what seemed like hours of endless walking. Then she worked something out.

'I think we should be seeing daylight by now. You are nearly at the end of your second candle.' Said Katina.

'That's true. I had about a quarter of a candle left on the way down. Can a tunnel be longer going out than in'?

'Doubt it.'

There was the tug of a small boy on Katina's cloak. 'Yes, Puppy.'

'Mum and dad haven't taught me about this type of thing yet, but we have been travelling between our world and various spiritual ones. I very much doubt distance will be consistent with our world.'

'That's worrying.' Replied Hawkyn.

'It is, isn't it. Any suggestions?' Added Katina.

'In my dragon form, I can see better in the dark than Humans. I could go on ahead.' Suggested Puppy.

'Sure Puppy, you lead.' Replied Katina.

'We're going to have to come up with a better name.' Suggested Hawkyn.

'I do have a real name, but I have become quite fond of Puppy.'

'Puppy it is then, for now at least.' Replied Katina.

The small boy walked forward, then when clear of Hawkyn, shimmered, changing into his dragon shape. He walked ahead, clearing rocks and debris to the side with his tail as he went. From time to time, he also breathed orange fire that lit the way forwards for a few seconds.

'At least I'm not falling over rocks all the time.' Said

Hawkyn.

'I can feel the fresh air, but still no daylight.' Replied Katina. Then she groaned. 'It's night-time.' She added.

'Well, let's get out of this place anyway. We can get some rest knowing we're back in our world.'

'Agreed. I think we would all feel a lot happier.'

'Erm, the ramp has gone, and the entrance is not cleared.' Said the now boy shaped Puppy.

'Eh. So, we are in a different tunnel.' Replied Katina.

'We did turn the correct way at the bridge, didn't we?' Asked Hawkyn.

'Yes, definitely.' Replied Katina.

'Now what do we do?' asked the boy.

'We can't go back. We don't have enough candles.' Said Hawkyn.

'Then we must get out and hope we are somewhere we know.' Replied Katina.

It took some time, but the three of them cleared enough of a hole to get themselves and the horses out.

'Damn.' Said Hawkyn looking around. 'We are not in the same place.'

Katina looked at the sky, and then with a worried expression on her face, slowly spun around, looking into the distance. She then swore loudly and profusely. Hawkyn, having seen the angry Katina, looked about and simply said, 'Shit.'

'I'm missing something.' Said Puppy.

Katina pulled herself together then said to Puppy. 'You grew up in a cave and didn't get out much. So, you probably don't know about navigation.'

'You're correct.' Was the response.

'See that star.' Said Katina pointing at the brightest star in the cloudless night sky.

'Yes.'

'It's called the North Star and stays in a constant position in the night sky. It was behind us when we came out. It should have been to our left. Also, the fire mountain should have been behind us, but I can't see it at all.'

The boy shaped Puppy looked worried.

'If we could still see the fire mountain, Katina could work out roughly where we are, at least in terms of where we went down.' Replied Hawkyn.

'But I can't do that with only one point to refer to.' Added Katina.

'So, we're lost. You guys are amazing at this wilderness stuff, so what's the next step?' Asked the boy form Puppy. Katina and Hawkyn took a few seconds to calm down, then.

'Well, as we know where the North Star is, so the other directions are also known.' Replied Hawkyn.

Katina thought for a few seconds then said. 'We want to go east.'

'And if we find the coast before something recognisable, then we go north.' Said Hawkyn, nodding.

'If I can't see our mountain first.' Added the boy shaped Puppy.

Katina looked at him.

'If I fly high, I can see a long way, I may just spot it.'

'It's worth a try.' Suggested Katina.

'I'm not sure. There's no chance of us being in friendly territory. Every Goblin tribe within a hundred miles would see a thirty-foot long flying dragon and will be down on us in a day.' Replied Hawkyn.

'I don't have to be a dragon to fly. I could do a bird of some sort, something that would not attract attention.'

'Can you do anything?' Asked Hawkyn.

'No. I can only take three or four forms. I have a Human form and a dog form. I should have one or two more.'

'Then I suggest you think carefully about that. While it would be useful, you will be stuck with it. Let's get a few hours' sleep and see how things look in the morning.'

Suggested Katina.

Hawkyn applied the honey to Katina's shoulders, arms, and hands, then they both lay down on their bed rolls. Puppy reverted to his dog form and snuggled in, falling asleep quickly.

Katina woke up shortly after first light. The prolonged lying down reminded her of the severe burns she had received at the gates to the underworld. Letting the others sleep, she watched the sunrise over the grasslands to the east. The various shades of oranges and yellows were amazing. She buckled her belt with scabbard and sword, slung her quiver of arrows across her back with a wince, picked up her longbow and walked to the top of the small hill that covered the entrance to the tunnel they had come out of the night before. There were no signs of any settlements. Katina berated herself for not checking the area was safe before they settled down for the night. She did see plenty of herds of wild cattle and sheep. But, judging by the amount of running, predators too. There was also no sign of the fire mountain, which must be hundreds of miles away. She groaned.

Walking back down, Katina realised the tunnel opening was also gone, although it was clear something had been there from the state of the side of the hill. No going back that way then. She thought to herself. Wandering over to Hawkyn, she gently shook him awake.

'It's time we got moving.'

'Sorry, I stayed awake for some time last night, just in case. Nothing came anywhere near us apart from a lone wolf who checked us over and moved on.'

'The tunnel has gone. Also, no signs of civilisation but plenty of wild cattle. Can't see our mountain either.'

'Hmm. We should probably check what supplies we have and whether we need to get more before we move on.'

'I will have a look around the immediate area, see what's about.' Katina turned round to see a young Golden Eagle stood on her bedroll.

'Are you going to look around too?'

Squawk.

'Be careful and don't be too long. When we have finished here, we will head east.'

Squawk.

The juvenile eagle flapped its wings and quickly soared into the sky, initially circling the camp then heading further out. Finally, after a few minutes, it went off east. Katina looked at Hawkyn, who was packing up his bedroll. He simply looked back at her and nodded.

She trotted off across the grasslands, starting her first circuit about half a mile out, then went wider. There were signs of small animals such as rabbits and wildfowl in addition to the wandering herds of cattle and sheep. However, she didn't see any signs of civilisation or the passage of anyone, let alone Goblins or Plains Devils.

Apart from filling her water skin from a small stream, she completed her circuit and went back to camp. When she arrived, Hawkyn had packed the gear, saddled the horses and was ready to go.

'There's nothing here but grass and wild animals. Let's get moving. I'm sure Puppy will find us when he wants to.'

They continued at a slow canter for an hour or so before Katina saw the shape of an eagle slowly gliding in the cloudless sky. They stopped as it landed a few feet in front of them. The eagle then shimmered, and the familiar small boy appeared.

'Well, I have done a bit of a look around. As far as I can see, north south and west, apart from the odd lone tree or low hill, is a flat grassy plain. The best part of twenty-five miles east from here is a sizable river with the remains of some long-abandoned town on the other side. Five miles further east from that is the beginnings of a forest with some tall trees in it. They are way bigger than anything I have seen. I did not check out how far it went, but it is extensive. No sign of our fire mountain, though.' Said Puppy.

'We could go to this abandoned town and spend a day or two restocking supplies. Just a thought.'

'And a good one too, Hawkyn. It might also be possible to find something that indicates where the hell we are.' Said Katina.

'Wherever we are, there's no sign of anyone living here.' Said Puppy.

They continued their eastward travel for the rest of the day, cantering for part of it, walking for the rest, periodically stopping to rest the horses and to eat. Come dusk, Katina said.

'We'd better make camp here. I think we still have another five miles or so to the river. That is too far for today.'

'Sure. I'll set up camp if you want to have a look around.' Replied Hawkyn.

'Thanks, I will.' Katina dismounted and with her bow in hand, ran off through the tall grass.

Thinking as she searched, in truth, she was finding the current situation odd. Puppy was right. There was no sign of any civilisation. She had only ever been in areas either populated or regularly travelled by either Humans or Goblins and usually, both. Here there were wild cattle and sheep, wolves, some bears by the looks of the tracks and the usual birds and small animals. So, the current risks amounted to bears and large packs of wolves. Not being anywhere near help, severe injury or illness could be an issue. While the regular dangers appeared not to be relevant, being far from anybody for an extended period held different problems, professional repair, or replacement of anything broken would be impossible. Over time, arrows would become broken, as there would be no replacement heads, she could make the rest; repair of damaged armour would be impossible, as would replacement clothing. The list went on. Still, it is the hand the gods had dealt her, so make do she must.

Katina returned to the others deep in thought, having completed a circuit. When she arrived, Hawkyn had secured the horses. He had laid out the bedrolls and made the fire.

'No signs of anything but wild animals. I found tracks of bears and packs of wolves, so we will need to keep alert.'

'Freki size wolves?' Asked Hawkyn.

'No normal ones.'

'That's something.'

'We'd better take it in turns keeping watch. I'll go first.' Offered Katina. Hawkyn applied more honey to her shoulders, arms and hands. Puppy came and relieved her after several hours and the night passed without incident.

In the morning, they struck camp. Katina took half an hour to forage for food and came back with a couple of wildfowl and wild vegetables. These she stowed quickly, and the group moved on.

They travelled eastwards at the tribe's familiar slow run. A family of brown bears sniffed the air, then completely ignored them. A large pack of wolves didn't even do that, just loped past them.

'That's a fair-sized river.' Said Hawkyn.

'Looks about the size of the one at Warameth.' Replied Katina.

'It does, doesn't it. Swimming that will be unpleasant.'

'Don't see we have a choice. There won't be a bridge. But, Puppy, could you fly our bags across?'

Bark.

'Thank you.'

They continued to the riverbank and removed the packs from the horses. Puppy changed into a dragon and flew across the river, looking around.

'We will go a fair way upriver before starting to cross, so we end up somewhere near you on the other side.'

Puppy picked up a few bags in his front claws and flew

across. Katina and Hawkyn, leading the three horses, walked northwards. After about half a mile, Katina stopped.

'Shall we try here? It's a fair way upriver.'

'Sure. How are we going to do this, we've got three horses between the two of us?' Replied Hawkyn.

'We tie the three together. Put the strongest at the front, the keenest at the back and the weakest in the middle. That would be yours, packhorse, then mine last. You go with yours. I go with mine.'

Hawkyn led the train of three horses into the river. Then, holding the saddle, he urged him across. Katina clung on to her horse at the back of the three. Slowly they made progress through the fast-flowing cold water but drifted substantially downriver. The spot Puppy had chosen came and went, but they did eventually make the other side and scrambled up the far bank. They checked their horses over before leading them past the remnants of stone buildings back towards where Puppy was waiting.

As it turned out, they weren't that far away and found him quickly. He had put the belongings in the remains of a stone building near the river. It was a thirty-foot wide square structure that still had two feet thick walls above door and window lintel height. Puppy was waiting outside.

'Good choice, Puppy. This place should keep the worst of the wind off us.' Said Katina.

Just then, as Hawkyn was leading his horse to the front door, Katina pulled him back.

'What was that for?' He said as the wooden lintel gave a cracking sound and several courses of stone blocks fell where Hawkyn would have been.

'Oh.' He continued looking at the pile of stone blocks in the doorway. 'How did you know?'

'I got a second or two's warning.' Replied Katina.

'Thank you. What happened?'

'I got a short vision of the wall falling on you.'

'So, you are starting to get visions of the future. That

could be useful.'

'I don't know that one short vision two seconds ahead really counts as future sight.'

'It was enough this time.'

'True.'

Puppy barked as he pressed down on the remains of the heavy wooden lintel. It snapped easily.

'The wood is rotten. The two window lintels will probably be the same. We still may have three usable walls, though.' Said Hawkyn.

'It's a good start. Let's have a look.'

'If we can find somewhere that can keep this constant wind off us, then great. Last night was fairly cold.'

Katina went inside. It was clear that at one time, the building had internal walls. Several bits of stone could be seen and join marks on the outer walls. It appeared to have had one big room that was the width of the building at the front and several smaller rooms at the back.

On the floor, mostly buried in soil and muck, Katina found a plaque just the other side of the leftmost doorway. Using her fingers, she uncovered it, finding some writing, two words one above the other.

'Hawkyn.' Katina shouted.

'What's up?' He said shortly later when he entered the building.

'I found this. Any ideas what it means?' Said Katina.

'I don't even know what the top language is, but the bottom one is the old tongue used at the time of the old empire.' Replied Hawkyn.

'Oh. Any idea what it means?'

'None at all, but you've got another plaque over there.' So, they went over and dug it out. Again, two words, but this time Hawkyn simply said 'Oh.'

'What's that supposed to mean?'

'Look at the bottom word.' Replied Hawkyn. Katina looked.

'Aelfcynn.' She read out loud.

'Yeah. It could mean "Elves" or something like that. It sounds right.'

'It does, doesn't it. In which case I may know where we are, the area we are in, anyway.'

'How so?'

'Well, I was taught that the Elves had several strongholds. The Woodland Elves lived in a great forest near our plains, but their nobility, I think they were called High Elves, had a realm in the Great Central Plains. If we can find evidence that Elves ran this place, then we will be at the Elven stronghold on the Great Central Plains.' Said Katina.

'That sounds like a long way from home.'

'It does, doesn't it, but home is east, that much I'm certain of.'

'We'd better set up camp if we are to stay and look around.' Suggested Hawkyn.

They brought the horses into the remains of the building, after which Katina went foraging for firewood. She walked east, away from the river, along what looked like it had been the main street. The stones sticking out of the ground reminded her of long-abandoned structures. Not much was left, but enough to suggest many buildings.

She looked at what remained of the stonework. It was expertly shaped and fitted together very tightly. Also, the door or window surrounds had, even at this stage of decay, ornately carved plants or trees on them. She imagined a wide well-paved street running between tall, well-built ornate stone buildings. Katina believed that in its prime, this town would have looked stunning.

After walking about a third of a mile, the place seemed to open out into a large flat area, with a raised part on the other side. A central square, she thought. Several trees left some deadfall for firewood which she collected and went back to camp.

Hawkyn started to build a fire as Katina explained what she had found. He looked at her and then said, 'Are you thinking of staying a while?'

'I think we should check this town out and make sure we know who lived here. This place would provide a good base for several days.'

'Not for long, though. If you are right, we have a long way to go. But, unfortunately, it's only a matter of time before Warameth gets hit hard and the days are passing rapidly.'

'I know Hawkyn. These tasks and becoming the Oracle are all good, but we must get home soon. There's no point in being the Oracle if everyone else is dead.'

The fire was now well alight and Puppy, in his dog form, was curled up near it dozing, apparently not listening to the conversation.

'I'd better go and see if I can find dinner.' Suggested Katina.

'I'll check the horses out.' Replied Hawkyn.

Katina went in search of food and started at the riverbank. There was a fair amount of reasonable sized fish. Unfortunately, she only knew the basics of fishing, having never needed to improve her skill. Perhaps the stay here was a time to do that, but not now, so on finding a game trail, followed it through the remains of the town.

The complete absence of inhabitants meant wildlife was abundant. Tracks of rabbits, wildfowl and small game were frequent. Katina decided to get an idea of its overall size, so she went exploring. The first thing she discovered was that the town itself was about half a mile across and had no defensive walls. The open area found earlier was at the back of the town furthest away from the river. The buildings were larger than in her home, sturdier and more densely packed together. This place would easily hold a thousand families.

She stopped her exploring, deciding it was time to catch

dinner. The most convenient food source was a colony of over thirty rabbits in the open just outside town. Approaching silently from downwind, Katina prepared her bow as she went. Releasing three arrows in quick succession achieved a kill with each and let the rest of the colony escape. One for each of us, she thought and went to collect them. When doing so, Katina noticed an awful lot of wild wheat, most of which seemed ripe.

When she arrived back at camp, Hawkyn was sat on the riverbank with a rod and line. He had already caught several fish.

'I didn't know you could fish.'

'Oh yes, not that I get the chance often.'

'Can you teach me? I've only ever had basic training and that was years ago.'

'Sure. Sit down and I'll talk you through it.'

So, Katina spent several hours of the late afternoon learning how to make and use a rod and line for fishing. She even caught one near the end. They spent the evening talking of past times while skinning rabbits, filleting fish and cooking on an open fire. Puppy just lay down listening and watching. At the end of the evening, Katina lay down to catch a few hours of sleep before it was her turn to keep watch.

In the morning, at breakfast, Katina said. 'The lands surrounding the town have a lot of wild wheat. If we harvest a bag full or two, that will give us some long-term food possibilities. There were also the remains of some large buildings on the other side of a big open area that I think may have been a market or main square of the town.'

'We'd better do food harvesting first.'

Katina led Hawkyn along the riverbank to the edge of town. Then they started harvesting the ripe wheat. After an hour or two, they had a whole bag each.

'I think we have enough, for now. Perhaps we can go exploring these buildings you mentioned?' Suggested

Hawkyn.

'Sure. Follow me.'

Katina led him from the fields outside of town directly to the square in front of the large buildings. The nearest was a rectangular structure that appeared to be tall but of one story and considerably longer than wide. Near the back end was a large rectangular lump in the grass. Katina approached it and exposed the top. It was polished granite. She uncovered some of the front of the stone block to reveal an ornate carving of a lythe figure.

'Looks like an altar. We should look for a hidden rear compartment.' Katina said. Hawkyn just nodded.

Katina went around the back of the altar and removed the grass and earth that had built up over time. Unfortunately, on this occasion, there was no moveable back or side panels.

'Perhaps there isn't one this time.' Suggested Hawkyn.

'Maybe. I doubt every temple has special stuff. Perhaps this one wasn't important enough.'

'Katina.' Said Hawkyn, staring at the carving on the front of the altar while removing the remaining dirt and earth.

'Yes, Hawkyn, what is it?'

'Does this carving remind you of anybody?'

Katina went round to the front and stared at the carving. It was a relief of a thin lythe athletic and muscular person with leather armour, bow over the shoulder and thin-bladed sword in one hand and long hair. Katina thought.

'Now imagine the skin with a slightly green tinge and brown hair.' Suggested Hawkyn.

Katina gave a startled cry. 'It's Arturous, but perhaps a bit older.'

'I think you were right. This is one of the Elven strongholds.' Said Hawkyn. Katina swore.

'What's wrong? We've now got an idea where we are.'

'We know the valley is about three hundred miles long,

right.'

'Yes.'

'And we know our fire mountain is at the western end of it or further.'

'Yes.'

'And we know Puppy has no sign of any mountains.'

'Yes.'

'Then Iredan is at least six hundred miles away, on the wrong side of an unknown mountain range.' Concluded Katina. Hawkyn then swore too, badly.

'Our enemy is bound to throw everything he has at Warameth as soon as he can. We're not going to make it in time to save them. So not only do we have to get home, but we also have to convince all the tribes to do a mass migration to the valley and get them there. That's going to take at least a year on its own. With the months that have passed already and more that it will yet take us to get home, the others will have been flattened by then.' Said Katina, almost in tears. 'If only the gods hadn't dumped us so far away, if I'd kept to being an atheist and not risen to this Oracle idiocy, we'd be home and in with a chance.'

Hawkyn put his arms around the distraught Katina, held her tight and kissed her. He then thought for a while.

'Militarily, that is not necessarily true.' Hawkyn replied after a few minutes of consideration.

'How can you say that?'

'Tiranimeith is a vast place. We already know that. You said the Elven stronghold was in the Great Central Plains. We also know that the Lord of All Evil doesn't have enough forces back home to win, or he would have already squashed both us Plains People and the valley folk. So, he's got to move more warriors in from somewhere else. They could easily be a thousand miles west of us. They certainly haven't been through here yet. In any event, you can't move large amounts of Goblins together, or they end up killing each other. So, my best guess currently is that our enemy is going to have to use forces from elsewhere and move them long distances in such a way as they don't destroy each other before they get to us.'

'Do you believe that?' Said Katina.

'Yes. We're here for a reason. There's no way, after everything they have invested in us, the Gods of Light would deliberately make it so we can't get home in time. I must be right.' Replied Hawkyn. 'We can't hang around, though. We're going to have to concentrate on getting home as quickly as possible.'

'You are right. We can't afford to waste more weeks chasing down tasks for my Oracle quest if it means our tribe gets wiped out. Getting home quickly must be the priority.' Said Katina.

The sky became stormy and the clouds dark. A vicious storm appeared to be building. Katina looked up at the sky, held her arms out wide, then said out loud.

'Huntress, Light Bringer, Farmer, Warrior, Lord of the Gates, other Gods of Light. I still want to be your Oracle and am willing to do your tasks in due time, even if it kills me, but I must get to my people first, or we all lose. Sorry, but it is just the way it must be. There is no other choice.'

While the sky remained dark and the clouds black, the heavy atmospheric pressure of a heavy storm abated.

'Wow.' Replied Hawkyn. 'A "we're very angry with you" appears to have changed to a "we're thinking about it".'

'Yes, I agree. The Gods of Light have to return in force if our enemy is to be defeated, but we Humans must survive as free people also. We cannot blindly follow one at the cost of the other and right now, the mortal world needs our attention as messengers.'

'We move on in the morning?' Said Hawkyn.

'Yes, I think we do.'

'What do you think of trying to find the main Elven city. It is probably in the large forest Puppy saw to our east.' Asked Hawkyn.

'Why not? We're going to have to go through it anyway. We can't stay long, though.'

'Let's go back to camp.' Suggested Hawkyn.

'Sure. I think I have had enough realisations for one day.' Concluded Katina.

They found Puppy keeping a watchful eye on things, but when they entered the remains of the building that was camp, Puppy looked at the sky then looked at them with a "what have you been up to expression".

'We have realised a few things, which has altered Katina's mind on what is of most importance. First, our new friends didn't like it much, not that there's any choice.'

Puppy whined.

'We'll still try to do as they ask, but we must get home first, is all.'

A sad-faced puppy curled up by the fire, looking like he was going to sleep. Katina and Hawkyn talked for a while over the cooking and eating of the evening meal. Then Katina herself lay down to sleep feeling very sad about her decision but had no doubts that it was the right one. She even forgot about her burns.

13 – THE GREAT TREE

Katina woke the following day full of sadness and the distinct feeling she had missed the point. Perhaps so. The Gods of Light were, in part, correct, Humans could not defeat The Lord of All Evil without them. As with many things, one side's view however, was not the whole picture. They would only overcome their enemy with everyone working together. The Southern Plains peoples would be crucial in that victory, if she took too long chasing Oracle tasks, then her people would be in the wrong place when it mattered. Katina still felt that going straight home was terrible though.

She decided to get up. First light had been around for a while and the sun was now peeking above the south-eastern horizon.

'Good morning Hawkyn, time to be moving, I think.' Said Katina while bringing the fire back to life and putting a kettle of water on it.

'Sure.' He replied, then looking at her continued. 'Why the long face?'

'I somehow feel my decision to go home is wrong.'

'That will be the Gods of Light trying to influence you into doing what they want. You know what I think of the Gods, they are to be worshipped and regarded with awe, but you have a greater responsibility. You must consider the necessities of achieving a military victory. To accomplish that victory, you must offer advice and tell the leaders of the tribes at home what is needed elsewhere. When the Gods stop being upset with you and consider what you are saying, they will understand and could even offer you advice or aid. While I hate to say this, especially as strategic thinking was never my strongest point, militarily there is no choice but to go straight home. Sooner or later, our enemy will throw The Host of Evil of ancient legend at Warameth. We must be there when it arrives.'

An awake Puppy looked at the pair of them with a very stern face. Katina didn't know how she knew but there was absolutely no way Puppy was going home abandoning Hawkyn and her to face hordes of Undead alone. And he didn't care what anybody else thought about it, parents or otherwise.

The kettle boiled, so she made both Hawkyn and her a mug of tea. Katina considered the situation as she sipped her drink, then decided to try and pray. Clearing her mind, she cast her thoughts out, not sure the Gods would answer them.

"Gods of Light, I beseech thee, please hear my prayers. Please be assured I will continue with the tasks for becoming Oracle as soon as I can. If any occur on the way home, we will attempt them, but we must go home. It is a long way through the wilderness and hostile lands."

To her surprise, there was an answer.

"Thank you for talking to us. Odran, the Warriors' Vaettir, spoke to us all at length last night of the military situation and the difficulties you face. We now appreciate the delicate balancing act you are attempting to achieve. I wish I knew where my warrior brother was. I sorely need his counsel. I must go now." And with that, The Huntress' presence vanished.

'They appear to understand our situation, that's a start I suppose.' Said Katina out loud.

'They sent someone to talk to you, that's good. I noticed you preparing yourself. Now let's pack up and move on.' Replied Hawkyn.

This they did quickly, led their horses out of the building, mounted and headed eastwards up the street towards the main square and temple. They did not go near it this time but rode over a low hill on the other side.

'A stone raised platform for the remains of a large building, I would think.' Suggested Hawkyn.

'Agreed. Some sort of main town communal building like our chief's hall or perhaps an administrative one like they have in Kersladen.' Replied Katina.

The area behind the raised platform was flat with a few trees of varying sorts and lots of wildflowers. They continued with Puppy ambling along beside them. After about half a mile, Hawkyn said.

'Look at the ground, Katina. These were once fields. You can see the remains of the field boundaries.'

Katina thought Hawkyn was probably right. So they continued through the miles of grassland, wild wheat and corn towards the huge forest. The sun shone and the bitter easterly wind had gone, just leaving a gentle cool breeze.

As they approached the forest, Katina wondered what type of trees it had as they all appeared the same. From the overall shape, colour and appearance, she would have said Oak, but a great deal taller, easily two or more times larger. The other thing she noticed was that the trees looked distinctly odd somehow. At first, Katina couldn't make out what was strange about them. Then as they got nearer, she realised it was the branches. Typically, even the lower limbs were a long way up off the ground with large, tall trees. These, though, were very low. So low it would be a challenge even to crawl under them and they seemed to intertwine with the next tree along.

'That's weird. It's going to be tough work getting through those.' Said Hawkyn breaking the silence.

'I'll get down and have a look in.' Replied Katina.

She dismounted and approached the trees. Moving some small branches and leaves out of the way, she peered through. The next line of trees looked about fifty feet away and in a neat row. Again, the branches were low to the ground and close together. She pulled her head out and backed away. Looking up and down noticed even the outermost trees were in exact rows.

'This place is distinctly odd Hawkyn. Did you notice the branches?'

'Yes.' He replied.

'It's the same for the next row fifty feet inside. I am

thinking of crawling through and seeing what I can from the next row. If it keeps on, it will be tough getting through the forest.'

'More like impossible in our time scale.' Said Hawkyn.

Katina approached the trees again and started to squeeze through some branches that ran horizontally about waist height. Finally, she got her head and shoulders through when there was a slithering noise. Hawkyn shouted at her to back out now as he jumped off his horse. Then, some branches wrapped themselves around her ankles, and others made a determined effort to grab her arms. More were getting too close to her neck for comfort.

Katina clutched the large branch above her and pushed the top half of her body back away from the branches. Her legs, though, were pulled out from under her. She fell to the ground as the tree started to drag her under the lowest limb into the forest.

Then Hawkyn was there. He grabbed her under her shoulders and yanked, pulling her hips and upper legs out from under the tree branch. Katina freed her arms from entanglement. Puppy, in dog form, started biting and pulling at the small branches with his teeth. Katina's knees were now clear. Finally, as she thought she would get free, more small branches grabbed her legs and pulled.

Katina screamed with pain as the branches tightened their grip on her ankles and feet. Puppy then shimmered into his dragon form and breathed fire into the air.

'Enough. Let Katina go, or I burn the lot of you.' Came a strange deep rasping guttural tone from Puppy.

Everything then stopped for a few seconds. Katina was neither released nor pulled further. Finally, after what was definitely the longest three seconds of her entire life, the tree released her, and the lashing tendrils retreated into the oak tree branches. Hawkyn, with his arms still under her shoulders, pulled Katina clear of the trees.

'Well, Goblins aren't getting in there in a hurry.' Was

Hawkyn's first comment, much to Katina's annoyance, as she would have preferred a more personal question. Then, as she started to get up. 'Oh no, you don't. I need to check you over first. It will be a miracle if you haven't broken anything.'

'I don't think I have. While it all hurts, none of it is the sharp, searing pain of broken bones.'

'Well, let's see. First, I will take your boots off and check you over.'

Hawkyn undid the straps on her knee-high leather boots and carefully removed each one. Puppy looked on anxiously. Even this soon, the ankles were bruising rapidly and starting to swell. Hawkyn gently felt and manipulated the ankles and feet. Feeling the odd sensations and stiffness, Katina said.

'I think I have some dislocation.'

'I agree.' Replied Hawkyn.

'Are you capable of doing the manipulation to reset? Sorry for asking, but I don't know how far your knowledge goes.'

'I am familiar with it. Prepare yourself. Left foot first.'

Katina readied herself when Hawkyn gently took hold of the left foot and ankle. He gradually increased the strength of his pull. Puppy held her shoulders in his front claws. The pressure on her ankle increased. Then, feeling a bone move back into place, she gave a large exhaling of breath struggling to control the pain.

'Now, for the right one. You ready?'

'Yep.' Katina replied as she took a deep breath in.

Again, Hawkyn gradually increased the pull on her right ankle as Puppy held her shoulders. Again, she felt the bones pop back into place, with a large exhaling of breath. Then lay back on the ground breathing heavily.

'Stay there. I will have to splint both ankles, no walking for a few days. You will have to ride. Don't know how we are going to get you on your horse though.' Said Hawkyn

'Easy, I lift her on and off.' Replied Puppy.

'I didn't think your dragon form could speak Human languages.' Said Katina.

'We're not supposed to until we are at least what you would call Young Adult. We can if it's a special occasion. I thought that having one of my carer's legs pulled off by a tree counted. I must say the things you have here are much more interesting than my cave. Never even heard of moving trees before.' Replied Puppy.

'Why did you think they would listen.' Ask Katina.

'I can sense something else. I thought that pointing out the consequences of its actions may help. I also think it isn't tied with the other side. I doubt the creator of Undead would be interested in animating trees.'

'He's probably right, Hawkyn. There's no way whoever set this up plays for our enemy.'

'We were wondering if this place is an Elven homeland. You're thinking of Elven Druids, aren't you?' Replied Hawkyn.

'Yes, I am. It would fit if they were still about.'

'What are Druids? I thought the Elves had their own god.' Asked Puppy.

'They do, but it wouldn't be much of a stretch to think that like us Humans, some may have gone to worship a specialist rather than their racial god. As for Druids, I don't know much, but they are nature specialists and worship Mother Nature, otherwise known as The Mother Goddess, wife of the Father of the Gods and mother to the Gods of Light.'

'How did you know that? It's not in our teachings.' Asked Hawkyn as he finished applying the last splint.

'I appear now to have a basic knowledge of who's who.' Responded Katina. Then looking at Puppy, she asked, 'You said you could feel something else.'

'Yes, I can. Not a clue what, though.'

'I wonder if I can do that.' Replied Katina.

'I wouldn't have thought so.' Opined Hawkyn. 'An Oracle is about asking questions and giving advice. Sensing spirits and stuff sounds more like an Oswald and Luka type of thing.'

'Anyway, we need to be moving. Puppy, can you see if we can go round this forest.'

'I will go and have a look. But, first, let's get you on to your horse.'

Katina sat up, and gently Puppy picked her up in his front claws and slowly lowered her into the saddle. He then flew upwards quickly, climbing to the treetops. Puppy didn't stop there though but kept climbing. Finally, after about ten minutes, he started to descend, gliding gracefully in large circles. They waited patiently for him to return.

'Trees as far as the eye can see in both directions.'

'Damn. Puppy, can you look at ground level and see if the trees go back to normal at any point. If you head north, we'll head south for a few miles and meet back here.' Suggested Katina.

They headed off in their directions. Katina and Hawkyn rode along the forest's edge a few hundred yards out at a mile eating canter. After about five miles, they stopped, turned around and headed back. There was no sign of the ending of the tall oaks with low horizontal branches.

They returned to the agreed spot to find the small boy version of Puppy lying on the ground waiting for them.

'No change our way.' Said Katina.

'Nor mine.' Responded Puppy.

'It's too far to go round. We must find a way through.' Said Hawkyn.

'But we can't force it. We don't want to anger the Mother Goddess.' Said Katina.

'Then, we must find the right spot and seek permission.' Replied Hawkyn.

'Puppy, did you see anything that might look like an Elven city.' Asked Katina.

'I saw a tree that was a bit bigger than even these. It's about ten miles further in.'

'Which direction?' Asked Katina.

'Roughly that way.' Replied Puppy, pointing east south-east.

Katina turned around and looked at the town, then looked back at where Puppy had been pointing.

'We need to head south a bit.' She said.

'What have you got in mind?' Asked Hawkyn.

'There must have been a road between the town we were in and their main city. So if we can get in anywhere, it will be there.' Replied Katina.

They headed slowly south, carefully looking at the tree line and the ground for any signs of an old road. After about half a mile, Katina noticed a few things she had missed the first time around.

'Look, they're very spaced out, but a line of stones heading back to the town.' Both Hawkyn and Puppy looked.

'And the trees just there are a bit further apart.' Observed Katina.

'I suppose somehow we need to knock on the door and ask politely, if we may enter without getting eaten by a tree.' Said Hawkyn.

'Well, we know whatever it is knows our language. So perhaps I should simply ask.' Suggested Puppy.

'Worth a try.' Replied Hawkyn.

Katina rode a little way forward, then shouted. 'I am Katina of Iredan and seeking to return to my home in the plains a long way east of here. I, Hawkyn and our young companion here simply wish to travel through your lands on our way home?'

Katina gently edged her horse forward. There was a rustling of branches that waved threateningly towards Katina and the others.

'I take that as a no.' Observed Hawkyn.

'We mean you no harm or disrespect. There doesn't appear to be any way round. Please may we pass?

The threatening waving of branches continued.

Katina tried again. 'I am known to several Gods of Light, The Huntress, The Farmer, The Light Bringer, and The Lord of the Gates. We have even met the Warrior's Chief Vaettir. I have agreed to do the tests for becoming the next Oracle of Light. I mean you no disrespect or harm. May we please pass?'

The threatening, waving branches stopped.

'You're making progress. Try offering them something in exchange for our passage through their lands.' Observed Puppy.

Worth a try, Katina thought.

'Recently, we have done various tasks and tests for some of the Gods of Light. If there's something we could do for you in exchange for our passage through your lands, we would be happy to oblige.'

The forward-facing smaller branches returned to the larger main horizontal ones. Then they turned ninety degrees to reveal a paved road beyond, heading into the depths of the forest.

The group slowly edged forwards, keeping a very wary eye on the branches which did not move. Once they were past the entrance, the branches return to the gate closed position. It took some time for Katina's eyes to adjust to the darkness under the forest canopy. There were half a dozen rows of defensive trees before a normal Oak Forest started. She then realised they were travelling along a two-cart width cobble paved road, though suffering from lack of maintenance. A wide variety of smaller plants struggled to reach the sunlight when hidden under the much larger trees. There was also an abundance of smaller animals going about their daily lives without any care over the new strangers.

They rode along what in the past had been a well-used

road. In places, you could see grooves in the cobblestones from the cartwheels. Yet strangely Katina felt relaxed and at peace when travelling this part of the forest. It was clear to her that here at least, there was no danger.

After a brief discussion, they decided not to hunt for food here. It was unnecessary due to earlier foraging trips, and there were plenty of small streams from which they could obtain fresh water. Puppy could still feel the presence of something with them, so considering the earlier hostilities, everyone was polite and respectful of where they were.

Katina didn't notice at first, but slowly things seemed to change. After several miles, the air started to smell stale and as they progressed, it became more unpleasant to breathe. While the giant oak trees seemed unaffected, the small plants and animals were not so resilient. The abundance of animals decreased rapidly with evidence of abandoned birds' nests. The small plants became withered and black. Even the bark of some great oaks had fallen off, although the trees themselves still seemed sound. By the time they saw the tall solid defensive walls of a city, even some of the ground was black and oily.

They stopped at sights that were both amazing and bizarre. The only stone fortification walls she had seen had been the castle in the mountain pass and the city walls of Kersladen. These were simple walls of straight lines and square angles that were roughly twenty feet high and fifteen feet thick that was not accurately carved or fitted together. By comparison, whoever had built this place had done so to an entirely superior level of skill and vision.

Katina found herself looking at the moat first, if only because it was closest. She had on occasion come across defensive ditches before. Some had water in them, others had wooden or metal barbs to hinder those uninvited guests wanting to cross. However, this moat took that to a whole different level. It had big sinuous bushes with large and razor-sharp thorns several inches long. She wondered if they moved and grabbed things like the border trees did. No sooner than the thought came to mind, the plants started to writhe and wriggle. The death toll of crossing that moat would be horrendous.

She realised that it would also achieve virtually nothing. For behind the moat were the city walls. She just stood there open-mouthed at the tallest constructed object she had ever seen. Probably several hundred feet high and nearly the height of the trees that were now behind her. They also were not simply vertical walls but rather a very thick base that gracefully curved up to a lot thinner top. The quality of the stonemasonry appeared perfect. There were no signs of joints or stone marginally out of place. If you made it to the bottom of the wall, there were no hand holes that you could use for climbing. There was no way ladders or ropes were getting up that.

The bizarre aspect of this was that the black oily goo covered most of the moat plants and walls. However, like the great oaks, it did not appear to degrade what it covered very much.

Katina found herself lost in thought. Given the capabilities of the Goblins and Plains Devils, how did The Lord of All Evil defeat this place? She must have been thinking out loud because Hawkyn answered.

'The place is cursed, so my guess would be high end dark divine magic and Undead.'

'You are probably right. Let's go in.'

The road they had been travelling along headed straight to a gatehouse. The drawbridge was down and the gates open. Despite the age, the wood of the narrow one cart wide drawbridge appeared solid. Cautiously, they rode across. After proceeding through the main gate, they entered a one cart wide one hundred foot long passage through the city walls. The sidewalls and roof all had arrow slits in them. Katina wasn't a military expert but could see the defensive advantage here. Traditional attacks on this place would be costly in soldiers.

To her surprise, once they left the passage, they entered a large rectangular open area about one hundred feet wide and two hundred feet long. The courtyard's exit was not opposite the corridor they had come down but on the left-hand side at the other end. She looked up at the vertical walls containing arrow slits and crenulations on all four sides.

'Attacking here is a death trap.' Observed Hawkyn.

They rode on in silence, turning left through the next gate and corridor like the first one. Only when they exited were they in the city, entering a large plaza with rampant black goo virtually everywhere.

This city, though, was quite different from Kersladen. The first thing Katina noticed was a large Giant Oak tree, at least a hundred feet high, taking pride of place in the centre of the plaza. Although one side abutted the city wall, the remains of large opulent buildings were around the other sides. Each had its own giant oak tree that the city's occupants had manipulated to support and augment the building attached to it.

Katina then noticed the lumps in the black goo. She realised they were skeletons of the dead. The lumps were everywhere, as far as the eye could see. They carefully continued onwards, occasionally finding remains that were exposed. Katina noticed the skeletons not covered had a green tinge to the bones. It was not moss or mould but a slight hint of colour.

'Guess they'd be Elves then. Arturous had a green tinge to him. Look taller than Arturous, quite a bit taller in fact, but not as tall as us.' Observed Hawkyn looking at a pair of skeletons that appeared to be hugging each other.

They continued along what appeared to be the main street towards a huge tree about half a mile away that looked completely black.

'Seems like the tree is the centre of your curse.' Suggested Katina.

'We'd better go and have a look.' Replied Hawkyn.

The black goo was so prevalent now it was not possible to avoid it. They tied the horses on the last patch of clear grass in the area. Katina carefully dismounted, her feet and ankles hurting from the weight of her body.

'Stay put. We are going to have to put your boots back on.' Said Hawkyn. They tried, but with splints and bandages, it proved impossible. Hawkyn removed the splints and rebandaged the feet. The boots then just about fitted.

'Puppy, you mustn't walk in this. With our knee-high hard leather boots, we should be protected from this goo, but your paws won't be.' Said Katina. Puppy changed into his young eagle form and started to look about carefully. After a few minutes, he flew to a statue at the base of the tree and perched on the head. Puppy started examining the tree closely.

With Hawkyn holding Katina's arm to steady her, the pair left the horses and walked towards the base of the tallest Giant Oak next to the statue Puppy was perched on. They took their time being careful not to tread on any bones.

'Thoughts, anyone?' Asked Katina.

Puppy looked towards the top of the tree and squawked.

'He's right. There's something up there.' Said Hawkyn.

'I'm going to have to go up and look.' Said Katina.

'I wouldn't be keen on that if you were healthy but climbing several hundred feet up a tree covered in goo with damaged feet. No way my love.' Said Hawkyn. The eagle form of Puppy gave an angry squawk too.

'You are worried I'll fall, I understand, but these are my quests, and I must deal with them. Somehow.' Said Katina.

'Then we must give it some thought.' Replied Hawkyn.

Puppy took off from his perch, changed into dragon

form mid-flight, then breathed fire over an area of black goo. It caught fire but petered out quite quickly, burning off about one hundred yards in the process. He then landed in the cleared grassy area and changed back into a small boy.

'That was lucky. I was starting to worry how far it would spread.' Said Puppy after Hawkyn and Katina walked over.

Katina thought for a few minutes, then said, 'This is one of the Elven strongholds, or at least we think it is.'

'More than that, I think it is the original Elven stronghold.' Puppy said. 'If I am right, then this place is the homeland of the High Elves. From what mum told me, they were quite tall and believed themselves superior to anything else.'

'Then I believe there are two things we need to consider doing.' Said Katina.

'Go on.' Replied Hawkyn.

'Firstly, try and clear this area and as much of the tree as possible of black goo. Give it as much chance as possible to survive.' Said Katina.

'Yeah.' Replied Hawkyn.

'Secondly, the goo is thickest around that tree and there is something up it near the top. I need to see what's up there and dispose of whatever is creating the goo. Hopefully, that will allow whatever it is that's still living here the chance of killing the rest of the stuff.' She continued.

'So, I do several short flame breaths and hope they burn out before the fire meets something natural that burns.' Suggested Puppy.

'That would be a start.' Replied Katina.

Puppy changed back into his dragon form and did a short breath towards the patch of ground the horses were on and another towards the tree. After a few minutes, the fires died down, leaving an irregular shaped patch of ground from where the horses were, extending to near the base of the big tree.

'Dare we risk burning up to the tree?' Asked Hawkyn.

'I don't like burning the ancestral tree of the Elves either, but the lowest branches are a long way up. Being a big tree, it should be resistant to modest ground level burning. We dare not go higher up, though.' Replied Katina.

Puppy nodded and gave a small burst of fire around the base of the giant tree. Again, that area cleared and again the fire petered out. This time though, it was clear that black goo slowly oozed back into the freed area from up the tree.

'I'd better work out how to get up it, or this place will be overrun again.' Said Katina.

'I could grab you in my front claws and try flying you up. I should be able to get you near enough to one of the bigger branches close to where whatever that is up there.' Suggested Puppy.

'But start her close to the ground for a while. I don't want Katina one hundred feet up in the air when you work out that you can't carry her.' Said Hawkyn.

'Certainly.'

Hawkyn retrieved the horses while Katina started removing things that she was not likely to need up a tree. She took off her longbow and quiver of arrows, her longsword, backpack and waterskin. Katina kept her dagger and retrieved a spare. When down to an absolute minimum, she looked at Puppy and said.

'Ready.'

'Arms out sideways, please.'

Puppy took off then stabilised himself before gently picking up Katina under the arms. Initially, he flew just ten feet off the ground, then after a minute or so rose to twenty, then halfway, then up to near the top of the tree.

'Are you ready?' Puppy asked.

'Yes, let's go for it.'

Puppy flew around the top of the tree. Katina could see him looking for a suitable branch. He approached one which was slightly above a black humanoid glob resting between two major branches and the trunk. The branch Puppy had chosen was almost devoid of black goo. He slowly approached, setting her down with her legs on either side of the thick branch before letting first one arm go, then the other.

Katina grabbed the branch and clung on tightly. She was not a person frightened of heights, but this was a very long way up. Gradually she pulled herself along the high branch towards the trunk of the tree.

When she got to the trunk, she lay face down and looked at the thing they had seen from the ground. It looked a bit like a Plains Devil in body and head but was smaller. The skin and scales were a mixed brown and black colour, it had large leathery wings from behind its shoulders on its back and it seemed to be excreting the black goo from various exposed areas of its scales. It also had four arrows sticking out of its abdomen and had several oak tree branches wrapped around its legs. In its arms was a black box about a foot cubed.

Katina edged towards the centre of the tree without touching the black goo. The creature suddenly let go of the box and lunged at her. Katina drew her dagger and swung it at the incoming claw but did no damage. Its other claw, however, pinned her to the trunk of the tree. She struck again with her dagger, pressing it into her enemy's neck, but again no damage. Then it tried to shove her off the tree. With her left hand, she desperately clung on. Several small branches of the Great Oak grabbed both the creature's arms wrenching them off Katina.

A thought occurred to her as she watched it writhe, trying to get free of the small branches that now held it. Her hand tingled as she pulled an arrow out of the abdomen of the creature. Holding it at the mid-point of the shaft, Katina shoved the arrow directly through the neck. Then grabbed a second arrow and plunged that into the creature's left eye socket and beyond, making large circular motions with the shaft. Whatever it was, stiffened and then went limp. The tree let go and it fell. After a few seconds, there was a thump as the body hit the ground several hundred feet below.

Katina lay there for a while as the realisation that she had just had a fight with an unknown creature several hundred feet up a tree hit her.

'Great Oak, you have my most sincere thanks. Without your prompt help, I would have probably died.'

Then she remembered the box. It lay on its side at the junction of branch and trunk about two feet below her. She looked at Puppy flying just at the edge of the tree.

'I will take the box further out. If you can then grab it and take it to the ground before coming back for me, please?' Puppy nodded. Katina gingerly picked up the black goo covered box and slowly edged along the branch with it.

It wasn't that long before Puppy swooped in and grabbed the box in his front claws, then glided down to Hawkyn waiting below. Within minutes he was back up, slowly flying in with front claws outstretched. With arms held out straight, Katina was collected and gently taken to the ground.

'Are you alright? I couldn't see what was happening. It looked very dangerous.' Asked Hawkyn.

'Thanks to the tree, I am fine. If it hadn't grabbed that things arms, then I would have been shoved off rather than him.' Replied Katina. 'And thank you, Puppy.'

'You're welcome.' Puppy replied.

'My dagger didn't harm it at all, but the Elven arrows did, and they tingle to the touch. We should keep an eye out. It would be useful to find more of those.'

'It's got to be worth a look. Puppy, can you burn that thing? Then perhaps we look at the box.' Puppy went over to the remains of the creature and pursed his lips as he breathed fire. What came out was the blue flame Katina had seen before. There was an unearthly screech as the remains turned to black ash.

They went over to the box. Katina got out her dagger and bent down, intending to try and open it. Puppy held his front claw up to stop her. Then he gently breathed orange fire on the box, setting light to the black goo that still covered it. The goo burnt off quickly, leaving at black coloured foot cubed metal box with a locked lid.

After allowing the box a few minutes to cool down, Katina forced it open with her dagger. Inside was a twelve-inch square gold and jewel-encrusted equal arm cross and an opaque white crystal. Hawkyn took a deep breath.

'These must be the Elven Temple's cross and their version of the crystal we found at the small Light Bringer's temple we restored.' He said.

'Unless we receive guidance to the contrary, these must go to Arturous. I can sense the power in these.' Replied Katina.

'I agree, somehow we must get these back to Warameth.'

PART 8 – LONG TRIP HOME

14 – THE POLISHED WALL

'Now we need to work out what to do next.' Said Katina.

'What happens next is you sit back down on the ground, and I put those splints back on your ankles.' Said Hawkyn in a no-nonsense tone. Katina sighed. He was right, so she sat down on the burnt remains of the grass. Hawkyn removed both boots, then unbandaged her ankles, applied the splints and re-bandaged them.

When he was satisfied, 'Now we can discuss what happens next.'

'We have retrieved the Elven religious artefacts and know who they need to go to.' Replied Katina.

'Are we going to do anything about all this black goo.' Asked Puppy.

'I think we need to know two things. Whether there's any more of that creature creating the stuff and whether it will burn with normal fire.' Said Katina.

'The second one is easy.' Replied Hawkyn as he went over to a two feet long broken branch, picked it up, turned to Puppy and asked,

'Would you do the honours please?'

Puppy obliged by breathing a little orange fire at the end of the stick. Hawkyn then walked to the edge of their clearing and put the flaming stick against the goo. It did not burn.

'Oh dear.' Said Katina.

'Actually, that kind of makes sense.' Responded Puppy.

'How so?' Replied Hawkyn.

'Well, that thing that produced the goo, must be a

created or cursed being of some kind. Perhaps some form of demon. It will have taken dark spiritual magic to make or summon it, so something special will be needed to harm it and destroy what it produces. Those arrows were probably blessed somehow. My fire, because of what us dragons are, is also part spiritual and part magical.' Said Puppy.

'The arrows did tingle to the touch.' Added Katina.

'My family's sword would be a good bet too then.' Said Hawkyn.

'Yes, I would think so.' Responded Katina. 'Puppy, can you clear our local area, without burning the city to the ground.'

'I can try. If I limit it to major roads and open spaces. Let one area burn out before I do the next. I should be able to clear a fair bit. It could easily get out of hand though.' Replied Puppy and wandered off to the edge of the cleared area and breathed his orange fire. The black goo caught alight straight away. Puppy watched it burn, then as it died down moved on to the next patch.

While Puppy was doing his thing, Katina thought.

'Hawkyn, you know more about these things than I do. How likely is it that whatever it was up the tree was the only one?' She asked.

'Unlikely. From what we know, the smallest group our enemy operate in is units of ten or twelve. Given the Elves had some weapons that harmed these things, not all the unit will have survived the initial attack. So, there's probably more out there.' Hawkyn replied.

'How do we find them?' She asked.

He thought for a while. 'Try looking for thicker concentrations of the stuff and places where it flows back into cleared areas.'

'Of course.' Said Katina.

They collected the horses and led them towards Puppy, then explained what they were looking for.

'I think we need to find and identify any further sources

of the goo before we leave. We can't stay and purify the whole city, but I hope we can at least stop it spreading and maybe over time it will weaken.' Said Katina.

It took a while to clear the central square. They removed a lot from the tree without setting fire to it. Most of the small branches and leaves that were already diseased did burn, but the major branches and the trunk of the tree survived without any significant damage. The remaining goo on the tree seemed to be slowly running off by gravity alone.

By the time the sun fell below the horizon, Puppy had cleared the main square. He found several more of the strange creatures, who tried to attack him, but Hawkyn decapitated them. Puppy then incinerated the corpses with his blue flame. Katina managed to recover some arrows that tingled to the touch. They would need cleaning and new flight feathers, but otherwise looked in good order.

A large oval public building at the eastern side of the central square seemed particularly heavily infested with thick black goo. The Elves had manipulated two trees into creating a large covered, seated, meeting area. There was also a significant gap around it. Puppy solved the problem by the simple expediency of setting fire to the whole area. It burnt fiercely destroying the two trees that created the building but did not spread to its neighbours.

After further discussions they decided to spend the night camped in the now clear main square on a patch of scorched grass near the central tree. The burning building seemed to be dealing with the rest of the black goo in the area. They ate there evening meal, fed, and watered the horses then settled down for the night.

Katina woke at first light. The public building at the eastern side of the square had pretty much burnt itself out. The fire had cleared the goo from around it and a good part of the road next to it heading east. She woke the others, they ate a breakfast of bread and cheese and readied the horses to leave. Katina, although a good deal better, still required help to mount her horse.

'Something is bothering me.' Said Hawkyn.

'Oh?' Responded Katina.

'Why did the whole place not going up when Puppy breathes his fire?' Said Hawkyn.

'It's bothering me too. The city should have gone up like a torch.' Responded Puppy.

'I guess there are some things we just don't know yet.' Said Katina. 'I'd better sign in with upstairs and tell them what we are going to do.' She closed her eyes and cleared her mind.

"Hello. Anyone there?" Asked Katina.

"Yes, it's my turn on watch. What do you want?" Responded an unknown voice that Katina couldn't work out if it was male or female.

"Hi, I don't think we've met."

"No, we haven't. How can I help?"

Katina gave up trying to find out who it was. *"We think we should move on now. We've cleared a part of the city of that black goo stuff and eradicated several of those weird flying creatures. We have rescued the symbol and power stone of the Elf God, which in due course we will give to Arturous. We have a long way to go and can't afford the time to clear the entire city."*

There were a few seconds of silence, then. *"You are right, you have done all that can be achieved at this time. Now that the ancestral tree is free and several main concentrations of infection cleared, the city should be able to clean itself up. As for the religious items, while it will take time to accomplish, Arturous is a good idea for now."*

Katina felt the presence go.

'Well?' Asked Hawkyn.

'That was a strange one. I've no clue who I spoke to. They seem to be alright with our ideas for now.'

'That's a start. So, what's your plan?' Said Hawkyn.

We continue following this road east. Burn our way out

if we must. Destroy any more nests we find along the way and go home.' Said Katina.

So, they continued along the east bound road. Puppy in front. Hawkyn next, ready for any surprises and Katina leading the spare horse. Every few hundred feet Puppy had to clear the way, after which they waited for the fire to die down before continuing. Slowly they inched along the wide ornately decorated paved road, with large houses set into manipulated giant oak trees on either side. Elf skeletons were plentiful, usually in small groups and completely unarmed.

'Where's all the warriors.' Asked Katina.

'Good Question. City walls I'd imagine. The place must have been overrun from the air.' Replied Hawkyn.

'We need to get that passed on. Flying creatures that require special weapons. It will need careful thinking about.' Said Katina.

They found a group of four near the eastern gate with multiple arrows in them. Hawkyn quickly decapitated the creatures with Puppy incinerating the bodies afterwards.

This left Katina feeling somewhat useless. Despite her training and experience she had no means to fight these new creatures, which, she thought, was probably why they were used against the Elves.

All three of them kept a look out for more blessed arrows as they continued along the street heading east. Occasionally one was found. By the time they reached the eastern gate the group had retrieved several dozen. None were useable yet, but in due course she could fix that.

The eastern gate was like the western one they had come in by. You had to pass through a fortified courtyard to get out. They discussed looking for a barracks or similar, but decided against it, wanting to be clear of the cursed area before they ran out of supplies and water.

Katina felt a certain relief when crossing the drawbridge leaving the city. The infestation was markedly less severe outside. The thorny bushes were still present in the moat and although there was still infection, it was patchy and less noticeable. Even the smell of death and decay in the air lessened.

Like the west road they came in by, the east one was a well-made cobblestone road with signs of regular use. As they had seen elsewhere, there was a gap of several hundred yards between the moat and the giant oaks which made up this part of the forest. The entire area was still diseased, trees included, but the black goo affected less of the forest the further out they travelled. Puppy cleared the base of the city walls for several hundred yards in each direction of the gate.

'Puppy, do you need a break from that?' Katina asked.

'No thank you, I'm fine, but I will be glad when we are past it.' He responded.

And so, they continued slowly forward. After about half a mile.

'What's that funny noise?' Asked Puppy. 'Sounds like one of Hawkyn's stews boiling dry.' He continued.

'It does, doesn't it.' Added Katina.

'Look, the black goo stuff is bubbling.' Said Hawkyn in a surprised tone.

'Puppy, you thought these creatures were created or summoned using black magic or dark divine magic.' Katina asked.

'I think so, from what I know. It's the only thing that fits my fire killing it and your fire not.' He replied.

'Can someone help me down please.' She asked.

Hawkyn came over and helped her off her horse. She took off her leather glove and touched the stone roadway in several places.

'Yep, there's a slight tingle. The place is blessed or has spiritual power now.' Said Katina.

'Which is harming the black goo stuff. Impressive.' Concluded Puppy.

'Does that knowledge help us?' Asked Hawkyn.

'Yes, I think it does. It means that divine magic can be placed on land to prevent some of the more serious creatures of our enemy from getting in.' Said Katina.

'We're not the ones that need this information though, Luka and Oswald do.' Said Hawkyn.

'We'll work that bit out later. Can you help me back on my horse please?' Asked Katina as she put her gloves back on. Hawkyn obliged, then touched the ground himself.

'I can just feel something also. The faintest of tingles, but I can feel something. Do you think that means anyone can feel it?'

'Doubt it.' Replied Puppy.

'Puppy is probably correct. You are questing for the Gods of Light to become an Oracle's Protector and have completed several tasks. There's bound to be some things you will be able to do, that normal people can't.' Said Katina.

They continued slowly on their way, ignoring the pangs of hunger. Everyone wanted to be clear of the cursed area before stopping. It took several more miles, but at last the final traces of the goo were gone, the animals and birds were back, as was the sounds of the forest and the small plants that give it life. Katina could see the faces of both Hawkyn and Puppy relax. They decided to stop before continuing further. After they had eaten and rested the horses.

'I think we should work out how we are going to do this. We have no knowledge of the area and just a vague idea that home is east. Any thoughts.' Asked Katina.

'Our methods have worked well so far. We keep heading east, with Puppy in his eagle form supplying the next ten or so miles of general terrain information. Once we are out of this forest, we can spend some time foraging for food, then perhaps move on at a faster pace.' Suggested Hawkyn.

'I'll go look ahead.' Added Puppy, who changed form to

an eagle and flew off up through the giant trees. Hawkyn helped Katina onto her horse, then they continued along the paved road. The slow canter seemed to eat the miles and it wasn't long before Puppy returned telling them they were about halfway to the edge. They continued, reaching the thick horizontal branches of the giant oaks that marked the boundary of the forest after the sun was down.

Katina took a deep breath then said.

'Guardian of the Forest, please may we leave.'

There was a rustling and moving of branches clearing the way to the grasslands beyond. They kept going for several hundred yards outside the forest before stopping to make camp for the night.

'I feel a lot happier now we're clear of the place.' Said Hawkyn.

'Me too.' Replied Katina.

Then with a thoughtful frown Hawkyn said 'You know in two days we appear to have wrestled with some trees, investigated a city, burnt lots of black goo stuff, climbed a giant tree, fought a strange monster and travelled about fifty miles through forest. Any idea how that works?'

'No, afraid not.' Replied Katina. Puppy just shook his head.

'No, me neither.' They discussed watch shifts while they ate a cold meal, then settled in for the night.

Puppy woke Katina at sunrise saying, 'I will go and have a look around, while you guys have breakfast and pack up camp.'

'Sure. Not too far though. We will continue east if you're not back before we leave.'

Puppy nodded, changed into his juvenile eagle form, and flew off. Katina went over to Hawkyn, explained what Puppy was up to, then started breakfast. Just as they were about to leave, Puppy returned landed and shimmered into his boy form.

'About five miles east there is another abandoned town

on a large river about the same size as the one on the west side. This time there's a stone bridge. No signs of any occupation.' He said.

Crossing the grassland at a canter they reached the town quickly.

'I don't see any need to stay and look around. We know who this area belonged to. We might as well just keep going.' Suggested Katina.

'Agreed.' Replied Hawkyn.

The town was like the one on the other side of the forest and in a similar dilapidated condition, so was ignored.

After crossing the bridge, they continued at this fast pace day after day, heading directly east, often scattering herds of wild cows, sheep, or horses. There were signs of wolves in the area, but none seen. No sign that anyone lived there, not even the outlying villages and farms that are always near population centres. Katina took a bit of time each morning to exercise and manipulate her ankles, while Hawkyn and Puppy hunted to build up their stocks of supplies. They even took a day to rest the horses as Hawkyn attempted to make some more tallow candles.

Katina had lost count of the days riding through endless rolling grasslands when a range of mountains became visible on the eastern horizon.

'That'll be The Spine, which I think is about halfway.' Said Katina.

'How do we cross it.' Asked Hawkyn.

'No clue.' Responded Katina. 'I only have a dim memory of an old story.'

They continued east. Two days later when Puppy came back from scouting,

'We've got a north / south road several miles ahead. It's wide and appears well maintained, but no one around currently.' Said Puppy.

'We'd better go and have a look.' Suggested Katina.

They rode through the tall grasslands towards the road.

It was a hard-pressed gravel road about two carts wide that ran along the edge of the foothills, perhaps some twenty miles away from the mountains themselves.

'Which way now?' Asked Hawkyn.

'Good question. Somehow, we need to find a way across the mountains. Blindly ploughing straight into them is not likely to get us through.' Said Katina.

'The road is maintained, and therefore well used. There must be something at both ends or it would be neglected.' Replied Hawkyn.

'Let's head northwards for a while and see if we find anything.' Said Katina.

They headed up the road making quick progress with Puppy, in eagle form, scouting ahead. After about five miles, there was an abandoned rectangular town with defensive stone block walls. While nowhere near as grand as the Elvin City, at fifty feet high and regularly spaced large square stone towers, the defences were formidable.

'Wow, they didn't do things by halves around here did they. Twice the height of Kersladen and a lot better made.' Observed Hawkyn.

They approached the town with caution. Hawkyn held the horses while Katina and Puppy scouted inside. The pair crossed the solid oak drawbridge and entered the town through the single cart width gatehouse. Katina noticed large vertical grooves in the walls when walking through the building. When she looked up, suspended above her was some sort of heavy metal gate that had spikes on the underneath. A yard or two behind that was an open heavy wooden door. There were also arrow slits in the walls and holes in the ceiling.

The town itself comprised of stone and wooden beam buildings with pitched slate roofs either side of cobble stone streets. What would have been an excellent town was only marred by the abandoned old clothes, food and the odd unburied dead Goblin body or skeleton.

Katina looked inside several buildings she passed on the way. Some were houses, others were shops with living quarters above. The buildings had been abandoned for some considerable time. The street approached a large central square from the south. Other streets came from north, east and west.

Katina decided to go back, the eagle form Puppy joining her on the way. After they returned to Hawkyn, Katina explained what she had found. Puppy added.

'The east street continues out of the town and straight towards the mountains, the west one goes back to the grasslands. I didn't follow either very far. No sign of anyone around.'

'It looks like we can stay the night then and head east tomorrow.' He suggested.

'I think so. There will be a reason for the road heading into the mountains. It might be a way through, you never know.' Said Katina.

After some searching, it became clear that Goblins stayed in the town often, but not for long. Eventually they found a building with a decent roof near the east gate and stayed there the night. A quiet time was spent out of the wind. Having removed all signs of their presence, the three of them left the nameless abandoned town at sun-up.

The east bound road heading towards the mountains degraded after a short distance. They had to slow there pace considerably or risk the horses falling on the uneven surface. After a few miles the originally straight road curved around foothills and through large fields of wild ripe corn. There were remnants of side roads with small groups of derelict buildings visible a mile or so off the road.

'If I had to guess, I'd say this used to be a farming region.' Said Hawkyn.

'I agree, but who for?' Wondered Katina.

They continued along the unmaintained road, rounding the last hill when the sun was low in the western sky. Katina looked on the valley before her with confusion. The sides were vertical rough rock walls with low hills beyond. The floor was flat compressed gravel and devoid of vegetation. A solid vertical cliff in the mountain formed the rear of the half mile wide, half mile deep area before her. She tried to see more detail but could not as the sun reflected off something at the back of the valley.

'Wow, I bet that took some work. I suppose we'd better keep going.' Said Hawkyn.

'Yes, I think we had.' Replied Katina.

They rode across the gravel ground towards the cliff face of the mountain a half mile away. As they approached, the reason for the sun reflecting off the mountain became clear. While the incline had been cut back, in the middle of the valley was a one hundred feet wide by one hundred feet high vertical polished stone wall.

'How in the hell did they do that?' Exclaimed Katina.

'Not a clue. Where's the door? I can't see someone building a twenty mile long road, excavating a half mile wide valley and polishing a stone wall unless there was a door.' Said Hawkyn.

They picketed the horses and in the fast-fading light, looked for a door, but with no luck they spent the night camped on the gravel.

15 – THE GATEWAY

At first light, Katina, who had been on the last watch, woke the others. While Hawkyn prepared breakfast, she took the horses to a stream letting them drink and graze on nearby grass.

Thinking while the horses ate, Katina considered a few options. Firstly, that there was never anything here. Not a possibility given someone had built twenty miles of road and carried out significant amounts of terrain alteration. Far too much work for there to be nothing at the end of it. Another, that what was here was gone now. She considered this unlikely, the tendency to use large stone blocks would leave a trace and probably actual buildings. That only left one choice, whatever was here was very well hidden. She rounded up the horses and took them back.

'Breakfast is ready.' Hawkyn handed her a bowl of porridge.

'Thankyou. I'm thinking that whatever is here is well hidden or concealed. Puppy will your special dragon sight help?'

'Sorry no. Tried that last night. My sight sees through magical alterations of appearance. If there's anything here, then it is physically concealed, no magic involved at all. Are you sure something is here?' Puppy asked.

'Far too much work has been carried out for there not to be. It would have taken a lot of men a long time to create that road and this valley.' Replied Hawkyn.

So, once they had eaten breakfast and packed away the camp, the trio started to examine the cliff face. They carefully looked at every square inch of the polished section of the wall from the ground to as high as they could reach. Observing and carefully feeling the surface hoping to find a crack that might be a door or button to press. Several hours later they had completed the whole width of the polished stone section.

'Now what?' Asked Hawkyn.

'We take a break for a few minutes and try again.' Said Katina.

The three sat down heavily on the gravel.

'There's no sign of any sort of imperfection in the polishing that might be a crack surrounding a door, button or leaver. I suppose we had better try something else.' Said Katina.

'How about somewhere, rather than something?' Suggested Puppy.

'Why in the name of the Gods would you go to all the trouble of perfectly cutting and polishing a huge area of stone mountainside, then go and put the door someplace else?' Said an exasperated Katina.

'Haven't a clue, but it's definitely not in the polished bit. You two are just too good at finding things for the both of you to have missed a large stone door.' Replied Puppy.

'Perhaps they were drunk.' Suggested Hawkyn with a smirk.

'Makes about as much sense as anything else round here.' Said Katina looking at Hawkyn with a grin. 'Alright, let's try Puppy's idea. Why not start to the left of the polished bit.'

So that's what they did. Each to a section. Puppy started at the corner with the stone lined hillside, Hawkyn at the other end where the cliff face became polished and Katina in the middle about a third of the way along from Puppy.

And so, they searched, felt, and examined, hour after hour, from ground level to about seven feet up. None of them found anything, accept at one point Katina found a small hole about four feet off the ground. That was the only aberration found by anyone. Just about big enough to get your little finger in, but probably not big enough to get it out again afterwards. The sun was setting, so they stopped for the night, set up camp again, ate and talked.

The little hole started to nag at her. Normally it would not be an issue. Stonework was never that good. Holes and small gaps were common from carving errors or faults in the stone itself, and that is what she had assumed it was. But everything else here was just so perfect. One hundred feet wide by one hundred feet high of polished stone and not a single fault or carving error. The more she thought about it, the more she became sure the hole was deliberate. Curiosity getting the better of her, she went over to it, ignoring the calls of the others.

Katina could not see much of the hole in the moonlight. It was perfectly round, so it was handmade and not badly carved or a stone imperfection. She looked around for something long and thin. There was a suitable twig a few yards away. Picking it up she started to feel out the hole. The others came over.

'What's up?' Asked Hawkyn.

'We have a created hole. Several inches of solid stone then an open space for a few inches then solid again.' She replied.

'So, we either push against the solid end or there's something in the open space we move.' Suggested Hawkyn.

'Like a key in a lock.' Replied Katina.

'Yes, but key holes are normally a hole and a slot.' Said Hawkyn.

'What about one of your metal meat skewers, would that be strong enough to push anything at the back of the space?' Asked Puppy.

'Probably, I'll go get one.' Responded Hawkyn. He came back a few minutes later. Katina put it in the hole and tried to move the other end of the cavity.

'It is not going to budge. I can tell that the open space goes downwards.' Said Katina.

'So, if anything needs moving it's in that cavity. I think we had best leave this to the morning.' Said Hawkyn. They returned to camp, agreed watch shifts and settled in for the night.

Katina awoke in the morning having spent a considerable part of the night trying to work out how to see round corners without a mirror. Having failed, she was now tired and worried, but was convinced that there was something here. The big question was how to get in.

At breakfast Katina said. 'Alright folks, I am out of ideas. I cannot work out how to see what's in that cavity and we need to if we are to work out what to do. Any suggestions?'

'Hmm. Whoever built this must have a device that works what is inside the cavity. Whatever it is we will have to push or pull it. Given its narrow size and the bend necessary, I am having trouble with pushing. Pulling might be possible with a hook.' Suggested Puppy.

'My fishing line and hook might work if it pulls.' Suggested Hawkyn. The others agreed, so he carved a slot in the end of a stick, put some fat in the slot, fed his fishing line through allowing several inches of line between the end of the stick and the hook.

'What do you think?' He asked.

'Worth a try.' Replied Katina.

The three of them wandered back over to the hole found the previous day.

'You had better do this Hawkyn. Of the three of us you have far more experience of hook and line.' Said Katina.

'Sure.' Was his response.

He put the hook in the hole and pushed it a little way up with his finger. Then in went the stick with Hawkyn trying to look up the hole at the same time.

'I've pushed the hook into the cavity I think.' He said.

Hawkyn slowly pushed the stick as far as it would go, then gently pulled it out. There was no resistance. He tried again angling the stick so that the end was on the righthand side of the hole until it reached the far end of the cavity. He then manoeuvred the stick, so the end was on the left-hand side of the hole and gently pulled the line out.

'It's caught on something.' He said, continuing to pull on the line. The line went slack.

'Damn, it's come off.'

He tried again several times and on each occasion the hook caught, it came off when he tried a significant pull. Hawkyn then appeared to think things over for a few seconds.

'Katina, I believe you need to do this.' He concluded.

'Why?' She responded.

'I just do. Trust me.' He replied.

Katina took the stick from Hawkyn and tried several times as he had done, putting the other end of the stick to the right-hand side of the cavity, then gently moving left and pulling out. The hook repeatedly caught on something but broke free. Then she tried something a bit different, angling the stick slightly downwards and gently forced it a little bit more. Just that fraction of an inch further and held it still for a few seconds. Then gently pulled it back out.

The hook caught on something. Gradually she pulled on the line. After a few seconds, the hook came free and there was a loud clunk behind the stone cliff face and a loud grating sound.

'Well, something has happened.' Said Katina.

'The sound came from inside and off to our right.' Replied Hawkyn.

'Let's go and have a look.' Suggested Katina.

The three walked slowly along the cliff face towards the polished stone section paying careful attention to the stonework. When they got to the polished section.

'Look up there, a gap. Not a very big gap, but a gap none the less.' Said Katina.

'Where the polished stone meets the cut stone. Slightly wider at the top I think.' Replied Hawkyn.

Katina pushed against the polished stone. It didn't budge. 'There must be another hole.' She suggested.

'Perhaps in the section on the other side of the polished stone.' Said Hawkyn.

It took the three of them a while, but in the end, Puppy found another hole. Katina inserted the hook line and stick into the hole and as before pushed it to one side and all the way in. Then angling down pushed a little further and gently pulled back. The hook caught something, she pulled but it slipped off. After a fair few more tries there was another loud clunk followed by a grating sound behind the stone.

This time the grating sound continued. They stepped back and watched, mouths open as the entire one hundred feet wide polished stone section of the cliff face fell backwards at the top several yards, then the whole thing slowly rose into the cliff above.

In front of them was a three yard wide trench into which the polished stone section of cliff face had sat. Beyond that was a few yards of gravel surface before a fifty feet high crenulated defensive wall. In the middle was a wooden drawbridge in the upright position. The cave itself was considerably wider than the door and about one hundred feet high. While it was too dark to see the roof, the sides of the cave were cut to the same flawless standard that outside had been.

'This is going to be fun, all that time getting that stone moved, and having done so, we still can't get in.' Observed Hawkyn.

'How do drawbridges' work? Perhaps I could fly over and lower the thing myself.' Said Puppy.

'Worth a try.' Said Katina.

'Well, there are two chains which should attach to the inside of the drawbridge at the top. One to each corner. Those chains should go through the wall to a large barrel shaped winch. It will have some sort of catch that you can release to let the drawbridge down.'

Puppy changed into his juvenile eagle form and flew over the wall out of sight. After a few minutes, the drawbridge dropped quickly with a clatter and a thump. Katina and Hawkyn walked across the lowered drawbridge towards the gateway in the wall. Puppy waited in his small boy form on the other side.

'Nobody home. There's another set of much larger winches.' Said the boy form Puppy.

Behind the fortification wall, the cave opened out to an area several hundred feet long. Around the edges were some large rectangular buildings each made of stone and two or three stories high. In addition, there was a stable building for horses, a warehouse and a large open area running up the middle to a large tunnel at the far end.

'What do you think this place is for?' Asked Puppy.

'This must be a defended entrance to a people who lived underground. Merchants from outside probably came here, stabled their horses and traded at the warehouse before going home again.' Suggested Katina.

'Do we go through the tunnels on the hope we find a way out?' Said Hawkyn.

'I don't see we have much choice. There's no known way over the top of the mountains. Having found this, we must hope there's a way under.' Said Katina.

'This could go terribly wrong. If we get lost or can't find our way back, we're in serious trouble.' Replied Hawkyn

'Yes, I know, but can't think of any other choice.' Concluded Katina.

Hawkyn nodded, then said 'You two have a look round. I'll go get the horses.'

Hawkyn spent about half an hour packing up the camp, then brought the horses in. Meanwhile Katina and Puppy had a look around. Puppy showed her the drawbridge winch and another much larger one that had massive chains running up into the roof. Once Hawkyn had re-joined them.

'I think if we are going to try and find our way through, we should seal this place up again.' Said Katina.

'Yes, I agree. We don't want to find this place full of Goblins.' Replied Hawkyn.

'Erm, how much food and water do we have? We've been hunting every day. We live off what we catch that day or perhaps the day before. Given we don't know the way and you won't be able to catch rabbits in caves, do we have enough food and water?' Asked Puppy.

'Actually, Puppy, we have three days food, two days of water and minimum horse fodder.' Replied Katina.

'Puppy's right though, that won't be enough. We will need more of each, especially water. We'd better sort that out before we shut the door. I'll secure the horses while you go forage. Not sure where we will put it all though.' Added Hawkyn.

'Make litters with those tent poles, like I did to move you up that hill.' Suggested Katina.

'That would work.' Said Hawkyn.

Katina left Hawkyn to get on with it. A juvenile eagle flew overhead towards the hills, she slowly ran over the drawbridge heading to the plains and wild wheat fields they had passed on the way there. After several hours Katina came back with bags of grain, some wild berries and apples.

'I've found a well near the stable building. The water is clean, I've checked and refilled our water skins.' Said Hawkyn.

'Great. I've got some grain and fruit.' Said Katina.

'Puppy's been back with a few wild fowl and rabbits. Leave the grain to me and I will make some flat bread. You get some more.' Said Hawkyn. Katina nodded and headed back out.

And that's how it was for the rest of the day. Katina and Puppy foraged, Hawkyn ground grain into flour, made and cooked flatbread, wild fowl and rabbits. By the end of the day there were two litters full of supplies. They camped in the stable building that night along with the horses. In the morning breakfasted and broke camp.

'We'd better shut the door.' Said Hawkyn once everything was ready. Katina simply nodded. She wasn't really looking forward to spending days underground with no sky, but there wasn't a choice.

They went to the gatehouse winch room where Katina and Hawkyn, using the handles on the barrel winch, lifted the drawbridge easily. They secured it in an upright position with the locking bar, then went to the much larger winch.

'Well, here goes.' Said Hawkyn.

They both grabbed handles on the wheel and held tight, then Puppy released the locking bar. Slowly Hawkyn and Katina unwound the huge barrel winch to loud grating sounds.

'The polished stone door is coming down from the roof and two large stone blocks are rising up the walls of the cave.' Said Puppy.

The pair exercising every ounce of strength to keep hold of the winch handles, just grunted. Ten minutes later there was a resounding thump as the polished stone wall arrive back in its original position. They both sank to the floor, arms shaking from the exertion.

16 – WE DON'T WANT TO GET LOST

Katina lay on the floor recovering from the extreme exertion of lowering the outer wall with Hawkyn. Her mind wandered, but eventually it started to focus. She noticed there was still a low level of light. About every twenty yards had a protruding rock in the roof of the cave that glowed. It didn't amount to much light, but it was enough to stop you from bumping into things.

She got up, then looked out of the window staring at the massive stone wall that now blocked the entrance. While there were no feelings of actual fear, the roof above her looked awfully heavy now they had sealed the doors.

'Are you alright love? You're looking a bit . . .' Hawkyn left it hanging.

'I'm not used to being locked in a confined space that's all, even if it is huge.' Katina replied. Hawkyn smiled at her, got up and gave her a hug, then suggested.

'I suppose we had better get moving.'

Katina nodded. Then said 'I wonder who lived here? There's no sign of conquest.'

'Perhaps we will get a clue as we go through.' Suggested Puppy.

'Well, we know it's not Elves. We also know it's not Goblins, this construction is much too advanced and well-built for them. I don't think it was us Humans either. There's no way we could build that door and those lights. If it were us, somebody would have bragged about it. I have absolutely no idea who lived here.' Replied Hawkyn.

Katina thought for a moment. The various Gods of Light came to mind from somewhere previously unknown, as they had done before. She knew there were gods of each of the races. The Lord of the Gates for Humans, The Elf God, The Goblin Lord and, well now.

'How about Dwarves. I know that there is a god for them, and we carry his hammer. Though I don't know anything about them.' Said Katina.

'Dwarves! If that is true, they are way better at building than we are.' Said Hawkyn.

They collected the horses and led them towards the tunnel that exited the cave. It was about fifteen feet high and a similar width with vertical sides for about ten feet and a flattened arch for the roof. Katina's horse became resistant to continuing and stopped dead, its eyes wild looking. She did have some sympathy for what her horse felt, but there was no other choice. It took some time and persuasion, but eventually, the hesitant horse dragging one of the litters of supplies, moved forwards.

The floor was a reliable flat surface made of compressed gravel. The glowing ceiling stones continued about every twenty yards or so. While not perfectly smooth, the walls were reasonably uniform and showed signs of alteration to make travel easier and a more consistent tunnel shape.

After a while, they came to a new cavern, not as wide or as high as the first one, but longer. Again, the glowing ceiling stones supplied a low level of light. There were many modest rectangular stone buildings, but on the left-hand side by the entrance was another smaller tunnel with a plaque above.

'Runes. Any ideas what it means?' Katina said.

'No.' Was the universal response.

'I'll go a short way up and have a look.' Said Katina.

What she saw was a large room carved out of the rock, with racks for weapons and shields, and stands for suits of armour. The beds stools and tables were lower to the ground.

'A guardroom for about twenty men. Pretty standard save it's a cave. The armour has a different body shape to us, shorter but wider. Perhaps it is Dwarves.' She said after returning to the others.

'I wonder where everyone lives. All these buildings seem functional rather than occupational.' Said Hawkyn.

The current cave had several side tunnels, but they appeared to be of a more minor nature being smaller overall. They decided to follow the major one. The next cave had two such tunnels, the first they tried led to a large barracks with multiple buildings, parade ground and training area. They went back to the other one. That tunnel appeared to be a hewed out natural cavern, had the usual solid gravel surface and fell slightly on a constant slope. Katina lost all sense of time and distance. They stopped occasionally to rest the horses and eat when her stomach complained of hunger.

Caves with buildings and other smaller tunnels were frequent and seemed to be roughly consistent in distance, though it was impossible to tell. Some of these caves were larger than others, but they all had signs of extensive excavation. The smaller side tunnels they checked seemed to have occupation areas built directly into the sides of them. Some of the larger caves had paths cut into the sides that meandered forwards and backward slowly climbing upwards. These had many entrances hewed out of the rock. Each had a small, recessed porch area and a six feet high solid door. Some appeared to have a small window next to the door. Katina assumed these were the equivalent of people's houses.

They kept going straight along the widest tunnel on a steady decline. Everywhere there was a fist sized glowing stone set into the ceiling every twenty yards or so. After about a dozen caves, they started to feel tired, so continued to the next cave, found a building and slept.

They all woke about the same time, got ready, ate a cold breakfast, and moved out, continuing slowly downwards and ever onwards. Several caves later they entered the bottom of a large cavern which stretched ahead of them. Katina could not see the top, it disappeared into darkness above her. There were plenty of those glowing stones, some on the cavern walls, others at the top of thick poles near the sides of the "street" that lay ahead of them.

The cavern quickly widened to several hundred feet with what appeared to be row after row of workshops along the side walls. One thing that Katina had never seen before was a pair of iron bars set into the hard gravel surface. They were about two feet apart running into the distance. They walked on.

Later, two major tunnels entered the cavern from right and left. Both had a pair of these iron bars in the ground that turned heading further up the cavern in front of them. They followed.

A while later, when the cavern widened further, there were row after row of four wheeled carts resting on other pairs of bars set in the ground. Each row having dozens of wheeled carts. Each cart was about three feet long, three feet wide and about two feet high. A quarter were full of iron ore, a quarter were full of coal and half were empty.

'Iron tracks for carts to run on. Very clever. The contents of those carts would make an awful lot of iron. We definitely don't want our enemy finding this place.' Said Hawkyn.

'I wish the occupants were still here. These people would be seriously useful.' Replied Katina.

They followed the lines of carts. Katina saw several large machines or devices some of which she recognised, but others she did not. The first machine she didn't recognise had a large flat surface and a heavy rectangular block hanging above it on chains. It looked as if the chains raised and lowered the block. Hawkyn saw her looking and explained.

'I have seen some of our artisans convert ore into iron, so I think I know what each of these machines does, though ours do it by hand with hammers and small fires with pots. The one you are looking at will crush the iron ore rock to powder. The ore then goes into one of those furnaces to produce iron. A process repeated several more times to get the impurities out. The finished iron will then be given to artisans to make things with.'

'The people here are better at it than us?'

'Yes, by miles.' Said Hawkyn.

He went over and had a good look at the large pounding machine and the furnaces. Appearing to try and get every detail of how they worked committed to memory. After a few minutes.

'Are you thinking of telling our own tribe about these machines?' Asked Katina.

'Yes I am. Our people do marvellous work, but they could do so much more and better with these.'

Katina and Puppy left Hawkyn to his investigations. They fed and rested the horses, ate a cold meal and looked in nearby buildings. Most were warehouses of iron and maybe even steel blocks of varying sizes. One appeared to be an administration building with books and records. Puppy found several leather-bound books containing sheets of blank parchment. He also found a pot of ink and several unused quills.

'I think we should give these to Hawkyn and let him take notes. Clearly whoever these people were, they knew what they were doing.' Said Puppy.

'I agree.' Said Katina. They gave the books, ink and quills to Hawkyn, who at once started to create drawings and write notes on each machine and what it did. It took him several hours to finish.

Ignoring the other ways up, a good while later they reached the other end of the cavern, passing the heavy industries of mining and smelting of iron ore on the way.

Continuing along a similar sized tunnel for what seemed like longer than usual, they came across another cavern. This time though, the ceiling was only twenty feet above them. A wide path went each side of a lake of water as far as they could see. Hawkyn bent down and tasted the water.

'It's clean.' He said, so they refilled all the water skins

and gave the horses a good drink.

'Which way?' Asked Puppy.

'Let's go right.' Suggested Katina and off they went. The water filled cavern was longer than she could see from where they entered, the occasional side tunnel inclined upwards. At the other end was a major tunnel, but it was not well lit. One just before it however was wider, paved and much better lit.

'What do you think about trying that one? It's a lot higher quality tunnel.' Said Katina pointing to the paved tunnel.

'True, but we need to be careful. Our best chance of getting through is travelling in a straight line on the major tunnels.' Said Hawkyn.

'Perhaps we go up a little way, to the first major junction and see what's there. Then come back.' Suggested Puppy.

'He's right. It doesn't matter what we find there if we get lost and can't get out.' Replied Hawkyn.

They went up the tunnel which rose more steeply than other gradients. It eventually opened into a large cave with a flat paved floor. Most noticeable was an ornate stone marble building inside a ten feet high perimeter wall. Outside the wall in the rest of the large cave were several other equally ornate stone buildings and a group of workshops in one corner. There were also a few other tunnels entering the cave.

'We need to make sure we know the correct one to go out.' Said Hawkyn.

'I'll remember.' Said Katina.

'Where first?'

'Let's look at the workshops, there may be something of use in them.' Suggested Hawkyn.

They wandered over to the workshop compound and when rounding the corner of the central building's perimeter wall saw a tall statue in front of the main gate.

'Is that a statue of a Dwarf?' Asked Katina.

'Yes, I believe so.' Replied Hawkyn.

'It's very well carved isn't it.' Said Katina.

'It is, yes.' Replied Hawkyn.

They spent a few seconds admiring the statue, then continued over to the workshop compound, tying the horses up at the gate. There were no tools left in any of the workshops they looked at. Most of the buildings were completely empty, but one of the workshops had a six foot long large wooden box by the door.

'Looks like they forgot one.' Said Puppy.

'Easily done when moving house.' Replied Hawkyn.

'Lid is nailed shut.' Added Katina pulling at the box.

'I'll get an axe and hammer.' Said Hawkyn as he went to his horse.

He put the blade of the wood cutting axe where the lid of the box joined the sides near one corner, then hit the flat back end of the axe blade with his hammer. The corner of the lid came off the box slightly. Continuing this elsewhere on the box slowly loosened the lid. Eventually Katina and Hawkyn lifted the lid off.

Inside were several long thin bundles wrapped in heavy cloth. They lifted one out, placed it on the floor, and unwrapped it.

'Oh my.' Said an awestruck Hawkyn staring at the shining multi grey coloured surface. Katina just staired open mouthed.

'Why the surprise, it's a sword. A nice-looking sword, I'll give you that, but still just a sword in bits.' Asked Puppy.

'How many are there?' Asked Hawkyn, ignoring Puppy's question. Katina went to the box and rummaged around inside.

'Six including that one.' Replied Katina.

'Oh wow. This one has all the bits, blade, hilt, handle, pommel. They're just not assembled and the blade not finally sharpened or polished.' Said Hawkyn.

'Could we put them together and sharpen them.' Asked

Katina.

'Probably not. I doubt our sharpening stuff would even touch it.' Said Hawkyn.

'Hey, what's so special?' Asked Puppy with a little exasperation in his voice.

'Sorry Puppy. I don't know anyone who can get anywhere near making one of these.' Said Katina.

'Although unfinished they look exactly like the blade of my family's sword. These are the base weapon for the enchanted swords of legend. It looks like steel mixed with iron somehow. I don't think we can make steel and certainly not mix it with iron. This is the best type of sword that we can imagine, and there isn't anyone who can make them. Give one of these to a Lord Guardian and I doubt even Plains Devils would stand a chance.' Added Hawkyn.

'It would go straight through my long sword if I tried to parry it.' Added Katina.

'Looks like I'm walking then.' Replied Puppy. They both looked at him puzzled.

'Well, we can't leave them behind can we.' He responded.

'We'd better wrap it up and put it back in the box.' Said Hawkyn.

'Hold on.' Said Katina as she bent down and touched the blade. 'No, it isn't.'

'Shame, but they are still incredible swords.' Replied Hawkyn. They re-wrapped the sword.

'We'd better check the others.' Suggested Katina.

'Right.' Replied Hawkyn. They removed each of the remaining five bundles from the box, unwrapped it, checked it had all the required bits, checked it was not damaged or cracked, checked if it tingled and then re-wrapped it. There were four bastard swords and two of the shorter and more slender long swords. After Hawkyn put them back in the box, he nailed the lid shut and tied it securely to Puppy's horse.

'Now for the big house.' Said Katina.

They untied the horses and led them across to the gateway in the perimeter wall of the central building. Once they had entered, they secured the horses near the gate and looked at the building in front of them.

Katina had not seen anything like it. There was a raised white stone platform with a dozen steps at the front in the middle, but just vertical sides elsewhere. Smooth columns lined the sides of the raised platform with graceful, curved stone archways between each column and its counterpart on the other side. These supported a slate pitched roof. The building was about one hundred feet wide and several hundred feet long. The front had no walls, but it appeared the very back did.

They climbed the steps, took a few paces forwards and looked in. After about ten feet, there were a dozen steps down. Either side of the steps and down each side of the sunken area were seating platforms that were in line with every other step. The raised section at the other end of the building had a large stone throne with again, a dozen steps leading up to it. A wall with a door in it stood a few yards behind the throne. Several stone frescos adorned the rear wall either side of the door. Large beams and purlins supported the roof, with more glowing stones regularly spaced amongst the beams.

'Judging by the throne, these Dwarves appear a bit shorter than we are, but a good deal wider.' Said Hawkyn.

'This must be the Dwarven royal family's cave.' Suggested Katina.

'Agreed, hence the superior weapons here.' Said Hawkyn.

The three of them looked around the large hall and went up to the throne. As Katina expected, it was of superior quality of stone and carving. It was also surprisingly comfortable and gave Katina a distinct feeling of superiority when she sat in it.

'Enjoying the seat?' Asked Hawkyn.

'I'm not sure I like the feeling that attaches itself to this chair. I am not comfortable with thinking of myself superior to others.'

'You'd better get used to it my love, because as Oracle, you will be.' Replied Hawkyn with a grin.

She got up off the throne and they walked to the door in the wall behind it. On the other side was a large room, with an oval stone table surrounded by eighteen wooden chairs but was otherwise empty. There were other doors, the rooms behind them were also empty. One appeared to have been a library, but all the scrolls and books were gone.

'This was a planned evacuation, not a military defeat or a retreat carried out in a hurry.' Said Hawkyn.

'They took with them everything they could carry, including their knowledge. Then locked the place up.' Said Puppy.

'I wonder where they went. Shame we can't spend the time to look.' Said Katina.

'But it is possible they are still out there. That would make another race that might fight.' Said Hawkyn.

'Possible yes, but we can't say that for certain.' Said Hawkyn.

'We're becoming side-tracked, let's move on and see if we can find our way out.' Said Katina.

They returned to their horses and led them back down the tunnel they came up in.

'Is this the right one?' Asked Puppy.

'Yes. Katina remembered correctly.' Replied Hawkyn.

'Don't worry Puppy, we aren't going to get lost in here.' Said Katina.

About ten minutes later, they reached the lake cave and turned right along the water's edge then up the tunnel at the end of the lake. It wasn't long before they came to another major settlement and after that several smaller ones. Finally, after more overnight stops and a fair few more settlements, they came to another entrance cave.

'Here's a thought, after we have got things open and got out, how do we get the door shut without one of us being caught inside?' Asked Katina.

'I wonder if the big door thing, can be convinced to lower itself. If so you and the horses leave. Drawbridge gets lifted and I fly out before the door closes.' Suggested Puppy.

'It could work.' Said Katina.

'Depends how fast the door closes.' Added Hawkyn.

'It would be worth finding out where those two holes are beforehand, just in case.' Suggested Katina.

'Agreed.' Said Hawkyn.

They walked to the gatehouse tower and looked over the two winches. They both appeared to work, but the stone door one was extremely heavy to turn.

'There's something wrong here.' Said Puppy.

'Oh, what?' Enquired Katina.

'Well, that other door was opened by a small hook on a bit of line pulling on something. Nothing like the effort needed to move that.' Puppy said pointing at the large barrel winch.

'Puppy is right, there must be an easier way.' Said Katina.

'Let's think this through then. Most of the weight of the door is taken by those huge counterweights on the sides of the cave. So, for it to be as easy as pulling on that hook, something else must happen.' Said Hawkyn thinking. Then he looked at the counterweights through a window in the gatehouse. 'Of course.' He said.

'There's a smaller additional counterweight above the main one. Whatever we pulled with the hook, drops this extra counterweight on top of the main one which will tip the balance and the door opens all by itself. Once the door is open there will be another winch or two somewhere that resets the smaller counterweights.' Hawkyn concluded.

'So, to close it, we lock this winch, reset the two smaller counterweights, release this winch again and run for it.' Said Katina.

'Or fly for it in my case.' Suggested Puppy.

'Let's go find the lever or whatever it was for the smaller counterweights.' Said Katina.

They looked at the outer walls passed the large stone door. After some searching, they found a small barrel winch and a cord coming out of the wall running to a leaver on the winch. Katina pulled the cord. The leaver disengaged the lock on the barrel winch which then turned on its own. High above them the smaller counterweight slid onto the larger one. Some further searching found a second small barrel winch on the other side of the cavern. Katina pulled the cord for that one and the same thing happened. Both the large counterweights started to drop and the one hundred feet by one hundred feet stone front door rose slowly into the roof.

They went back to the wheel room in the gatehouse and lowered the drawbridge. Hawkyn also applied the lock catch to the main door winch, so the door didn't start to close on its own.

'We should reset the little counterweights now.' Said Hawkyn. This they did using the smaller winches at the side of the cave and returned the locking catch and cord to their correct locations. Puppy went outside and quickly found both the small hook holes just in case they needed to open the door again.

As Katina led her horse through the gatehouse the sun blinded her for several minutes. Eventually her eyes became accustomed to the sunlight, and she crossed the drawbridge. In front of her was a valley about half mile wide at this end. The grassland and various small copse of trees were a welcome sight. It was also late afternoon. She joined Puppy waiting outside. Hawkyn followed a few minutes later.

'I think we stay here tonight, get a fresh start in the

morning.' Said Katina.

'Do we leave the big door open until we leave?' Asked Puppy.

'No. Close it now. The less chance of our enemy seeing what's here the better.' Said Katina.

'Can you do the drawbridge on your own?' Asked Hawkyn.

'Yes, I think so. Drawbridge first, then release the big winch locking catch and run for it.' Replied Puppy.

Katina watched Puppy walk back over the drawbridge. A few minutes later and it started to rise. A few minutes after that, once the drawbridge was up, a loud clunk followed by a constant grinding sound indicating that Puppy had started the main door closing. A juvenile eagle then flew very quickly over the defensive walls. He shimmered and changed into the young boy form of Puppy. All three watched as the huge stone door slowly ground its way into position becoming part of the cliff face with a loud clunk.

17 – HEADING SOUTH

Katina looked up at the sky and gave a loud sigh, feeling the tension of the last few days evaporate as she exhaled. The anxiety at being underneath endless tons of rock was gone.

'It's good to be outdoors again, isn't it?' Said Hawkyn.

'It most definitely is. Just the smell of the fresh air, the sounds of the birds, and the open expanse of sky. They rid me of that enclosed oppressive feeling.' Replied Katina.

The horses seemed equally pleased at being outdoors as they tried to pull away from their reins to run. Everyone just wandered around for a few minutes enjoying the open space, the feel of the grass and wind. Then they set up camp for the night.

'I'm going to find some firewood, why don't you two go and have a look round.' Suggested Hawkyn.

'I'll go a bit beyond your usual mile or two.' Said Puppy as he changed into his juvenile eagle form and flew off.

Katina also headed off. Now though she paid more attention to where she was. Either side of the valley was a mountain high enough to have snow on its peak. The valley widened out to about a mile across and snaked its way eastward between the two mountains. The strange part of it was that there were not the usual slopes of a valley. Its floor was flat, with vertical sides of twenty plus feet. There were several mountain streams, waterfalls and a small lake which held fish. One for Hawkyn she thought. There were also wild fowl, rabbits and the occasional sheep, goat and wild boar. She walked for several miles without coming to the end of the valley. Katina caught a few wild fowl and rabbits, then went back to camp.

When she got there, the fire was going nicely. Hawkyn prepared and cooked a rabbit and two of the wild fowl by the time Puppy got back.

'You were gone a long time, find anything?' Asked Katina.

'Erm, yes. The valley is about five miles long and ends behind a large rocky outcrop in some trees. It connects the lower slopes of the two mountains either side of us. From the outside, this valley is impossible to see unless you are flying over it. That's the good news.'

'And the bad?' Asked Hawkyn.

'Well, in the hills some ten miles northeast is a large Goblin settlement. Several thousand I think.' Replied Puppy.

'Damn that's close. Getting out of here without the Goblins seeing us will be difficult.' Said Katina.

'In here, they won't unless they start climbing mountains, but getting out of the area will be a challenge.' Said Puppy.

Katina thought. 'The best choice is for us to get away from the area without the Goblins knowing we were here. Yet again, we are going to have to hide and run, rather than fight and kill.' She said.

'If the tribe is north-east, then we will have to go south south-east in the foothills for a while before we can cut across the plains.' Said Hawkyn.

'Puppy, could you do some extensive aerial scouting tomorrow. North, south and east. Find out where the main Goblin centres of occupation are and patrol routes if possible.'

'That's a lot for one day, Katina. Any more occupation sites will be thirty or forty miles away. Looking for patrols as well will take a lot of time.' Said Hawkyn.

'I should be able to do that sort of distance in a day, but active searching rather than casual looking will take me a lot longer.' Replied Puppy.

'Tomorrow, look for our routes out and patrol patterns. If you find out enough information to allow us to leave, then great. If not, then we will just have to wait another day.' Katina replied.

They spent a quiet restful evening talking and relaxing

by the campfire. Puppy, in his dog form, curled up in front of the fire and went to sleep. Katina woke in the morning cuddled into a sleeping Hawkyn. She carefully extricated herself without waking him and made breakfast.

'Here's some tea for you.' She said, shaking him gently.

'Thank you.' He said groggily.

Puppy looked at her and changed into his juvenile eagle form.

'We will stay in the valley today. Hawkyn will probably do some fishing and I will see how to get out.' Said Katina.

Squawk was the response and he flew off. Hawkyn and Katina packed up the camp, put the fire out and headed off down the valley. When they got to the lake.

'Do you want to try your hand at fishing.' Katina asked.

'If you don't mind. I will look after Puppy's horse and catch up with you in a few hours.'

'Sure.'

She rode around various small copse and across the grassland until a large group of mainly oak trees blocked her path. At this point the ground returned to the usual uneven sloped surface of a mountain forest floor. Katina considered this was to protect the valley from any passing curiosity.

Eventually the sixty feet tall outcrop that blocked the entire end of the valley came into sight. With various other large sharp-edged rocks on it, slipping here would result in serious injury. She tied her horse to a tree nearby and walked on further to see if there was any way through or round. There was none. Slowly and carefully, she climbed to the top on its right-hand side. The trees continued the other side of the rocky outcrop as well as up the slopes of both mountains. Despite not being completely above the line of the treetops Katina kept her profile as low as possible.

Carefully she looked along the slope of the mountain to the left of the valley to see if there were any signs of a way through, a pathway, a hidden door or passage that might get them out but found nothing. That did not surprise her given how difficult it was to find the entrance to the Dwarf city. Katina climbed back down and retrieved her horse.

Thinking as she walked back through the trees, there was simply no workable way out near the rocky outcrop. Her, Hawkyn and Puppy could get out by climbing, but no way the horses could or most of their belongings, especially with the Dwarf God's Hammer or the half dozen new swords they had picked up. They would have to find another way.

From the edge of the copse, she saw Hawkyn coming across the grasslands leading the two horses.

'Hi. I caught a fair number of fish which we can prepare and cook while waiting. Any luck with finding a way out?' Said Hawkyn.

'Great with the fish and no, nothing. The outcrop is about sixty feet high with lots of jagged rocks and sharp edges. No way we can get the horses over that. I didn't see any candidates for possible hidden doors. Given the workmanship of Dwarves we've seen so far, it could be right in front of us, and we'd never know.'

'Very true. So, we're going to have to come up with our own way out.'

'Yes, I think so. A way which the Goblins can't find.'

'There will be a way, I just know it. The problem is, finding it.' Said Katina.

'There's plenty of animals in here, how would they do it? If you were outside looking for an animal that you had lost track of, where would you go to find its movements?' Hawkyn asked. Katina thought.

'Well. I think I would check the slopes of the mountain for game trails.'

'Then that's what we must do, look for game trails up the mountain slopes and try and go round.' Said Hawkyn.

They secured the horses, then Katina retrieved some

dead branches and made a small fire while Hawkyn prepared the fish for cooking. When the camp was set up, all the chores done, and the fish were slowly cooking over the open fire, Katina said.

'I'd better go and look for this game trail if there is one. We have several hours of daylight left. I'll be back by sundown.'

'Alright, see you later.'

Katina walked off back up the valley towards the Dwarf stronghold. She found one game trail quite quickly, but it didn't seem to go any distance, so walked further up the slopes of the mountain and towards the edge of a copse. Then outside the limit of the trees, continued around the mountain. The terrain was manageable at first, but soon became littered with large boulders and sharp rocks. She considered it would be difficult to move the horses over that terrain so climbed further up the slope of the mountain and sat on a large boulder.

Assessing the area, Katina looked for any signs of a possible route out for the laden horses. After a while, she noticed a small deer disappear behind some bushes at the bottom of the cut back side of the valley. Katina watched for several minutes. The deer did not re-appear. Then she remembered the very narrow gorge to the castle in the mountains. Could it happen here? Could there be something behind that bush? She decided to go and see, so climbed back down the slope of the mountain.

Even relatively close, there was no sign of anything there. Just a wall of plant tendrils and leaves. No sign of anything at all, not even the deer that had gone behind the bush the best part of an hour before. Then it hit her. There must be something there, or else where did the deer go? Katina walked closer to the bush.

She was almost on top of it before she realised. The cut back vertical side of the valley seemed like a straight solid wall, but various large bushes from below and hanging plants from above, hid the fact that the straight vertical side to the valley was not in fact a straight wall at all. It was an optical illusion involving the clever use of colour and shape of rock, of placement of bushes and hanging vines. Quite brilliantly, she could not see an alcove several yards deep, and a few yards wide even when stood right in front of it.

Inside the illusion was an alcove with wet walls covered in vines. She knew there must be a way forward, but Katina still could not see it. Only when touching the walls did her hand find the gap in the rock to her left. Parting the vines revealed a two yard wide passageway in the rock that headed roughly southeast. Katina pulled the hanging vines to one side and went through.

Behind the wall of vines, the crack in the rock was damp and dark. The floor was strewn with small boulders and rocks, the walls covered in moss and slime. Katina investigated further, carefully walking along the narrow passage. While she thought it broadly continued in a south-easterly direction, the passage turned often. After about a quarter of a mile Katina decided it was time to follow it from the top outside.

The various bushes and vines that obscured the edge of the valley prevented her from finding the beginning of the passage. Katina, however, knew where it started and picked it up a few yards in. The long grass, large boulders, bushes and constant changes in direction made the passage difficult to follow. With care, she was able to track it as far as the trees on the slope of the mountain. As the sun was, by this time, low on the horizon Katina headed back to Hawkyn.

Puppy, in his human boy form, was lying by the fire while Hawkyn prepared the evening meal.

'Did you find anything?' Asked Hawkyn.

'Possibly. I found a hidden gap in the slope of the mountain to our south. It heads off south-east in the direction of outside. I followed it for a while, inside and above until it got to the trees. The horses will have trouble, it is damp narrow and has rocks and boulders in it. However, round the outside of the outcrop at the end of the valley is just not possible.' Said Katina.

'You will have to walk this gap of yours, from end to end and check if we can get the horses through.' Said Hawkyn.

'That will have to wait until tomorrow.' Said Katina.

'Of course.' Replied Hawkyn.

'What did you find Puppy?'

'The Goblins to our north-east carry out extensive patrols, but only for about ten miles or so out from their town. There is another large Goblin town about twenty miles to our south-east, but again they only regularly patrol about ten miles or so out. There appears to be a gap in the middle. We may be able to travel through if we are careful and quick.' Suggested Puppy.

'I will get up first thing, go the full length of this passage and check where it goes.' Said Katina.

'Puppy will go with you to the beginning of the passage, so we know where it is. I will pack up camp. Then we will wait for you this end.' Said Hawkyn.

They all ate a meal of cooked fish and talked, before having an early night. Waking up at first light, they had breakfast, then Katina and Puppy headed off to the beginning of the passage. She went through the hanging vines leaving Puppy to return to Hawkyn.

The floor of the passage soon developed into a small stream, littered with stones and boulders. If she hadn't followed it above ground the night before, she would have lost all sense of direction.

After a good while, tree roots started to protrude from the side. Not enough to prevent progress, but sufficient to impede it. Katina believed she now knew where she was and that progress with the horses through this section was still possible. Eventually a large bush barred her path. Forcing it to one side she stepped through and climbed out of a bank of earth behind a large tree.

Katina looked about. She was in a major forest on the other side of the rocky outcrop that blocked the valley entrance, so climbed a tree to see where she was. Behind her and heading both south and north were a line of mountains. The foothills were in front and each side. There was a glimpse of the plains beyond them.

While climbing back down she carefully looked around to check if anything was in the area. She went back through the bush and returned to the other end of the passage where Hawkyn, Puppy, and the horses were waiting.

'It's going to be damp, muddy and will involve lots of unloading and loading of the horses, but we can get through.' She informed.

Katina took the reins of her reluctant horse and led it into the rocky alcove, pulled aside the hanging vines and after some persuasion, took her horse through. Puppy and his horse followed, with Hawkyn and his entering last.

After about two hundred yards, they reached a point where the width of the passage was too narrow for a horse with packs to get through. They had to unload each of the horses, drag them reluctantly through the narrow gap and load them again afterwards. A process repeated every few hundred yards. They were still a long way from the end of the passage when they lost the last light of the sun. There was no choice but to continue.

'At least we have a full moon on a clear night. This would be impossible if it were cloudy.' Said Katina.

'It's not brilliant now.' Replied a wet muddy sour faced Hawkyn.

Eventually and a long time after the sun had come up, they exited the passage through the bush covering the end. Katina did her best to replace it in the original position and hide any signs of the passing of three loaded horses. Unfortunately, there were still obvious signs of damage, but Katina considered, given a few weeks, the bush would recover. With luck, no one would notice.

'We can't stop, if we're seen here then the Goblins will find the valley and possibly the entrance to the Dwarf caves. We must avoid that.' Said Katina.

'I don't like the idea of continuing without rest, but don't think we have a choice.' Replied Hawkyn. Puppy sighed. Katina looked at him.

'Where do you recommend?'

'I think we're on the edges of the land patrolled by the northern Goblin town. I would suggest a few miles southeast before heading due east.' He replied. They followed Puppy's advice.

Katina was worried. They were looking at a long hard day trying to pass unseen between two large Goblin tribes. That was a challenging task at the best of times. However, they had worked all day and night to get out of the hidden valley. The three of them were all tired, dirty and hungry. The horses were no better. In Katina's thoughts, they had to travel probably thirty miles before the odds of bumping into Goblins reduced and that assumes there isn't another tribe right in front of them after they got through.

What to do? How were they going to safely rest? If they had Freki or Helghyer it would be easy. Pass the job of being lookout over to them and get some sleep. Puppy was far too young and inexperienced for that level of responsibility. Ignoring the fact that being either the dog or the eagle was not his natural form, at best he was a juvenile novice. Yes, he had done great work. Yes, he had fought in some serious combat. He hadn't been in a Goblin war-zone before. It would be too much to expect him to guarantee finding Goblin patrols or combat groups without years of specialised training. Far too much to expect of a child.

'What's wrong?' Asked Hawkyn as they rode through the forest.

'I'm concerned about rest and food. We're all hungry and tired, especially the horses. At most Goblin patrols are only a few miles away. They could probably run us down in less than fifteen minutes. We'd have no time to get away and be far too outnumbered and too tired to fight.' Katina replied.

'We were bound to bump into heaps of Goblins sooner or later.' Added Puppy.

'Travelling over six hundred miles of open wilderness was never going to be easy my love. When the time comes, we will fight regardless of tiredness or hunger.' Replied Hawkyn.

'I know, but it would be better if we can get some rest first.' Said Katina.

'True, but that is not always possible. We fight with what we've got. Our mission is to get home. Between us we'll work out how to do it.' Replied Hawkyn.

'What's the reason for us keeping going rather than having a rest here while there's no one about?' Asked Puppy.

'We don't want to be seen too close to the Dwarf lands. We can't risk the Goblins taking over their caves and producing steel.' Said Hawkyn.

'Why don't we go back into the mountains, but head south rather than between the Goblin settlements and hide out somewhere for a few days.' Suggested Puppy.

'Get cleaned up and rested then go round to the south before heading east.' Said Hawkyn.

'Good idea. Could we get round the other Goblins that way though?' Asked Katina.

'I think so. They are over ten miles out from the mountains on the edge of the foothills.' Responded Puppy.

'That area is unlikely to be heavily patrolled, they would have no reason to, but the route we are currently taking will be. I suggest we try Puppy's idea and maybe we find somewhere to hide out for a day or two.' Said Hawkyn.

They turned round and rode back towards the mountains, but further south from where the hidden valley was. Then continued broadly south through the foothills, on the edge of the mountains for about another five miles.

'I think we go to the next valley and find somewhere to hide.' Suggested Katina. The others nodded, their faces drawn and tired.

In the next valley where the hill met the lower slopes of a mountain, there were plenty of small groups of trees and no signs of habitation. A little further on the slopes of the mountain and they came across a small grassy field with a stream in it, hidden in some trees. Katina got off her horse, handed the reins to Hawkyn, then had a good look round the clearing.

'There's no signs that anyone has been this way. The trees to our east should conceal our presence to anyone outside the clearing. The hills and trees supply shelter and the stream water. This should do for a few days, or at least until we are rested.' She said.

'This is the best we are going to get I think. We should make camp nearer to the trees and keep the fire small. That should minimise the risk of being seen.' Said Hawkyn.

'I agree.' Replied Katina. They set up camp quickly and ate a meal of cooked fish from the lake in the hidden valley. Puppy refilled the water skins and watered the horses. They agreed the watch shifts for the night with Hawkyn taking first watch. Several hours before dawn, Puppy woke Katina.

'Your turn.' He said quietly. 'A pack of wolves checked us out, then went away. Other than that, nothing.'

'Thank you.' She replied. 'Now go get some sleep yourself.' He curled up by the remains of the fire.

Katina got up, stretched, then with sword belted to her waist, quiver of arrows over her shoulder, and bow in hand, went for a look around. She didn't go far from the camp, just far enough to get the feel for the place. No more than a few hundred yards. She took a spot a bit away from the camp and settled down to watch the area while the others and the horses slept. Dawn came and went and everyone else remained asleep. Katina let them sleep, stirred up the fire and prepared breakfast. That did the job of waking Hawkyn and Puppy.

'Good morning. Tea?' She asked.

'Yes please.' Replied Hawkyn. Katina handed him a mug of hot tea.

'What do you think for today, keep going or look about first?' Asked Katina.

'The horses look very tired.' Added Puppy.

'Currently the Goblins don't know we're in the area. The longer we are this close to their lands, the higher the risk of discovery. If we're found here, then we'll be trapped.' Replied Hawkyn.

Katina looked at the horses. Despite a night's rest, good grazing and a stream, their heads still drooped and their hooves dragged. Puppy was right, the horses were exhausted. Unfortunately, so was Hawkyn. There was no choice.

'Alright, I will go scout ahead. You pack up camp and follow me leading the horses. Let's see if we can't get a few more miles or perhaps a couple of valleys further down. Puppy, where's this Goblin town?' Said Katina.

'That way about ten miles.' Said Puppy pointing east south-east.

'Alright, that's good enough. I'll go south on a line a bit east of here. You follow, but closer to the mountains. I'll come back and check occasionally.' Replied Katina.

She packed away her gear on her horse, checked her sword, bow, quiver and dagger, then headed eastwards into the forest at a slow run.

There was plenty of space between the trees and bushes of the wooded valley, making travel a lot quicker. Slowly she climbed to the crest of the hill, then ran along it. To her dismay she needed to concentrate on her woodland craft or leave signs of her passing, but then again, it had been a while. There were no signs of anything other than wild animals.

Quite quickly Katina was some four or five miles away from the others and decided this was far enough. A large rock stood on the crest of the hill. Keeping a low profile, she climbed it and looked at the valley below. A group of Goblins were hunting several wild boar.

Some of them were a little way up the valley making lots of noise shouting and banging sticks. Further east was half a dozen or so others in a spread-out line holding spears. Katina nodded to herself. It is how her tribe did it. The family group of wild boar charged the line of spearmen. Four bigger ones were in the front with the piglets running behind as fast as they could. Katina heard a command shouted and to her surprise the Goblins stood aside for one of the bigger ones and the piglets to go through. They went for the other three though. Two of the spears were true, but the third one snapped on impact with the boar. The two tusks of the boar hit the unfortunate spearman in the stomach. With a scream the Goblin went flying hitting his head on a tree when landing some yards away. The boar kept going. The other Goblins repeatedly stabbed the two speared boar.

Well, it happens if you are unlucky. Anybody can suffer a weapon breaking at an inopportune time, that's why being a hunter is dangerous, Katina thought.

The Goblin giving the orders went over to the unfortunate one who had suffered the broken spear. After checking over the crumpled heap's head and stomach, plunged a dagger into its chest.

Katina sighed, sometimes that is necessary after two boar tusks to the stomach. She had no care for Goblins but had understanding for someone having a very bad day. She watched as the other Goblins picked up the two dead boar, retrieved a litter that had been laying unseen on the grass, put the boar on it and headed back east taking the litter with them.

Katina stayed put a while and watched them leave. Then keeping out of sight went to the Goblin left behind. The stomach wound was severe, he probably would not have survived. Katina left him and did a slow run up the hill on the other side of the valley. Beyond it was another valley, with more Goblins hunting food. This time it appeared to be rabbits and wild fowl. She ducked back behind the crest of the hill and watched them hunt. When they had filled their litter, they left also. Katina then ran back up the valley towards the mountains hoping to see the others as they headed south. There were no signs of anyone passing, so finding a convenient spot that had an all-round view, waited.

A good while later, Hawkyn and Puppy appeared leading the three horses along the slopes of the mountain. She went to them.

'Hello.'

'Hi.' Replied Hawkyn.

'You should know that these valleys are used by the Goblins for hunting. I saw one team hunt wild boar in the last valley and in this one, wildfowl and rabbit. They were in the eastern end and both teams left before coming very far up the valley. We are going to have to be careful though.' Said Katina.

'Why don't you cross into the next valley and then check it out. We'll continue to walk the horses today across to that valley and find a place for the night's camp.' Said Hawkyn.

'Sure.' She replied and headed off.

The next valley along was far more open. A mountain stream meandered its way down the middle of the valley which was perhaps three miles wide. The predominant grazing animals appeared to be sheep in the valley and goats nearer the mountain.

She ran eastwards along the ridge line checking for any more hunter teams but saw none, so she went into the valley itself. Katina found Goblin tracks near the stream.

So, they hunt here too she thought and went back to the others.

'Hi. I think we are going to have to move on a bit further, this is far too exposed. While they are not here now, Goblins have been at the other end of the valley.' Said Katina.

'Yes, we should move on.' Replied Hawkyn. They continued south towards the next valley.

What they found was that the hill ridge line dropped before it reached the slopes of the mountain to their west. This left an area obscured from the east where the Goblins were.

'I think we have found our spot for the night.' Suggested Hawkyn.

'It doesn't look like there will be anything better for some time.' Said Katina. They set up camp, stayed the night and set off shortly after first light, being careful to remove as much trace as possible of anyone being there.

They crossed several more valleys of grassland before deciding to try heading east again. This time there was a forest with a wide variety of trees in it heading down the valley and possibly beyond. They crossed through the uphill end of the forest. The first thing that Katina noticed was that the hills stopped running out from the slopes of the mountains but started to run parallel to them. Trees covered the entire area.

'If we go a decent way into that forest, we should be able to pass through undetected.' Suggested Hawkyn.

'So long as we can keep our sense of direction.' Said Katina.

'No problem, I'll just go have a look where the sun is occasionally.' Added Puppy.

They continued south into the edges of the forest for a way, then headed south-east. While the forest was wild and unmanaged, it wasn't particularly overgrown, so they travelled quickly stopping for the night in a small clearing deep in the forest and many miles from where they had entered.

Being on the last watch, the following morning at dawn, she packed away her bed role and poked the fire into life. Everything was dead quiet. No birds or other forest sounds. It felt very wrong. She woke Hawkyn quietly putting her hand over his mouth. His eyes said he understood. She belted on her sword, slung her quiver of arrows over her shoulder and holding her bow with arrow nocked ran quietly into the forest.

After about a hundred yards she stopped, crouching behind a tree. Within seconds, Puppy in his juvenile hunting dog form was a few trees to her right. There was a slight noise behind her, of Hawkyn entering the forest to her left. There were also noises further into the forest. She crept forward to the next tree in front and peered round. A group of Goblins to her front with no scouts out were talking to each other. Puppy had also gone forward several trees and was a bit further away. Hawkyn at this point just stayed still, hiding behind a tree, arrow nocked and bow partially drawn. Wise, she thought. Hawkyn was a warrior and not as adept at the silent approach as the trained hunter scouts were.

Puppy was looking somewhere else further out. Katina quietly looked in that direction. Another group of Goblins. Oh dear, that's a lot for just the three of them. No chance of getting away unseen and they are bound to find the camp if they go forward any further. There was only one choice. She stood up while staying behind her tree and slowly drew her bow. Hawkyn had done the same. Puppy was shaking his head. She sighed quietly and eased the draw on her bow. Hawkyn did the same.

The Goblins still oblivious to their surroundings now approached thirty paces away. Puppy was still shaking his head. He was looking deeper into the forest. Katina knew the Goblins would see her if she looked.

Then there was the sound of tearing flesh and a scream, followed within a second by several others. More Goblin shouts and the sounds of running feet followed. Katina risked a peak and edged round the tree. A pack of Great Wolves had attacked the group of Goblins near Puppy and had taken several down. Three great wolves were amongst the twenty or so Goblins still standing. At first, she thought the wolves were in trouble, then half a dozen or so more who had circled around behind the Goblins attacked. They put down six more Goblins, the remaining ones just fled, chased by some of the wolves.

Two of the wolves stayed behind and looked directly at Katina. She slowly removed the arrow from her bow and put it back in her quiver. They continued to stare.

'We're just passing through heading to our home back east. We live near the range of the pack run by one of your kind known as Geri. We understand we are a long way from our home. We will not be staying in your range long. I hope that is acceptable.' Katina said to the largest wolf.

'I don't think they understand our language, they're just animals, not like Freki.' Said Hawkyn.

The two Great Wolves just stared at him with stern faces.

'Well, that's me told.' Hawkyn added.

The wolf then looked at Katina then gazed into the forest in a specific direction.

'We go that way then?' Said Katina.

Bark.

'Thank you.' She replied. The two wolves disappeared into the trees.

'They're huge.' Said an amazed Puppy.

'Yes. We call them Great Wolves. One of my friends we left in the valley runs with one called Freki. They can pretty much fully communicate with each other. The wolves seem to understand our language and respond by barks and growls. If you phrase the question correctly, you can get a lot of information from them.' Said Katina.

'They don't like Goblins.' Added Hawkyn.

'I gathered.' Replied Puppy.

'Time for us to pack up and move on.' Said Hawkyn.

'It seems so.' Replied Katina. They returned to camp, ate breakfast, packed up and followed the directions given. Katina considered the prevalence of Goblins this far out and the absence of birds and animals. She was missing something, but the question was, what.

18 – THE THIN LINE

They continued through the forest in the direction recommended by the Great Wolves. Although they didn't see them again, the occasional dead Goblin or two in various stages of decay made it obvious who owned this part of the forest.

At the end of the day, they came across a small clearing, so stopped for the night. Hawkyn set up the camp and fire, while Katina went looking for deadwood and dinner. Puppy had a scout round. An hour or so later and they were all sat in front of the fire eating cooked wildfowl.

'May I ask a few questions please?' Said Puppy.

'Of course.' Replied Katina.

'Two things really. When you first met me, you started to teach me how to hunt. That basic knowledge has been very useful, but we haven't done any more of that lately. I am wondering, given one of my forms is human, could you continue to teach me some skills. It would enable me to be helpful in your society and fit in better. I would also like to learn how to use a sword and bow.' Asked Puppy.

'Certainly, we can continue training and instruct you in relevant wood-craft and hunting skills. We can begin to teach you bow and sword, but your human form is quite small, you will need to be bigger and stronger before you can be taught properly.' Said Hawkyn.

'We are also behind on our own fitness and practice. Sitting on a horse all day doesn't do us any good either.' Said Katina.

'We could return to running and leading the horses. Perhaps practice and exercise for half an hour after breakfast each day.' Suggested Hawkyn.

'And the other thing.' Said Katina.

'Well, you live in this area don't you. A long way east, but this area between the western and northern mountain ranges.' Said Puppy.

'Yes, in a very broad sense.' Said Katina.

'I was wondering how much you know about where the Goblins are around here. I've listened to Hawkyn talk strategically and wonder if that information would be useful.' Said Puppy.

'When I fly, I can look a good way beyond the immediate area. I should be able to look roughly thirty miles away without much difficulty. Finding activity and settlements themselves should be easy enough to achieve without much risk.' He continued.

'That knowledge would help the tribes a great deal. Where the never-ending stream of Goblin tribes come from is something that we have always assumed, we've never actually looked. It would allow some strategic planning back home.'

'So, we start Puppy's wilderness education tomorrow morning then?' Said Katina.

'I think so. If he were of our tribe, he would be starting now anyway.' Said Hawkyn.

'So, tomorrow morning it is then. That alright with you Puppy?' Said Katina.

'Yes of course.' He replied.

'Great. Time, I think I got on with sorting out those arrows we got from the Elves.' Said Katina as she went to one of the packs, pulled out some of the elven arrows, a sharpening stone and a cloth. Then sitting by the fire started to clean the muck and dirt off the arrows and remove the dilapidated fletching.

'They look shorter than your arrows.' Observed Puppy.

'They are. Our bows are what's called high poundage long bows. The arrows are a lot longer so you can draw the bow back more. Those arrows will travel a lot further and penetrate the target a lot deeper. Elven bows do not seem so powerful, probably because Elves are shorter than we are and don't have the arm length to draw the bow as far.' Said Katina.

'The Elven arrows are special?' Asked Puppy.

'Yes. They appear to have divine magic on them and can harm creatures that normal weapons can't. I don't have any others that can do that, so I must clean and repair them.' Said Katina. She started her scrubbing and cleaning the arrows while Hawkyn grabbed two stout sticks and started to teach Puppy the basics of sword use.

After an hour or so of working on the arrows, Katina, feeling increasingly jumpy, went for a scout around the area. Firstly, a complete circuit a quarter mile out, then another at a half mile, then back to camp. She took the first watch as there was no sleep in her anyway. Back against a tree a bit away from the others Katina considered her mood. They were missing something very important, but for the life of her, couldn't work out what it was. Eventually, it was Hawkyn's turn, so she woke him and tried to get some sleep herself.

After breakfast the next day, Katina took Puppy scouting and started to show him the tracks of various animals. They did this each morning. There were sheep, boar, wolves, and a few others. Each time she showed him a few occurrences of the chosen animal and then told him to find others. As the days went on, he started to recognise tracks on his own. He learned the rudiments of scouting ahead and hiding, in addition to finding food. Recognising edible plants took longer. They covered types of trees and bushes as they went on through the day. Then one morning.

'What is that? A five clawed foot about the size of your feet.' Said Puppy. Katina went straight over and started swearing.

'Of course. I'm a dumb twit.' She said followed by more swear words.

Puppy looked puzzled as Katina examined the tracks more closely.

'We'd better go back to Hawkyn. Life just got

interesting.' She continued. So, they returned to the night's camp.

'Hawkyn, we have a problem, Plains Devils.'

'It was bound to happen sooner or later. We are in enemy territory.' He replied.

'Unfortunately, they have been near us for some time. Since the meeting with the wolves, I think.'

'Why. If they were, they would have attacked by now.'

'I can't say why they haven't attacked, but Puppy found tracks and we have had a distinct lack of wildlife about for ages.'

'Surely, that is the wolves.'

'Maybe. That is what I thought, but we have tracks less than a day old.' Said Katina.

'How do you know that?' Asked Puppy.

'Over time, the tracks degrade and things like twigs and leaves fall into them. They haven't been around for long.'

'So, do we find them? Hunt them ourselves?' Asked Puppy.

'They usually operate in squads of ten and are far better at combat than Goblins. It would be too much for Katina and me.' Said Hawkyn.

'So, what are the options?' Asked Puppy.

'I've never known it, but a scout could be out on his own. That we could handle.' Said Katina.

'If we move on from a squad or individual without taking them out, what happens?' Asked Puppy.

'We get followed if they find our tracks.' Said Hawkyn.

'We are assuming they are actually after us. They may not be.' Said Katina.

'So, what's the plan?' Asked Puppy.

Hawkyn and Katina looked at each other for a few seconds. 'We sneak away. If they follow, we will know it's us they are hunting.' Suggested Katina.

They packed up camp carefully and quickly. Katina then went to the effort of removing all the traces of their presence.

'Not that way. Go towards the birdsong and away from the footprint. We can head east later.' Said Katina.

They travelled in a north easterly direction for a while then went back to heading east. Katina and Puppy took it in turns scouting ahead. After one such trip Puppy came back and said. 'No bird noise ahead.'

So, they turned south for a while, then south-east, then back to heading east. As they were progressing through the endless forest something caught Katina's eye.

'Stop. Don't put your foot down.' She shouted. Hawkyn froze.

Giving the reins of her horse to Puppy, Katina went forward to Hawkyn who was still standing on one leg, his right leg suspended in mid-air while holding on to his horse. She took hold of his right leg and placed it on the ground as far back as it would go. Then grabbed the left leg lifted it and moved it backwards, placing it on the ground next to his right leg.

Hawkyn just looked at her with a straight face and didn't move.

'What was all that about?' Asked Puppy.

Katina picked up a sturdy fallen piece of branch nearby and poked it at a pile of leaves lying on the ground where Hawkyn was going to put his right foot. There was a loud clang as two serrated semi-circular iron jaws snapped shut severing the end of the piece of wood.

She looked at Hawkyn and Puppy. 'This is a man trap. We are being hunted.' Katina said.

'That's pretty specific. How did they know we would be here?' Asked Hawkyn.

'I don't know.' Replied Katina.

'Perhaps they are looking for someone or something else in the area and we just happened to come across it.' Said Hawkyn.

'Either way, I will have to go first and we will need to be

extra vigilant.' Said Katina.

The pace slowed to allow time for Katina's increased observance. Just as she was going to say it was all over, she found a covered-up hole with spikes in it.

'This is going to be annoying.' Commented Hawkyn.

'It is. Any suggestions?' Said Katina.

'Would changing direction help?' Asked Puppy.

'We've been going southeast for some time and should be well past that other Goblin town by now. We could head due North for a while. It would bring us closer to the right direction anyway.' Suggested Hawkyn.

'We need to be unpredictable. If they are tracking something else, then going a different direction may help. If traps still turn up, then we will know somehow they have the drop on us.' Said Katina.

They went round the spiked pit and continued southeast for several miles, then turned north. Katina searched long and hard with Hawkyn leading her horse as well as his own. There were no signs of any further traps or suspicious tracks. After a long day, they found a clearing and made camp for the night.

Katina had the midnight watch and as was her custom she stayed away from the fire, keeping a lookout from a distance. About an hour later she heard Goblins talking. Damn she thought and staying hidden silently ran into the trees while readying her bow. They were a hundred yards or so into the forest south-west of where her sleeping friends were. Keeping herself well hidden behind a large bush, she saw the Goblins and listened.

There were just two of them having a heated discussion which was only marginally short of an actual fight. She couldn't understand Goblin, but got the general idea from the shouting, arm and hand movements, that one wanted to keep going, taking them straight into the camp, but the other, wanted to head north-west, roughly Katina imagined in the direction of one of the Goblin towns. Where were the others in their squad? She thought. Perhaps they had become separated from each other or fell afoul of the local pack of giant wolves.

The one who wanted to go home appeared to be trying to explain his idea more calmly now and was struggling to convince the other to relax and think about things. After some time, the other Goblin appeared to agree to go home. They turned and headed off north-west. Katina considered following them but decided against it as her friends would be unprotected. Instead, she shadowed their path placing herself between them and the camp.

After about fifteen minutes she returned to her original shady tree vantage point. To her amazement there was a dark grey haired Great Wolf lying on her spot. It looked at her most sternly, got up and wandered off. Well, that's me told she thought. The wolf clearly considered her investigation had gone too far from the camp.

The rest of her shift passed without issue. Katina wondered, as she woke Puppy, whether that was because no one was around, or because the Great Wolves were. Either way it was a quiet watch. In the morning, the human form of Puppy had re-awakened the fire and was making some tea.

'Good morning, Katina. I stood watch in my dog form and got visited.' Said Puppy. Katina who figured she knew what was coming, just nodded.

'A huge dark grey wolf came over. Apparently, you wandered off during watch. He was not impressed. Gave me extensive advice on doing one's job properly, regardless of what two legs says.' Puppy continued.

'I don't know what to be more surprised about, Katina apparently leaving her post, or you Puppy being able to speak to wolves.' Said Hawkyn.

Puppy got in first. 'Because one of my forms is a dog, I can speak dog. Wolf is very similar but more advanced. I got the gist of it.'

'As for me, I heard Goblins approaching the camp and went a little way into the forest to check things out before waking everyone up. There were only two who appeared lost. They headed off north-west after a heated discussion. The dark grey wolf showed himself to me and made it clear he did not approve of my choice of action.' Said Katina.

'His opinion has merit.' Observed Hawkyn.

'I know, but if we all had engaged, the Goblins would be dead and our presence would be known.' She replied. Hawkyn just nodded and let it go at that.

'I have missed something I probably should understand.' Said Puppy.

'As you are young, you will not have experience of working with others in hostile situations.' Said Hawkyn.

'Until I met you, no, but we've come a long way and I have learnt loads.' Puppy replied.

'In terms of skills yes, but it is also important to learn how to act within your group. One of the first things to learn is that you must trust the others in your group. Each of us, daily, makes decisions on things that could affect the lives of the others. If we are to survive this enormous journey, we each must trust, respect and accept the decisions of the other two. Anything else will kill us.' Said Hawkyn.

Katina looked at Hawkyn's face and concluded that he did not like her actions but was not going to say anything. She would not say anything either. That would not be helpful. Had she made a wrong decision? Perhaps. She had assumed the two Goblins were the only ones in the area. Given the presence of the wolf that was clearly wrong. She was losing her edge and would have to attend to that.

Katina continued to think while they packed up camp. Once they were on their way again 'Hawkyn, I've concluded that I am losing my edge. I will have to spend more time hunting and tracking.' She said.

'Do not read too much into one issue this morning,

which didn't actually go wrong.' He replied with a smile.

'Maybe, but what we do know is that we are being shadowed by Giant Wolves and I didn't see those at all.'

'I wouldn't be too hard on yourself about that either, they are incredibly skilled and perfect hunters.' Replied Hawkyn.

'He's right Katina. I can see invisible and magically hidden things in any light. I didn't know the wolf was there until it tapped me on the leg.' Said Puppy.

Katina was unhappy with herself but had to admit the two of them had a point. There were limits to what anyone was capable of. Despite that she strongly believed she needed to do better if they were to make it back home.

They continued northwards for another day, then turned east. It was slow going as Katina had to continually keep an eye out for traps or snares. They found several, but no trace of anything following them. She still couldn't find where the Great Wolves had gone.

While Puppy got some combat training the following morning, she scouted the area. At first, when a fair distance away from the camp Katina found some footprints of Goblins. Then she noticed the departing of animal and birdsong. So, she thought, Plains Devils were entering the area and hid herself behind a large tree. Looking around saw nothing and decided to go hunting.

Paying special attention to her craft, Katina silently advanced several trees into the rough area the creature might be. Using the thick undergrowth and a variety of large and misshapen trees, Katina was able to progress further forward to where there was no animal noise or bird song. Now she waited for several minutes in the unnatural silence of an ancient forest. She even controlled her breathing. Slowly and silently, Katina prepared herself to fight this enemy alone and readied her bow.

Eventually, coming slowly through the woods, constantly looking at the ground and bushes was an eagle headed six and a half feet tall reptilian creature armed with a short bow, scimitar and dagger. That was her Plains Devil. Question was, were there anymore? She thoroughly looked at the surrounding area. No signs of any others, so lifted her bow and took careful aim.

The creature now approached fifty paces then stopped, ducked down and unslung its bow from over its shoulder. While it did so, the Plains Devil's reptilian skin blended into the background, although there were still signs. She saw the ripples in the appearance of the trees and bushes of the forest as her opponent changed position. There seemed to be movement of limbs and perhaps a slow movement of the head. Then a sudden movement as an arrow hit the tree next to her.

Katina held her nerve and waited for her ideal chance. Patience she thought. Barely breathing and with only the slightest of movements she kept her aim on the Plains Devil while keeping the leafy evergreen bush between her and her quarry. Slowly she exhaled, held a second then released her arrow. Good straight and true, right where she aimed it, the neck. There was a gurgling cry and her foe fell to the ground.

She mustn't leave any evidence, so went forward and retrieved her arrow. Then in the customary style, beheaded the creature to avoid the risk of it coming back to life. On its belt was a pouch with several silver coins in it and some others. She took those but left everything else before trying to remove traces of her presence. It was not perfect but concluded the deception by heading off south rather than to the west. After going a fair way Katina circled back to the camp.

'Hi. Got some bad news.' Katina said as she entered the clearing.

'Oh?' Replied Hawkyn.

'Just killed a Plains Devil scout to our east. On his own and had some silver coins on him. There must be a major settlement around here for that.' She said.

'So, we keep going north for a while.' Said Hawkyn.

'And hide our camps better. Probably no fires.' Katina replied.

'Do you want me to have a look around in bird form?' Asked Puppy.

'It's a thought.' Said Hawkyn.

'But a dangerous one. He's not Helghyer and they may have access to dark magic.' Said Katina.

'If there's a major settlement in the area, then we must know. Because of what I am, magic of any sort, dark or otherwise, doesn't really affect me that much. And who's Helghyer?' Said Puppy.

'Helghyer is a huge Gyrfalcon that is somehow linked with another hunter that stayed in the valley we told you about. She's now a priestess of the goddess The Huntress, well a spell casting Initiate at any rate.' Said Katina.

'Oh. My mum told me about this. A few of the old Lord Priests and Lord Guardians used to get allocated some kind of special spirit that could be put in an animal to help them. I can't remember much about it. From what mum said, it's not a good idea to get on the wrong side of one of those. They were former living Lord Priests or Lord Guardians and kept spell-casting and combat knowledge. Very dangerous.' Replied Puppy.

'I just thought they were a spirit from your chosen god.' Said Hawkyn.

'They are, but without fail they were all high ranking people in their former life and maintain all their knowledge. Also, the god set up a full mind link with the worshipper to whom were allocated. I don't know much more as I didn't really pay attention. Anyway, do you want me to go look about. I will keep my distance and fly high.' Said Puppy.

Katina thought about it and the more she did so, the more it made sense. 'It's risky and I don't like it, but we must have some knowledge of what is about.' Said Katina. 'What do you think Hawkyn?'

'I don't see there's much choice. If you spot Plains Devils, come back. Katina and I could probably handle a squad of Goblins, but not Plains Devils. We would have to run and hide from those if we get the time.' Said Hawkyn.

Puppy changed into his juvenile eagle form and took to the air. Hawkyn and Katina hid the remains of the campfire and removed other signs such as the small pile of food waste. Usually, they would have continued in their chosen direction, but this time they did not, they just waited. After what Katina thought was about an hour, Puppy returned and changed into his boy form before he even touched the ground.

'Difficult to see these Plains Devils of yours aren't they. Fortunately, I have better eyesight than you do. About five miles east of here is a line of these things running for about ten miles, one every half mile or so with another line nearer. That nearer line has a hole in it though.' Said Puppy.

'That hole will be the one I killed earlier.' Said Katina.

'About ten miles south-west is a group of mixed races, slowly heading in this direction.' Said Puppy.

'We're being herded.' Suggested Katina.

'To a group they believe can take us out.' Added Hawkyn.

'Or rather, take out whatever it is that's being hunted. They may not be looking for us. As far as we are aware, they don't know we are here. Puppy, did you see anyone else?' Said Katina.

'No, I didn't. However, once I found the hunting party I came back. I didn't think I had the time to spend looking for more before the hunters turned up.' Replied Puppy.

'He's probably right Katina.' Said Hawkyn.

'I agree, two or three miles won't take long to cover even when searching. The closer line is probably already nearly on us. No more than a mile away.' Said Katina.

'So, our options are to run north-west or fight our way through the east lines. Thoughts?' Said Hawkyn.

'If we go north-west, we will end up being trapped by vastly superior numbers against mountains we can't cross. Widen the hole in the front line and take one out in the next should give us enough space to get through though. We'll have to go like the clappers afterwards to get some distance between us.' Said Katina.

They travelled north a little way to get as far away as possible from the hunter group, then Katina handed the reins of her horse to Hawkyn and ran off to the east. It took a few changes in direction to work out roughly where the nearest Plains Devil to the one she had already killed was. Then slowly she advanced tree to tree and bush to bush ever forwards.

After about ten minutes, she heard noises. The sound of a stick hitting bushes. Keeping low to the ground and being careful not to even break a twig, Katina continued forwards while readying her bow. With arrow nocked and bow partially drawn she advanced silently, slowly closing on her chosen prey. The next tree had a convenient hollow in the ground just before it. Sitting in that Katina waited. The only noise was the ever-closing crash of large stick against bush. No sound of the others, they should be to her south just now.

Looking from her hole Katina could see distorted shapes of background bushes and trees that moved forwards through the forest. Aiming carefully for the large head, or at least where it appeared to be, she fully drew her bow and released the arrow. It went straight past and into a bush behind the creature. Damn that wasn't the head Katina thought.

Her adversary spun round and jumped to the bush. Drawing its scimitar, it vigorously attacked the bush. Oh well, Katina thought, perfect target. Her second arrow didn't miss, straight into the back of the head. The Plains

Devil went down with a groan. She ran over, pulled her arrow out of its head and seeing her first one recovered that too. Then decapitated the creature, took its pouch of silver coins and headed east.

Hearing horses to her southwest she ran quickly southeast to put her ahead of Hawkyn and Puppy, remembering that the next line was nearby. After about a mile Katina slowed down and started to be cautious despite the abundant sounds of the forest and continued eastwards.

As the forest sounds decreased, Katina crept forward quietly, again taking exceptional care. Hearing noise ahead of her, she crouched behind a tree and waited. This time though there were several noises, possibly three. There would be no quick silent kill and be gone for these ones. She readied her bow and moved round to their flank going from tree to tree giving them no direct line of sight to her. They were not using their camouflage skin. Two were talking and one keeping watch ahead as they advanced.

She was side on, took aim and released her arrow. It went straight into the watch keeping one's side. He spun as he fell and lay on the ground groaning. The other two crouched and stared into the forest around them. Quickly they readied their bows and one released an arrow into the bush a yard to her right. A young deer fell forwards with a squeal followed by a swear word from the archer. Crouching low and hidden, she carefully watched her prey as they scanned the area for the enemy they knew was there.

As one was looking elsewhere the other looked down at the groaning Plains Devil on the floor. She released another arrow and again achieved a hit in the stomach. It too fell groaning. The last one jumped up and drawing its scimitar ran directly at her. Katina dropped her bow, drew her sword and ran towards her attacker. Then a loud noise came from the trees above, followed by a whooshing sound. The top half of the Plains Devil vanished, its sword falling to the ground and a wriggling pair of legs flew up to the sky, disappearing over the treetops.

She quickly dispatched the two wounded Plains Devils, retrieved her bow and arrows, grabbed two pouches of silver coins and headed to the sound of approaching horses. Hawkyn was pulling all three of them.

'Where's Puppy?' She asked.

'He went off to find you.' He replied.

'Hmm. For the second hit, there were three of them. I put the first two down, then the third one's top half disappeared and his legs flew off above the trees.'

'Oh. Wonder what happened there.' Said Hawkyn.

Katina mounted her horse and they rode eastwards. A few minutes later Puppy stepped out from behind a tree. As he got on his horse Katina asked.

'Puppy, was that third Plains Devil you?'

'Yes.'

'What did you do?' She asked.

'I ate him. Wouldn't recommend it, they taste disgusting, even worse than Goblins.' He replied as they cantered off through the forest.

19 – MR. A. FARMER

They rode on east at as fast a speed as they could manage in a forest, covering many miles quickly. Katina was worried though, the area showed increasing signs of maintenance and travel. She called a halt.

'This part of the forest is regularly used. There's a settlement near here, probably a major one.'

'It will be quite close. People don't usually go that far into the woods apart from hunters like yourself.' Replied Hawkyn.

'We're going to have to try and get through. Let's keep going and see what we can find out, then work out how to get past it.' Said Katina.

The group rode on, but at a slower pace. Half an hour later and Katina could see a stone walled city in the distance from the edge of the forest. In the foreground Humans were working on the farms but overseen by Goblins.

'So, do they look like slaves or regular free farmers?' Said Hawkyn.

'Bit of both to my eyes. All are definitely being watched by Goblins though.' Said Katina.

'Some Humans appear to travel to the city unguarded. Do we try and bluff our way through?' Asked Hawkyn.

'I don't think we have the space to go round the edge of the forest.' Observed Katina.

'I don't like this.' Said Hawkyn.

'Neither do I.' Replied Katina.

They headed around the forest towards a stone building on the edge of the nearest farm. Katina watched carefully, only making a run for it when the supervising Goblins were looking to the fields rather than where they were, then dismounting at the hidden side of the barn. Katina looked through a back window. Inside had a cart, several horses and stalls, a good number of large sacks full of something, tools, barrels and a large trough.

'It's a fully kitted out barn.' She told the others.

Hoping no one noticed them, the three walked the horses around to the front of the barn and entered straight away, closing the large door as soon as they were in. Hawkyn quickly tasted the water in the trough and nodded. They let the horses drink. Puppy changed into his dog form.

The barn door creaked and opened slightly. Hawkyn and Katina both spun round drawing swords. A dishevelled muddy middle-aged farmer, a bit less than six feet tall with greying hair stepped through and shut the door quickly.

'What the hell are you doing here?' Then looked at them as they advanced towards him. 'Better still don't tell me, I might live longer that way. No please don't kill me. You are too well equipped and far too healthy to be resident here. I know what you are, I've heard stories. You are either passing through or here to kill someone. There's no way you will get into the city looking like that. You appear fitter and better equipped than even the Goblins' best warriors and I'd imagine those devil spawn things too. I really don't want to know what you are up to or who's side you are on. And I certainly don't want to give my name. Let's try and get away with "A Farmer".'

'Well, "Mr. A Farmer", let's just leave it at passing through shall we. Better for everyone.' Said Katina.

'Fine by me.' Replied the farmer. 'In case you don't know, there are three ranks of Humans. Slaves, The Free who are little better than slaves, and The Informers who actively do the work of our Goblin lords. I am the latter. I chose this so I can run my own farm and better support my family and slaves. I am aware that your kind would kill my family, with about as much emotion as squashing an ant.'

'He talks very fast doesn't he.' Hawkyn observed looking at Katina. 'We kill all those who worship the Evil Lord.' Hawkyn continued.

'Then in return for you not killing my family, I will help

you get through the city. Do we have a deal?' Asked the farmer. Hawkyn just looked at Katina while she thought. They could kill him now, but then the fact that warriors from elsewhere were here would be known. Best to play along for now then kill him later.

'Alright we will agree.' Said Katina.

'I have a brother on the other side of the city. I can say I am taking him seed grain and tools. Mostly, that should do. There's no way you will get through looking like that. Those swords are a real give away, as is your height. Not even the best of our warriors use swords like that and you are a good foot taller than most of us Humans here. Hooded cloaks and stooping, together with hiding those huge swords in my cart might work if they don't search us. Concealing that chain mail will also be necessary.'

They helped the farmer load the cart with bags of grain and a box of tools. Hawkyn put the box of swords from the Dwarves as well as Katina's and Hawkyn's own swords on the cart also. They loaded extra bags of grain onto their own horses. Puppy in his dog form just stayed quiet and out of the way. Katina sat hunched on the front seat of the cart next to the farmer. Both her and Hawkyn's bows and quivers of arrows were put on the cart under a canvas near her. Hawkyn, who had secured the three horses in a line attached to the back of the cart, opened the barn door and they all left.

The farmer took them down a hard earth track with hedged fields full of ripening wheat or corn on either side. Within a mile a group of Goblins stopped them at a crossroads. Katina kept her hunched stance but had her hand inside her cloak on her broad long bladed dagger.

'Where are you going?' The Goblin leader said in a rough aggressive voice.

'Kind master, I am taking some seed grain and tools to my brother's farm on the eastern side, third district.'

'Who are these?' Pointing to Katina and Hawkyn.

'Two of my strongest workers. The grain bags are heavy.' The Goblin looked at the cart and horses laden with bags of grain and waived them through. The group turned right towards the city and slowly continued their way.

'Well done.' Katina said quietly. The farmer nodded an acknowledgement.

About a mile later Katina began to feel distinctly odd. She couldn't put her finger on what was wrong and gently put her hand behind her onto the cart's heavy canvas covering. Puppy, lying asleep on the canvas, gave her hand a gentle nip. Good, he understood. She looked about passing her gaze over Hawkyn and saw that he had untied his cloak, but held it closed.

A group of riders approached from behind and rode past both sides of the cart. At first it seemed that the ten heavily cloaked riders would continue without bothering them, however a little way up the road, the leader stopped turned his large black stallion around and walked back. He threw back his hood and opened his heavy cloak as he approached.

Katina desperately tried to keep control of her emotions, but what she saw surprised her. The face was almost identical to Arturous but appeared a little older and not quite as tall. The skin rather than having Arturous' green tinge to it had a grey tinge instead. He wore light weight black enamelled chain mail armour and two slender long swords. The only noticeable difference was he had no bow and quiver of arrows over the shoulder. He did however seem to exude a sense of overwhelming evil. The others in the group had returned now as well. Cloaks open ready for combat. They were warrior Plains Devils and fully armed. Katina glanced at the farmer driving the cart expecting to see a gibbering wreck, however he was cool, calm and unafraid.

'Farmer, have you seen any strangers today? They are wanted for the deaths of several overseer guards.

'No master. We have only seen the Goblin guards at the crossroads a bit back. There has been no one else since leaving the farm.' Replied the farmer. Katina thought this answer was rather clever because it was actually true.

The grey tinged elf looked the group over, then replaced the hood of his cloak over his head, wheeled his horse and rode off towards the city. His subordinates turned and followed.

'Thankfully, we've only got one of those.' Said the farmer.

'He was quite something and you were not frightened at all. I am impressed master farmer.' Said Katina.

'I wasn't always a farmer. While some things do frighten me, those don't.'

Katina considered that this farmer was more than he seemed, then thought.

'I wish I could tell Hawkyn all this.'

'Relax, he's worked most of it out for himself already and so has your dragon.' Replied The Huntress.

'I'm not looking forward to fighting an evil version of Arturous very much.' Replied Katina.

'We aren't keen on that either. I must go now, or the priests will sense me. Careful what you think here, you are very close to some of their religious centres. Call on one of us by accident and you will stand out to a black priest like a fire beacon.' And with that The Huntress was gone.

They continued towards the city, which Katina could now see was at least several miles long and probably more. The walls seemed higher than Kersladen's and better made. There was also a queue to enter the city. The guards checked everyone. Oh dear, Katina thought.

There was a farm access track approaching to their right with a small squad of Goblins stood at it. When they approached the farmer shouted to them.

'Master, may I have a word please.'

A senior Goblin walked over. 'Yes.'

'I can see you all have a busy day. We don't have any business in the city as I am delivering seed grain and tools to my brother in the east. If it would save your people's time, we could take the farm roads round the city.' The farmer said.

The Goblin looked at the long line of carts waiting to get into the city and seemed to think for a few seconds.

'It is a long queue.' He said to himself, then shook his head. 'No, I have orders, everyone through the city.'

'Thank you, master.' And moved his cart onwards to the back of the line a mile or so away where they waited.

Slowly the group edged forwards with every cart in front questioned and searched. Katina was concerned as the gate guards appeared to be Plains Devils rather than Goblins. The farmer's iron nerve held. He didn't appear to be in the least bit concerned. Eventually it was there turn, the farmer slowly edging the cart forward. Hawkyn looked as if he was dozing leaning on the back of the cart. Puppy, seemingly asleep, lay on the canvas covering where the box of unfinished swords lay.

'You, what is your business here?' The cloaked Plains Devil said with a rasping thickly accented voice.

'Good master, we have none in the city, we are just passing through. I am taking seed grain and tools to my brother on the eastern side. I asked the Goblin masters to let me drive round the outside of the city, but they refused.'

'Do you or your workers carry weapons?'

'Only long bladed daggers just in case someone tries to rob me.' Replied the farmer.

'Show me.' The farmer put his hand inside his cloak and pulled out an eighteen-inch blade good quality dagger and showed it by holding it flat across the palms of his hands. The guard thought and grunted.

'And your workers?'

'Similar.'

The guard looked at Katina and said, 'Show me.' She put

her hand in her cloak and pulled out a dagger also showing it on the palm of her hands. 'You at the back.' Hawkyn without changing position or even appearing to wake up, held a dagger by the tip of the blade, showing it to the guard.

'Let's see these bags of grain then.'

The farmer climbed down off his cart, walked round to the back, opened a bag near Hawkyn's feet and showed the contents. Then walked over to the nearest horse and again opened a bag. The guard leader nodded and started lifting various bits of the canvas and checking a few bags. He didn't really pay attention though, did not bother to move either Puppy or Hawkyn and as a result did not check what they were laying on. A minute or so later and the guard waved them through. The cart slowly edged forwards over the wooden drawbridge and through the stone gatehouse.

The inside of the city was very different from Kersladen. Although the houses were large and a mixture of stone and wood, even those on the main streets did not appear to be regularly maintained. Although the main road was wide, most of the people within were not, it seemed, free to wander. Thin, unkempt dishevelled Humans carried out all the heavy lifting.

One dark haired and exhausted Human woman of middle age chained by the ankle to the man in front dropped a large sack of potatoes at the feet of a Goblin guard and exhausted was unable to pick it up. The Goblin guard drew his sword swung it hard slicing into her back causing her to scream and collapse. He then chopped off the ankle holding the chain to the man in front and told him to get moving as he kicked the bleeding dying woman to the side of the road. The man with a heartbroken look on his face turned away and walked on.

'Please don't do anything, just ignore it. We mustn't interfere.' The farmer whispered.

Katina saw many instances of cruelty. Mainly Goblins

beating Human slaves with sticks. More interesting to her was the number of Humans. Although Goblins were common and Plains Devils every few minutes, Humans were easily the largest in number. Most Humans were slaves, although a few seemed to be better off and a couple, like there farmer were actively running a business of some kind.

Goblins questioned them often, but it appeared more out of the desire to annoy people than any actual wish to investigate what they were up to. As soon as any questioning Goblin worked out the farmer was an informer, meaning they couldn't freely kill any of them, they wandered off. If they couldn't be violent, they lost interest.

She also saw scuffles and worse where competing groups of Goblins fought each other. They just left the seriously injured or dead behind.

'This is the Human portion of the city. The Goblin families live on the north side. We are not allowed in there. The eastern gate is about half a mile.'

'What's that large compound over there?' Asked Katina.

'The Overseers Mansion. It's huge, about half a square mile of grounds and gardens.' The farmer replied.

They continued through the muddy dilapidated streets, then without warning.

'Gotcha Finullas. At last, you are alone without that pesky wife of yours to protect you. I'm going to slice the throats of your two slaves, then gut you like a fish. After that I will take your dog and eat him alive.' Said a gravelly voiced Goblin much taller than the usual ones. He wore badly fitting chain mail, an open-faced metal helmet and a blue tabard.

Katina could hear Hawkyn moving and Puppy turning round. She could also see another group of Goblins approach from about twenty paces behind it, wearing brown tabards.

'Oh shit.' Replied the farmer.

'Get down woman. You slave at the back get down and come over here. I'm going to kill you both nice and slowly, so I want lots and lots of screaming.'

Katina hunched herself and stepped off the cart. Turning slightly to conceal her movements placed her hand inside the closed cloak and held the handle of her dagger.

'Please don't.' Said Finullas the farmer. The Goblin just looked at him and gave a wicked smile. Katina was fairly sure however, that the farmer's comment was not meant for the Goblin. It was though, too late for niceties.

'Kneel.' Said the Goblin to Katina and put his left hand on her shoulder and pushed her down.

As she started to kneel, Katina's left hand grabbed the Goblin's arm and pulled down hard. It lost balance. Her right hand whipped out her dagger slashing the throat of her falling assailant. Then Hawkyn grabbed the falling Goblin by the helmet, lifted him up from behind and slit its throat so completely he nearly decapitated the creature. As the corpse fell to the ground, Katina stuck her dagger into the eye just to make a point.

The lead brown tabarded Goblin simply laughed loudly.

'That didn't work out very well for you did it Krandar. You always did forget that not all slaves were always slaves. Chop him to bits.'

Then looking at Finullas the farmer, while his own men swiped their swords at the deceased Goblin, said. 'Your slaves have done me a great service, so be gone. I was supposed to fight a dual with him at sundown for rights to my wife. I will deal with the effects of this, but don't do it again.'

'Certainly master. We are leaving now.' Replied Finullas and the cart was moving before Katina was back on board.

They continued along the street, leaving sounds of swords hacking at dead flesh behind them. Katina saw a glimpse of a movement as a cloaked medium height individual turned from looking out of a side alley and ran down it.

'You butchered him pretty thoroughly and very quickly. I'm right, you are Plains People. You're a long way from home. No need to say anything.' The farmer said.

Slowly they made their way towards the now visible east gate. Again, people were being stopped and searched on the way out, so they joined the back of the queue. Katina noticed that the Goblins manning the east gate wore brown tabards. As they approached, the lead Goblin just looked at Finullas nodded and waived him through.

'I'm surprised, we must have done those brown tabarded Goblins a serious favour.' Said Katina.

'The two tribes hate each other. Don't know why. The one you killed was serious trouble for everyone including his own clan.'

'What's the bit about your wife?'

'She was one of you but got captured. I was given her along with my freedom for services rendered as a dark mercenary. When Krandar tried to kill me, she defeated him and chased him off. We've been happily married ever since.' Then with a sad face continued 'I will never see her again, will I.'

Katina looked at him and sternly said 'I am afraid not, no. It is too risky to let you live.'

Finullas sighed, then said. 'Well, I have twenty years of wonderful marriage and she has three strong sons to help her run the farm. That is quite an achievement for a Human.'

They rode in in silence through the farmland of wheat and corn, the face of the farmer looking down cast. They turned left after passing several crossroads heading to a farm to their north.

As they approached Katina noticed the pigs cowering in a corner. So, this was it, she thought. Then put her hand under the canvas covering the back of the cart, checking the location of her bow and arrows. A further movement found the handle of her sword. Puppy crawled forwards until he was right behind the farmer. She could hear Hawkyn moving. They went through the gateway and entered the courtyard of the farm buildings. There was no one about at all.

'Where is everybody?' The farmer said.

'Don't care.' Was Katina's curt reply as her bow and several arrows came out from under the canvas. Hawkyn jumped down off the back of the cart and walked towards her. She put an arrow to her bow and drew the bowstring back.

While ducking forward and sideways, two arrows went past her head. She released her first arrow into an open window followed by a second to its neighbour. Grabbing her sword in her right hand while holding the bow and arrows in her left she jumped off the cart and ran for the nearest open barn door.

As she reached the door *"Roll NOW."* Sounded in her head so she dived for the floor, curled up into a ball round her bow and sword. There was a thump on the floor behind her. She rolled to her feet and spun round.

The grey tinged elf was down on one knee, both his long swords were stuck vertically point down in the ground in front of him. There was a ledge above the door, Katina considered he had jumped from that. Could have worked too, she thought. He stared menacingly at her as he slowly rose to his feet and shrugged off his cloak while pulling his swords out of the ground.

Personally, Katina wasn't interested in all the theatrics and was firmly of the view that if you were going to kill someone, you should simply get on with it. So, she dropped her sword, grabbed her last arrow held in her left hand along with her bow and took a snapshot. Glancing hit to the outside of the lower left arm, penetrating the chainmail and out the back hitting the inside of the falling cloak. The dark tinged elf winced and dropped the sword in his left hand.

Dropping her bow, Katina picked up her sword. The dark tinged elf drew a smaller dagger from his belt and walked forwards. Puppy ran through behind him shortly followed by several arrows, all heading for a pile of logs off to her right. She heard various screams and curses from outside. Katina couldn't worry about that now and had to concentrate on business.

The grey tinged elf swung aiming to hit her left upper torso which she parried with her long bladed dagger and then countered with a swing from her long sword to his upper torso, which he parried with his dagger.

This clang clang routine continued for several minutes, while two Plains Devils chased Puppy around the large pile of logs. They were having about as much success as the elf was. That was not to say that he wasn't skilled, he was. It's just that she seemed to know where he was going to try and hit a fraction of a second before he did it. This made blocking his blows easy despite his superior swordsmanship.

She didn't spot one though. While blocking an overhead blow, she missed the simultaneous kick to the stomach and fell landing on her back. Knowing the elf was lunging forwards, she rolled over several times and jumped to her feet, then parried incoming attacks from both longsword and dagger. What she didn't see beforehand was the step forward and headbutt to the nose. Blood everywhere. Before he could step back though her longsword nicked his left arm where the chainmail was damaged and her dagger struck his armoured side. He then took two steps back.

This exchange continued, an unpredictable move following every attack on her. After several minutes Katina was covered in small bleeding cuts. The grey tinged elf paid for those injuries. Every time he made one of these extra attacks, he was for a fraction of a second out of position and got hit by sword or dagger. After about five minutes, they were both looking distinctly worse for wear.

The change came quite suddenly. The first thing she saw was that puppy was getting bored of being chased around various piles of wood and farming equipment. When running behind the wood he simply vanished.

Katina realised she could also predict where the elf was going to parry, so waited for the right opportunity. After a series of attacks by the elf, she swung her longsword at his left shoulder. He parried with both his weapons. While they were out of position, she thrust her dagger upwards into his chest and kicked him hard in the groin. The elf fell.

Before she had a chance to react, two Plains Devils knocked her flying by jumping at her. One landed a few feet away, the other sat on her hips. It raised its scimitar in both hands preparing to administer a fatal blow. While raising her longsword and dagger to try and deflect the attack, she realised it didn't have a head neck or most of one shoulder. A fraction later and the head hit the second Plains Devil in the stomach.

As she was forcing the dead devil off her, the farmer said 'No master, you cannot beat them this time, they are too skilled. You must leave, come now.' Finullas quickly helped the grey tinged elf out of the barn and onto one of two horses. As Katina got up, the second Plains Devil ran. She grabbed her bow and ran back to the cart for her arrows.

About ten seconds later and Katina stood next to the cart, an arrow nocked into her bow aiming at two horses galloping off into the distance. She released the arrow hitting the farmer in the back beneath his left shoulder blade.

'That was not a mortal hit Katina.' Hawkyn chided.

'I know.' She replied sadly.

'That will come back to haunt us.' He said.

'Perhaps.' She replied.

20 – THE FINAL STRETCH

Katina watched as Finullas and the grey tinged Elf disappeared into the distance. It was only then that she saw Hawkyn's condition and the bloodbath that had happened outside the barn. There were bits of Plains Devils and Goblins all over the place. Some sliced and diced, others chewed and bitten. Hawkyn was holding his ancient family's sword in his right hand and his original personal sword in his left. He stood breathing heavily, covered in blood and worse of his slain foes. His drawn face and stooped shoulders a testament to the seriousness of his battle in the farmyard.

She started to check him over and shouldered her bow but winced with the pain.

'You are no better off than I am my love.' Said Hawkyn. Katina nodded.

Puppy, in boy form, came out of the barn, his right arm dangling loosely.

'There were four Plains Devils in the barn, not just the two you saw. "Were", being the important word here.'

'Your arm Puppy.' Said Katina.

'Got swiped by a scimitar.' He replied.

'Can you ride?' She asked.

'Yes.' Puppy Replied.

'Then we'll look at that later. Our two escapees will reach the city soon. We must be moving, like now I'm afraid. Half an hour and hundreds of them will be here.' Said Hawkyn.

'Agreed.' Replied Katina, who picked the boy form of Puppy up and sat him on his horse. Katina then untied the various bags of seed grain from the horses. Hawkyn retrieved the equipment hidden in the cart and distributed it amongst their mounts. Within ten minutes they had secured all their belongings and were riding away from what to Katina appeared to be a well-maintained large farm, with two barns, a blacksmith's workshop and a large wooden timber frame farmhouse.

They rode fast to get as much distance as possible. Within a few minutes Katina realised something. All the corn and wheat in the fields had young plants in. Finullas the farmer didn't need to take seed grain to his brother. The entire thing was a hoax. She shouted her thoughts to Hawkyn and Puppy.

'And a Human too. I had serious doubts about your tribe's belief that all who have dealings with The Lord of All Evil should be killed. Perhaps you are right after all.' Said Puppy sadly.

'He talked a particularly good lie. However, we must remember if he hadn't of brought us this far, we may well have not made it passed the city.' Added Hawkyn.

'Strange how things turn out sometimes.' Said Katina.

The terrain changed from cultivated farmland to abandoned fields and finally grassland as the three galloped east at speed. A full moon on a cloudless night followed the setting sun. An hour later, with a small stream in front of them and mounts shaking badly, they stopped for a rest. All three cleaned themselves up while the horses drank.

Katina looked at Puppy's right arm. The cut was minor, but the bruising was significant.

'A blow from a scimitar you say.' Said a confused Katina expecting a severe wound on the arm.

'Yes. I was in my normal form. The scimitar was made of poor-quality metal, so couldn't get through the scales very easily. All it really did was a bit of compression damage. I'll be alright in a few days.' Puppy replied.

'It looks like you've pulled a few muscles though.' Said Katina.

'If that's all Puppy gets from fighting four Plains Devils, then he got off lightly.' Said Hawkyn.

'Talking about getting off lightly, how are you doing Hawkyn? I want to have a look.' Said Katina. He grinned and as a result Katina blushed, then said 'Oh come here.'

'Yes dearest.' Hawkyn replied.

He had several deep cuts which he had cleaned properly but would need bandaging, which she did. Hawkyn then looked at Katina. She had the same, which he cleaned and bandaged. Katina could feel the bruises coming out.

'We'll have to walk the horses, they're bushed.' Said Hawkyn.

'We're not much better.' Observed Katina.

'Let's go then.' Said Hawkyn. Each holding the reins of their horse walked off east into the darkness.

'We're going to have to get some sleep. It's been a very long day and the horses will not be able to go much further. Any idea if we are being followed?' Asked Hawkyn.

'No, I'm afraid not. Do you want me to go and look?' Replied Katina.

'Question is, could you go far enough behind on foot for it to make a difference and still get back to help when mounted Goblins come looking?' Said Hawkyn.

'Probably not. On flat grasslands I'd have to go a fair way and as you say, I'd be too far away to help or warn you.' Said Katina.

'Afraid I can't fly until my arm is better and besides, eagles don't have good night sight anyway.' Added Puppy.

'I suppose I could do a trip back. Say five miles, then return. If you two are walking, I should catch up in an hour, perhaps two.' Suggested Katina.

'After the day we've had, I don't like it, but there's no choice really I suppose.' Replied Hawkyn.

'I don't like it either, but that's the way it is.' Katina handed her reins to Hawkyn and ran off west.

She travelled at a modest pace, partly due to tiredness and partly due to darkness. Although with the moonlight, she could see quite well. For the first few miles there was only grass and the odd scrawny tree. Then, she climbed one of these trees and looked further west.

After a while, at the very edge of what she could see, there was a group. It stopped for a while, then split into two parties, one went north, the other south. She watched them for about ten minutes, then climbed down and ran back to the others.

'Alright, we are being followed, or at least it's possible. There was a group about three miles behind us, but they have split up. Some went south and others north but none straight on.' She told them.

'Damn, we need to keep going then. I was hoping for a rest.' Replied Hawkyn.

So, they kept moving for a few more hours through the darkness. They didn't make many more miles, but they did do some. Eventually the horses had to rest, so they risked a few hours' sleep until dawn.

As soon as first light hit, Katina grabbed a few bits of cold cooked meat, an apple and prepared to go scouting. Hawkyn got up and started to pack up camp.

'Don't you two ever stop?' Said a yawning Puppy.

'It's part of our training and way of life I suppose. There are times when small deep patrols need to operate like this, so we are all trained and conditioned for it. Katina, you go off and see if it is clear to keep going. We'll stay put for a bit.' Said Hawkyn.

Katina headed off south to start with, going at a slow run while eating breakfast. She was roughly a mile away in less than ten minutes, stopped and looked around. No sign of anything. She then ran north-west for several miles. Again nothing. Then north-east before turning south-east and back to camp.

'No signs of anything, so we can head out east. I will go that way first, then loop round in a circle a few miles out and catch you up.'

Katina slowly ran off ahead leaving Hawkyn and an exhausted Puppy bringing the horses. It was a while before she found anything. The unmistakable footprints of a

Goblin party heading north lay in front of her. After further examination it became clear that the footprints were old. Perhaps yesterday, but certainly before they had got through the city. A possible path for regular patrols then, but they would be long gone now. Worth noting. So, she decided to head south for a few miles and check if anyone else was coming.

Unfortunately, they were. A slow dawdle by the looks of it, but on their way none the less. She ran back to the others and said.

'There's a squad coming up from the south about three miles away. It looks like this area is on a regular patrol route. I haven't checked north or west yet.

'We'd better mount up and ride quickly say, north-east.' Said Hawkyn. This they did until finding a stream. The group rode along it south-east before leaving the stream on the eastern bank and continuing their journey.

After a further day of hard riding, they made camp for the night in a small copse. Katina did the usual perimeter search and restocked their supplies with wild fruit and a few rabbits. They appeared to have outrun their pursuers as Katina found no trace of anything following them, for now at any rate. They did take things a bit easier for the next few days but kept alert and continued to cover up all traces of an overnight camp.

Puppy's arm improved so he started some short distance flights in his eagle form to look around. He saw parties of Goblins to their west, but these appeared to be conducting regular patrols. As his arm got better, he flew a bit further. After one such trip Puppy said

'Something has been bothering me. I know the Goblins are careless and slapdash, but they are not that bad. So, I went and had a look. Our tracks have gone, there's nothing for them to follow.'

'We're being helped, aren't we?' Said Hawkyn.

'We may be, but I can't check as asking may give away

our location. So long as we stay vigilant and careful, the three of us will get through this.' Responded Katina.

They continued with Puppy checking ahead to the east. There appeared to be no one around for miles. So that night, Katina decided to ask about the tracks. Calming herself down and composing her mind she cast the thought out.

"Is one of you helping us? If so, thank you."

"Yes I am. None of us much liked the idea of you fighting that Dark Elf on your own again. Currently he and his squad are about fifteen miles behind you trying to work out where your tracks are. You are occasionally receiving the benefit of one of my divine miracles. Hides the tracks of a small group for a while." Answered The Huntress.

"I'm amazed, thank you."

"As an Oracle, there will be times when you can call on our specialist divine miracles because you will be connected to all of us. I should leave you now." And The Huntress was gone.

In the morning, before her scout around.

'I spoke to The Huntress last night. Yes, she is helping us. Apparently, it is one of her divine miracles that hides our tracks for a time. The Dark Elf, is fifteen miles behind us trying to work out where we've gone.' She said.

'So, we keep going as fast as possible.' Said Hawkyn.

'Yes, I think so.' Katina replied.

While Hawkyn and Puppy packed up camp and did their best to hide its presence, Katina did her usual scouting circle to see if any unwanted guests were in the immediate area. All appeared good, so she returned to camp and they headed off.

This is how it continued for the next few days. Puppy rested his right arm as much as possible, until about a week later when he felt able to engage on longer flights. In his eagle form, he ranged out about thirty miles in a day and reported on seeing nothing but grass and the odd tree. A few days later and he found a town. The following day he found several more.

'There's something not right about them, but I can't work out what. I am sorry.' Said Puppy.

'Don't concern yourself with that. Despite your time with us you are still very young and inexperienced. Becoming a master scout cannot be hurried.' Said Katina.

'We'd better go and have a look, hadn't we?' Said Hawkyn.

'Yes, I think we should.' Replied Katina.

They closed on the nearest of the newly located towns, found a nearby hill, hid at the top and watched. It was a modest wooden built town, with a palisade and sturdy gates.

'Puppy's right, something is off.' Said Katina. All three spent some time looking and watching the town. It was Hawkyn that noticed.

'Where's all the warriors, or for that matter, the males in general? There are a few warriors at the gate and standing guard over the workers in the fields, but not many. We've seen no evidence of patrols. They appear to be massively short on men.' Observed Hawkyn.

'Do you want me to check the other towns for the same thing?' Asked Puppy.

'Good idea. We'll continue heading east.' Said Katina.

Puppy changed into his eagle form and flew off. Katina and Hawkyn took the three horses and continued east. They tried to remain hidden. While there weren't any patrols, there was no point in taking risks.

Puppy caught up with them about six hours later. 'The others appear the same. Five towns in total and hardly any male Goblins about.' Said Puppy.

'So, either they are off someplace else, or the war casualties are taking them far harder than we thought.' Said Hawkyn.

'We're going to have to know which one.' Said Katina.

'How do we do that?' Asked Puppy.

'I suppose we'll have to look.' Said Hawkyn.

'Depends on how long they've been gone. That sort of

numbers would leave a huge trail you could probably follow by flying.' Said Katina.

'There would also be regular supply wagons. That number of soldiers would require lots of feeding.' Suggested Hawkyn.

'So, all I really need to do is find a group of supply wagons and see where they are going.' Said Puppy.

'Or at least the direction.' Replied Hawkyn.

Puppy remained with them the rest of that day and the night. He left at first light saying he'd be gone several days at least. Hawkyn and Katina continued generally east. It was about a week later that Puppy finally returned, just as Katina was starting to get seriously worried.

'I've found three groups of large wagons spread out and heading south-east. At the slow rate they are travelling I think they're two days apart from each other.' Puppy said.

Katina looked at Hawkyn who thought for a while. 'I think they have moved the bulk of their soldiers somewhere south-east. We are talking about a lot of Goblins if every settlement has been stripped bare.' He replied. They continued for about a further week when.

'I recognise this area from some of my deep patrol missions. There are Goblin settlements about. We're nearly home.' Said Katina. Then she had another thought.

'You'd better be cautious about changing form now. We are in territory where we might meet warriors and scouts from our tribe or some of the others. We dare not have them find out that you can change forms or that you are a dragon. They might be alright with it, but it's a big ask, they are going to have a lot to chew on.' Said Katina.

'I recognise this area too. I think Katina is right.' Agreed Hawkyn.

'Let's find one of the settlements, sneak around and see what we can find out.' Said Katina. Hawkyn believed he knew in which direction a settlement was, so for a change they followed him as Katina took his horse and let him run ahead. She saw him crouching down, run into the distance. After about half an hour he returned.

'Well, that was unexpected. I didn't get close, but it looks abandoned.'

'Let's go see.' Replied Katina.

As they approached, she could see Hawkyn was correct. As they got closer, she saw the place was covered with carrion birds. Abandoned was not the right description. The Goblins had not evacuated the half mile diameter wooden palisaded settlement, but there was clearly nothing living in it. When they got to within one hundred paces, both Katina and Hawkyn drew their swords. The settlement's gates were smashed in rather than left open. Attached to a post in the middle of the forced open gateway was a wooden board that had scratched into it.

'Here lies the remains of an enemy of the Iredan.'

'Oh dear.' Said Katina.

'Puppy, you are quite young. I think you should wait outside.' Said Hawkyn.

A very long looking sad faced Puppy replied, 'Inside is how your people do war?'

'Yes Puppy, it will be, but please remember that our enemy offers or gives no quarter. As a result, our people offer no quarter at all either. I agree with Hawkyn, you should wait outside and not see this.' Said Katina.

'You are both good people, you can't be as bad as the Goblins.' Replied Puppy.

'I am truly sorry to say this Puppy, but to our enemies we are worse, much worse. You should not see this.' Said Katina.

'I will come. I am part of your war now. I should know what your war means.' Replied Puppy with a face that clearly showed that he was not looking forward to it.

'From a military education perspective, it's also what happens when you put your army in the wrong place.' Added Hawkyn.

'Well, let's go then.' Said Katina and led her horse through the gates with sword drawn in her right hand. Hawkyn and Puppy, in his boy form followed.

Inside the gates were mud brick walled round houses with steep thatched roofs, or at least they had been once. Doors broken, houses burned and walls shattered. Every building was destroyed in some manner or other. Carrion of all forms were abundant amongst the fallen Goblin warriors and other males. The stench of death was everywhere. Also common were the signs that Goblins had been trapped in their burning houses.

'I see dead warriors, but no women or children. Where are they?' Asked Puppy.

'They'll come later I'm afraid.' Said Katina.

She was correct, though not being a large settlement, later was not that far away. When they got to the central square, Puppy for a few seconds looked at the horrific sight with a stunned expression and was then horribly sick. The Goblin females and children had been corralled into the central square, then butchered and left to rot. The carrion was feasting on the rotting flesh.

Once Puppy had got control of his stomach, he said. 'Your people have become your enemy.' Katina gave a long sigh.

'No Puppy, we have always been this way. It is how we have made war since the beginning of time. They became us, well in some respects anyway.' Said Hawkyn.

'You see Puppy, to be a worshipper of The Light, does not, for most of them at least, require you to be a good person. It requires you to stand up against supernatural evil and Undead. You do not have to be a good person to do that.' Said Katina.

'That will be why the elders of my kind required us to be no part of this war then. You Humans are not good people.' Said Puppy.

'While us Plains People do not make war in what you

might call a civilised way, I have met plenty who are good people. Oswald Shamus, the first divine spell caster, argued most strongly that we should behave better. Now is not the time for that though, we need to win first.' Said Katina.

'As I remember it, there were four major Goblin settlements, we should check the other three.' Said Hawkyn.

'Agreed.' Said Katina and they left.

They headed roughly north for the rest of the day and entered that settlement the following morning with the same results. In the next few days, they checked the last two. They were the same.

'Goblins have been eradicated from this area then. We didn't see many in that last town. The nearest significant concentration is that city we went through, and even that was mainly Human.' Said Katina.

'It seems in our absence the tribes have gone on the offensive. Do not be fooled by this. The Goblin settlements were all but bereft of their warriors and males before our tribe attacked. I would think a massive Goblin army is elsewhere looking for blood. The question is where?' Replied Hawkyn.

They continued east for a week, then about mid-morning.

'Puppy, we are entering tribal lands now. Suggest you take on your dog form and stay that way.' Said Katina. Puppy jumped down off his horse and asked.

'How far?'

'Three days, two if we push it.' Replied Hawkyn. Puppy changed from his boy form to that of a young hunting dog. Katina grabbed the reins of Puppy's horse and with him running on ahead slightly, they all rode at a faster pace.

'Do you want to push it?' Asked Hawkyn.

'I think so, let's get home.' She replied.

So, they rode on at the fastest pace Puppy could run at for a long distance. They made frequent stops to allow Puppy to catch his breath. It was in one of these stops, that

Hawkyn got up and walked towards some approaching horsemen. Katina followed.

'Hello. Are we pleased to see you. You won't believe how far we've come to get home.' Said Hawkyn.

'Brother.' One of the helmeted riders exclaimed in a loud surprised voice.

'Sulien.' Hawkyn shouted running over.

Sulien jumped off his horse and ran to Hawkyn, face smiling with a big grin. They embraced in a serious hug for a few minutes,

'It is so good to see you. We didn't think it was possible you were alive.' Then turning said.

'Hello Katina, you found them I see.'

'Yes, all of them and made new friends too. What I have to say though, must be told to the entire tribe.' She replied.

'Yes of course. The rest of you complete the patrol. I will return home with my brother.' Said Sulien.

'Of course, Sulien. See you at home in a few days.' One of the riders responded.

The rest of the horsemen continued their patrol, while Katina, Hawkyn, Puppy and Sulien proceeded quickly towards their home, but not at a full gallop. Sulien asked some ordinary questions, such as were they all alive and well, that sort of thing, but did not pry further. Hawkyn and his brother talked a lot, but mainly about old times. Gently re-establishing the family bonding after years apart. The journey went quickly with the terrain becoming ever more familiar.

When it came to make camp for the night, Katina found it very hard to stop, but she knew she must. Puppy certainly needed to, as he was very tired. As usual, Hawkyn set the camp up and Katina went for a scout around. After a clear circuit they went back to camp.

As she sat doing her part of the night watch, a large dark grey great wolf came out of the tall grass and walked straight over to her. She looked at him for a few moments then said.

'Hello Geri, thank you for stopping by.'

He inclined his head slightly.

'While I have come a long way, I am afraid I don't speak wolf yet. Freki, though he has been in a lot of fights and hunts, is well and if possible bonded even closer with Tara than they had been before.'

Another inclining of the head. Katina was not sure how she knew but got the distinct feeling that Geri's pack were going to head off somewhere else.

'Thank you for telling me. Will we meet again?'

The great grey wolf nodded his head.

'Then until that day, may all your hunts be successful and your pack prosper.'

Geri gave her a long stare, headed back into the grasslands and disappeared into the night.

'Well, that was weird.' Said Sulien.

'He just wanted to come say goodbye. We've been gone a long time. They are going travelling.' Said Katina.

'You can speak with animals?' Sulien asked amazed.

'No, of course not. However, it is not only us Humans that don't like our enemy or his creatures. We are most certainly not alone in this fight.' Replied Katina.

'Really, what help can they be?' Sulien said.

'Ask someone who's been thumped by a bear.' Replied Hawkyn from his bed roll.

'Either way, our Great Wolves are off.' Said Katina.

'My turn.' Said Sulien and he took over the watch.

Next morning, they left early and rode hard. Everyone wanted to be home now and by late afternoon, the familiar sight of the circular wooden palisaded hill came into view. People were working in the surrounding fields. The scouts clearly visible at the edges of those fields and warriors were patrolling the tops of the Palisade. As they approached the gate Katina thought out loud.

'We've made it, we're home.'

'Yes, we have.' Said Hawkyn.

Then someone shouted, 'It's Katina and Hawkyn.' And the place went nuts. Everyone rushed over and surrounded them all talking at them at once. Puppy became quite frightened by the sudden throng of people and hung close to Katina. There were simply too many people too close. After a few minutes, the chief came out and barged his way through.

'It is so good to see you both again. I have many questions but seeing you two together answers one of them.' The chief said.

'My Lord, we must speak to the whole village as soon as possible. Everyone has a stake in this and it would be unfair for some to know before others. There's much to tell.' Said Katina.

'No kidding.' Said Hawkyn.

The chief turned to one of his guards and said, 'Get everyone together.' Then looked back to Katina and Hawkyn and said, 'Follow me.' They were taken into the great hall.

PART 9 – THE LOST TEMPLE

21 - THE MEETING

Katina stood in the great hall, a large two hundred feet wooden long-house that acted as the tribe's meeting place. She faced the seated chief with Hawkyn one side of her and the dog form Puppy the other. The four visiting tribal chiefs sat in their own chairs either side of the Iredan leader. Each of the personal guard stood respectfully a yard or so behind the tall backed large wooden chairs of their ward. Many Iredan people crowded into the hall angling to get the best vantage point to see and hear what was going to happen next.

There was not an ounce of timidity or even humility in either Hawkyn, with his two sheathed bastard swords slung over his back, or Puppy, who alert stood on all fours just inches from her left leg. Katina took a long deep breath as she prepared to give her first public speech and seriously hoped this didn't go sideways. Neither of her protectors were in the mood for games. The tribe would be in for a serious surprise if they gave trouble or caused offence. Before she had a chance to start.

'Hold.' Came the Shaman's voice from the doorway behind her. 'Katina and Hawkyn have been away from the tribe, there are certain ceremonies that must take place.' Several people gave a groan.

Katina turned to the Shaman and said. 'In our travels Hawkyn and I have learned the purpose of the rituals. They are necessary and wise. However, they are long and tedious. There is a quicker way revered Shaman and it does work.' She removed her leather glove on her right hand and offered it to the Shaman in greeting.

'The gods require proper ceremony and ritual. A simple holding of the hand is insufficient.' He replied.

'For a vast majority of things, you are right, but not for this. Try me, Hawkyn will comply too.' Said Katina.

'Give it a try. If it doesn't work, I will order them both to go through the ceremony. If it does, then it saves us all waiting around for an hour or two.' Said the Iredan Chief.

The Shaman nodded and with a significant look of nervousness clasped Katina's right hand in both of his and developed a look of pure shock. He quickly clasped Hawkyn's hand then stroked Puppy.

'I am most surprised my chief. I see many auras, several shades of white on all three of them including their young hunting dog.' Said the Shaman.

Katina had had concerns about the authenticity of the Shaman. Clearly, in her absence, things had improved.

'Each God of Light passes on to those connected their own shade of white aura. What I have to tell you will explain things.' Replied Katina.

The chief nodded and bid her continue. She started to talk. From time to time Hawkyn added to her narration as the events of the world elsewhere were laid before those gathered.

Once they had finished, the Iredan villagers and visitors from the neighbouring tribes were in complete silence. Katina could have been in a hall of statues as the gathered considered the description of the events and situation elsewhere, the difficulties and challenges facing the valley folk, the return of divine power and the missing Goblin army.

'Well now, what a story. And what responsibility you place on the tribes. You were sent to find a new safe home, but rather than that, you desire all the tribes to fight in a battle that could easily see our complete extermination.' Said the Agrini tribe's chief after some moments silence.

'That's not the worst of it though is it. To give us this news and return to their tribe as they said they would, they have reneged on oaths given in person to two Gods of Light. They risked damnation of their souls for eternity by not completing a divine quest. I don't know whether to be honoured or appalled.' Responded the Iredan Chief.

'The Gods of Light weren't pleased but did understand.' Said Katina.

'Eventually.' Added Hawkyn wryly.

'As for a safe new home, even if we were to find one now, it would not stay safe. Believe it or not, presently the eyes of our enemy are firmly on the valley and those that live within it. Once he destroys the valley folk, he will concentrate on us as there will be no one else left. The distance his forces have to move give us some time, but only a little.' Said Katina.

'If the valley falls, we will follow.' Added Hawkyn.

Katina saw an elderly man sat at a table amongst the gathered lost deep in thought.

'Well now uncle, I think it is time that we tell our secret. After all, two of our tribe's souls are at stake, we must help.' Said the chief.

The elderly man slowly stood up and started to speak as everyone looked at him.

'Nephew, we are sworn to secrecy. We must protect our secret and cannot explain or assist.'

'Keep secret, from whom? Clearly the Gods of Light are happy with Katina and Hawkyn knowing, or they wouldn't have given them the quest in the first place. It's time uncle.'

The elderly man sighed. 'Nephew, we cannot.'

'No uncle, you choose not to. Katina and Hawkyn have risked more for this tribe than anyone since ancient times. If you won't, I will.'

'You will condemn us both nephew.'

'It is not me who condemns us uncle.' The chief then looked at those gathered and continued.

'You all know my uncle failed his leadership quest thirty years ago. The Gods of Light considered he was not worthy. A few of you may remember that previously he had my build and strength. Failing the quest resulted in him becoming the thin weak cripple he now is. Some may remember that I was his companion, despite only just qualifying as a warrior. What none of you know, is where we went. The quest led us to the Temple of the Oracle, where we met one of the Gods of Light. We swore silence and privacy in return for our lives. Katina and Hawkyn, if you wish it, I will order my uncle to take you, but you must get one of the Gods of Light to release us from our oaths, at least as far as you two are concerned.'

Katina didn't hear the elderly uncle's response. Her mind switched to the total attention of the Spirit World as she felt the approaching presence of a God of Light.

"Hello Katina of Iredan, Duthac gave his oath to me, I am the one he met at the temple. Just so you are aware, I will be visiting him tonight in his dreams to confirm I will partially release him from his oath. He may show you, Hawkyn and the one you call Puppy, but no others. For now, its location must be kept secret."

"Thank you, Divine Light Bringer. Should I tell him?"

"You can try. I doubt he will listen."

"Understood and thank you." The presence left.

When she came too, Hawkyn tightly held her by waist and arm.

'Are you alright Katina?'

'She is fine my chief. Katina goes completely blank and inattentive when she is spoken to by one of the Gods of Light.' Replied Hawkyn. He then turned to Katina.

'Who was it this time?'

'Apparently elder Duthac spoke to The Light Bringer on his quest. He is willing to, for want of a better way of putting it, allow a variance to the oath so that he can take Hawkyn and I to the temple he visited. He was quite specific the location is to remain secret for now.'

Katina then looked at the elderly Duthac and said. 'Just to forewarn you, the Light Bringer will come to you tonight and confirm this personally.' Duthac visibly sniggered. 'You do still know where the temple is?'

'Yes, I do. Although we were living somewhere else then, I am sure I can still find it.'

Katina looked at Hawkyn, he just nodded.

'If we could have a word with you in private Duthac, it would be appreciated?'

'That can wait, I think tonight the tribe should celebrate your return.' Said the Iredan Chief. Katina looked back to Hawkyn and made a small tying of knot hand signal to him. He just nodded again.

'My Chief, not only have we travelled a long way and are tired, but we also have things that we must discuss with our families. It would be great to meet everybody and chat, but right now may we be excused for a while?'

'Certainly Katina, you may.' Replied the Chief. Katina bowed, turned round and walked away. When nearing the door, her grandparents and younger brother came out of the crowd. He ran forward and gave Katina a big hug.

'I am so pleased you are back. I have missed you so much.' Said her brother.

'But you refused to even speak with me.' Replied Katina.

'I was selfish and stupid. It took you leaving for me to realise that. I am better now. Oh, I passed my Warrior tests yesterday. The chief himself gave me father's sword. I was so nervous during the ceremony that even my hand tingled when I held it.' He drew the sword from over his back and held it crossways in front of him. 'I had to redo the leather of the hilt last night as it had all perished. It had strange symbols carved into the hilt and a clear needle shaped crystal that had light in it set in the steel of the hilt. They were all covered up, so I re-covered them this time.' Katina could feel the colour drain from her face as the shocked realisation of what it could be hit her. She made a move to pick up the offered sword and got the distinct feeling that her touch was unwelcome.

'You've kept the blade sharp I see.'

'No sis, it wasn't needed.'

'It never needs sharpening. A bit of oiling and polishing and the occasional replacement of the leather binding on the hilt is about it.' Added her grandfather. That confirmed it, Katina thought.

'We'd better talk in private.' She then turned to Hawkyn who was nearby talking with extended family. 'I know you have plenty to discuss, but as soon as possible can you join us with your ancestor's sword.'

Hawkyn looked at her face, gave a barely perceptible nod, then said. 'Certainly, Katina.' Hawkyn's father having looked at the pair of them then quietly whispered to Hawkyn who with his immediate family walked towards their hut. Katina followed her Grandparents and brother to their own hut to discover two aunts, an uncle and several adult cousins already there.

'Here, have some mead.' Said her uncle handing her a goblet. No sooner had she sat down and taken a sip than Hawkyn, with his mother, father, younger brother and sister walked in. The place was distinctly busy.

'Katina and I would like to consult our two families on something.' Hawkyn then paused, moved towards Katina and put his hand on her shoulder.

'Yes, we would wish to be allowed to marry. We have travelled long and far together, have faced many dangers and have come to love each other dearly.' Katina continued.

'And it looks like we will be going on more journeys together for as long as we live.' Concluded Hawkyn. Katina noticed her grandparents looking at Hawkyn's mother and father. Before they had a chance to say anything, Katina's brother came over to her, gave her a big hug and said. 'Congratulations sis, he is a wonderful man. I can't think of anyone else I would prefer you to go through life with.'

Katina hugged her brother back and simply replied 'Thank you.' She looked round at Hawkyn and saw his sister had done something similar. There were smiles around the room.

Her grandparents, somewhat overtaken by the reaction of others, responded. 'Hawkyn is the one you truly want?'

'Yes grandma, it is.' She replied.

'Then you shall have our approval.' Her grandfather said.

'And ours.' Added Hawkyn's father with a smile. 'But there's something else, something more serious. I could see it when you looked at each other.'

'Yes father, there is. Our journey has been long and our adventures many. In our travels we came across the remains of a tall brave warrior that had succumbed to an attack by six Undead. He killed them all before he fell.' There were many words of admiration.

'I hope you gave him a suitable send off.' Said Hawkyn's father.

'Yes father, we did.'

'The real question is how did he do it.' Interrupted Katina's grandfather.

'Yes, grandfather, it is, and I asked. It appears that the sword is a spirit sword. A specially made steel weapon that exists on both the spirit world and ours. That means it can harm and kill Undead as well as the living. It has been used to fight and kill a demon.' Said Katina.

'You have been busy brother, I'm impressed.' Said Sulien.

'And I thought my warrior qualification quest was bad.' Added Hawkyn's other brother.

'It goes further. The gods informed me that the warrior was a direct male line ancestor of Hawkyn, though several hundred years ago. It is Hawkyn's family sword. I am proud to say we have been able to return a long lost family heirloom to you.' Said Katina. There were various sounds of approval.

'That's great, but it is still not all, is it.' Added Hawkyn's father.

'No, it is not. The Gods of Light have told me that when The Lord of All Evil returned, the Mages and Weaponsmiths of the empire collaborated with the last Priests of Light and created some Spirit Weapons. The weaponsmiths used only the highest quality of steel and iron, making the weapons very strong and sharp. To this the Mages added magical enchantments making them the sharpest weapons known and impossible to break by conventional means. To this potent weapon the last High Priests added divine and spiritual enchantments blessing the weapon and allowing it to kill spirits and Undead.'

'So, there are more of these swords then?' Added Katina's grandfather.

'Yes. There are several identifiable aspects. Impossible to break. Incredibly sharp without the need for maintenance. Very Very old, at least five hundred years old I would say. And lastly have strange symbols or runes on the hilt under the leather of the grip.' Said Hawkyn.

'My brother's sword is one.' Added Katina. Everyone stared.

'Then I must hand my sword on to a more worthy warrior. I am newly qualified and can't have a sword that special.'

'You can't.' Replied Hawkyn. 'The sword is tied to a bloodline and once it accepts a master from that bloodline that's it.'

'I don't want to appear a coward in front of other warriors, but I am far to newly qualified to be fighting Undead.'

'Knowing the limits of your skill is not cowardice.' Replied Hawkyn. The other gathered warriors all agreed.

'I will speak to the chief about further training for you. He must know this anyway.' Responded Katina.

The meeting broke up then. Hawkyn and his family returned to their own home, while Katina washed and changed clothes in private. A while later and she left the family hut to find Puppy waiting by the door. He looked at Hawkyn's family hut, then barked.

'Yes Puppy, we should get Hawkyn and go in together.' She walked over and knocked on the door. 'Hawkyn, are you ready.'

'Yes Katina, coming.' A minute later, the door opened and Hawkyn stepped out. The three walked over to the meeting hall. They moved through the crowd and presented themselves to the chief.

'My chief, if I may raise a matter with you.'

'Please proceed Hawkyn.'

'I have the pleasure of informing you that our families have agreed that Katina and I may marry.'

'That is wonderful news. I am pleased to hear it.'

'There's something else we would like to discuss with you in private my chief.'

He thought for a few seconds, then got up from his seat and said, 'Follow me.'

Katina signalled her brother to come too and he quickly ran up behind her. There was a concerned look by the two guards on duty, but the chief waved these off. He took them round behind the grand chairs to a modest size room with a trestle table and nine stools. The two guards shut the door behind them.

'Place your swords on the table side by side.' Said Katina looking at her brother and Hawkyn who drew their swords and placed them on the table.

'They are both wonderful weapons. Any family would be proud of such antiques to go on their wall.' The chief commented. 'But you didn't get me alone to show me a nice pair of swords. There's more to this.'

'As ever my chief, you are wise and sharp. While the swords are the reason, my request is for my brother to be removed from front line duties and thrown back into the toughest warrior training that can be envisaged, with enhanced training on mental strength and fighting fear.' Said Katina.

He leant forward. 'No my chief, do not touch either sword. They are tied to bloodlines and will harm you.' Said Katina after receiving a quick vision of him writhing on the floor in agony. He halted.

'Divine Magic.' Added a surprised chief.

'And Elemental Magic too. Katina, you had better explain.' Said Hawkyn.

So Katina told the chief of Hawkyn's Ancestor and the fight with the demon, the advice she had been given, the symbols, the sharpness, the age of her brother's sword and the final conclusion that her brother with his sword could kill any Undead.

'And that is why we wanted to see you privately, to ask for additional training for my brother so he would be up to the challenge when the time came.'

'That is a very big ask of one so young, no disrespect meant.'

'None taken my chief. I have already asked if the sword could be presented to another as I consider myself without the experience for this, but apparently the sword has chosen me and that's the end of it.'

'My brother is correct. We don't know very much about them, but with our skill and training there will be a few people who will be able to face the Undead of our enemy.' Said Katina.

'Do not worry about your brother's training, I will handle that myself. I have faced an Undead, during Uncle Duthac's trials.'

'Without divine help, how did you defeat it my chief?' Asked Hawkyn.

'Threw him in the river. The one I faced didn't like fresh running water.' He replied with a shrug. Then the chief's face appeared thoughtful. 'Well now, I wonder.' He said and walked to the end of the room. He took a bastard sword off the wall, where it had hung since the tribe arrived at this place and put it on the table next to the other two.

'What do you two think?' The chief asked.

'Who's is it?' Said Katina.

'It's the symbol of the Iredan Chief and mine until someone else is appointed.'

Hawkyn checked the sword. 'The blade's sharp, the steel very hard. The hilt grip leather is in a shocking state. We could unwrap it.' Observed Hawkyn.

'Go ahead.' Said the chief.

'You had better do it my chief. If it's your sword it will harm anyone else.' Katina said.

The chief started to unwrap the perished leather of the handle. About a quarter way down the hilt, the first symbol became visible.

'Tough steel, sharp blade, very old sword, with runes on the hilt. I think it is one.' Replied Hawkyn.

'I had better arrange to get this combat ready then.' Said the chief.

'Do it yourself rather than delegate. Use it, bond with it.' Replied Katina.

'Be careful who you hit with it in training. It will cut through virtually any weapon or shield put in its way.' Added Hawkyn.

'There are several of these with our tribe and our neighbours. All the chiefs have one and a fair few of the older families. All are up on walls for display.'

'Then some select people must become bonded with these swords and trained to fight Undead if they haven't got existing experience.' Suggested Katina.

'It will be done. Undead has always been our weakness. If we can get divine spellcasting as well, then we have a real chance.' Said the chief.

'That is why we must go to Warameth. It is where the

divine knowledge is now.' Replied Katina.

'The tribes must all discuss that. We should return to the gathering.' Which they did.

Most families talked to Katina at some point over the next few hours, especially the families of Tara and Luka. She was polite, respectful and gave what information she could. Puppy stayed close to either Katina or Hawkyn but spent equal times between the two of them. After several hours of talking and well into the night, Katina sat in the middle of a long bench, head sagging and back slumped, completely exhausted. Puppy lay next to her, his head on her lap, not asleep as such but resting. Hawkyn came over and sat next to her putting his arm around her waist.

'You two need to go to bed.' He said.

'We're not the only ones.' Katina replied with a weak smile.

'Yes, I am exhausted too. Somehow we must make our excuses.'

'No need to. Go and rest.' Were the words of the chief from behind them.

'I will escort them, my chief.' Said Katina's brother.

'As will I.' Added Hawkyn's youngest brother.

After they had left the Great Hall, Hawkyn gave Katina a long kiss, then said. 'I will see you in the morning. Puppy, please look after her.' Puppy just looked up at him.

'Come on sis, let's get you home. I will stand guard tonight.' And led her to their hut.

'Stand guard?' Katina replied after a few seconds.

'Oh yes sis. You are a candidate for the Oracle. Certainly, someone the gods talk to, I saw that myself. By morning, the warriors will have selected your small personal guard probably headed up by Hawkyn. Until then I am guarding my sister. Now get inside and get some sleep.' Katina thought about arguing, but knew it was pointless. She entered her hut, went to her sleeping area and realised her bed was already made. Too tired to think about that now, simply collapsed onto her bed. Puppy jumped up next to her and both fell asleep.

She woke the next morning to the sound of Puppy growling. Judging by the light a long time after daybreak. There was a young woman cooking by the fire, making porridge and tea by the looks of it.

'It's alright Puppy, she's a close friend.' Then looking at the stranger continued. 'Saldina, you should not have done that, Puppy was about to attack you.'

'He's only a small dog, he could not have hurt me.' She replied.

Puppy had played his young stupid dog part very well since they got to the village, but the facial expression definitely fell this time.

'Still, it is best not to surprise him.' Katina responded.

Saldina had been a childhood friend whom she had gone through the hunter training with as young teenagers. She was reasonable at most hunter tasks but moving unseen through the woods she was hopeless. Their tutor often said she left a trail a blind deaf Goblin could follow and as a result had been unable to complete her training. Without having a profession and with no suitors showing interest in her she survived by helping short-handed families with running their households.

'While it is great to see you, what are you doing here?'

'I am currently at a loose end. You will have a family set up around you and Hawkyn, with bodyguards and helpers. They will all need feeding, clothing and somewhere to sleep. The chief will appoint a more senior woman, but in the meantime, I will help my oldest friend get things set up, provide meals cleaning, washing, repairs and the like until my replacement is assigned.' Saldina replied.

'We will not be here long before we are off again. Setting a new family up round Hawkyn and I is pointless. Your help until we leave again would be appreciated but is likely to be only a matter of days before we depart.'

'I will help as much as is needed. Now have your porridge and tea. I've found some scraps of raw meat for your puppy.' Which Saldina thew on the floor for him.

Both Katina and Hawkyn over the next few days tried to explain that at this time setting them up as a senior new family was pointless, but the tribe was having none of it. What had happened to them, the position that they were now in with the gods and the experiences they had, left no other choice. They had to be a senior family with a seat on the council. One existing elderly council member even stepped down as he had no heirs anyway. By the end of their first day, they had four guards and a steward of the house. The four guards were newly qualified youngsters, and the Steward was a retired former warrior who walked with a limp. Katina's only success was keeping Saldina as Matron. Hawkyn explained to the steward that he wanted the four guards to continue training and made sure all five of them knew what they both had experienced so far.

The Steward responded by saying that they did not have to justify orders.

'True, but on this occasion, I think it will help. Extensive training and field experience are why we are both not already dead.' Replied Hawkyn.

22 – LEAVING AGAIN

Katina and Hawkyn decided that their marriage should wait until after they got back from completing the Oracle tasks. Weddings take time to prepare and time afterwards also. Delaying the completion of the Oracle tests that long was not an option. The horses were generally fine but did need a few more days rest.

Hawkyn took this time as an opportunity to gather the Iredan blacksmiths and related artisans to discuss the manufacturing techniques discovered in the Dwarven stronghold. They were initially sceptical. However, the attitudes changed dramatically when shown the unassembled swords and his notebook, in the face of significantly superior metal and craftsmanship. The blacksmiths immediately took it in turns to copy Hawkyn's notes and every one of them listened intently to his explanations of what he found. They asked many questions and decided to build smaller scale machines to see if they could make the new ideas work.

The chief believed the journey would be several hundred miles south-west in unoccupied lands. Some people wanted to come along, but Katina was firm in her refusal. The Light Bringer had been specific, only her, Hawkyn and Puppy could go with Duthac. No others.

A week after arrival and surrounded by their families, they were leaving the village again. This time with Duthac as well. He did not offer any guidance or indeed say anything at all for several days. Both Katina and Hawkyn tried to engage him in conversation, but he refused to talk. This made things difficult with Puppy. They were used to talking with him normally, have him change into his eagle form to help with scouting, or any number of other matters. Now they had to treat him as a normal hunting dog in training. The situation was difficult for all of them.

Although the tribe accepted that they could not come

along, they dealt harshly with any trespassers to their land, even more ruthlessly than usual. Katina hoped they didn't keep that up as it would be clear to the other side something was going on. On the plus side, it did mean that the first few days were easy going. Progression was quick as Katina did not need to scout for the enemy. Duthac's age and infirmity did not hamper his speed on horseback either.

After three days, having left Iredan lands, the forward clearance by the tribe stopped. It wasn't until the end of that day when they had made camp for the night, did Duthac say anything.

'Well now, as we are clear of any prying eyes, or ears for that matter, I think I should say something.' Said Duthac as they all sat by the fire. Katina noticed Puppy, ostensibly asleep, ears prick up.

'Please proceed Duthac.' Said Hawkyn.

'You will not be able to find the temple as it is magically hidden. I think you are a fraud Katina and I will not break my oath. Visited by The Light Bringer, my arse. What did you do, get some hallucinogenic herbs from that charlatan of a Shaman of ours and put them in my ale that night? To think you expected me to believe I had had a god sat on the end of my bed. Ah what rubbish. I will stop you and destroy you, I will not let you harm our tribe with your delusions. You will never be Oracle or survive long enough to have our tribe believe you.' Said Duthac.

Katina could feel a great anger building in the area around them. An extreme inhuman rage. Duthac's tirade stopped abruptly as he cried out in pain. With a sharp intake of breath, he clutched his chest. His face became pale and his skin suddenly looked clammy.

'We must help him.' Said Hawkyn.

'I'm not sure we can, I can feel extreme divine rage.' Said Katina. Then she went over to Duthac and held him with his head against her chest.

'Please Duthac, apologise to the Gods, quickly. Think it

if you can't say it. You are a good man, don't die for this.'

'Never, you are a fraud Katina.' Duthac just about managed to whisper through gritted teeth.

Katina wondered what to do. Her treating the injured was pretty much limited to sword cuts and arrow holes. Duthac was beyond her. That only left one choice. She looked at Duthac who was now on the floor, crying with pain as his skin started to have a blue tinge to it.'

She tried to gather her thoughts and calm herself down.

"Gods of Light please here me."

"Hello Katina." Said a voice she recognised as The Light Bringer.

"Hello. May I please ask you to stop hurting Duthac. He means well and simply wants to protect his village, that's all. He's not an evil person, just thinks I am a fraud. Please stop hurting him." Said Katina.

"He would stop you completing your mission and would endanger all three of you. We cannot allow that. Your mission must succeed, he must die." Replied The Light Bringer.

"Then at least don't make him suffer like this, he's a good man."

"Alright, we will take him now." Said The Light Bringer. The crying stopped and his lips also turned blue. Hawkyn went over to Duthac and put his hands on him.

'He's dead.'

'The real shame is that he was only doing it because he thought we were frauds. He was simply trying to protect the tribe. I would have much preferred to convince him he was wrong. I hope the gods understand that and aren't too harsh with his spirit.' Said Katina.

'The extent that they are willing to go to is surprising. They really want us to complete this quest don't they.' Said Hawkyn.

'Yes they do, very badly.' Said Katina.

'We should dispose of the body.' Added Hawkyn.

'It will have to be burnt to prevent use by the other side.' Said Katina.

'No problem.' Responded Puppy, now in his dragon form. Katina and Hawkyn moved the corpse of Duthac a distance away from the camp, then Puppy breathed a long breath of fire until the corpse was fully incinerated.

'Well, that's us stuffed then. Our guide is dead.' Said Hawkyn.

'Not necessarily.' Said Puppy now in his boy form. 'If what he said was right and we are looking for a wide river and magically hidden things, then I should be able to see through it. Even if I can't do that, I will see the magic protecting it. There can't be many of them around.'

'So long as it is still south-west of here.' Said Hawkyn.

'Yes, but we should be able to get a fair bit of leeway on that too. If I fly, I could cover much more area.' Replied Puppy.

'How accurate do we think his south-west was.' Said Hawkyn.

'That's a thought, he may have taken us in completely the wrong direction.' Suggested Katina.

'I don't think so. He went on his earlier quest from our old village. You were very young when we left there, so you probably won't remember, but it was a long way south of here. Our neighbours were east, so all tests headed either further south or west from there. That makes where he went either south or south-west of here.' Said Hawkyn.

'We also know that our chief threw an Undead into some fresh running water.' Said Katina.

'I could fly west a few days, see if I find a major river.' Suggested Puppy.

'If you do find a river, we head down stream until we bump into large amounts of magic.' Replied Katina nodding.

They camped that night taking it in turns to keep watch. At first light Katina said 'Puppy, we will head due west. Reduce the risk of you not finding us.' Puppy turned into his juvenile eagle form, squawked and flew off.

They packed up camp, spent some time foraging, then mounted their horses and rode west. The day passed uneventfully and they camped just behind the brow of a hill. During the night though, Katina awoke to Hawkyn putting their small fire out.

'Look south.' He said in a whisper. Katina got up and crawled to the brow of the hill. She could see hundreds of campfires a few miles away.

'Damn.' Katina muttered.

'If it's twelve Goblins a campfire, that's a lot of Goblins. We need to move out and now.'

'Yes Hawkyn. I suggest north-west for a bit then south-west to put us back where Puppy will expect us.' Replied Katina.

'If we'd followed Duthac, we'd have walked right into them.'

'Yes, I know. Do you think he would have done that deliberately?' Asked Katina.

'I think we know what the Gods of Light think.' Replied Hawkyn.

They struck camp quickly. Katina removed the signs of fire and other disturbance. She left little evidence of their passing. Neither Hawkyn nor Katina would say it was perfect, but anyone not deliberately looking would miss the signs that someone had been here.

They rode quickly north-west chancing that the Goblin scouts and advanced parties were not yet that far north. Their luck held and nothing was encountered. Within a few hours they were about ten miles away.

'We've left a significant trail.' Said Hawkyn.

'Don't think there's anything that could have been done about that. It would have taken far too long to cover our tracks. We would have been overrun.' Replied Katina.

Luckily, after a few more miles, they came across a fair sized stream heading south-west. It was slow moving water that gently trundled through grassland, several copse, various stone outcrops and heavy brush. They followed it for about an hour. Although keeping aware of her surroundings, Katina took the opportunity to enjoy the scenery. They finally left the stream by traversing a large stone bank then up a rocky outcrop. It was several hundred yards before they had to cross soft ground making it unlikely the Goblins would find the tracks even if they were looking in this area.

They then headed west again and after a further few hours came across a hill with a few trees on top. Katina climbed one and had a good look about. There was no sign of Goblins or their passing. She climbed down and informed Hawkyn.

As it was only late afternoon, they kept going across the tall grassland occasionally interrupted by small groups of trees or shrubs. After a few more miles of steady progress.

'Hawkyn.'

'Yes dear?'

'Something is starting to bother me.'

'What's that?'

'Where are all the Goblin Tribes?' Katina asked. 'If we're being pushed to extinction by overwhelming numbers, where are they all? They haven't just temporarily moved, there's no sign they were ever here. It's not just here either, we've travelled vast distances with hardly a village in sight.'

'The continent is huge and Goblins are being sent in large numbers to where we are at the time. Lots of settlements do exist, we just don't know where.' Replied Hawkyn.

'So how do we win then?'

'We don't know that we can yet. What we need to do is work out where all the Goblin tribes are and what empty space there is. Once we know that, we can consider the options of where and when to attack or retreat. I'm not a strategist, this is something better suited for Daxx.' Said

Hawkyn.

'You've got an idea though. I can see it in your face.'

'Yes, I have. If we're right and all us plains tribes work together, then something may be possible. It will depend on where the Goblin villages are. They would be weak as their warriors would be elsewhere. It would require better thinking and co-ordination than I can do to achieve that.'

'But the first step is to know where the Goblin tribes are though?'

'Now it is my turn to say, "You've got an idea, I can see it in your face".' Replied Hawkyn.

'I do, but I'm not even sure if it can be done. I don't know if an Oracle could remote view where Goblins are at any given time.'

'Now that's an interesting thought.' Hawkyn said finally.

They rode on for another hour or so before making camp for the night. Once set up, Katina went foraging while Hawkyn cooked dinner. They took turns keeping watch which passed uneventfully. They struck camp in the morning and continued west.

'I'm getting worried about Puppy. He's late.' Said Katina.

'We don't know how far he had to go and we did have to change direction. I wouldn't start worrying just yet.'

Katina's worries were unfounded as a few hours later she noticed an eagle approach from the east, behind them. It circled around and landed in front of them, then changed shape into a boy.

'Good to see you back, I was starting to worry.' Said Katina.

'When I saw all those Goblins, I decided to have a look about. I also wondered if you had gone home and warned your tribe, so I checked that too before I came out this way. You're a bit off course.' Puppy replied.

'We had to divert around the Goblins and try to avoid leaving any trail that could indicate where we were going.

How far out are we?' Replied Katina.

'Not that bad really, ten miles or so too far north.'

'What did you find?'

'Quite a lot. There are thousands of Goblin warriors plus hangers on heading to your village. Two large packs of those Great Wolves are tracking them. Some are bigger than most ponies. I saw them shred the Goblin scouts. Your tribe and some others are still patrolling the area north of where the Goblins are so they will see them soon.'

'We needn't worry about home then. They will know the Goblins are coming. One of the sets of wolves will be Freki's old pack. As for the other, it makes sense for there to be more than one. Any luck with what you were actually looking for?' Replied Katina.

'Hard to say. About one hundred miles west of here is a significant river that heads south. It's a few hundred feet wide and quite fast flowing. A little way down river smack in its middle there is a thin line of very powerful magic that goes for miles. I flew right through it several times. I can't figure out what it does. To set up any magic spell that goes on for that distance would take stupid amounts of magic energy. It didn't seem to do anything at all, which makes no sense. So, I quit trying and came back.' Said Puppy.

'That must be it.' Observed Hawkyn.

'It's got to be.' Responded Katina. 'The Oracle Temple must be inside Puppy's magic spell.'

'Yes and if you don't do things right the spell spits you out the other side rather than letting you in.' Added Hawkyn nodding.

'So, what do we do?' Asked Puppy.

'Try and figure out how to get in.' Replied Hawkyn.

'There must be a way.' Said Katina. They continued another hour or so then stopped for lunch and to rest the horses, Puppy riding Duthac's horse.

The group continued for another week across the grasslands, before they met the river and turned south, downstream. A few days more and they got to the spot where the magic started.

'Does anyone know how to build a raft?' Asked Puppy.

'I have done it once, though it was a very long time ago. The problem with building a raft is that it requires several tall trees cut into straight lengths. They just don't exist here. We would also need a lot of strong rope or something to bind the logs together, we simply don't have the stuff.' Replied Hawkyn.

'We'd better have a look further down the river and see if we can find something to help us.' Said Katina.

'What are we looking for.' Asked Puppy.

'Well, I'm thinking that if there is a major temple on a hidden island, then in the old days there must have been a method of getting there. It might have been a bridge, or perhaps a ferry, but there must have been something. A collapsed bridge could have left signs on the bank of the river, as would the landing stage of a boat.' Replied Katina.

'Of course, look for the original way across.' Said Hawkyn.

The first walk along the riverbank, the entire length of Puppy's magic field found nothing, so they walked back the other way and still found nothing.

'I suppose it's become hidden with the passage of time.' Suggested Hawkyn.

'Covered in dirt, bushes and grass. That would make sense.' Replied Katina.

So, they started their third riverbank search. This time making a careful examination of the topography of the riverbank, carefully probing with sticks or uncovering any irregularities. After several hours they found a large flat stone block buried under dirt and a large bush. Uncovering it found a second block next to it, giving a width of about six feet near the riverbank.

'The base for a jetty perhaps.' Suggested Katina.

'Possible. No sign of a boat, raft, or bridge though. How

do we cross?' Said Hawkyn.

'The river looks deep. It will be hard to cross with the horses carrying us and our equipment.' Said Katina.

'There's no way we could swim it on our own with the equipment and Puppy can't fly it across. Should you ask?' Said Hawkyn.

'I don't think so. Duthac couldn't have asked the gods and he got over, so that's not the answer.' Said Katina.

'So, it's not divine knowledge.' Said Hawkyn.

'It's not likely to be magic based either, unless Duthac was a mage in disguise.' Said Puppy.

'If it's not divine or magical, then it must be physical. There should be an actual way in. Some sort of door or path that is not visible.' Concluded Katina.

'More than not visible, get it wrong and you will simply appear on the other side.' Added Puppy.

Then Katina had an idea and her face lit up.

'What is it?' Asked Hawkyn.

'If it's a bridge or something like that, we should be able to find it.' She replied.

'How so?' Said Hawkyn.

'Well, we know from Puppy that if you fly into the magic, you get spat out the other side. A bridge or causeway must have width.'

Puppy groaned and just said 'Of course. We'll have to spread out though and be staggered otherwise we'll all disappear at the same time.' Then after a few seconds added 'I should be able to sense magic like that if I think about it.'

'Let's try it then. Puppy, can you fly around and see if you can sense the magic?'

'Sure.' Then he changed his shape to an eagle and flew up to the upriver end of the magic.

'I'm lost here.' Said Hawkyn.

'It will be obvious if it works and I'm not sure I can explain it.' Said Katina.

Puppy then circled and started back. He landed about a

hundred yards upriver of where they were. Katina and Hawkyn led the three horses up to where Puppy had stopped.

'Where is it?' Asked Katina.

'Between us, about a foot in front of me. It's very thin and heads off towards the river and away from it.' Responded Puppy.

'Puppy, can you walk away from the river and see if you can sense where the magic gets wider?' Said Katina.

Puppy changed shape into a boy and slowly walked away from the river face deep in concentration. When he got to a large bush about twenty yards away, he disappeared from one side of the bush and reappeared on the other.

'That's it. We've found the gateway.' Exclaimed Katina. Then she looked at Hawkyn and asked. 'Do you understand now?'

'I think so.' He replied. 'As the magic moves you to somewhere else, we can see that and workout where the gateway is.'

'Which side do you think the entrance is?' Asked Katina.

'Probably my side as it is in a straight line to the river. I think you had better go in first Katina.' Said Puppy.

Katina and Hawkyn led the horses to where Puppy was. She gave the reins of her horse to Puppy then turned to face the bush. Taking a deep breath, extended her left hand in front of her and stepped forward. As she approached the bush her arm vanished. Feeling no unusual sensations, she stepped through.

23 - THE TEMPLE

The magical entrance she had walked through was two bushes, one each side of a six-foot wide light grey granite stone bridge with balustrades. It was flat, very long, with a stone archway at the end. The temperature was comfortable with no breeze. She could still see the sun, sky and riverbank, but the appearance was as if seen through a window of distorted glass. Then her mind realised the error of her eyes. If, when looking out from the bridge, you only saw the river and both its banks, where did the bridge go. Especially as it was way longer than the width of the river.

An idea then occurred to her. Look over the balustrades and try and see where the bridge went. Unfortunately, all she saw was her own back. Her head had come out of the magic wall opposite where she had put it in. Stepping back between the bushes, returned her to normality. The bridge vanished.

'We've found our way across. It's a stone bridge. Only six feet wide, so we will each have to lead our own horse and walk single file. I will warn you though, what you see is very weird.' Said Katina, who then took the reins of her horse from Puppy and led him onto the bridge. She walked a little way on before Hawkyn and Puppy followed her.

'This is amazing. I can't even begin to understand what is happening here.' Said Hawkyn.

'The level of magic knowledge and power necessary to do this is beyond comprehension. It can't be an illusion, due to the disappearing reappearing bit, which means whoever did this must have altered where things are. Incredible.' Observed Puppy.

They walked along the bridge slowly and carefully. Despite being many hundreds if not thousands of years old, it was sturdy strong and unaffected by the erosion of weather or time.

After ten minutes or so of walking in stunned silence,

they reached the stone archway at the other end. Carved on the top of it was "Gweledd O Pentef"

'What does that mean?' Asked Hawkyn.

'No idea.' Replied Katina as they walked through.

She then stopped and looked about, taking in the sights around her. They had just walked into a large village of rectangular buildings, mainly one story high, made of an off-white stone. They were on a large island. The shore opposite was what Katina thought were the banks of the river. The place looked abandoned.

Then she saw another building to her left, down river. It was enormous. The only thing that rivalled it was the city walls of the High Elves home. A pyramid shaped building and its walled grounds, occupying the entire down river end of the island. Each of its thirteen levels was about twenty feet tall, made from off-white stone and slightly smaller than the one below it. Every level also had a blue stone structure in the middle of one side that protruded slightly and contained a twelve feet tall arch. At the very top was another blue stone arch with a dozen statues in two rows either side of it. The entire structure was inside a perimeter wall some ten feet high, the only entrance being a twenty feet high arch set inside a blue stone gatehouse.

'Wow that's big. No guesses for where we're supposed to be going.' Observed Hawkyn.

'We might as well find somewhere to leave the horses then get on with it.' Said Katina.

They walked towards the compound. Despite the abandoned nature of the place none of the buildings showed any signs of decay or dilapidation. Nearby were several thirty feet square buildings, so they picked the nearest one and secured the horses inside.

As they walked towards the entrance to the compound Puppy changed into his natural dragon form and said.

'Seems appropriate.'

'You're probably right.' Responded Katina.

The three passed through the large blue stone arch side by side. Katina in the middle, Hawkyn on her left and Puppy to her right. As they entered, a tall, even for them, very elderly dark-skinned man holding a quarter staff walked in front of them from her right. He bid them to stop by holding up a hand. Despite his apparent age, his movements were so graceful he seemed almost to glide across the marble paving slabs. The long white cloak with multi-coloured border trimmings opened to reveal a strong and athletic physique.

'No one may enter the Temple of the Seers at this time, please leave.' Said the elderly man.

Katina thought for a few seconds. She didn't need Puppy's special sight to know that this man was not at all what he seemed, so decided to be cautious.

'Honourable sir, I am Katina, daughter of the Iredan tribe of Plains People. The goddess The Farmer has asked me to become an Oracle. My friends and I have experienced lots of hardships and challenges getting here. We hope that this is the place where I can present myself for adjudication of my worthiness for that honour.'

'And I suppose you dreamt this task.' Replied the old man with a snide smirk.

'Nope. The Huntress and Farmer both turned up in person at a campfire meal and asked Katina directly. Brought some potatoes with them too as I recall.' Replied Hawkyn.

'Actually physically turned up in person?' Was the elderly man's surprised response.

'Yes sir.' Responded Katina.

'Any other contacts?'

'We've met The Lord of the Gates, his Wolf and The Bridge Keeper. Spoken with The Huntress many times, and the Light Bringer a few. Been subject to six tests and am still looking after the Dwarf God's Hammer, which I will return when I can find him.' Said Katina.

The elderly man then concentrated and whispered a few words under his breath.

'I see you are telling the truth.'

'Yes sir we are.'

'Then you should know there are twelve tests and a long ceremony carried out at the Temple of the Oracle. While a ceremony can take place here, you have only done six tests. Continuing will most likely kill you.'

'I believe that if we were bound to fail, then one of The Gods of Light we've been working for would have told us. We should proceed.' Suggested Katina.

'I agree.' Replied Hawkyn.

'Then I will conduct the ceremony for you, but the dragon should wait here and not take part. His kind are not supposed to be involved in this.' Said the elderly man.

'We have faced death together, and quite literally been to hell and back. There's no way I am sitting this one out if Katina and Hawkyn's lives are at risk.' Replied an angry Puppy.

'No, I guess not. There will be consequences for you.' Replied the elderly man.

'Nothing new there then. I have been faced with consequences ever since I set foot outside my cave.' Was Puppy's reply.

'Which is why your kind are supposed to stay put.' Replied the elderly man with a frown. 'Please follow me.'

He led them across the immaculately kept paved courtyard lined with flowering trees and sweet-smelling red roses. The old man took them towards a blue stone building that protruded from the side of the pyramid by several feet. It had an archway eight feet wide and twelve feet tall. After stepping through the first blue gateway the elderly gentleman turned round and holding his quarterstaff horizontally across the gateway barred their progress and said.

'Who is it that seeks entrance to the Temple of the

Seers.'

'I am Katina of Iredan and seeking to become the next Oracle.'

'I am Hawkyn of Iredan and betrothed of Katina. I wish to be the Oracle's Protector.'

'I am Kerlon of Draconis Isle. Son of Lord Kalan and Lady Sanrina. I seek to share the cost my friends will pay in their submission, so they have a better chance of success.'

'You each understand that to progress beyond this gateway may result in your death.'

'I do.' Was the unanimous response.

'Then please follow me.' Said the elderly man.

He led them through the blue stone archway and along a smooth black walled passageway that inclined slightly towards a light at the other end. Hawkyn walked beside Katina with Puppy following behind. Katina wondered if Puppy would have any problems fitting in the corridor. As if he knew her concerns said.

'I hope this doesn't get any smaller.'

They continued up the passageway towards the light. As they got closer Katina could see the archway at the end with a stone frame lining the inside. The archway keystone had a symbol of a sun carved on it. Just before passing through the elderly man who was leading the group stopped, held his hands up over his head and quietly muttered some words Katina could not hear.

The glare of the sunlight through the archway into the tunnel seemed to waver and alter. Slowly a humanoid shape appeared out of the sunlight.

'Who seeks my bonding.' Came a powerful voice.

'I, Katina of the Iredan tribe of Plains People. I seek to be an Oracle of the Gods of Light.'

'And who are those with thee.'

'The man is Hawkyn also of my tribe. He's my betrothed and wishes to be my protector. There's also a young dragon who has accompanied us on many of the tests and whom we affectionately call Puppy.'

'What tasks have you undertaken to entreat my support.'

'We have restored a small temple of yours to spiritual operation by locating and replacing the Spirit Stone. We also restored the altar.'

'Your submission is accepted. You may pass.'

As they started to follow the elderly man through the archway. A bolt of what appeared to be translucent lightening that originated at the keystone, hit Katina. She felt a searing pain and a bit drained. There were groans from both Puppy and Hawkyn.

A bit shaken and legs a bit wobbly Katina tried to walk through the arch, but her body would not do it. She just stood there for a few seconds, then Hawkyn asked.

'What happened?'

'The cost of being tied and approved by a god. It takes some of your spiritual energy.' Replied the elderly man.

'Is this for each god?'

'Yes Katina, that's right. If you're spiritually not strong enough, then you will die before you get to the top.' He replied.

'Oh.' Responded Hawkyn.

'How many die?' Asked Katina.

'Virtually everybody. Those that go with them die as well. Your average Human simply doesn't have the spiritual strength and those that do, tend to become Divine Priests to a specific god.' Replied the elderly man in an emotionless tone.

'Puppy, you had better think of sitting this out. You have no need to prove your loyalty to us. For you to die to the hosts of our enemy is one thing, but dying to the Gods of Light is unnecessary.' Said Katina.

'Thanks for the consideration, but I will stick with it as long as I can.' Puppy replied. Katina nodded, an expected reply.

She looked out from the tunnel to the bright light of the

day outside and saw the archway opened out onto a narrow six feet wide ledge running left and right. What surprised Katina once her eyes had adjusted, was seeing that they were in the middle of a lake. It was large, about a mile wide and extended several miles downriver where it turned east and disappeared behind a forest. The air was still and the water smooth, the wildlife happily going about its business. A huge difference from the straight fast flowing river she had seen from outside. The only elemental magic previously seen was Puppy's illusions of a few cubic feet in size. Katina just stood there stunned as the enormity of the vanishing act pulled by the mages who did this sank in. Her mind recoiled from even trying to understand how they achieved this scale of magic.

A path had been created by the next level of pyramid being slightly smaller than the one on which it rests. Realizing they were now on the opposite side, she walked around the perimeter. The paving slabs were perfectly laid, which was just as well as there were no walls, railings or balustrades. A trip here and you would fall straight over the edge. Not that much of a problem at this level, however a few more up and it would be. The party walked single file following the elderly gentleman until they got to the opposite side of the pyramid and protruding stone archway standing above where they entered. She gathered her thoughts before entering the archway and the tunnel beyond leading upwards to the next test.

'Now for The Huntress.' Commented the elderly man. They just nodded and entered the dark unlit tunnel, following him up the slope to the light at the end. As they walked on Katina wondered if there would be another batch of pain. Then she saw the stone lined archway. The keystone had the symbol of a bow carved into it. Katina considered that she would find out very soon.

Again, the elderly man held his hands up over his head to stop the group passing through the archway and quietly muttered some words. Slowly a humanoid shape appeared out of the glare of the sunlight.

'Who seeks me.' Came a female voice.

'I, Katina of Iredan. I seek to be an Oracle of the Gods Of Light.'

'And who accompanies you.'

'The man is Hawkyn also of my tribe. He's my betrothed and wishes to be my protector. There's also a young dragon who has accompanied us on many of the tests and whom we affectionately call Puppy.'

'What have you done for me to justify my support.'

'We have followed tracks and located the young dragon that now accompanies us. We treated his wounds and have helped him to learn new skills. We have spoken with you on several occasions and carried out where possible what you desired.'

'I accept your proposal. You may pass.'

As they started to follow the elderly man through the archway, Katina was again hit by the translucent lightening that originated at the keystone. She again felt a searing pain, but this time a bit more drained. There were more groans from Puppy and Hawkyn.

With shaking and wobbly legs, Katina gave her body a minute to settle down before she tried to continue. As she waited.

'I'm going to need a few seconds.' Said Hawkyn.

Once everyone had recovered, they bid the elderly man continue, proceeded through the archway and walked around the six feet wide ledge to the next level. This time it was The Farmer. Katina recounted the time spent at the lost Iredan village and the discussions at the castle. The now familiar searing pain followed acceptance of her submission.

Katina though started to worry. She could see the debilitating affects her submissions were having on both Hawkyn and Puppy. Her own condition was starting to suffer significantly also. Aside from feeling physically weak, she felt ill. Her body was starting to run a temperature and was becoming sweaty.

They proceeded to The Warrior whose appearance brought a surprised look from their elderly guide. He looked somehow more translucent and less defined than the others. His lightning also lacked the strength and force that they had encountered before. Then came the Elven God. Each encounter brought the now familiar searing pain and debilitating effect on health. She was also feeling a distinct lack of energy and a growing feeling of tiredness. The faces of her two companions were starting to look drawn and reddened.

The Dwarf God was interesting, because all Katina could say was, they had retrieved his hammer from the Demon Cruach. She was told bluntly to go get it, which she did while the others waited. On her return she presented it to the Dwarf God's spirit and was informed that he would take it from her if she reached the top. Everyone else must leave it alone if she died first, including the elderly guide. That left a shocked look on his face.

Next came a real surprise, the God of the Goblins, who introduced himself as The Goblin Lord. He was not at all keen on having a member of the Iredan tribe as his representative, given the tenacity with which they committed genocide against his people. Katina was not keen on helping Goblins either and had not expected them to be considered a light bearing race at this time. However, Katina realised there really wasn't a choice. If they were to defeat The Lord of All Evil, then the Goblin Lord must get his people back. She explained this to the god and said her people kill all followers of The Lord of All Evil, whatever race. Those of his people that worshipped him and not their enemy would be helped. Discussions continued, but in the end so long as she stuck to her word that day, the Goblin Lord would support her for Oracle. She confirmed she had no intention to deceive, those that followed him, she would help.

The next four were The Healer, The God of Knowledge, The Lord of the Sea, and The Thunder God. With each she had to admit not having undertaken a task and explain that she was putting herself forward at the personal request of the Farmer. She was allowed to proceed but the pain and drain on her was far more severe. Each time all three of them were brought to their knees.

On the last occasion, progressing beyond the Thunder God, Puppy screamed, collapsed, and passed out. When Katina and Hawkyn came too themselves, they checked on him. He was still alive but unconscious. Despite all efforts, they could not wake him.

'We're going to have to move on and leave him.' Katina said.

'We have no choice. In his current form we can't take him with us.' Replied Hawkyn.

'We've only got one left, the Lord of the Gates.' Said Katina.

They walked through the archway looking back at Puppy lying on the floor.

'It feels strange moving on without him. He's been so central to our journey.' Said Hawkyn.

'True, but he would be too weak to sustain another archway.' Said Katina.

'Yes, I know.' Said Hawkyn

'We can go back to him afterwards, I hope.' Said Katina.

The pair followed their elderly guide onto the walkway now about two hundred feet off the ground.

'We're both very shaky and need to take care. We must not fall off here.' Said Hawkyn.

Katina looked at him and was worried. His face was drawn and pale. His eyes had gone deep set. His face was wracked with pain and he looked as if he could barely stand up. She seriously doubted he could take another blast of that translucent lightning. They clung to each other as they walked around to the far side of the stepped pyramid, being careful on the narrow walkway. Katina considered herself and concluded she was not any better off than Hawkyn was. She could feel the burns on her shoulders, back and chest from the lightning strikes. Stiffly she held on to her betrothed as they walked to face their final god.

They entered the archway and slowly walked up the tunnel to the light at the end. As they reached the arch the familiar spiritual shape of the Lord of the Gates appeared.

'I am your penultimate task. Katina and Hawkyn of Iredan, what is it you seek of me.'

'I seek your support in becoming the Oracle of the Gods of Light. Hawkyn, Puppy and I freed you and your associates from the imprisonment of the demon Cruach and enabled you to re-open the gates to the underworld.'

'You three have my support, now and always.' The Lord replied. Then continued 'What happened to Puppy.'

'He's still alive but was rendered unconscious by the archway of the God of Thunder.'

'I see. You may continue.' Replied the Lord of the Gates.

They walked around the parapet again to the final entrance arch. The elderly guide entered, turned and looked at them.

'You do not have the spiritual strength to survive the ceremony. You will both die.' He then turned back and walked up the steep steps that took them up to the ceremonial area at the top of the pyramid.

Katina stopped, looked at Hawkyn, smiled and straightened her stooped stance. He gave a weak smile back, let go of her and stood straight too. Side by side the pair stood at the base of the steps to their final task, the ceremony itself.

Despite the pain, injuries and bone weary tiredness, her heartbeat raced and blood pumped as they climbed the steps towards their death. She was not afraid and neither was Hawkyn, she could see that. No Iredan was ever frightened of dying. They had done their crucial task, warning her own tribe of what was happening elsewhere. It was a critical task and they had done it. They both could face their ancestors with heads held high.

The steps led to a flat area about one hundred feet square and entered at the middle of the side nearest the village. About twenty feet in from the far side was a large twenty feet tall blue stone arch that had some form of filmy distortion inside it. The elderly guide stood in front of it. The twelve statues of the Gods of Light stood six each side and appeared to be solid and alive. The exception was the Warrior, who like previously appeared transparent and vapourish.

'Katina of Iredan, do you still wish to be an Oracle of the Gods of Light?' The elderly guide asked in a loud voice.

'Yes, I do.' She responded firmly.

'Do you have any offering to support your petition.'

'Yes, I do. We have recovered the Hammer of the Dwarf God from the demon Cruach. I offer to return this now.' Katina replied.

She stepped forwards several yards, placed the hammer on the ground and stepped back. The Dwarf God held out his right hand and the hammer flew directly into it.

'The offering is accepted.' The Dwarf God responded.

'Gods of Light, Katina of Iredan seeks to be your Oracle and Hawkyn her Protector. Do you agree.'

'We do.' Came the simultaneous response of all twelve gods.

'Katina, you must pass through the archway to the realm of the gods. Retrieve the goblet on the other side and return. Be warned that being mortal and still of physical form, your strength will dissipate quickly.' The elderly guide said.

Hawkyn took Katina's hand and side by side they

walked towards the archway and simultaneously stepped through.

Before she even had time to contemplate what lay beyond, Hawkyn groaned and collapsed onto the blue stone base of the other side of the archway. She bent down and touched his neck. His heart had stopped. Then it dawned on her that her own heart wasn't beating either. She knew she didn't have long. In front of her perhaps twenty feet away was a three foot high circular marble pedestal with a gold and silver goblet on it. She ignored the bright colours of the wild-flower meadow that dominated her peripheral vision and focused on her target. Already feeling light-headed she ran over, grabbed it, stuffed it down her front and turned to run back to Hawkyn.

He was gone. Head spinning and dizzy, she ran back towards the archway. At halfway, she fell. Crawling, she got ever closer. Finally, just feet from the archway, her strength failed her. She lay face down breathless and motionless fading into unconsciousness. A large claw grabbed her right arm near the shoulder and started to drag her, then all went dark.

TAIL PIECE

BACK AT THE VALLEY

The mismatched group of Scout Plains Devils, oversized Goblins, a Black Priest and a Goblin Commander, carrying one unconscious Light Bringer Priest ran almost blindly across the open country west of Warameth in the middle of a dark cloudy night. The cold wind bit at their faces and the tall grasses whipped at their legs.

'Commander, why don't we stop and fight the petty villagers who chase us. A bunch of farmers won't cause us trouble.' Came the guttural tones of Dragrish, a decade plus subordinate Goblin and kin of the group's leader.

In one movement the commander drew his sword and with the flat of the blade hit Dragrish in the stomach. He went down like a dropped bag of potatoes.

'How dare you question me, now get up and run. Take a leg of the White Priest while you are at it.'

'Yes commander.' Was the guttural winded response of Dragrish as he got up off the muddy grasslands and ran to catch up.

'Those petty villagers killed a hundred Goblins with ease. They also killed my cousin and his squad. They are not meek as we were told, but still commander we outnumber them, we could lay an ambush.' Was the rasping question of one of the panting Plains Devils.

He was acting strangely for a Goblin Commander in not assaulting a human farming village. He acknowledged that to himself. However, his instincts told him something was very wrong here and attacking the villagers was not the correct tactic. Hence the sneaky grab. He was an experienced established Nihtgenga commander who had had a lot of success for his tribe and overlord. That is why he had been volunteered to lead a team to capture this new village priest and take him back for execution. His orders expressly forbid killing the priest on route.

He hadn't realised why until he grabbed his prey and sensed the bright white glow of a Divine Light Bringer priest. An odd experience he had never had before, but somehow, he knew. What was even stranger was the Black Priest could not, it seemed, sense the captive's divine aura. Part of him was curious why, but a vast majority of him was more interested in living beyond the next few hours. Grabbing this one would come with serious consequences.

'We need to know who is following us. The fastest runner of you scouts drop back briefly. See if you can tell what we're up against. Not long and absolutely no engaging them. Not yet.' Was Thogrish's guttural command. The six Plains Devils looked at each other as they ran. One turned north towards a small hillock his scales changing colour as he climbed. The rest of them ran on through the waist high grass.

The scout caught up a few minutes later. 'They are perhaps half a mile behind. I saw the Elf. The Great Wolf is with them too. There are five Humans, all dark-haired locals, none of the Southern Barbarian butchers, but they are very well equipped. They don't seem to need to check for tracks. The oldest Human is in charge. He looks as if he is carrying a bastard sword and along with another is mounted, although it is hard to say for sure at that distance.'

'We have no chance of ambushing our pursuers with both the Elf and wolf present. The oldest is most likely a Lord Guardian. Faster, they are only minutes behind us.' The leader commanded. The others all looked shocked.

'Run faster or get slaughtered. We don't have a chance against whose chasing us.' Thogrish replied.

They had several dozen miles to cover before any hope

of help. They ran as fast as they could. They ran as if the Lord of All Evil himself was hunting them. Thogrish suspected, from his own scout around the village before they grabbed the White Priest, that the dark-haired Human part of the group contained the Lord Guardian known as The Hawk and his family. If he was right, the pursuers were a very special group that would never tire, never miss a track, and would go into Hell itself if they needed to. Thogrish wished the Lord of All Evil was after them, it would be preferable to this lot. Then he spotted something. Great, a small river.

'Head upriver, quick now.' He ordered.

The others looked puzzled but said nothing. They ran into the river and headed up its middle in a generally south direction towards the hills, and away from help waiting in the forest west of Warameth.

'Sir, do you want me to hang back and keep watch, see if we have shaken them?' Asked the rasping voiced scout from earlier.

'Not yet, but when there is a solid rock that you can stand on, maybe.' Thogrish replied.

They kept running. A few minutes later and he spotted a modest flat stone at the side of the river of about two square feet in size.

'Use that one. No longer than thirty seconds and you absolutely must not get seen.' Thogrish ordered.

The fast scout runner nodded, jumped onto the flat rock and crouched looking behind. The rest of them kept running. Even the Plains Devil Scouts were starting to have laboured breathing. Thogrish thought they would have to stop and rest soon.

A little while later he heard a quiet splash as the Plains Devil Scout caught up with the group.

'I can't see them.' The scout said.

'We're going to have to chance it, we need a rest. Head for those low hills, let's see if we can hide behind them for a few hours.' Said Thogrish.

A short while later and they were running round the back of some low hills, stopping behind some large bushes. They dumped the White Priest on the grass and all dropped to the ground breathing heavily.

After a few minutes Thogrish got up and went to check on the captured priest. He put his hand on his forehead. The strong white glow of his aura was as powerful as ever. Thogrish also realised something.

'He's not unconscious, just pretending.' Thogrish said.

'Then we must gag him so he cannot speak, or he'll cast Divine Magic on us.' Said the Black Priest.

Dragrish threw over a long piece of cloth which Thogrish placed in the Priest's mouth and tied round the back of his head. The White Priest opened his eyes and gave a surprised long look at Thogrish.

One of the Plains Devil Scouts came running back from the top of the hill.

'Sir. No sign of pursuit yet. One of us is up there keeping a lookout.' The scout said.

'Good. Work out a watch and get some sleep. One, maybe two hours is all we've got.' Thogrish replied. He then looked at the White Priest and said in the Human language.

'Try and escape and we'll kill you. Things are much too dangerous to be keeping you alive unnecessarily.' The White Priest nodded.

After a little over an hour's rest, Thogrish felt most strongly that they should be moving quickly. He roused everyone and recalled the watching scout.

'We head south-west deeper into the foothills.' Then looked at the scouts. 'Hide signs that we were here and catch us up.' They picked up the White Priest and headed off.

Thogrish led them through the foothills north-west up the valley, keeping the group on the mountain side of any obstacle hill or group of trees. He split up the Plains Devil Scouts, one forward, one behind, and one on the valley side of the group. The remaining three he kept with him but swapped them around regularly.

At the end of the day the forward scout came back. 'Sir, the Elf and two of the dark-haired Humans, are ahead of us. They are going in the same direction as we are.'

'Go get the other scouts.' He ordered.

'Yes sir.' A short while later and they all had returned.

'Any signs of the others?' Thogrish asked.

'No sir. More worryingly we can't see that wolf.' One replied.

'You probably wouldn't see that wolf until he was on you anyway. We can't go into the mountains, there's no way through. No signs of the rest of our pursuers on the grasslands?'

'No sir, none.'

'That's the way we must go then.'

'But commander.'

'I know Dagrish, I don't like it either.'

They ran all day and night, onward through the waist high grass rapidly approaching the Great Forest where help waited. Thogrish also knew from the occasional scouting activity that the pursuers were gaining. With the first light of pre-dawn in the sky behind them and just as Thogrish thought they might reach the rest of the unit, a scream came from his right. A Plains Devil's leg went down a rabbit hole and snapped, bones visible. He looked at the injured creature and looked behind.

'Keep going, we have barely a few hundred yards.' He yelled to the others, who instantly ran off.

'I must leave you.' He drew and raised his sword ready for the killing stroke.

'No commander let me fight them. It will give you a little time.' Thogrish nodded turned and ran after the rest of his squad. He had travelled no more than a few hundred yards when he heard the guttural screams behind him of a Plains Devil dying.

He ran on trying to catch the rest of his squad but lost sight of them when they reached the trees. The wolf was closing fast as were the galloping horses. Damn, he was not going to make cover. At the last instant he dived left, rolled to his feet drawing his scimitar and swung it at the passing wolf's flank. It hit the fur but did not bite deeply. The huge wolf turned to face, snarling.

Two galloping horsemen approached from his right. Bastard swords held high to strike. One of the two approaching was The Hawk. That face was burned into every Nihtgenga commander's soul. Such merciless violence even after surrender, only one other Human came close. The scale of butchery those two dished out in the Goblin Raids rivalled that of the last Human princess five hundred years before.

He had no hope, so took a chance and dived directly at the lead horse's forelegs. With a resounding thump his ribs broke, and the horse and rider fell. He rolled to his feet screaming with pain. Retrieving his scimitar and drawing his long dagger he turned to face his opponents. A mounted leather armoured dark haired woman approached rapidly, the Human called The Hawk was pulling himself out from under the fallen horse, the Elf and two more Humans were missing, the Great Wolf snarling was preparing to attack.

So, this was it for him. Well, if he was to die, he was damn well going to take one with him. Weapons to the fore, Thogrish dived for the prone struggling Human still partially trapped under a fallen thrashing horse. His opponent produced a dagger that blocked his scimitar. His own though penetrated the chain mail armour and cut deeply into his adversary's side. Then, before either of them could do anything else, a set of wolf teeth bit heavily into his right shoulder and wrenched him off the Human who had now freed his leg from under the horse. He struck the wolf's right forequarter with his dagger who yelped and let go.

Thogrish rolled to his feet again, right arm dangling limply barely able to hold the scimitar. Dagger in his left hand, he stared at the mounted woman and a very angry bleeding Giant Wolf. Then as his opponents started to move, a guttural shout in the Human language came from behind him.

'Hold, or we kill him.' Thogrish turned to see Dragrish with his dagger held at the captive's throat while the Black Priest and one of his Nihtgenga held an arm each.

'Harm our commander and the priest dies. That Elf and his friends remain hiding, and the priest dies.' Dragrish continued.

He felt the blade of a large sword at his neck.

'Harm the priest and your commander gets impaled alive and burnt at the stake.' The Hawk replied, shortly followed by the Elf and two dark haired Humans, bows ready and arrows nocked, coming out from behind trees a hundred yards or so away from his squad. Hands went to remove his scimitar and dagger.

'Stop. Do you want your priest back or not? Leave our commander and his weapons alone.' Dragrish continued looking at the Elf to his side. The hands retreated from Thogrish, but the sword at his neck did not.

'What are your terms?' The Hawk replied.

'We exchange. Your priest for our commander, and we all go home.'

'I'll do it father.' A young man said who had just caught up carrying the head of the fallen Plains Devil. The Hawk nodded. 'Come on you, let's get this done.' With a sharp longsword at his neck the young man pushed Thogrish.

As they walked, his head started to spin and he coughed up a little blood. Then more. The pain increased and he felt light-headed. He kept his face taut to not show weakness to his enemies.

About a third of the way the young man stopped him. 'We wait here.'

'Why, you are all butchers, you will kill me anyway.'

'If he is unharmed, you will be allowed to go. If he is wounded, you will die.'

'He is already wounded. Three arrows in the back and a thump to the head during capture. Also, he has been dragged for miles, but in time he will recover fully.' Thogrish replied.

'If it stays like that, so will you. Oh, our village is not for the taking. Now move on. Remember I have a bow, so no tricks.' Thogrish nodded and walked towards Dragrish.

At about fifty yards Dragrish stopped. Thogrish kept his hands in plain sight and well away from his weapons. He also made sure he walked several yards away from the Light Bringer Priest coming in the other direction.

Unfortunately, he lost control of his stomach, was violently sick with a good deal of blood showing. He collapsed, but was still conscious.

'Hold priest. Move a step and we fill you with arrows.' Shouted Dragrish as several of his Nihtgenga came out of the forest bows in hands. He didn't need to look to know the pursuers were doing the same. He saw Dragrish running towards him and heard his Human escort do likewise as he coughed up more blood. Then he saw the Black Priest approaching quickly and heard a set of galloping hooves.

'This is going to get out of hand. Priest can you heal me, that way we all get to go home alive. Otherwise, lots of death all round.' Said Thogrish.

The White Priest looked about. The young Human took his gag off and untied him.

'You are probably right. Unfortunately, as you are not Human, I can't heal you.' The White Priest replied.

'Damn, we're all dead then.' Thogrish replied.

With weapons drawn, Dragrish and the Black Priest, faced a mounted dark haired lady warrior and the young chap who had escorted him.

'Not necessarily. You have a grey-white aura, so you aren't linked to the Lord of All Evil, but a God of Light. Who are you tied too?'

'Like all Goblins, I follow The Lord of All Evil.' Said Thogrish.

'Wrong, auras never lie. You follow one of the Gods of Light.' Replied the White Priest.

'The White Priest is right. Sorry commander, I saw you pray to our old Goblin Lord before we left.' Said Dragrish.

'Blasphemy. I knew you were a heretic Thogrish. I'll kill you for this.' Said the Black Priest, who's face then went blank with concentration. Sadly, for the Black Priest at least, that's as far as he got, as Dragrish neatly decapitated him in one blow.

'Simple praying does not give you an aura. There's more.' Said the White Priest.

'Well, my father did cut my hand as a small boy and have me hold our statuette of the Goblin Lord while reciting some words. Can't remember what I said.' Replied Thogrish.

'Subject to what the statuette was, that could work. It has been known. So, you are a Priest of the Goblin Lord.' Said the White Priest.

'Absolutely not, I'm a military man.' Replied Thogrish.

'Are you by chance a Lord Guardian?' Asked the Hawk who had approached during the talking.

'No. I passed the skill tests but was not accepted by The Lord of All Evil.'

'And so, you pray to your race's old god?' Said the White Priest.

'Occasionally. Why?' Thogrish responded.

'That explains it. I have the honour of presenting to you the first Divine Lord Guardian of the Goblin Lord in longer than I know my history. The Goblin Lord was one of the original twelve Gods of Light.' The White Priest paused. 'You could do the spell casting yourself by praying to the god you worship. I'd hurry though, you don't look good.'

Thogrish nodded.

I'll guide you through divine spell casting. I know you will be able to do some, but haven't trained Lord Guardians so do not know how far you can go.' Said The White Priest.

'What do I do?' Asked Thogrish.

'Go on.' Gasped Thogrish through his sickness and pain.

'Clear your mind and think of your Goblin Lord.'

Thogrish did this.

'Now place your hand on your ribs that are broken.'

He did this too.

'Now imagine in your mind four overlapping ellipses.'

Thogrish did this also.

'Now add to this image a jagged line emanating from a central point.

'Alright, done. My hand is tingling though.'

'Add a second jagged line. Then say the words Iach Grym Grym.'

'Iach Grym Grym.' Repeated Thogrish.

He felt power funnel through his hand and into the injured ribs. Then he went very lightheaded.

'Commander, let me help you.' Said Dragrish as he lifted the Nihtgenga commander to his feet.

'I'm not sure that was such a good idea master priest. Teaching the opposition how to cast divine spells.' Said The Hawk.

'He is a God of Light Divine Lord Guardian. They don't grow on trees. It is proper that we render aid, and I will continue to do so. My decision is final.' The White Priest retorted harshly.

'Well, that's me told.' The Hawk replied. Thogrish noticed that Dragrish was just as surprised at the exchange as he was.

Then they backed away slowly, Weapons drawn.

'Now, run for the trees.' Thogrish shouted.

And they both ran for it, the pain of his ribs almost causing him to lose control of his stomach again. While they felt a good deal better, they were not fully healed. Thogrish could hear running feet behind them, but they were not chased or shot at.

As soon as they reached the cover of the trees, he saw the remaining Nihtgenga, but not the Plains Devils.

'What happened to the others?' Thogrish asked.

'We couldn't keep up carrying that priest, so they abandoned us.' Dragrish replied.

'Without them we have no hope of fighting our way out, so we had to get you back if we were to live. The exchange was all we could come up with at short notice.' Dragrish added.

'Hmm, that choice is a discussion for later, right now we must get out of here. As soon as the priest is safe, they will be back. We run deeper into the forest.' Thogrish replied.

'Certainly commander, but what happened to our Black Priest?' One of the Nihtgenga asked.

'He was going to kill our commander. If he'd done that our pursuers would have killed us all.' Dragrish said. The Nihtgenga nodded. They all ran off, Thogrish desperately trying to avoid screaming with pain.

'Revered commander, we're leaving a trail that is yards wide. A blind child could follow us.' Dragrish observed.

'Being careful won't help against those following us. We need distance.' Thogrish replied.

Several hours later and well into the morning. 'We must stop and rest. Dragrish, go see if anyone is following us. No risks at all. Use your best skill, in addition to the Elf and Giant Wolf, there's one of two Human legendary Lord Guardians on our tail.'

'Yes commander.' Dragrish replied with a worried face. Slowly and carefully, he headed back into the forest the way they had come. They all collapsed onto the ground breathing heavily.

'Commander please let me look at your shoulder.' Said one of the other Nihtgenga. Thogrish got up and went over. The wound was quickly cleaned.

'We have no time for bandages, that'll have to do.' Said Thogrish.

'I saw what happened with the White Priest and saw your spell casting.' Said the Nihtgenga. 'That makes you a worshipper of a God of Light.' The Nihtgenga continued. The others jumped up drawing weapons.

'Surely you can't expect us to attack our commander while running from Humans.' One responded.

Dragrish came crashing through the forest at a run. 'What is happening here?' He shouted scimitar drawn.

'He has been seen spell casting and he's not a priest of the Lord of All Evil.' Said one of the Nihtgenga.

'Our esteemed commander is a Lord Guardian and the only reason we are still alive.' Dragrish responded. 'You pray to our race's old god.' Dragrish continued looking at his commander.

'Once as a child, once before my first major command, and before this mission as I was sure we would die.' Thogrish responded.

'You must each decide if you follow your commander and the ways of the Goblin Lord or return to the tribe and the ways of The Lord of All Evil. This is a religious choice of your own conscience. The Goblin Lord was one of the original twelve Gods of Light.' Said Dragrish.

There was a stunned silence as the others looked nervously at each other.

'Enough conjecture for now. Dragrish what's going on behind us.' Thogrish ordered.

'The Elf and wolf found both our tracks and those of the Plains Devils but are following the others.'

'That'll do for now.' Thogrish said.

'Commander, you must heal your shoulder. It is bleeding badly.' One Nihtgenga observed.

He drew a symbol of four overlapping ellipses with the jagged line next to it on a patch of earth in front of him and concentrated hard. Remembering the prayer to the Goblin Lord his hand tingled. He placed the hand on the shoulder wound and said

'Iach Grym.'

The wound partially closed over and became less severe. There were gasps from the other Nihtgenga.

'We have wasted enough time and must move now.' Thogrish ordered.

'Where too commander, we can't go back up the valley or to the Humans.'

'For now, to the mountains. We look for a cave to hide and a source of food and water.' Said Thogrish.

Here Endeth Book 2

The story will continue in Book 3 – Light Ascendant.